Hannah Wakefield was raised in Massachusetts and educated at
Tufts and Berkeley. She visited London in the mid-1970s intending

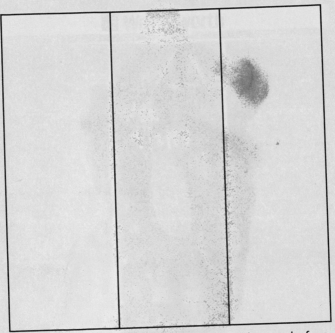

This book should be returned, or renewed, on or before
the latest date shown on this label.

Wandsworth Libraries
24 hour Renewal Hotline
01494 777675
www.wandsworth.gov.uk

L.749A (rev.5.2001)

Also by Hannah Wakefield from The Women's Press:

The Price You Pay (1987)
A February Mourning (1990)

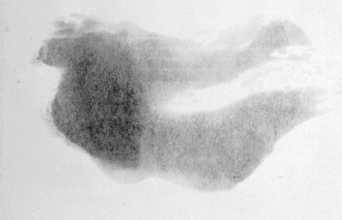

CRUEL APRIL

HANNAH WAKEFIELD

F–T
WANE

500130075

First published by The Women's Press Ltd, 1996
A member of the Namara Group
34 Great Sutton Street, London EC1V 0DX

British Library Cataloguing-in-Publication Data
A catalogue record for this book is available from the British Library

ISBN 0 7043 4475 0

Typeset in Goudy by Contour Typesetters, Southall, London
Printed and bound in Great Britain by
BPC Paperbacks Ltd

Author's note

Many thanks to Sarah Burton for her inspiration, friendship and advice. Dee Street would not exist without her.

Thanks also to Helen Armitage, Salma Badrul, Jane Battye, David Collier, Caroline Davies, Owen Davies, Michele de Larrabeiti, Helen English, Josie Fairney, Kathy Gale, Sandra Gulland, Maya Isaaks, Blanche Marvin, Gwilym Owen, Phil Parker and Wendy Savage for their comments at various stages; to Elaine Steel for her support; and to Faber and Faber Ltd for permission to quote from *Collected Poems 1909–1962* by T S Eliot.

Apologies to the residents of Spitalfields for packing another neighbourhood into their dense environs.

April is the cruellest month, breeding
Lilacs out of the dead land, mixing
Memory and desire, stirring
Dull roots with spring rain.

T S Eliot, *The Waste Land*

Dedicated to the memory of
Janey Riordan.

– If only we'd known. –

One

The final phase of my friendship with Janey Riordan I date from that day in late March when she was supposed to meet me at Whitechapel Hospital. She'd promised that by ten she meant ten, but she wasn't in reception when I arrived and I spent the next fifteen minutes flicking through the problem pages of the old *Woman's Realms* on the table and wondering about the other people waiting and attempting to work out whether fresh paint over the institutional yellow of the walls, carpet over the dark floor tiles and a less functionalist front desk would warm the place up. Answer: probably not.

I got to my feet and stretched – the moulded plastic chairs needed replacing too – then walked over to the main door. How I loved crisp March sunlight. Why had I rushed? Wasn't she always late?

I made a vow: I'd use the ladies' room and if she hadn't arrived by the time I'd finished, I'd seek out the doctor she was supposed to be introducing me to. There was no point in two of us being rude, and it wasn't as if Janey were necessary. She was the go-between, that was all; the business was between me and – I fished my diary out of my bag – Dr Sophia Khan. I was dying to know what 'useful information' she had about my young client Amin Ali, whose murder trial was starting the following week. My fear was that Janey was exaggerating the hotness of the tip and that, in my desperation, I'd bought it.

The ladies' room was through the double doors and to the right. It seemed empty and I paused to glance at the new, thinner version me in the mirror. Wearing a straight skirt – what a feeling. Then I noticed that the last of the four stall doors was shut. I went into the nearest one.

I was fastening the latch when there was a sharp cry from the other cubicle. The chord of pain touched the base of my spine and raced to my shoulder blades. I undid the bolt and hurried over to the closed door. I could hear the other woman hyperventilating.

'What's the matter?'

She moaned.

I pushed the door. It resisted.

'Can you undo the lock?'

She struggled to control her breathing and I heard a bit of fumbling on the latch. This stopped and she squeezed a few words out. Unfortunately they weren't English. Then she let out another sharp cry.

One option was to try to kick the door in, but brute physical strength was not at the time one of my attributes. Instead I told her to hang on, then hurried back out to the corridor and down to the reception area, where I compelled the receptionist to sound the alarm.

When I re-entered the ladies' room the sharp cries were coming regularly, like my worst fantasy of a hard childbirth. A thin trickle of watery blood was coming from under the door.

I'm not a churchgoer or a religious person in any conventional sense, but I prayed that if there were any benign force it would bring help before whatever was about to happen happened. I started murmuring to the woman behind the door as soothingly as I could, telling her how quickly help would be here and encouraging her to hold on until it arrived. At the same time I filled a sink full of hot water and pulled a great drape of blue cotton towel out of the wall dispenser.

Several long minutes later two nurses and a woman doctor hurried in, followed by a maintenance guy in a boiler suit carrying a tool kit. I stood there uselessly as they huddled around the door, talking quickly among themselves about the chances of unscrewing the hinges, while the woman's cries became more urgent and frequent and breathless and animal. Abruptly the guy in the boiler suit said, 'It will take too long', and threw his kit hard at the handle area. It gave.

The doctor, who looked Indian or Pakistani in origin, put her head into the cubicle and spoke quickly in the language the woman had used. This time I recognised it: Sylheti, the Bengali dialect spoken by most of the local Bangladeshi population. Within seconds she'd slipped around the opening, got the poor suffering woman clear of the door, opened it wide and started guiding her out. The patient was young – twenty at most – and looked terrified. The loose tunic top and trousers of her lilac shalwar kamiz were blotched with wet purple stains.

I watched, half fascinated, half appalled, as she collapsed on to the mattress the nurses had made from the blue toweling. There was a lot of blood – much much too much. And the sharp cries stopped abruptly while they were still on the ascendant, with the climax yet to come.

The long silence which followed was all wrong.

The nurses and the doctor, I realised, were on their knees, almost at prayer.

I felt suddenly stifled, in desperate need of air. I'd miscarried myself once and being so near someone else going through it brought it all back. The depression afterwards had been like nothing I'd ever experienced and made the funks caused by lost cases and business problems and heartache seem lightweight and passing. Even my tortuous split with the baby's father paled.

I didn't want to remember.

I pushed past the scene and back out into the corridor, where I took a big lungful of air. It wasn't enough. I carried on outside and took a bigger swallow. That was much better. I concentrated on my breaths, inhaling and exhaling, inhaling and exhaling until the knots in my gut had relaxed.

I was making my way slowly back towards the door of the hospital when the doctor I'd seen in the ladies' room came through it, spotted me and hurried over. This time I got a clearer sense of her: thick black hair, well cut – almond skin – dark skirt and white blouse under the white doctor's smock – wedding ring. Thirty-five. Large eyes that smiled and reassured. Always running late but always time for *your* pain.

'Are you all right?' Her accent had a confident clarity that made me think Oxbridge.

'Yeah,' I said feebly, 'fine. Thanks.'

My own accent sounds American to British ears and English to American ears. She picked it up at once. 'You're not –. Are you Dee Street?'

I nodded. 'You're Sophia?'

She put out her hand. '"Sufiya". Janey's always late, isn't she?'

I shook it. 'Tell me about it.'

She glanced at her watch. 'I just need to check that patient again –'

'Did she – miscarry?'

She sighed. 'I'm afraid so. It's not a good area for full-term pregnancies. The spontaneous abortion rate has doubled just in the four years I've been here.'

'Really? I'd heard something about birth heart problems –'

She nodded. 'Heart problems, lung problems, cancer problems.'

'God. Do you have any idea why?'

'Not the diet, not the water, not lead or carbon monoxide. The grant I'm about to start – number five – is paying for tests on the fabric of the primary school and the mosque and for monitoring the health of a group of upwards of 2,000 local women. Janey's providing the premises for that in fact.'

'Good. That's terrific. So, is there a link between your research and Amin Ali's case?'

'Janey didn't tell you?'

I shook my head.

She checked her watch again and thought quickly. 'How's this,' she said. 'You get us coffees from the canteen – better get three – and I'll meet you on the ward?'

'Fine by me,' I said. 'Janey –?'

'She knows where it is. Special Care Baby Unit. Second floor. Garden Wing.' Then she waved and hurried back into the hospital.

Get coffee: it should have been quick. Instead, thanks to a queue of nursing students and a beginner on the till, it was twenty minutes before I found my way to the ward. I peered through the glass-panelled double doors. It was long and narrow, with drawn curtains and dim lighting, and was crowded with incubators and life-support systems. About half a dozen had young Asian women standing watch beside them, and Sufiya, her white coat making her stand out, was down at the far end, talking with one of them.

Still no Janey.

Hmmm, I thought, in other circumstances I could start getting seriously worried about this.

Sufiya glanced over at the door. I waved and she gestured for me to come in. Squeamishness rose in my gut. I spent a moment getting on top of it, then pushed open the doors with the coffee tray and headed through.

I didn't intend to look but couldn't help myself. Each incubator contained a brown baby, comprehensively wired up to the drugs and other apparatus. The poster-sized kids' paintings and strings of handmade cards and bright polka-dot fabric patches on the walls behind the equipment were obviously meant to warm the place but, for me, just accentuated what a chilly limbo it was.

As I approached Sufiya, she laid her hand supportively on the shoulder of the young woman beside her. 'Hello again,' she said. 'This is Amin Ali's sister, Nasima.'

I was so surprised it took me two tries to make my voice work. 'Sister!' I squeaked at last. I'd met Amin's British-Bangladeshi aunt and uncle and a couple of cousins; all his immediate family (he'd told me) were still out in Dhaka.

Nasima pushed her scarf back slightly from either side of her face and gazed solemnly into my eyes.

Sufiya gestured to the nearby incubator. 'And this is her son.'

I looked down, conscious of Nasima's gaze still on me. The technological nest he was lying on emphasised his smallness, but he was bigger than most of the others – definitely not a newborn.

I looked back at Nasima. She was so young. How did she cope?

Sufiya said, 'She says she knows Amin didn't kill the policeman.'

'Fantastic!' I grinned into the solemn eyes. 'That's wonderful.'

'There are just two problems,' Sufiya went on. 'She's here illegally and the alibi involves hashish.'

Yes, I thought, just another simple criminal defence case. 'Right,' I said, 'is there somewhere more comfortable we can discuss this?'

Three-quarters of an hour later I was heading towards the tube station so preoccupied rethinking the brief that it was only when I got out my purse and saw the pathetic few coins in it that I recalled the other reason – the original reason – Janey and I had been meeting. The small non-profit organisation she directed owed my small practice a big chunk of fees and today was pay day.

The chunk was big because it stretched way back into the good old days, before a new accountant had pointed out that our careless billing practices and growing list of uncollectable hardship cases would mean no more caring sharing services to anybody by the end of the year. We'd all sworn oaths on a tougher system, warned clients of the monthly invoices they could expect and given last deadlines to clients with long-standing debts. We tried to be fair and reasonable in this: community groups like the one Janey Riordan ran got time to adjust their grant applications and do whatever else they needed to do to raise the money. The results had been mixed, but Janey – until that moment – I'd counted as a success. She'd needed a couple of extensions but she'd come up with ninety per cent of it.

Or so she'd said.

When she'd pulled the Sufiya Khan 'favour' out of her hat two days earlier, my partner – a long-time Janey cynic – muttered at me to steel myself, Janey could be up to tricks. I'd taken this lightly: I'd known Janey half my life and was one of the few untouchables she'd never pulled 'tricks' on.

Had my partner been right – my turn had come? There was one way to find out. Janey's office wasn't that far away. I'd go there and see. I checked the local map on the station wall, oriented myself and headed through the warren of back streets between White-chapel and Brick Lane.

I emerged ten minutes later at the corner by the ex-church, ex-synagogue that served as the mosque. Elders with chin-strap beards, dressed in ankle-length kurtha robes and boxy topee caps were standing talking in knots of two or three on the pavement in the early spring sun, and the restaurants and cafés I passed all had their doors open, saturating the air with the many smells of curry.

I walked on past the old brewery and under the Shoreditch train bridge and came in sight of the block-long queue of people outside the bagel shop. The office of Weaverstown Housing Association, Janey's base, was across the street (a wonderfully fattening location) and as I approached I saw a white threesome of sober-suited and blue-rinse types chatting as they filed in the narrow front door: obviously Management Committee members – they had to be . . . which meant I was in luck. Janey might skip out on a meeting with me, but with her executive board? Never.

The front door was on the latch, so I let myself in and climbed the narrow stairs towards the party noises coming from the first-floor reception office. Its door was wide open and fifteen or twenty people were milling about drinking tea and munching sandwiches in a space designed for half that number. A pall of cigarette smoke hung unfashionably above their heads and I could hear the overly elocuted voice of Janey's boss, Evie Maguire, rising from somewhere in the back.

I was surveying the scene for Janey when someone gripped my arm from behind and said my name. I turned, realised the hand touching me was attached to Evie Maguire's son, Tim, and pulled my arm away faster than was cool or kind. It didn't matter: the guy's ego armour shielded him from my response. He didn't see himself as a dumpling-shaped middle-aged hustler whose trendy leather suit and permed rock-star ringlets looked completely ridiculous, therefore no one else did. Quite the opposite: he assumed that every woman he met fancied him as much as he did.

'Tim, hi,' I said without enthusiasm.

He looked me up and down with an inane expression that was probably supposed to be wolfish. 'Jesus, Dee, you been on a diet or what?'

I was tempted to tell him I had a highly contagious fatal disease but refrained. 'Seen Janey?' I asked instead.

He gestured upwards with his thumb.

I carried on up the stairs to the top floor and knocked on her office door. 'Janey, it's me, Dee.'

She called out to me to enter and was standing leaning against her desk in that willowy way of hers, arms extended, when I came through. It hadn't been that long since we'd last met up – three or four months – but as I approached her to accept the hug, I was surprised at how much her face had aged. She was in her late forties, ten years my senior, but that day she could have been my mother. The 1950s cut of her suit and the severe French-twist hairdo that showed off her grey streaks only heightened the impression.

'I'm sorry I couldn't get there, love.' She swept her arm over the half-collated piles of papers she was obviously working on. 'Emergency meeting. Did Sufiya deliver?'

'Did she ever. Thanks a lot.'

She smiled and kissed the air by my cheek. 'Good.' She glanced at her watch. 'Look. They're waiting for me –'

The moment had come. 'You were going to give me a cheque.'

She hung her head and let out a deep sigh, then looked up at me again. In her eyes I saw the hard truth: I was no longer exempt from 'tricks'. Anger, hurt, betrayal surged together in my diaphragm.

'There are problems –' she began.

'We've been through them all.'

'Yes, well, since the warehouse conversion fell through –'

'That's not new.'

'Well, I'm sorry, you'll have to wait until the playground site grants come next month –'

I leaned in at her and looked as menacing as it's possible for me to look. 'You don't understand, Janey. We can't wait until next month. We can't wait until next week.'

She didn't back away. 'And *you* don't understand, Dee. The pot is empty. That's what the emergency meeting's about.'

I don't remember what I said next but I'm sure it referred to the length of our friendship and the amount of understanding and credit she'd had from us going back a dozen years and posed the question How could she? several times. She didn't protest, didn't say a word, just nodded. When I'd burned myself out, I turned and huffed out of her door and down the stairs. She didn't call after me.

Given the inevitable dire impact of Janey's news on my firm's finances, hiring a taxi to take me from Bethnal Green Road to my office in Camden Town felt profligate. On the other hand, it was important that I share the bad news with my partner instantly if not sooner and this was the means to that end.

As the cab turned off Parkway and pulled up to the kerb

opposite my little building, I spotted the racing-green Mercedes two-seater parked in what was coming to seem like its spot in front. It belonged to a new client, a wealthy antiques trader, and with the sun glinting off its hood it made our humble premises look infinitely more decrepit than the fond image I carried with me. And as for the worn name sign in the window that we'd long accepted as post-feminist and ironic – 'As all t eet, Solicit s' it said instead of 'Aspinall Street, Solicitors' – the joke suddenly seemed pathetic.

Twelve and a half years it had been since Suze Aspinall and I had set up our partnership in the ground floor and basement of this same building. As I let myself in, I wondered: was it really to be unlucky thirteen?

The small reception area, where bright curtains and hanging plants were struggling to cover over ageing paintwork, was pretty full and the kids' area was turbulent. Our receptionist, the imperturbable Jackie, was juggling the phone, a courier and a gloomy couple who had to be waiting for Simone, my colleague with the family caseload. She still managed to give me a smile and a cheery hello.

Some days every one of the five associates, all half a dozen secretaries, both clerks and the cleaner seem to need to besiege me on the stairs up to my office. Other days it's as if the whole place is heads down. Fortunately that was a heads-down day.

My office, Suze liked to tell people, was an effort to reconstruct the southern California climate I grew up in, from seed. That's an exaggeration – I had maybe 100, 120 plants – though it is true that on a hot day in July the place could feel like the temperate zone glasshouse at Kew Gardens. (Smell like it too.)

I crossed to the interconnecting door between our offices and was lifting my hand to knock when I heard her burst into a husky laugh and say something in her throatiest, most down-home, roots-Yorkshire lilt. A male voice said something back to her, something that made him exaggerate his rolling Scots 'r's, then started to laugh kind of huskily too.

Hmmm. I'd thought Mr Antiques seemed unusually attentive. Good! Suze could do with feeling fancied. Her husband was just so much hard work.

I decided to send up a coded signal. I filled my watering can and banged around among the plants near the interconnecting door. She received it: a minute later chairs scraped back and first one, then two sets of footsteps crossed Suze's floor. Her main door opened and shut and they walked by my office to the stairs, both still laughing.

I went over to the window and looked out. A moment later he emerged on the front path. His white hair said 'ageing' but his lean frame and springy step said 'under control'. He turned and gave Suze a wave and I caught a glimpse of his patrician profile. He was straight off an old Roman coin, this guy, gene carrier of the Caesars.

There was a knock behind me and Suze came in. It was one of her firecracker days – light red shoes, deep cherry suit, explosion of hennaed hair, zippy step – and I'd barely turned to greet her when she was beside me. She looked out of the window too and as we watched the Mercedes pull away she said, 'Speaking of Janey Riordan . . . Guess who threw Marc Felici our way?' She laughed. 'I thought, uh oh, if she's done us *two* favours –'

I turned and looked at her again, and the instant she saw my expression her jokiness went. 'Shit. She really didn't pay?'

'No. She didn't.' I slumped into my desk chair and for a moment thought I'd cry. 'What a mug. What an ass.'

She pulled a client chair around so she could sit beside me, then put her hand over mine. She didn't remind me that she'd predicted trickery. In fact she didn't say anything.

I said, 'We won't come near our income target.'

She nodded. She'd predicted this consequence if she was right about the trickery. 'I think we've got to face it, Dee: we've done our best and we still have this big core of uncollectables. Unless one of our possible investors puts in about ten times more than any of them seems inclined to –'

'What about Mr Antiques?'

Suze feigned a shiver. 'I don't want Marc Felici to know we've got financial worries – not until I've done more work for him. Look, we said that if this was the position we found ourselves in at this point, we'd bite the bullet and look more closely at the other options. I vote we get going *fast*.'

I sighed. My heart felt just so so heavy. Collecting old debts and looking for investors – they were ways of staying as we were. Anything else meant fundamental change: laying people off, working fewer hours, moving, merging. I didn't want any of those things.

Suze watched me think all this. She squeezed my hand again. 'I don't want any of them either. But what if the miracle doesn't come, Dee? We've got to be ready.'

This was so simple and so patently true – so reasonable – that my brain belatedly re-engaged. She was right. We had reached change or die point, and indulging fear and sadness – that way lay death.

Two

Amin Ali's trial began the following Monday, so the actual work of investigating our survival options fell to Suze. I kept up by phoning her every morning and dropping back to the office every evening, but that was all. One debtor we'd written off surprised us with a cheque that cleared, and over a bottle of wine we shared a fantasy that all might go on as before. Then we found out how much our business taxes were going up and it was back to reality. The bump made us talk in much more detail about the firms we could imagine merging with, which in turn made us realise that our candidates, without exception, all had the same imbalance between needers and payers that we had. The next step was obvious: we had to identify a few that had the opposite problem.

On the third day of the second week I struggled back to the office at the end of the afternoon feeling equal parts exhausted and exhilarated. The prosecution barrister had finished presenting the police evidence, which hinged on two witnesses saying they'd seen Amin running away from the spot where they subsequently found the body of the murdered policeman, and on a transcript of what Amin allegedly said when he was arrested. The subtext was what the barrister and I had predicted: the investigating officer, a detective inspector with twenty years' experience, was a man of sterling character up against a fiendishly duplicitous defendant. We were going to turn that inside out and win – we had to. But I felt superstitious about too much confidence too soon – I'd seen it operate as a jinx. And before we'd had our turn was definitely too soon.

I came in to find a storage box sitting on my desk. Packed inside, filling it all, was the Weaverstown Housing Association file.

I picked it up, went and knocked on Suze's door, and without waiting entered her neat, uncluttered domain. As she looked up from her work I held it out. 'What's going on?'

She laughed. 'HM Queen Evie Maguire graced us with a telephone call.'

'I hope you were rude.'

'I tried to be. She talked right over me. You ready for why?'

I gritted my teeth. 'Sock it to me.'

'She wanted a lease Janey said you've got – for a playground? – sent to Weaverstown's new solicitor.'

I snapped my fingers. 'Natch. Free and gratis, no fees, no fuss.'

'You've got it. *And* – guess who the new solicitor is?'

I was too tired to try. 'Tell me.'

'Alex Maguire.'

'Her *son* Alex?'

She nodded.

'But he's only just qualified – and he's a tax specialist or something.'

She spread her hands and shrugged. 'Maybe he'll screw up.' She smiled. 'Wouldn't that be terrible?'

The defence case was built around proving that Amin Ali hadn't been anywhere near the scene of the crime and that, even if he had been there, he'd have been incapable of inflicting the heavy stab wounds that had killed the young police constable. We aimed to show that the senior investigating officer, sterling character or no, had been under such pressure from the tabloid press to make an arrest that he'd taken the word of known police informants with clear pecuniary interests and doubtful reputations, which he'd tried to keep from the court. Even more controversially, we aimed to show that he had taken advantage of Amin's weaknesses in English – heavy accent, limited comprehension – and edited or overseen the editing of the interview tape and the transcript so that it distorted Amin's responses.

The key witness our first day was Amin's sister Nasima, whom Sufiya had brought over to the Old Bailey twice to familiarise her with the atmosphere and help her to relax. But it was still intimidatingly white and European and she needed a lot of coaxing and reassurance from us both to get her through the front door. The wings flapping in my gut in the anxious minutes leading up to her taking the stand could have lifted a heron into flight But in the event she was softly but eloquently herself, and even the flat voice of the court interpreter somehow worked in her favour.

The story she had to tell began, she said, with the birth of her son. He was premature – twenty-nine weeks – and his heart and lungs were so weak his chances of survival were rated as very poor. The whole family was upset and tense, but her brother Amin was particularly affected – it happened not long after he'd arrived in London from Bangladesh and he felt it was somehow his fault, as if he'd brought bad luck upon his nephew and namesake. He got into a state of sleeplessness which led to a depression which led to threats to kill himself, and she was worried that he meant it. Her theory was that if he could just sleep properly for a few nights, he would feel better and see how ridiculous he was being.

By this point there wasn't an individual in the court who wasn't listening, rapt. When the door creaked open it sounded irritatingly loud and invasive and I, together with everyone else in the place, glanced over to see what idiot was responsible. Janey Riordan slipped in.

Typical.

Nasima continued: what she did was buy some very strong hashish from a source in the neighbourhood, then cook some in Amin's favourite cake. And it worked. When she left for the hospital to spend the day with the baby, he was unconscious on her sofa.

She hadn't come forward earlier because, for complex reasons to do with her husband's family's visa position in Britain – a situation she hadn't understood when they sent for her – she was an illegal immigrant. Her brother, who had the right papers, insisted she not put herself and her son in jeopardy. He was innocent, he said, and the truth would out without her incriminating herself. And she had acquiesced. Her son, miraculously, had lived – something which her brother also took as a sign. But now he had been bound so tightly in a frame of the police's devising that knowing he was innocent was not enough. This was why she was speaking up now.

She held up well in the cross-examination, which focused on her certainty about the effects of the hash on Amin in the period after she left him to go to the hospital. Issues we wanted to highlight – the 'lost' results of a blood test administered the day Amin was taken into custody, the floppy effects cannabis was known to have on him, the impossibility of him wielding a knife in that state – came out all. I know juries and jury body language: this group was impressed.

I allowed myself a moment of pure indulgence. I turned and glared at the person I knew beyond doubt was responsible for this whole despicable set-up, Sterling Man himself: Detective Inspector Keith Hamley. He came over as the quintessential new model senior policeman – no beer-belly laddishness, plenty of lip service to anti-racism and other liberal values, a showy eagerness to listen – but faced with pressure to produce results, he'd gone and behaved in the same old wearyingly stereotyped way. Mentally I plugged my thumbs in my ears and waggled my hands and stuck out my tongue at him. Uncannily he looked over at me, his expression as studiously neutral as my own. Was he projecting a hissing snake at me? So it felt. I shivered and turned away.

Outside afterwards all of us – Sufiya, Nasima, the barrister and I – were high. If everyone else hadn't been Muslim I'd have bought us a round at the pub, but instead we hugged and they flagged a cab to the East End and I set off to flag another going west. I'm sure I must have been skipping along the pavement when suddenly Janey caught up with me.

'Dee, hi. *Wait.*' She bent to kiss me and, though it was only late afternoon, her breath smelled of gin.

My first instinct was concern. Then I remembered what she'd done to me and Suze and the little firm we'd nurtured so long. If she'd paid us when she promised –. 'Hi,' I managed. I couldn't outpace her so I sidestepped to the kerb and peered into the oncoming traffic. Would she take the hint and go away?

But no. She followed. 'I know you're pissed off and I understand and I just want to say how really really sorry I am about the fees –.'

I spotted a black taxi and stuck out my hand. '"Sorry" unfortunately won't pay our bills.' The taxi headed towards us. 'Gotta go. See ya.'

'Dee –. Alex Maguire's screwing up the playground lease.'

'Well, I – you can hardly expect me to –.'

'There was no problem when *you* negotiated with Richard Farmer. I wondered – if you'd just phone him –.'

The taxi pulled over and I reached for its door. 'Janey, for God's sake. You fucked me over.'

'Evie made me.'

'*Janey* – listen to yourself. You're a grown-up. Nobody makes you shit on other people.' Then I turned my back on her and stepped into the cab. I was half-seated, pulling the door shut after me, when she inserted herself in the way. Bye-bye Janey the supplicant, hello Janey the bully. Like her tricks, her temper had always been something other people suffered, never me. Apparently my exemption had expired here too.

'I could lose three lots of development grant. I need them. You *have* to help me.'

'I don't "have" to help anyone.' I pulled at the door.

'If you don't, I swear to God, Dee, I'll –'

It was bluff and I called her on it before she made a complete ass of herself. 'Yes? You'll what?'

Satisfyingly, she bit her lip and let go of the door. I shut it and told the driver to pull away.

Before he could she leaned through the window and spoke the words she'd had the good sense to bite back a moment before. 'I know things about you. Don't forget that, Dee.'

All the possible old dirt Janey had on me swirled up in my mind. She knew I'd smoked my share of grass and not been above amphetamines when I was doing my law finals, and of course we'd trespassed together countless times back when we'd first met – but we were both squatting, that was what you did. And all these things had happened at least fifteen years before. Assuming a tabloid was having a dull day and used these old 'facts' to rubbish me – which was so unlikely as to be inconceivable – I couldn't see that any of them would seriously imperil my reputation now.

I shot her a look of pure disgust that gained in power when the taxi driver gunned the engine. She slapped the door with the flat of her palm as we pulled past and gestured 'Up yours' at me with a V sign. I'm ashamed to say I gave her the good old American finger.

When I got back to the office Suze was waiting for me, all keyed up. 'You won't believe what's happened. I found this old college mate, Charlotte McEwan, only I didn't realise it was her because she's called Ducane now.'

'As in Ducane Stafford?' They were a major City firm, right there in the heart of big money land.

'She's the founder's daughter-in-law. Been senior partner for a couple of years and runs the place from the sound of it.'

I sat down. 'Wow.'

'There's more. Get this – they've *just* moved into a bigger building and are *looking* for a merger partner with *our mix of skills*. They want to be able to offer "a full range of services to City-based individuals".'

'And hey presto, here we are. You told her we're all women?'

'She knew. She thinks it's great: if we joined, Ducane Stafford would become majority female.'

'Is she hoping her male colleagues won't notice?'

She laughed. 'She thinks their big question will be, Are we desegregating voluntarily?'

'And are we?'

She laughed again. How many times had we discussed this over the years? Way back in the beginning we'd been radical – fringe – marginal – notorious even for setting up a law firm run by women, for women. But these days half of all law graduates were women and it was a rare solicitors' office or barristers' chambers that didn't reflect this fact.

'Look,' she said, 'I'll go over there tomorrow, do the pre-liminaries I've done with the other possibles and set up a meeting for all of us. Is the trial running to schedule?'

'Yup.'

'Okay. Leave it to me. How was Nasima?'

'Terrific. Janey showed up. Pulled a number on me outside after-wards. Threatened to "tell tales". Like there's anything *to* tell.'

Suze frowned. 'Stay out of her way,' she said. 'Don't provoke her.'

But I didn't need to be told. We were finished, Janey and I. Fin-i-to.

The test came the next day when I arrived back from court to find a message saying Janey Riordan had rung to apologise and ask would I please please ring her urgently. I ignored it and the two she left on my answering machine at home. She didn't try again.

Less than a week later the jury did the only sensible thing and delivered a not guilty verdict on Amin Ali. It fell to me to make a statement to the press, which is how I came to be on TVs and radios throughout the land all that Thursday evening, calling on the Home Secretary to sack Detective Inspector Keith Hamley and legitimate Nasima's visa status. I avoid the news if I'm in it – I make me cringe – and that night, fortunately, Amin and Nasima's family made avoidance easy by whisking me and the barrister who'd presented the case, Abe Quereshi, to the best restaurant on Brick Lane for a celebratory feast. The place was already heaving with well-wishers when we arrived, Sufiya among them, though at that point she was so caught up in the conversation at her table that I waved and mouthed 'Catch you later' and passed on.

We were given seats at the head table, near the guest of honour, young Amin himself, in the head seat. Actually, 'in' gives the wrong impression. The poor guy was still flying. He 'hovered over' the head seat. What gave me the biggest kick was seeing how fast the premature haggardness he'd acquired during his nine months in a remand cell was vanishing. In another couple of hours he'd be back to looking twenty-two. By Monday (I hoped) he'd be instructing me to sue the police for malicious prosecution.

Tea appeared first, followed by spicy poppadoms, hot samosas, dry potato curry, chapatis and other delights. Then Amin and Nasima's father, who'd come over from Bangladesh for the trial, stood up and gave a short speech. His references to his daughter, who was sitting beside him, told me what the first part of it was about. Then I distinguished my own name. Everyone looked at me and grinned. His wife slipped out of the chair beside him, revealing the wrapped packages that had been on her lap. In mine was a shawl with gold threads running through it which he'd brought with him from home. I got to try out my few words of Sylheti and attempted to say thanks. They all laughed, which made me wonder what I'd really said, but they clapped too.

I slipped into the ladies' room to put it on and was in there primping when Sufiya came looking for me. She helped me adjust it around my head and shoulders and said congratulations, and I said it was all down to her and Nasima, and then I said, 'Is it me or are you a bit subdued?'

She sighed. 'It's me. I've got a problem. I hate to do this to you tonight of all nights, but I need to ask you a favour. In your capacity as a lawyer, I mean.'

'Shoot.'

'You know Janey Riordan was going to provide the premises for my health monitoring exercise with local women?'

'Oh, oh,' I said. 'What happened?'

'We were going to be in that new community centre she was supposedly doing up –'

'At the back of the playground?'

She nodded. 'The vendor pulled out. There's rumours he's sold to a development company.'

So: Janey'd been right to be anxious. I said, 'Wow, that was sudden.'

She nodded. 'It happened last week. They closed it to the kids the same day and they're already getting ready to excavate.'

'You're joking!'

'I wish I were. There's a round-the-clock vigil going on at the playground entrance and of course Janey's lobbying the vendor –'

'I know him. Richard Farmer. I negotiated her original lease with him. God, I bet she's in a state.'

'Terrible. Awful. Do you still represent her?'

'No.'

She smiled. 'That's what I'd heard. *We* want to hire you.'

'"We" being?'

'The three other groups affected by the collapse of the playground-site deal. We all feel Janey's concerned only about Weaverstown Housing Association's interests. We'd prefer not to break ranks but we feel she's left us no choice. I've managed to get an appointment with Richard Farmer tomorrow. Could you come with me? We want him to give us back the original building or give us an alternative.'

'Sounds fair. I'll need to check my diary but – what time?'

'Four. I'm going to try to get over to the playground to support the demonstration for a bit beforehand. Why don't we meet there?'

The celebrating went on past midnight and I got home to find my answering-machine tape had run out there'd been so many messages. I listened to the ones from friends and fast-forwarded over the requests for interviews. The media had had their bite of me.

By the time I arrived, gluey-eyed, at my office the next morning my colleagues had strung a big 'Congratulations' banner over the window and there was another pile of phone messages and faxes on my desk. I was going through them when Suze came in bearing a tray of coffee and buns, a crisp yellow wallet file tucked under her arm. I relieved her of the tray and when I'd set it down she gave me a hug and a pat on the back, allowed me thirty seconds to describe the party, then presented me with the yellow file. The neat new label said: Ducane Stafford and Co.

'We're scheduled to see them Monday morning.' She patted the file. 'That's so you're ready.'

I'd handled urgent items only for the three weeks of the trial and my desk looked like a model of the Peak District made from cardboard folders. I worked straight through until mid-afternoon at reducing it – no tea breaks, no lunch, emergency calls only – so letting myself out for my appointment with Sufiya felt like a reward.

I took along the Ducane Stafford file, and skimmed it in the taxi. The surviving founder partner was Sir Edward 'Teddy' Ducane, an old Labour Party supporter who was also a specialist in that most capitalistic branch of law, company and tax. His family were Quakers and in some circles he was credited with coining the term 'ethical investments'. The tragedy of his life was his eldest daughter's drug addiction and he'd won libel actions against *Private Eye*, the *Sun* and the *Mirror* for ill-judged stories about her. Two years before, on his seventy-fifth birthday, he'd handed over day-to-day management to Suze's old chum Charlotte.

All of which sounded wonderful.

– *But* merge *with them?*

– Our all-women hiring policy might seem dated now, but I was used to the special working environment we'd created.

– The first job I'd had, there'd been a patriarch at the top and I'd sworn never again.

– I loved our decrepit little building; could I really leave?

East End road-works led the taxi driver to cut through to Brick Lane and as we headed towards the junction with Bethnal Green Road I saw ahead a group of women, mainly white, with placards ('Save the Playground!') milling around on the pavement outside the Weaverstown Housing Association office. Janey came out of the door and as I ducked back, away from the window, she gestured to the woman as if to say, 'Troops, forward *march*.'

Whew, I thought, with any luck I'll be gone from the demonstration by the time she arrives.

We crossed into a neighbourhood of three-storey brick terraced houses, all of it ex-squatter property that Weaverstown Housing Association had acquired when the assets of the late Greater London Council were sold off. Making the places habitable for extended Bangladeshi families had proved a slow business. The two-thirds of them to the east were all done up and occupied. The third to the west were still boarded up and decaying.

We headed through these to the bottom of a cul-de-sac and turned right. The last time I'd rounded that corner I'd seen a playing field in the shape of the two streets of back-to-back houses that had been demolished there in the late 1970s. This time I saw a corrugated-iron fence, nine feet high, with a row of barbed wire along the top, surrounding the whole site. About fifty Asian women were marching in an ellipse in front of the padlocked gate. Some trailed children. Most were waving placards like the ones Janey's group had been carrying: 'Save our Playground', 'Save our Health Project', 'Save our Youth Centre'.

Watching from the pavement opposite were half a dozen young white men in suits and ties and preppie haircuts, almost City types slumming it except for their nose and lip rings and the three bulldogs they had with them. I'd heard the British National Party were trying to keep a lower profile – this was apparently it. A couple of them were still more legs than body, just boys out being *bad*. Go home, I wanted to say. Tell your mother she needs you.

As we pulled up to the kerb just past the demonstration I noticed a big flatbed truck with a crane on it parked at the other corner. A man with something familiar about him was standing in the road, hands in his pockets, talking to the driver.

I turned away to pull down the taxi window and wave to Sufiya when it came to me what I'd recognised: the permed hair. It was Tim Maguire. I looked back. My distance vision isn't great and he was a good way away, but that dumpling shape made me sure. It *was* Tim Maguire. He turned and walked off in the other direction.

What the hell was he doing, mixing it down here?

From his Enlightened Capitalist media image, you'd expect Richard Farmer's company headquarters to be in a small, ecologically sound building in some leafy neighbourhood. A top-floor suite in Broadgate, that monolith of imported Canadian postmodernism, had jarred when I'd first visited it years ago. Nothing had changed.

Sufiya and I were early, but Richard's secretary came and got us and showed us into his outer office, which was full of pieces of modern art like Zombar's *Four Sinks and a Toilet* installation and the cult painting *Maggie's Angels*. She offered us coffee and when she brought me mine a minute or so later she said, 'We've met before, you know.'

I looked into her face and saw youth and zip and mischief but nothing I remembered.

'You represented my sister Anji a couple of years ago.'

'Anji, of course!' She'd run over two guys who'd gang-raped her. 'How is she?'

'Okay. Better off in hospital than she'd have been in prison.'

'How long you worked for Richard Farmer?'

She opened her mouth to tell me but was cut off by the buzzer on her desk.

'Right,' she said instead. 'Follow me.' We fell in behind her. 'Be careful,' she added in a stage whisper. 'He's in a right tetchy mood.'

'Thanks,' I said. 'We've been warned.'

Richard Farmer had a build that my grandmother from Maine used to call 'a long tall drink of water' and as he bent to give my cheek a perfunctory old-time's-sake kiss and to shake Sufiya's hand, it was clear from his manner that only politeness had caused him to agree to this meeting – and that he wanted us out of there tout de suite. He gestured to us to sit down, for example, then perched. And he launched into a spiel that sounded rehearsed.

'I'm sorry for what's happened. Dee, you know I'm reliable. But as you also know, I'm a businessman. Bad investments were made without my full awareness. I had to sell something. The playground has planning permission.'

Sufiya leaned in. 'You donated money to the Health Monitoring project. You know we need premises.'

'I'm sorry. I'd like things to be otherwise.'

Now I leaned in. 'You have other properties.'

But at that moment a noisy hubbub burst into the waiting room beyond the closed door, as if one football team's fans had invaded the other side's pitch. All of us cursed and got to our feet. Richard was first and faster and was heading for the door while Sufiya and I were still giving each other startled looks.

Before he could reach it, it flew open and in swarmed the group of white women I'd seen leaving the Weaverstown office, led by

Janey. Bells and alarms and flashing lights all played across my forebrain. Instinctively I took a step back, as if I might somehow shield myself behind Sufiya. At that point, though, Janey was so high and so intent on what she was doing that she could see only Richard.

'You have a moral obligation,' she told him, 'to renew that playground-site lease.'

Richard made shooing gestures at her and her group. 'I won't be bullied or bounced. You've interrupted a meeting.'

This was the unfortunate cue. Janey looked over and saw us there. Then she looked back at Richard. Then she looked back at us. This time she registered us – first me, then Sufiya. Over her face came the expression of someone adding two and two and coming up with two to the power of twenty-two. She crossed the room so fast that she arrived in front of me giving off heat. Hands on hips, she said, 'How could you?'

But I of course had a store of indignation of my own. 'How could I what? Help a paying client? *Janey*. Get real.'

She switched her gaze to Sufiya. 'And you –'

Sufiya straightened, cleared her throat and stayed calm. 'The monitoring project needs premises. We can't be bound to you. You said so yourself.'

Janey laughed, a single derisory syllable. She gestured to me. 'And you're trusting *her* to help you?'

I was suddenly conscious of the audience crowded around the door – Richard, his secretary, the receptionist, the dozen women demonstrators who'd come with Janey. All were looking at me.

Someone at the back said to someone else, 'Who's she?' Another person said, 'That lawyer, you know. On the news.' A third said, 'Defended Amin Ali.' The first said, 'Yeah? Really? Hey.'

With as much dignity as I could muster I said, 'I'd be careful I didn't give these people the wrong impression, Janey.'

'By what? By doing what? Telling them you promise contracts that you don't deliver?'

'You fail to pay bills.'

'I put friendship before money.'

'Easier when you're the debtor.'

'Not in favours. And I don't forget who knows *certain things*.'

I clucked impatiently. 'Bullshit. There's nothing to know.'

She clenched her jaw and extended her arm full out, so the tip of her index finger came within inches of the tip of my nose. I took her speechlessness for evidence that she was scrabbling in her brain to make something up.

Three uniformed security guards came hurrying through the reception area, through the assembled crowd and right up to Janey. They grabbed her by the arms and she struggled to shake them off, but in vain.

Worse, the sight of me watching her struggle, not lifting a finger, acted as a goad. As the guards turned her around and led her out, she looked over her shoulder and said in a great big loud voice, 'I know you bloody lived with a convicted Irish terrorist.'

Then she was gone.

Three

'God,' was all Suze could say when I told her what Janey had come out with. 'She didn't.' Then she swivelled the chair around so she was looking out the window, her back to me, shaking her head.

I laughed a bit maniacally. I was still feeling much too hyper to stand still, never mind sit down. Pacing stopped me overheating. 'That's all *I* could think for about thirty seconds. It was like she'd gone 'doink' with a bad fairy-godmother wand and struck me dumb. Thank God for Sufiya. If she hadn't touched me on the arm I'd probably still be standing there.' I imitated myself frozen into a silly position and laughed some more but Suze didn't turn around.

'What did you tell Sufiya?' she asked over her shoulder.

'The truth! I said I went to West Belfast a few years ago with another lawyer to interview a witness, I collapsed and a woman from a Republican family took me in. To call her a terrorist, to say I "lived with" her, wilfully distorts the picture. More coffee?'

'No. No thanks.'

As I walked across her office to the sideboard to pour some for myself, I said, 'Richard couldn't handle it. I was surprised. He just disappeared.'

'You mean your meeting was a wipe-out?'

I nodded. 'On top of everything else.'

She sighed. 'No media about, let's hope.'

I recalled the group of women huddled in the doorway of Richard's office, watching Janey's explosion at me, and scanned their faces in my mind's eye. They'd looked ordinary enough, but what did that mean? Janey had brought them there because she hoped to embarrass Richard into doing what she wanted. Publicity goes with those kind of tactics and she'd spent much of her working life hustling the press.

'Who knows?' I said. 'I almost don't care if there was. Suing her for libel would be deeply gratifying.' I laughed.

She swung around and spoke with a lot more heat than seemed called for. 'Don't even joke about such a thing.'

I backed away, hands up. 'Okay, okay. Sorry.'

But her heat was gone, poof, like that. 'I'm the one who should apologise, Dee. I knew Janey'd do this one day, I *knew* it.'

'Yes, and you tried to tell me and I wouldn't listen. I can't believe I was so arrogant.'

She was shaking her head. 'No, I mean she isn't talking about –' But there the phone cut her off. She sighed wearily and picked it up. Then she heard the caller's voice and everything – her expression, her posture, her tone – lifted. She didn't say Mr Antiques' name, but she didn't need to. Eavesdropping revealed that they were going for a 'dinner meeting' in a couple of days. Forty seconds later when she hung up, the smile remained. 'I *love* being pursued. I'd forgotten what it was like.'

I had only the vaguest memory myself. I laughed for her. 'Any chance he'll catch you?'

'What, with Peter just starting AA sessions again? *Please*.'

I winced. 'What were you saying before the call? Janey isn't talking about "something" and I missed what.'

She thought for the quickest of half-seconds, then waved her hand. 'Nothing. It's hot air. It'll blow over. In fact it's probably vanished into the ether already. Now tell me, have you looked at the Ducane Stafford file yet?'

We spent the next half-hour reviewing the questions we wanted to ask at our meeting with them on Monday morning and it was while we were doing it that the finality of what we were contemplating hit me. Bye-bye Aspinall Street. Hello – what? Aspinall Ducane Stafford & Street?

No. It *sounded* cobbled together.

On the other hand, Dee Street, Bankrupt, didn't exactly have a catchy beat either.

When I got back to my flat my gut was still in a big knot over the merger idea, so I made some peppermint tea and stretched out on the Chesterfield to watch the news and the Gerard Depardieu movie that came after it. The next thing I knew the phone was ringing and when I opened my eyes an old *Cagney and Lacy* episode was on. I squinted at the digital clock: 11.50. A client arrested? My mother stricken? A friend in trouble? I stumbled over to answer.

An English male voice said, 'That Dee Street? This is the *Telegraph* Diary –'

'It's *midnight* –'

'We gather a client of yours claims you had an intimate relationship with an Irish terrorist.'

All grogginess fell away. 'She's an ex-client and she's stirring it.'

'Well, our information –'

'Your information is wrong. It's a matter of record and I would take appropriate steps were you to print it. I trust I make myself clear.' Then, with the dignity only the truly wronged can muster, I hung up on him. It felt good.

Normally when my work backlog is as big as it was then I spend Saturday and at least half of Sunday in the office, but I'd been invited to visit old friends in Dorset, west of Poole, had already cancelled once because of Amin Ali's case and felt I couldn't do it again. I boarded the train at Waterloo fretting – was Janey's appalling bit of defamation doing the rounds of the diarists? What was to be done? – and by the time I arrived I had a solution. I phoned the London journalist I trusted the most, told him I suspected malicious rumours about me might surface in the wake of the Amin Ali victory and asked him to tell me if he heard anything. After that I got on with relaxing, mostly on the windy beach near my friends' house, and reboarded the train Sunday night to return to London vowing, as usual, to let myself out of my work-dominated life more often.

When I got home there was a message from my journalist contact. He *had* heard a malicious rumour about me. Apparently I'd had a torrid affair with an Irish bomb-maker. He'd quashed it hard. 'In fact I got so carried away I told them you wouldn't hesitate to sue. It was late, I'd had a few – sorry if I went too far.'

I left a message on his machine to say thanks and not to worry: given the firm's precarious financial state, I probably *would* have to issue a writ if this lie, already larger and more hugely inaccurate than the version I'd heard, made it into print.

The next morning I got up first thing and was at the corner newsagent's when he opened. I bought all the papers and sat at the kitchen table skimming them while I was having my coffee and toast. Nothing. Not a whisper.

I closed the last of them and felt intuitively that I'd just had a very close call. I was last week's news. Rumours about me had decreasing interest value and came with libel threats. Another few days and the incident could be filed under Janey Blows Out an Old Friend, Number 1, 0, 5.

The thing I found least appealing about Ducane Stafford on paper was their location. Moorgate was too close to the centre of the establishment, and aesthetically, if I wanted to work in sky-scraper-ville I'd go somewhere like New York or Chicago, where they do it right. I might not miss the run-down-ness of my little office, but I'd miss being close to the park and within walking distance of home. I'd also miss the deluxe muesli of Camden's streetlife. The City was soggy grey cornflakes by comparison.

When I'd said this to Suze, she'd smiled and said, 'Wait and see. You'll like their new offices, Dee. Trust me. They have our taste – with money.'

I'd been certain she must be exaggerating, but standing in front of the entrance to the three-storey converted mews that was Ducane Stafford's headquarters I wasn't so sure. It was definitely several cuts above what we were used to. One wing was curtained and full of people taking off coats and filling coffee mugs and settling in to the day. The other had no curtains and I could see a couple of decorators painting away at the ceiling on the first floor.

I felt a little itch of excitement: we would fit perfectly in the vacant wing.

I liked Suze's old classmate Charlotte immediately, I liked the six partners she introduced us to, I liked the look of the staff and the organisation of the offices and the rapport I saw between Charlotte and the people who worked with her. Two hours later when Suze and I walked back out the front door we were both surprised at how much more euphonious Aspinall Ducane Stafford Street sounded. We bore with us Charlotte's full proposal document and an invitation to return on Wednesday for sandwiches and coffee with the patriarch, Sir Teddy Ducane, whose approval would be a formality on whatever merger plan we might agree.

Because I found Ducane Stafford so disconcertingly tempting, I made time between our meetings there to visit a couple of the other firms on the shortlist of merger candidates Suze and I had drawn up. She had been to all of them and convinced herself from that that Ducane Stafford were far and away our best bet. I wanted to be as convinced as she was.

It worked. Two visits later and I was sure.

I might still be feeling a strong inner resistance to the idea of merger and the changes it would bring, but if we decided to go ahead – and how were we to avoid it? – *which* firm was not an issue. Indeed, as Suze and I told each other at every opportunity, we ought to count ourselves damn lucky they wanted us.

Every time I looked up from my file mountain the next couple of days I tried to remind myself of that.

Suze was out all Wednesday morning, so we arranged to meet at Ducane Stafford just before our two o'clock meeting. I got there with five minutes to spare and, remembering that I'd wanted to look at the rock garden and waterfall in the reception, buzzed to be let in. As soon as I gave my name, however, I was told Sir Teddy had asked to see me the moment I arrived. I protested that I wanted to wait for Suze and Charlotte, but to no avail. As I was shown to the lift and told to go to the top floor, I reflected that if I were still alive and still working at 77, I'd probably get my way all the time too.

For a man who'd succeeded in keeping his picture out of the papers and off the television, Sir Teddy was a surprisingly colourful old boy with the straight posture of the wartime RAF hero he'd been and a walrus moustache and bright bow tie that together said he had a sense of humour about himself. His office was dark blue fabric against dark wood and looked as if it had been lifted whole from a Heal's display window.

'I hoped we'd have this opportunity,' he said as he showed me to a sofa in the lounge area. A pot of coffee was waiting on a hot plate surrounded by chunky mugs and when he invited me to help myself I was happy to comply. Only when I'd sipped and complimented him on it and sat back did I notice that he was holding his right arm behind his back.

He said, 'Am I right in supposing you haven't yet seen the latest *Private Eye*?'

Private Eye. Shit. I sat forward again. 'What about it?'

He brought it out from behind his back and handed it to me, open to the gossip column. A frog danced in my lower intestine as I read.

Only last week American-born 'progressive' lawyer Dee Street, co-founder (with former Socialist-Communist youth leader Suze Aspinall) of that bastion of legal and feminist political correctness, Aspinall Street, was lambasting the CID for corrupt values. Now comes news that Saint Dee is not immune. Disgruntled client Janey Riordan confronted her in public with claims that she overcharges, that she betrays confidences and that she once lived with a convicted IRA terrorist. Consulted on the latter, a spokesman from the Law Society refused to comment. Apparently there are no ethical guidelines on this issue.

I was rereading it when Suze was shown in. Sir Teddy greeted her in the same courteous way he'd greeted me and showed her to the sofa opposite mine. She gave me a puzzled look – why was I sitting there reading a magazine? – then she realised it was *Private Eye*. Anxiety flickered behind her eyes and she reached with alarm for the copy he was now holding out to her.

He came and sat down in the armchair beside me. His expression could not have been more sympathetic. 'I presume this is nonsense?'

'Absolutely.' I told him about Janey and the fees she hadn't paid and repeated what I'd told Sufiya about my trip to West Belfast and the hospitality I'd been shown when I'd collapsed there. I got pretty heated up about the stupidity of *Private Eye* for again printing a story without even bothering to check it, yet when I glanced at Suze for affirmation, I found she was staring out of the window at the sky, lost in her own thoughts.

Sir Teddy, on the other hand, was right there with me in my indignation. 'I've had to sue *Private Eye* twice. Both times I made them settle with me out of court and print bold retractions. If I were you, I'd issue a writ immediately. Stop it spreading.'

Suze murmured, 'Nobody believes what they read in *Private Eye* any more.'

'If only that were true,' he said.

I nodded. 'Sir Teddy's right. If we even lose one prospective client – at a time like this . . . And it *could* spread.'

'Also,' he said, 'Ducane Stafford upholds a long pacifist tradition. Allegations of terrorist affiliations are anathema. Given the nature of our discussions . . .'

But he didn't need to finish. I knew: we had to issue a writ.

I laughed harshly. 'Janey Riordan was our first client. What irony.'

Suze turned and looked at me then and I realised that her face had gone cadaver white. 'Suze? Are you okay?'

Sir Teddy poured her a glass of water, which she took and sipped gratefully. A bit of colour came back to her face and she said she thought in fact she had a migrane coming on – the first in years. He offered her a range of remedies but she said no thanks, with any luck it would pass, but if we could maybe move on to the next item on our agenda – how he saw the two firms' skill-bases combining.

That was fine by him and he launched into an answer, but he was only a few sentences into it when Suze lost colour again and put her hand to her head. He saw it happen the same moment I did.

'Please, my dear, there's a bed.'

'Thanks – thank you – but I better go home.'

'I'll come back with you,' I said.

'Absolutely not. That's ridiculous. Sir Teddy's reserved this time.'

He sighed. 'I fear it will be difficult to reschedule.'

'There – you must stay.' Then she shook his hand, apologised again, expressed utmost confidence in my ability to spread enthusiasm for Aspinall Street and said she'd talk to me later. I went with her out to the hall to wait for the lift but she kept her head down and one hand on her forehead, the other on her stomach, the way she does when she's got a migraine coming. When the lift door opened I repeated my offer to come with her and she repeated her rejection of it. I said, 'I mean to issue the writ when I go back to the office – you happy with that?'

The lift door was sliding closed. She shielded her eyes again with her hand. 'I'm happy for you to do whatever you think is best,' she said.

I spent another three-quarters of an hour with Sir Teddy and left feeling torn. I liked his track record, his energy, his charm and his goodwill. But: underneath I sensed a stern old Calvinist with a will to his own way that I'd not want to cross. I also sensed that, even though he was presiding over a wonderfully mixed stew of senior partners and associates, this just might have been achieved more in spite of him than because of him.

I was back in my office at 3.30 and an hour later libel writs were on their way to *Private Eye* and Janey Riordan. It definitely felt weird suing the person I'd always thought of as my first friend in London – so weird I reviewed every step of the logic of it again *and* phoned the lawyer friend I'd gone to Belfast with, Theresa O'Connor. Belfast was Theresa's hometown, she knew everybody in Irish nationalist circles and when she heard the allegation she agreed instantly to testify for me in the unlikely event that this action ever got to court.

As I handed the envelopes to the courier I thought, Sorry Janey, but you've left me – us – no choice. We can't front up to a smear campaign: we're too financially vulnerable. And we can't jeopardise the most promising merger possibility we have before we've even decided whether to accept it.

Deed done, I phoned Suze to check that she was okay. No one answered.

The reason for this was evident when I got to my flat: Suze was parked out front in her Mini, waiting for me. She wouldn't come in – insisted it was too confidential. We must drive around.

I crouched down to talk to her through the car window. 'This business with Janey's really upset you, hasn't it? What she's doing to me – it's what she did to you.'

She held open the passenger door. 'Get in.'

I obeyed – trying to argue with Suze when she's in this mood: I knew better. Anyway, I was curious.

She drove on to the Marylebone Road and headed up the Westway flyover. There was traffic but it was moving right along and after we were well out of central London she said, 'I have to tell you something, Dee. It's something I probably should have told you a long time ago, but –' she shrugged – 'the time came and then it went and it just didn't seem –'

'How long ago are we talking about here?'

She gave me a quick glance. 'Fifteen years.'

Don't know why this surprised me but it did. 'I don't even want to try to guess.'

'It would be pointless anyway. It's not something you ever knew about. Janey knows that, too. It's me she's getting to.' She shook her head. 'She must be incredibly strung out to be dredging up this old stuff. *Incredibly*.'

'Tell me,' I said.

She sighed. 'When Janey ran Squatters' Network, she helped a load of people on the run for political crimes.'

'Housing them, you mean?'

She nodded. 'It started with a pair of white South African college blokes who'd antagonised the old BOSS by speaking out against apartheid. She found them a place in Willesden somewhere and sent them to me for advice. A few weeks later three Germans turned up: Baader-Meinhoff members – tried to bomb the Bundesbank. They gave themselves up in the end. After that it was an American woman who'd done some armed robberies for the Weather Underground.'

'Not the one arrested last year?'

She nodded. 'Amazing, isn't it? On the run since I met her. Anyway, for two or three years Janey was first point of call for all sorts – including the Provisional IRA and the INLA and all the other nationalist Irish factions.'

'I'm not surprised by any of this. It's very Janey-as-she-was. But if I wasn't involved, how is this relevant to –'

She said the next two words quietly. 'Liam Mahoney.'

A thunderstorm seemed to gather instantly right over my head and, while it rumbled and blew, I couldn't speak. Liam: the man who'd felled me with heartbreak my second year in law college. Liam: the scruffy poet who'd showed up with his guitar case at my front door saying Janey'd told him I had spare rooms.

He'd stayed less than two months and we'd spent a lot of it in bed. That's partly why (okay – largely why) I'd been so upset when I'd come home and found his note saying he'd decided to move on.

'Let me get this right,' I managed to mumble. '*Liam* was in the IRA?'

'I'm sorry,' she said quietly.

'Did *you* know who he was before he moved in with me?'

She shook her head indignantly. That was *too* low.

'So when he left me like that –'

'I know –'

'But you knew how hurt I felt. If I'd known it was political –. Why didn't you tell me, Suze?'

'He was a client. Janey was a client and an old friend. You were still studying.'

'Okay, but none of that's been true for fifteen years. You could have –'

'I thought you'd freak,' she said. 'You used to be pretty naïve about certain things –'

A few gags of protest escaped my throat.

She wouldn't have it. 'Come on. You said yourself that before you went to Belfast you expected everybody over there to have a bomb factory in the basement and a stash of Kalashnikovs in the shed.'

I wasn't real keen on this revised version of the good old days, or on discovering what a Gullible Yank I'd seemed at the time to someone I'd admired as much as I'd then admired Suze. When I refocused on the present, though, I didn't like it much better. 'Why did you let me sue her?'

She glanced over as if to say, What else was I supposed to do?

It wasn't good enough. 'But I can't go to court knowing the truth.'

'She can't either. Whatever *you* did, she organised it. What happens to our reputations will be nothing to what will happen to hers. She'll apologise and retract. She can't not.'

Somehow I wanted to believe this more than I did.

After Suze dropped me back home again I ran a deep bath and, as I sank into it, found myself thinking about Liam Mahoney. When I got out I went into my hall closet and dug around in the bottom boxes where I kept my papers and bits from the past. Somewhere I had a picture. I opened the album with the worn black cover that was from about that time and flipped to the loose photos stuck inside the back. Yes, here it was. The back garden, a sunny summer day. Young man with a mess of long hair and a wild beard, no shirt on, lunging out of the deck chair at the camera, laughing. Between his fingers, a long hand-rolled cigarette that was probably a joint.

That's right, I remembered now: after he'd disappeared I'd wondered for a while if it had maybe been some dealing-related offence. The idea of him making bombs, planting bombs, killing people with bombs – it hadn't occurred to me then and it didn't sound right to me now.

But then, some people are able to keep these kinds of deep dark secrets.

Even people like my supposedly closest friend, Suze.

I went to bed full of anger and hurt and not surprisingly my sleep was light and pervaded by festering images of Liam and Janey and Suze. When I woke up for the fourth or fifth time at 5.30, I decided I'd fretted long enough. It was action time and priority one was to knock this libel charade on the head and get us all out of this quietly, with our reputations intact.

Because I'd sued Janey it wasn't on for me to ring her or even write to her. What I was going to have to do was arrange to bump into her.

Four

An hour and a half later I was standing discreetly beside a huge lavender bush at the corner of Janey's street, able to see her front door but not able, I hoped, to be seen. There I stayed for half an hour, an hour, ninety minutes. I was due at work – due to see clients – thinking I really really must abandon this idea – when her front door opened and she hurried out, slamming it behind her in her haste. She came down the stairs and down her path at a pace that was going to make 'bumping into her' a pretty contrived affair. And then – the unexpected: she turned not towards me and the hill and the street leading to the tube but the other way. I followed.

Several minutes later I entered Waterlow Park, where at first I thought I'd lost her. Then, in the distance, I saw her willowy form striding towards a pair of contractors' site huts. I was about to set off after her again when a tall thin man in a baseball cap emerged from beside a hut and headed towards her. The long drink-of-water build – I knew it. It was Richard Farmer, it had to be. They didn't seem to greet each other, just casually joined up and carried on walking.

What's this about, Janey? Last week Richard Farmer was your sworn enemy. You brought a demonstration into his office, you slagged him off. What are you doing with him now?

I got myself moving again and reached the spot where I'd seen them meet, but the thirty seconds I'd stood there thinking were unfortunately crucial: this time she – and he – really had vanished.

I was at my desk, trying to carve out a bit of time at the end of the day for stalking Janey near her office, when Sufiya phoned. I told her I'd chanced on Janey and Richard Farmer in the park and she said, 'There's a rumour going round that Janey's coming to the playground vigil at lunchtime to make a statement. Perhaps she's extracted something from him.'

'You'll be there for it?'

'Wouldn't miss it for anything.'

'Great. I may join you. Nasima coming?'

She sighed. 'Her baby's condition is not good, Dee.'

'Oh no. Will he – Is he going to –'

'Either way. He could go either way.'

I rescheduled several appointments and managed to get myself to the playground about 12.15. The gate was open and the crane truck I'd seen parked there two days before was backing in. This time there were hardly any demonstrators – a dozen, tops – and no British National Party spectators. And today the women weren't marching, they were huddled together, talking intently. Sufiya was with them. I asked the driver to wait and went over to find out what was what.

My Sylheti may be limited but as I got closer it was plain that the women were not happy. 'What's going on?' I asked Sufiya.

'I've only just got here myself. Apparently Janey came an hour ago, told everyone there was no point lobbying Farmer, they should be lobbying the Council planning sub-committee meeting – which started at 11 – then led them off to Weaverstown Hall. It's split the movement. These women think it's much too soon to give up on Farmer, and I agree with them.'

One of the others cut in, speaking rapidly and heatedly and gesturing towards the truck now disappearing inside the gate. Sufiya translated with the same feeling. 'They are saying Janey's been bought off.' She looked at the truck. 'That thing apparently showed up minutes after she led the other group away.'

I touched her arm. 'I'll go see what I can find out. You want to come?'

She shook her head emphatically. This group had to discuss next steps.

Weaverstown Hall wasn't far – twenty minutes on foot. The taxi drove me there in five. The breakaway group of demonstrators who'd followed Janey, plus observers, were gathered on the front steps. I felt sorry for the wedding party going in. Not only was it a bland building, but if this wasn't over soon, it was going to mess up their pictures.

The taxi dropped me off and pulled away, and as I fumbled my wallet back into my bag, I glanced over to check out the crowd again. I spotted yucky Tim Maguire and was just heading for the opposite side when he looked over, saw me and waved. It was childish and stupid but I pretended I hadn't seen him and carried on.

As I slipped into the group the front door of the building opened and a casually dressed Asian man stepped out, followed closely by Janey Riordan. Was she prodding him from behind? He certainly looked as if he'd rather be almost anywhere else.

At the top of the stairs they stopped. 'Our persistence has been rewarded,' Janey said in her best public announcement voice. She had that buoyancy she got when she felt on top of things, the buoyancy of the Janey she'd been when I met her. She gestured to her companion. 'Councillor – if you will.'

He cleared his throat, but when he spoke his voice didn't rise above a flat mumble.

Janey murmured to him and again he moved his lips. Finally she had to act as mouthpiece. '*He says the Council will be seeking to help* all three *projects which have been displaced by the sale of the Hodder playground and outbuildings.'*

A cheer went up. The councillor seized his chance: without so much as a glance at Janey, he turned and walked quickly back to the front door and into the building.

A teenage boy holding a 'Save the Youth Club' placard called after him, '*How long will it take?*'

'That's all he can say for now.' She stretched her smile as wide as it would stretch and waved in a way that suggested it was time to disperse. 'Thank you all for coming, and for waiting out here in good faith.'

'What if we're being fobbed off?' another of the lads called out.

Janey said, 'Believe me – things are working out for the best.'

'You say so,' another person called.

'How do we know?' said a fourth.

But she just waved again, then turned and followed her pet councillor back inside. I was among several people who went after her, but by the time we reached the foyer she'd disappeared and the receptionist wasn't saying which way they'd gone.

That afternoon my trusted journalist friend rang to tell me how fast word of my writ against *Private Eye* had done the rounds. He suspected when it was over there'd be a queue for the story to go with the headline 'Libel Lawyer sues ex-client for Libel' and I promised that if I ever told it, I'd tell it to him.

That evening I got away early and by five was leaning against the window of the bagel shop across the street from Weaverstown Housing Association, drinking coffee, eating a cream cheese bagel and keeping an eye on the comings and goings. The last light was on until eight-fifteen and when it went off I waited, murmuring at myself to stay calm. Alas, when the front door finally opened, the woman who emerged into the evening had the bouffant blonde helmet and hormone-replaced skin tones of Janey's boss, Evie Maguire.

'Disappointed' didn't even come close.

The next morning I played my last idea. I made my poor secretary Natasha phone Weaverstown and pretend to be a sociology student wanting to interview Janey for a project. The unexpected response was that Janey was on leave 'indefinitely'. Natasha pushed: would they forward a letter to Janey at her home? They said they would but warned that she wasn't there.

Wow, I thought, something had gone pop. Indefinite leave and not at home.

Hmmm.

It was at this point that I decided I had to adopt Suze's attitude: Janey had even more to lose than we did and on this new evidence was in an even more precarious state professionally. If I waited patiently she would contact me (surely) and we would settle. This thing could go no other way.

I had plenty to distract me: Amin Ali's civil action against Detective Inspector Kevin Hamley for malicious prosecution, Nasima's appeal to the Home Office for a resident's permit, Sufiya Khan's negotiations with Richard Farmer, an imminent Appeal Court hearing, a complex alleged social security fraud, the usual assortment of burglaries, thefts and drugs busts – and the unhappiness of several of our associates about the whole idea of merger. Surely, they said, we should be approaching them to work shorter hours and take less pay – anything to keep our independence and small, all-women, community character. It made Suze and me both feel guilty and ashamed of ourselves, as if we hadn't fought hard enough. Then her admirer Marc (she made me stop calling him Mr Antiques) returned briefly from a tour of former Soviet bloc countries and asked her to put together a complex set of multiparty international trade agreements. We summoned the accountant, sat down at the computer and went through our budget spread-sheet, plugging in the extra income and cutting salaries and seeing what happened.

It still didn't work – not unless we also lost two support staff and half an associate.

Faced with the latest financial facts, our colleagues too began to study the merger proposals with an eye to making the most of the details.

On the last day of that hot sunny April – the tenth morning after my vow of patience – my faith seemed to reap its reward. It was 7.30 a.m. and I was lying in bed half asleep listening to the Radio 4 news headlines when the phone rang. Don't ask me how, but I knew it was her – absolutely knew it – and sure enough, the familiar voice whispered, 'I haven't woken you, haven't I?'

I started to exclaim 'Janey!' but hadn't even formed the 'jay' when she cut in sharply. '*Don't say my name.* I have to see you.'

'Good! Yes! I'm ready when you are.'

'I'll be back mid-afternoon.'

'Where are you?'

'I'll tell you everything when I see you. Can you come for supper?'

I tried to picture my diary but sleep was still befogging my mental functions. Then a memory broke through: that night was the big Ducane Stafford–Aspinall Street staff get-together at their place. 'I could be to you by nine.'

'Terrific! Listen –' But at that point a computer-generated voice broke in and told her to deposit more money. There was an excruciatingly long pause during which it was easy to imagine her fumbling for coins. Then – a dial tone.

If I'd known it was a pay phone, I'd have taken her number, called her back. But never mind. She'd phoned at last and this whole miserable libel charade was as good as over.

The phone rang again. This time an operator with a south Wales accent asked me if I'd accept a reverse charge call from one Jane Riordan. I said of course.

A moment later she came back on and said, 'You must tell no

one,' as if we'd never been cut off. 'Not even Suze. And you *must make certain* no one follows you. When you get to me, come through the gate at the side and around to the back. Knock three times on the conservatory.'

I wanted to laugh at the paranoid stealthiness of her tone but bit it back. She hated being laughed at and the last thing I needed was to antagonise her. 'You can come to my place,' I offered.

'Thanks but I've got a debugging thing. Of course,' she said, dropping her voice, 'if anything happens to me –'

But this was allowing her melodramatic tendencies too much play. 'You'll be fine,' I said. 'See you tonight.' And I hung up.

My intention when I got to work was to go right in and tell Suze, but I'd forgotten that this was her Big Day Out trying to persuade a brace of newly victorious Labour local councils at opposite ends of the M25 to give her their work. She'd insisted she'd be back well before the Ducane Stafford party but hadn't reckoned on the Broken Gasket Theory of History. At 7 o'clock she phoned from the garage where she'd been towed to say there was no way she was going to make it, hoped it was jolly and would hear about it anon.

It was jolly in fact – so jolly it was going on 9 before I managed to extricate myself. Even our sceptics were still drinking and gabbing and contemplating the freshly refurbished, newly painted walls that could be theirs.

I caught the tube at Moorgate, and twenty minutes later emerged from Tufnell Park Station into the clear warm night. There was no ticket collector and this made me remember that I was supposed to be trying not to be seen. Silly, perhaps, but as I headed up Dartmouth Park Hill I glanced over my shoulder: a couple of women engrossed in each other.

As I neared the turning to Janey's street I checked again. People – singles, couples, knots – were coming along behind me and I slowed down, letting them pass. Only when the coast seemed clear did I head into it.

I'd reached her house, passed down the front path and had my hand out to push open the gate before it struck me: there weren't any lights on in her ground-floor flat. Well, if she were in her surreptitious mode, perhaps we'd talk by candlelight. Perhaps, even, she was waiting in the garden.

I checked behind me again – no one – then pushed the gate and slipped in. I closed it and headed along the path leading to the back. There too everything was dark and still.

That was when the thought first came to me: Janey was pulling tricks again.

No. She wouldn't dare. Mustn't be cynical.

I knocked on the conservatory door three times as instructed and waited. Nothing. I did it harder and waited some more.

Goddamnit, she really wasn't home. How could she do this to me?

How could I have let her do it to me?

I sat there on her back step for another five minutes, writing her an absolute stinker of a note in the dark, only to have second thoughts; I couldn't jeopardise the libel apology. I crumpled it up and tried another. 'Call me,' it said. But that seemed too minimalist. In the end I left her nothing, just cursed her and got the hell out of there.

The next morning first thing I had a meeting about the case coming up at the Appeal Court and didn't get to the office until about 11. When I arrived, there was an inky-blue new model Ford parked out front with a guy slouched in the driver's seat, waiting. I knew from the antennae that it was a police car and, even as I registered it, totted up the odds that it was there for me: 95 per cent? 98?

Which client, though?

I hurried in the front door and looked into reception, expecting to find a plain-clothes officer of at least inspector rank. There was only one candidate, a big, clean-cut guy with receding red hair, but the clothes were American, I was sure, and he gave me a smile whose width was beyond most English police. Then he said 'Hi!' in a voice that would have carried to my office upstairs. Yup – definitely American.

I said a quick 'hi' back and went over to speak to Jackie at the reception desk to see if she knew what was up. It's her sunny disposition that makes her so good on the job and that day's yellow sundress over her generous frame accentuated it. She was just ending a call. 'Mornin', Dee.'

'Hi! CID here?'

She nodded and ran a red fingernail down the page of the signing-in book. 'Holloway. Wanted Aspinall or Street. Suze's got him.'

'Whew!' I said, laughing. I thanked her just as the phone started again and was turning to go when the big huggy-bear American got up and came over in about three strides. 'Dee Street?' He put out one of his big hands. 'Hi, I'm Greg Tuttle.'

He had a slight Southern drawl and closer up the smile was white and even. His jacket and shirt and tie and chinos probably all had designer casual labels which would mean nothing to me. He looked like what I imagined my old high school boyfriend looked like by now.

'Hi Greg, what can I do for you?' I said.

'I need a lawyer. I saw you on the news. I thought you were just right.' The smile broadened. 'I like doing business with other Americans over here.'

Oh God, I thought: Mr Greenjeans. 'I don't do American law.'

'That's fine. It's British I need.'

'Okay, but if it's urgent, I hate to tell you, my appointments today are –'

'Your secretary said I could wait for a cancellation. I just wanted you to know who I was.'

'Great.' I smiled. 'Maybe see you later then.' And I carried on upstairs.

Suze's office door was ajar – her secretary must have nipped in with something – and I glanced in as I passed. What I saw caught me totally by surprise: it was devil man himself, bloody DI Keith Hamley. I'd heard he'd been transferred from Tower Hamlets without being disciplined and was intending to write to the Police Commissioner about it; it was on my list, anyway. So, Holloway had got him. *How insultingly close.*

What luck I hadn't been here to see him.

Five minutes later I heard the thud of Suze's door closing. I waited, assuming she'd come in and tell me what he'd wanted. But another minute passed and she hadn't.

I knocked on her door and opened it without waiting for her to summon me. She was sitting there, staring out the window. She didn't look around.

'You know who that was?' I said.

She nodded.

'Well?'

She said nothing.

Something alarmed me. I went to her side. 'What'd he *want*, Suze?'

Her voice was barely there. 'Janey. She's been shot. She's in – in a coma.'

I sat down in the nearest chair without consciously doing it. *Janey. Janey shot.*

It was ages before I could speak. 'When?'

'Last night.'

'Last night. Oh God –'

'She wasn't raped and they don't think she was robbed. She seems to have let whoever it was in.'

'What time?'

She finally heard the edge on my horror. She turned and peered at me. 'Didn't say. Why?'

'I – I was over there last night.'

'Shit. You weren't. She got in touch?'

'Early yesterday. Wanted to settle. Asked me over. Very paranoid.'

'What else is new.'

'Yeah, well –' My conversation with Janey played again in my mind. 'Looks like she was right to be. What did Hamley want?'

'A family contact. We're on page one of her address book. I said she was an ex-client but checked the records for him and found her father's address in Sydney.'

'So he didn't know about the libel action.'

'I told him.'

I grimaced.

'You're the one who always says "disarm them with candour". I played it down, said it was part of a boring on-going saga about non-payment of fees. Said we thought she was having mental problems – felt sorry for her. Said we hadn't heard from her since sending the writ. If *you* want to tell him –'

'I'm not telling that guy anything, especially not that I was anywhere near Janey Riordan's. Jeez, talk about inviting trouble.'

Her nod said she saw my point. Then she looked thoughtful. 'Your evidence might help determine the time it happened, that's the only thing.'

'Janey can tell them that herself when she comes around.'

'What if she doesn't?'

It was almost impossible to contemplate: Janey Riordan, a vegetable, even a corpse – just like that. 'Well –. Her life was in a bigger mess than we knew – obviously. She wanted to tell me about it and somebody stopped her before she could. If she *had* had a chance to tell me, I would be a very useful witness, I agree. She didn't. I'm not.'

'What if someone saw you there?'

'She went on so much about how I had to make sure I wasn't followed that I was careful *not* to be seen. There wasn't even a ticket collector at the tube.'

'What about the person who did it?'

I recollected how quiet it had been at Janey's – deathly still. It was possible the assailant had been inside the flat, but it felt, at that point, implausible. 'No,' I said emphatically.

I could see she still had reservations. 'Look,' I said, 'what's there to lose? If I say peep to Hamley he has an excuse to nose around us and make who knows what kind of trouble. Whereas if I say nothing he might just go off in some other direction. Like: the right one.'

'And if he catches you out?'

'How can he?'

'But if he does?'

'I'll tell the truth *then*. It's not as if I don't have good reasons for lying to this guy. Any judge and jury would grasp my motives.'

She studied me another moment, then nodded. 'You're right. No point handing him revenge.'

Back in my own office I telephoned a couple of people and made sure I was on the grapevine for news about Janey Riordan's condition. Then I tried to fortify myself against the storm of emotion going on inside me by getting on with some work. The results were mixed and within an hour I had a tense band of headache wrapped around my brow which even two fat pills didn't touch. When Natasha came in and told me my 12 o'clock appointment had cancelled, I was relieved.

'What about Mr Tuttle?' she said.

I didn't feel like seeing anyone, frankly, but it was not a time to be cavalier with prospective clients, especially the better-heeled of them. I told her to show him up.

A few moments later he came in, did a double take at my jungle atmosphere, whistled and said, 'Hey! Just like home.'

'You collect plants too?'

He was still looking around. 'No. I'm from San Diego.' He gave me that big clown smile. 'Lived back east most of my life, though.'

'Whereabouts?'

'New York. Went to Columbia. Then DC. Atlanta since five years ago. You?'

'LA. Dropped out of Berkeley, came here, ended up in law college.' I gestured to the chair beside my desk.

He was across the room in a couple of his long strides. 'So you been here a few years?' he said to me as he sat down.

'Half my life. *All* my adult life. You?'

He laughed. 'Four and a half months.' Then, abruptly serious, he leaned across my desk and peered into my face. 'Have you had a shock?'

I was so surprised I started. 'Yes – yes, I have. Someone I know has been – has had a – a bad accident.'

He continued scrutinising my face as if he were a doctor. He had green eyes with (I noticed now) a nice twinkle. Deals with people quite a bit, I thought. Perhaps a flirt?

'I'd say you could do with some fresh air,' he said. 'Want to talk outside?'

It was an odd, unexpected suggestion – and perfect. 'What a good idea,' I said. I checked my diary. I had loads of oughts and shoulds but nothing scheduled for another half-hour. I grabbed my dark pink cotton jacket and we went out.

As we headed up Parkway I was conscious of him being a foot taller than me and having to slow himself down to meet my pace. 'So,' I said, 'what's the problem?'

'Well, I'm an engineering consultant mainly –' he handed me his card – 'and I've invented a couple of products for the profession that I'm ready to market in Europe and the East. I need a lawyer I can trust to help me.'

I stopped and gave him my best look of regret. 'You've come to the wrong person.'

He stopped too. 'Wrong person?'

'New clients, I only handle criminal and libel work.'

He was frowning. 'I was sure I heard you did import-export.'

'Not me. My partner.'

'Drat.' The flirtatious smile came back.

Did I blush? God. 'Suze Aspinall is nicer than I am,' I said. I gestured back towards the office. 'She's even in if you want to make an appointment.'

He nodded. 'Yes. Thanks. I will.' Then *he* gestured towards the park. 'But why don't we finish that walk first.'

Twenty minutes later, after quick sprint to the wolf cages at the edge of the zoo and back, accompanied by some basic getting-to-know-you conversation, I left him with Suze's secretary, Annie, feeling as if I'd known him for years. Chatting with him was so easy. At the same time I felt that frisson of interest you only get when the other person's brand new. My headache was gone.

It was a good thing. When I got back to my office, Suze was waiting for me, her face saying it all.

'Janey?' I asked, needing to have it confirmed.

She nodded. 'She never woke up. They're treating it as murder.'

Five

Hamley was coming to interview us both at four and Suze, lucky sod, had back-to-back client appointments to keep her mind engaged till then. I just had a range of pressing deadlines which involved reading and writing. It was no contest. I kept catching myself staring at the wall, thinking about Janey.

Not just dead, *murdered*. Not just murdered, *shot*.

Why? By whom?

Had she done something stupid, like get involved in drug dealing to extricate herself from a financial mess?

It wasn't far-fetched: she'd done it way back in the last days of the original Squatters' Network – or there'd been a rumour that she had. She'd denied it but I'd thought at the time that it was the kind of risk she *would* take for something she was into. There'd been a rumour just after she came back from Australia too, when everyone knew she needed money to pay off her late mother's medical bills. She'd even asked me about getting a gun licence, ostensibly because of a conversion to the idea that women should know how to handle weapons.

Plus which, it would have been easy: the Pakistani hashish and heroin trade allegedly did a pretty good business in the neighbourhoods all around her office.

Suze eventually knocked on the interconnecting door. Her appointments, it turned out, hadn't been any more distracting than my reading and writing. 'I keep thinking it sounds like a drug deal gone wrong,' she said, propping the door open as she came through it with her perpetual cup of coffee. She sat down in the chair beside my desk.

I cleared an opening in the file mountain so we could see each other and nodded 'me too'. 'Passion's the only other possibility I could think of.'

'What, you mean jealousy?'

'It's not that outrageous. Remember how nuts Tony Riordan went when she left him.'

'Yeah, well, he was nuts to begin with.' She thought back. 'But I suppose . . .' A long moment later she said, 'What about blackmail gone wrong?'

My instinct was, No – too unlikely. I shook my head. 'She wouldn't.'

'She threw an old secret at you.'

'Yeah, but – we can't assume she wanted to keep Weaverstown going at any price.'

Her intercom buzzed. She knocked back a big sip and stood up. 'True. Can I assume you don't want to entertain Hamley in here?'

'I don't want to "entertain" him at all. I don't want to see the man again.'

She gestured to me to hush now and be a good girl and come with her into her room. 'I'm happy to do the talking.'

'Good.'

'Got a cassette?'

I fished one out of my desk and tossed it to her. Then I too stood up. I looked more rumpled than I'd have liked but it was a warm day; even Suze looked a bit rumpled.

The matt black and white decor of her office was cool and collected by nature, fortunately, and I positioned myself in a chair behind and to one side of Suze's, in a way that gave her prominence.

'Your gut okay?' she asked.

I could feel it undulating with trepidation. 'Tolerable. Yours?'

But then there was a knock and the door opened and he was in. Which philosopher talked about the normality of evil? Hegel? Heidegger? It was part of Hamley's good-bloke façade that he didn't look capable of framing a young Asian immigrant like Amin Ali for murder.

What might he do to me given half a chance?

We nodded at each other with scrupulous politeness and Suze gestured him to a chair nearby. 'Thank you for letting us know she died,' she said. 'I'd have hated finding out from the obituary column.'

'Thank *you* for giving me her family's address.'

'You reached them then?'

'Yes. Her father is flying out. He'll be here for the inquest.'

'Which is when?'

'Friday morning.'

'Who identified the body?'

'Mrs Evie Maguire. Now if *I* might ask a question or two?'

We both nodded 'fine'. Suze pointed to the cassette recorder. 'You don't mind –'

'Of course not. I run a straight investigation – always have done.'

The temptation to make a crack – even just smile – was strong.

Suze said, 'It's just this one we're concerned with, fortunately.' She pressed it on. 'Now – what can we tell you?'

'How long did you know Janey Riordan?'

'Since I first came to London. We lived in the same house.'

'Would this have been a squat?'

She nodded. 'The Greater London Council owned it. In those days Mrs Maguire was the GLC housing committee deputy in charge of trying to get us evicted.'

He turned to me.

'The same. I met Suze through Janey.'

'I see. Could you tell me more about your libel action?'

Suze leapt back in. 'I told you –'

'Yes. I'd just like to hear Miss Street's version.'

I'd expected this. 'Well, Janey owed us a lot of money and broke her agreement to pay, so we stopped doing her work. That's the context. The new solicitor botched a contract and Janey wanted just this one more bit of free advice. I felt sorry for her but I had to say no. Then I was hired by another party to the contract to negotiate with the same vendor. Janey saw us together, felt I'd betrayed her and –' *This was it, the crunch* –

Suze said, '– and said the first thing that came into her mind.'

He continued looking at me. 'About you and a terrorist.'

Suze said oh so coolly, and with just the right touch of weary 'seen it all before'–ness, 'You have to understand: Janey Riordan is – was – a volatile character when she got wound up. She's blown out at least eight old friends, myself included, by imagining betrayal and hurling pathetic over-the-top abuse at them. We'd have no doubt let this pass, the way they had passed, except that someone told *Private Eye*, who neglected to check it before printing it. We're in the middle of plans to merge with a larger firm. None of us could let a defamatory remark of this nature spread.'

'Of course not.' He was still looking at me. 'And did you see her again?'

'No,' I said truthfully.

He thought about that a moment and I used the time to pray he'd leave this particular topic there. Somebody heard me.

'Do you have any idea who might have done it?'

Suze told him our drug and jealousy speculations, but managed to resist his promptings to name any of Janey's ex-lovers.

At last he got to his feet. He put out his hand to her and she shook it. I held mine behind me and he got the message. Predictably he said, 'If you think of anything else –'

'Of course,' Suze said, just as ritualistically. Then he was gone.

When the door closed behind him, we waited in silence, listening until we heard the dim click of the outer door closing. She turned to me. 'Well? Have we disarmed with candour or have we disarmed with candour?'

'It doesn't pay to be cocky,' I said. But I shared her sense of relief and optimism. With any luck he wouldn't be back.

I bought the *Standard* on the way home and sure enough there was a brief piece on page eight about Janey's death. 'Local Campaigner killed by Gunman,' said the headline. Gun*person*? I wondered. Gun*woman*?

The only female contender was Evie Maguire, who turned up on both early evening local TV news programmes to comment on the murder. The studio lighting was cruel to her skin and her black suit heightened the artifice of her golden hair, but the grief in her eyes seemed genuine enough and only a churl would fault her soundbite summary of Janey Riordan's achievements in the housing field. She didn't mention the early squatting days but, what the heck, she wouldn't.

I switched off the TV and decided, No – Evie might be capable of murdering Janey but was way way too unlikely.

I'd ignored the blinking answering machine coming in and now went to check it. The tape was full again. I wound it back a bit and listened to one message: an old housemate I hadn't heard from in ten years. Wow. I wound back further: *News of the World*. Ugh. And further. My trusted journalist friend. I wasn't feeling extrovert enough to handle this – not yet. I got out a new tape, stuck it in and left the machine turned on.

I felt heavy-hearted about Janey: that she was dead – that the old her had actually died a decade ago anyway and never resurrected – that she'd been shot when she was the one ordinary person I knew here in the land of tight gun control who'd even ever worried about it. I heaved a sigh and headed for the hall cupboard, to that box at the back where I kept my bits and pieces from the past.

I'd left the old black album on top after I'd found the picture of Liam and now I picked it up again. This time I flipped through it from the beginning. There Janey was on page one, at the Squatters' Network office in Chalk Farm where I'd met her, looking young and innocent in those baggy bib overalls and that headscarf she'd worn all the time over her centre-parted hair. I'd walked out on that rat of an ex-boyfriend I'd come to London to join, had twenty-five dollars and the clothes I was wearing, and was desperate to avoid phoning my mother and admitting it had gone wrong. This was the woman who'd spared me that and without whom, really, I'd probably not have stayed in London.

Eighteen years ago it had been.

A long long time.

In the next one eight of us were lined up in front of the derelict terrace of late Victorian stucco houses in Maida Vale we'd just 'liberated', Janey in the middle. Then there were twenty, twenty-five shots of different groupings of us doing different bits of work – the roof, the kitchen, the garden.

How idealistic we'd all been, my God.

And how she'd inspired us.

Then the photograph of the unforgettable moment when the bailiffs came to evict us. If you knew where to look, which I did, you'd notice a blonde woman with bouffant hair watching from the side: the person who'd ordered the eviction, Evie Maguire.

I jumped ahead a few pages. Janey at the airport, the farewell party sending her off to Australia. Then another welcoming her back. She looked tanned but anorexic, as if the rigours of caring for her dying mother for two years had put her off food.

In the next shot, taken ten or so months later at the party to launch Weaverstown Housing Association, Janey had her old pasty colour back but still looked too thin. She also looked uncomfortable standing there beside Evie Maguire, pretending they'd always been on the same side. Why had she taken a job working under Evie of all people? No one from the old days could get over it and there'd been lots and lots of speculation. I decided just to ask her outright, which I'd done in the ladies' room at this party.

She'd laughed. 'Haven't you heard? Apparently her son Tim's my coke dealer and I'm hoping for family discount!'

'Seriously.'

'Seriously! Okay, no, it's a great job and I like Evie.'

She smiled at my efforts not to choke. 'I know, I know, but she looked me up when she visited Sydney and the way she was with my mum – it showed me another side. Give her a chance – you'll see.'

Remembering, I felt an upswell of guilt and remorse. Like some of her other old friends, I'd never managed to see what she did in Evie – and it had caused a breach, there was no use pretending it hadn't.

Tears rose.

When I'd cried myself out, I pulled myself together and made my way to the bathroom. It was in there that I thought, hang on, something's not right. I was on the top floor and there was a skylight in the bathroom that had been made secure after someone broke into a neighbour's a few years before. I hurried up the stairs to the roof and had a look at it. It appeared okay but when I grabbed it and tugged, it moved. If a burglar were clever . . . But burglars aren't into clever. They're into smash and grab. I hadn't noticed anything missing when I'd come in, but –

I hurried back down the stairs and straight through my front door to my bedroom. The desk – it definitely looked funny. I went over to it. It was folded down, had I left it folded down? (Don't be stupid, of course.) What about the papers on top? They seemed neater than I'd left them.

That was the trouble with my place: my housekeeping was so minimalist it made it hard to tell if someone had come in for a nose around.

But I definitely had this *feeling* . . .

I went back into the kitchen and stood there, testing the atmosphere. Then I started looking through the cupboards, one by one. Pans, stoneware plates and bowls, mishmash collection of drinking glasses. Dry food, tea and coffee, crispbreads. Part of me was telling me I'd better watch it, I was going off my nut; the other part was saying, Go with your instincts, go with your hunches. But there was nothing missing.

Nothing new, either.

Just this slight neatening of everything.

I went back out to the living room and surveyed it again from skirting boards to ceiling, in a clockwise direction, beginning at the front windows. Nope – nothing. My overwrought brain was making this up. I'd had a long, difficult day. Then I registered the airing cupboard. I'd check that and that would be the end of it. After that I'd go across the hall and bother my neighbours Grant and David.

I went and opened it and scanned it from top to bottom. The boiler looked normal, the vacuum and broom looked normal, the shelves of linens and clothes and tools looked normal. I felt around in them and was about to close the door and be done with it when I decided to be absolutely thorough about this. I got down on my hands and knees and peered into the cavity between the bottom shelf and the floor.

Something yellow was shoved under there. I pushed up the right sleeve of my shirt and reached for it. It felt rubbery. I pulled it out – a surgical glove. Oh God – with red encrusted blood on it.

And those black traces on the palm side – could they be powder burn?

I sat down hard on the floor and must have hung my head in my hands for ages. This was Janey's killer's glove: there was never the slightest bit of doubt in my mind. Janey's killer's glove. With her blood on it. In my flat. Hidden so I wouldn't find it, so if the police searched my place –

I remembered to breathe out.

God!

But what to do about it? Reporting it was obviously out of the question. Hamley would go into raptures. Hell, Hamley'd probably put it there.

Destroy it?

No. It must be evidence against *some*body.

I pulled myself to my feet, got to the phone and dialled Suze's number. It rang and rang, which meant she'd forgotten to turn on her machine or else was there and in the bath or else – But then someone answered. I heard a sniffle. 'Hello,' she said feebly.

'Me,' I said. 'Listen –'

'Dee! Thank God it's you.' She sniffled again.

'Suze, what is it?'

'Peter. It's Peter. He hasn't come home. He's gone out on the piss, I'm sure of it.'

I sighed. I felt too wrung out myself to help her through this again. I said, 'Come over. Stay over.'

She started to resist.

'I *need* you to come over,' I said, enunciating each word carefully. 'Please. It's about our earlier news and its messenger.'

The sniffling stopped. I could hear her thinking.

'Could be up to his old tricks,' I said.

She thought only an instant more. 'I'm coming.'

In the half-hour it took her to get to my place I searched all my rooms again, looking for listening devices or anything else that might have been planted with the glove. I found nothing more, but when Suze finally arrived and said, 'Dee! What's happened!' in a loud, alarmed way, I found myself saying, 'Shhh. Not here', and leading her into the kitchen and over to the sink, where I turned on the taps.

I reached behind the rubbish bin and retrieved the plastic Safeway bag which now had the glove in it. 'This was at the back of the airing cupboard,' I whispered.

She stared into the bag for ages before folding back the top of it so she could examine the bloody rubber more closely without touching it. Then she looked up at me, jaw slack with speechlessness. I'd rarely known her to be speechless. Maybe two or three times in fifteen years.

'Hard to believe, isn't it?' I said. 'That bastard Hamley really is setting me up. I mean, I *can* believe it, because I just proved he did it to Amin Ali, and I know he detests me for that, but I can't believe it because – well, because –'

'It's so cack-handed.'

'Yeah. Exactly.' I shrugged. 'But here it is –'

She nodded and scrutinised the glove some more. When she looked up again she said, 'You don't suppose it's a fake? To scare you?'

'There are easier ways to scare me than opening a vein on a rubber glove. I could believe Hamley might do it to test me somehow, but –'

'Maybe not Hamley. Maybe whoever killed Janey.'

'What, you mean they saw me and decided to set me up?'

She nodded.

'Why bother?'

'To divert the investigation from themselves.'

I thought about that. 'It would have to be someone who knew me – and didn't like me much.'

'Or maybe someone who just recognised you from the news and saw his or her chance.'

'Hamley could have seen his chance, too.'

She frowned at the floor. 'Mmmm.' She looked up again. 'Bit obvious.'

'Suze! Subtlety isn't the guy's thing. That's why we caught him out over Amin Ali. Look: maybe I should just brazen it out with him.'

'What do you mean?'

'Call him over here. Show him the glove. Tell him I'm on to him.'

She wrinkled her nose. No, she didn't buy it.

'Why not?' I said.

'Well, for one thing, I thought you said you were fed up being in the news.'

'I am. There's no reason this –'

'Come on,' she said. 'A major piece of evidence in a murder case shows up in your flat and you accuse a detective inspector of planting it to get even with you. Sounds pretty juicy to me.'

'All right, maybe he needs to be under the full glare again.'

'Yes, but do you? Do I? Does Ducane Stafford? And look – if Hamley did plant it, you can be damn sure he's going to be ready for you to say so. He's going to be ready with counter-accusations. And what's the proof? Your word against his.'

I opened my mouth to argue but the thought that came to mind was, She's right. I thought another minute, running through everything again. 'Okay,' I said at last. 'How about this. I phone my local police and report that I think my flat's been entered but nothing obvious is missing. They probably won't even come out but it'll put it on the record.'

She nodded. 'Yes. Good. Then get rid of this –' she gestured to the glove – 'and wait and see what happens. The question is –' The phone started to ring and she looked out the kitchen door towards the source of the sound.

I said, 'The machine's on. I can't –'

'It might be Peter.' She went closer to listen. All I could hear was mumbly maleness but she said, 'It is', and went out and picked up the phone. I didn't really want to eavesdrop (or to make her feel I was, anyway), so I waited by the running water, wondering as I watched it gush whether the killer really *might* have seen me. I found myself glancing around almost furtively. Had the killer stood here in my kitchen? I shivered.

Suze came back, big grin on her face. 'He took my car today – the battery was new *last night* – and it broke down again out in the back of beyond. The RAC was supposed to phone me. I've been through this whole negative fantasy just because they didn't. God, he just might crack it this time.'

I sighed. 'Let's hope so. When's Marc back?'

'Tomorrow.' She picked up the plastic Safeway bag with the bloody rubber glove in it and leaned over to me. 'I'll take it,' she whispered.

'And do what with it?' I whispered back.

'I have to run Peter over to catch a train in the morning. I'll put it in a –' and she gestured 'locker'.

It sounded as good an idea as any. We put another plastic bag around the first one and she slipped it in her handbag. Then she gave me a hug. 'You want to come back with me?'

I didn't fancy staying at home, in fact, but the prospect of Peter put me off. 'I'll be fine. Look, Suze, whoever's planted the glove, they're aiming for me to be searched and arrested. I'm going to meet a lawyer.'

She nodded as if she'd been quietly thinking that herself. 'Who do you want?'

'Theresa,' I said without hesitation.

She nodded again. Theresa was her choice too.

'If she's got time.'

'For you? She'll make the time. You know that. Will you tell her you went to Janey's?'

I shook my head. I knew I couldn't put her in that position. She couldn't lie for me.

'Good. Now, you *certain* you don't want to come home with me?'

I kissed her on the cheek. 'Positive. See you tomorrow.'

The moment the door closed behind her I picked up the phone and dialled Theresa. Her machine answered and I left a message saying, 'Remember the person I sued for libel? She's been murdered and I have a mighty big suspicion I'm going to be framed for it. Ring me.' Then I called my local police station and reported my feeling that things in my flat had been disturbed. As I'd anticipated, they took the details but didn't offer to send anyone around. There were enough unambiguous burglaries to be getting on with.

When I hung up from that second call, I looked around my sitting room. I could still sense the intruder and see the yellow rubber glove with Janey's blood on it. And what if he came back?

I decided I really would rather be somewhere else.

I threw my nightdress and robe and toothbrush into my big leather shoulder bag, locked up my place, crossed the landing and knocked on the door of the flat opposite. My neighbour Grant opened it. He's a therapist and sometimes, I have to say, can overlard the caring manner. But that night he was perfect: he took one look at me and hustled me firmly into his spotless white kitchen, where he administered Japanese herbal anti-shock remedy and asked me delicate questions. His new lover, David, a struggling playwright about my age, looked in once, saw what was going on and vanished again.

Dosed up on umeboshi plums and green tea, I spent the night on their sofa, sleeping more easily than I'd imagined possible.

Six

The knocking sound when it started seemed to be part of my dream. Then it penetrated, forcing me to wake up and realise it was coming from across the hall. From *my* flat. I checked the time: 6.58. My alarm would go off in ten minutes. I threw off the duvet and was hurriedly pulling on my robe when the bedroom door opened and Grant looked out. 'What's that?'

'Somebody for me, I think.'

He pulled the T-shirt he was wearing down like a leotard and did a quick tiptoeing stork-walk across the room and out into the hallway to the front door. I could see him applying his eye to the spy hole. He had a pert little behind for a man in his late forties. He turned around and stork-walked back. 'Not just somebody. Inspector Morse and his sidekick.'

I went out and took my turn at the spyhole. It was Hamley and the short-haired guy I'd seen waiting in his car outside my office the morning before. His sergeant, presumably. *Bastards*, I thought. You put it there and now you're here to find it.

They knocked again a few times and leaned on the doorbell. Then they conferred a moment, looked around to make absolutely certain I wasn't hiding behind a plant pot and headed back down the corridor towards the stairs. When they were long out of sight and the sound of their footfall had faded into silence, I let out the breath I'd been holding.

Grant spoke from behind me. 'You need anything?'

I touched the wooden door superstitiously as I turned around. 'I hope I've arranged it. Thanks, Grant.'

He smiled. 'Any time.'

Back in my flat I had a quick shower and was drying myself when the phone rang. I let the answering machine pick up and listened. 'Dee! Hello!' was all Theresa had to say for me to recognise her. Even after a dozen years in London, Belfast was plain in her voice.

I picked up the phone. 'Hi.'

'Hi. Well, this sounds a right mess.'

'That is one of the possible words for it. Can we get together?'

'I can offer you late this afternoon –'

I'd hoped for earlier. 'Mmmm?'

'I can offer you tomorrow night –'

I groaned.

'Or you can come jogging with me in about half an hour.'

Forty-five minutes later we were walking fast along the pavements of the area behind Kilburn High Road, where she lived, at a pace that was just a notch this side of a run. She looked so natural in a headband and track suit, going at that speed. I was a sodden sponge. Even my trainers felt squishy. Somehow I managed to tell her about Janey's murder, DI Hamley's freshly stirred loathing of me, the bloody glove in my airing cupboard and the crack-of-dawn police visit that I'd seen from my neighbour's.

'That's what's really made me think (pant) that he's behind it (pant).'

She was hardly even working. 'You genuinely believe he'd rather set you up (normal breath) than find the real killer?'

We were just coming up to a sturdy young plane tree and I stopped and grabbed hold of it and nodded. She ran in place.

'He did it to Amin Ali,' I squeezed out. 'I dread to think – if he finds out – my libel suit was – baloney.'

That stopped her. 'Baloney?'

I noticed a café a hundred yards away on the other side of the street and pointed to it. When I'd drunk half a cup of sweet tea and felt myself again, I told her about Suze's old lie.

Her response was essence of Theresa O'Connor. 'Liam Mahoney?' she repeated. She sipped her mineral water and squinted into the middle distance. I fancied I could see her leafing through her giant mental Rolladex, Irish nationalist sub-section. Sure enough: 'The name is definitely familiar,' she said. 'Can't quite think why. Leave it with me.' She glanced at her watch. 'Anything else?'

'Yes. Can I hire you?'

Her grin was immediate. 'Represent me old boss? I'd be honoured.'

It was only just 9 o'clock, our official opening time, when I got to the office, but a handful of people were already waiting. Jackie was standing on the wrong side of her desk, still in her long cotton coat, talking on the phone. 'I'm sorry, her secretary's line is engaged as well. If you could ring back.' She hung up and looked at me balefully. 'Watch,' she said and started to take off her coat by pulling the right sleeve. The phone instantly started to ring. Her gesture said, You see? She said, 'It's this murder –' I thought, Uh oh, the old joke. And sure enough: 'It's killing me.' She laughed and picked up the phone. 'Aspinall Street, good morning.'

I groaned out loud, as expected, then hurried down the hall and up the stairs to my office. Natasha was also on the phone and showing more impatience. 'No, she *never* gives interviews.' She waved at me and bared her teeth at the caller. 'No, it's not money –'

Maybe it should be, I thought as I passed on by and into my

office. Sell 'My Friendship with the Murder Victim by a Suspect' and earn enough to keep us going another x months.

I crossed the room, knocked on the interconnecting door to Suze's and, without waiting, opened it and looked in. Not there. I filled the watering can and gave the plants near the tap a drink, then refilled it and headed for the begonias on the windowsill. As I glanced out at the road and noticed the black Daimler idling by the kerb, I heard muffled but decidedly raised voices coming from the outer office. A moment later Natasha came through clutching a small sheaf of faxes and looking rattled. 'What?' I said. 'Speak.'

'Sir Teddy Ducane – he's outside in his car. His driver wants to know if you can see him *now*.'

No prizes, I thought, for what this is about. 'Sure,' I said without much enthusiasm. 'Invite him in.'

'Rightee-oh.' She turned to leave and got as far as pushing the door open before she remembered the faxes in her hand. She hurried back, dropped them on my desk and hurried out again.

The top one was from Vic Phillips, my trusty journalist friend. 'Writing Janey Riordan's obituary for the *Guardian*,' it said. 'Been trying to ring you. If you're ready to tell the libel story . . .'

Sorry Vic, I thought, I owe you, but not that much.

The next one was from Sufiya Khan. 'My patients are all talking about Janey Riordan's murder. Nasima's heard something she wants to tell you. We're both on the ward until mid-afternoon, then I'll be over at the primary school, Brick Lane, until six or so. Nasima's willing to come to you if needs be. Same schedule tomorrow. Let me know. Hope you are well.'

I kissed the piece of paper. Sufiya Khan had the makings of a long-term friend, that was for damn sure.

The bottom fax said, 'Forgot to ask you. Looking for an American expat speaker for an event. Urgent. Could we talk over lunch/tea/dinner? Call or fax. Greg Tuttle.

Mmm. Now that *was* tempting. What's more, the mere idea of it picked me up just that bit extra I needed to face Sir Teddy, whose unhappiness I could see writ large in his manner from the moment he crossed my threshold. There was little of the smiling bonhomie as he said good morning and glanced around at my jungle as if this alone raised new doubts about my suitability. I gestured to him to sit down, to which he said yes, and offered him tea, to which he said no.

'I'll come to the point,' he began. 'My partners are concerned that you're going to be drawn into a murder investigation.'

'Yes,' I said warily. He didn't sound concerned for *me*. 'So am I.'

'You must do what you can to eliminate yourself swiftly.'

I decided to ignore the double entendre. 'With all due respect, Sir Teddy, it's not in my hands – and I should tell you that the investigating officer loathes me.'

'That is unfortunate, of course. But you must co-operate with him, regardless. Do whatever you need to do.'

'But –'

'I know.' He glanced at his watch and stood up again. 'It won't be easy. But I'm certain you'll manage.' He shook my hand. 'Keep us informed.' And he said goodbye and was gone.

There it was, I thought: the authoritarian quality in him I'd sensed but hadn't seen until now. No wonder my antennae had twitched.

The moment after he left Natasha came in with more notes and faxes. 'The phone hasn't stopped,' she said. On cue it started up behind her.

'Just keep saying I'm not here, okay? I'll speak to Detective Inspector Hamley, that's all.'

'Okay.'

I handed her back the messages I'd gone through. 'Tell Vic I'll be in touch, tell Sufiya I'll try to make it to the school by 6, and tell Greg Tuttle –' Tell him what? Yes? It felt like the wrong time for a flirtation. I felt too oppressed by Janey's death and the trap being set for me. 'Tell him thanks but no thanks.'

I set to work on the stack of papers marked 'urgent' growing on the small bit of my desk I try to keep clear. My concentration lasted about sixty seconds, maybe forty-five. How long was Hamley going to make me wait? I wondered. Who *had* killed Janey Riordan? Was I really truly going to be framed for it?

Fifteen of the longest minutes I've ever endured passed. Then the phone rang.

I took a great swallow of air, straightened and picked up the receiver.

'Miss Street? Hamley here.'

He wasn't letting the grass grow, as Suze's mother would say. 'Detective Inspector. What can I do for you?'

'We have one or two more questions about Janey Riordan,' he said in a tone so polite it might have been a parody of politeness. 'Could you come down to the station?'

'Of course,' I said. 'I'd like to bring –'

'Your solicitor. Yes, I was going to suggest it.'

'We can't get there before 4,' I said, expecting argument.

All he said, though, was 'That will be fine.'

I hung up and put in the summons to Theresa.

The next three or four hours were as productive as any I've ever put in. In fact I got so absorbed in what I was working on that when Suze put her head in around one o'clock to say hello and catch up on the latest, I gave her a three-sentence summary.

Half an hour later she came in again; this time the look on her face made me stop everything.

'What?' I said.

'Bank manager.'

This was all we needed. 'Not the overdraft?'

She nodded.

'What did you tell him?'

'I said we were planning to merge with Ducane Stafford.'

'Just a slight overstatement. How much time did it buy us?'

'Thirty days.'

At that point it sounded like for ever.

Theresa and I met in front of Holloway Police Station about a minute to four. Both of us were wearing plain-cut cotton suits, hers in khaki and mine in dark royal blue. The message was neutral, professional. De-sexualised.

She kissed my cheek. 'You ready for this?'

'No,' I said, kissing her back. 'Look, however he plays it, I've got to be seen to be co-operating.'

She smiled. 'Of course! It goes without saying!'

'No – really. We're in – well, we're in merger talks.'

Incredulity swallowed the smile. 'Jesus Mary, you're not?'

I nodded. 'We are, I'm afraid.'

'But I thought – what about your commercial side?'

'Too little too late. Same with our private clients. We've got twice as many as we had six months ago, but it's not enough.'

'That's terrible. I am sorry.'

I sighed. 'You're not the only one.'

'So – what? You want him to search your place sooner rather than later?'

Was that what I meant? I decided it must be. 'Yeah. Let's find out what's really going on here.'

A woman police constable showed us into the police station interview room, which looked like all the police station interview rooms meticulously re-created on British television police dramas, right down to the high windows and the fluorescent lights and the chipboard table against the wall with a mounted cassette recorder on it. On the whole I'd rather have been home watching it than be in it live, and being in it live as a client was absolutely new to me. I almost sat in the lawyer's chair behind the interview subject's, out of pure habit. I only didn't because Theresa cleared her throat and pointed me right.

A moment later Hamley entered. (Did he only have the one suit? Or did he have a collection of them, all the same?) His sergeant followed him in but hung back by the door while Hamley crossed the room and sat down opposite me at the table. 'Miss Street – thank you so much for coming,' he said in the same tone of elaborate politeness he'd been using since this started. I hoped he intended to keep this up. Give me sarcasm over naked aggression any day.

I introduced Theresa and he shook her hand. Then he switched on the recorder and spoke directly at it: 'This is 2 May and it is –' he checked the clock – '4-0-8 p.m. Four of us are present: myself, Sergeant Adams, Dee Street and her solicitor, Theresa O'Connor.' With that he turned towards us again, his smile as forced as his tone. 'Now, Miss Street. Could you tell us where you were the night before last?'

I sat up straight, ready for the Big Lie. 'Certainly.' I smiled the way I do when I intend to disarm with candour. 'I left the office at about 6 with four of my colleagues. We all went to a reception at another law firm –'

'That would be?'

'Ducane Stafford.'

'Which is where?'

'In Moorgate.'

He cocked his head with some interest at this. 'Moorgate. And you left when?'

'About 9.'

'How did you travel?'

'By tube.'

'Did you go straight home?'

'Yes.'

'Did you stay there?'

'Yes.'

He gave me a long look which seemed like a genuine effort to read me. 'Did you visit Janey Riordan that evening at her house?'

'*No*, absolutely not,' I declared with such convincing indignation I worried myself.

Theresa touched my arm supportively.

'I have to ask,' he said to her. 'We've had a witness report a short, dark-haired woman in a dark jacket –' he turned and eyed my hair, then my darkish jacket – 'leaving the victim's flat by the front gate about 9.45. This was not you?'

'No!' I said even more emphatically. Inside I was a mess. A witness! Was this bluff?

Theresa cut in. 'She *told* you she went straight home.'

He reached into his inside jacket pocket and pulled out a small plasticised card which he unfolded on the table: the tube map. With his finger he traced the black line from Moorgate to King's Cross, then up to Tufnell Park. From there he retraced it to King's Cross and changed to the brown line, which he followed to Marylebone, the closest station to my flat.

Just the route I'd taken, in fact.

How had I thought to keep this quiet? Why hadn't I told Theresa? But no. It *was* just as well she didn't know. I glanced at her for help but she was already on the point of giving it.

'She could have done that – of course. But she didn't.'

He nodded and said to me, 'What time did you get home, then?'

'I didn't check. It probably took about half an hour.'

'You do anything like watch the news or talk to anyone?'

I shook my head.

'Okay. Now, you knew Miss Riordan owned a handgun?'

'No.'

'According to our records she applied for a licence ten years ago and gave you as a reference.'

I sighed. Good old Janey – way to drop me in it. I said, 'They ought to show she didn't persevere.'

'Mmm. Why was that?'

'The procedure made her impatient. She didn't want to spend her Saturdays at a shooting club.'

'So where do you suppose the weapon came from?'

Theresa leaned past me. 'How is Ms Street's supposition relevant?'

'It's okay,' I murmured to her. The truth was, I had a couple of ideas but they were so speculative I saw no need to tell him. 'Janey Riordan knew all kinds of people,' was all I said. 'Why? Did she use it to defend herself?'

I expected him to remind me that he was asking the questions but he merely shrugged and said, 'It's missing. We think it killed her.'

Here was news, and it took my speech away. Killed by her own stupid, illegally acquired, illegally possessed gun.

Hamley said, 'You know how to use a handgun, I understand.'

Theresa said in my ear, 'You *know* you don't need to answer that.'

But I opted to. 'I had one lesson years ago.'

He took that in with a nod and sat back in his chair, fingers fiddling with his lower lip, eyes at the ceiling. A former smoker, I decided, watching him. Out in the country he'd be chewing on a stalk of wheat. Then he looked at me. 'I want to go back to the libel again. How did you feel when Janey Riordan spoke these lies about you?'

'Irate. How would you feel?'

He gave me an intense look that dared me to break eye contact. 'Exactly the same.'

God, I thought, he means the court case. I willed myself to hold his gaze and as we were playing this game I heard the interview room door open and someone come in and say something to the sergeant.

Hamley said, 'Were you angry hurt or angry irritated – because of the trouble it would make for your merger deal?'

'Just angry. It was stupid and unnecessary. Neither of us could afford court costs. She was under stress for other reasons and, unhappily, ended up projecting it on to me.'

'And how do you handle anger normally?'

The disingenuousness of the question got right under my skin. 'Well, I don't shoot people, that's for sure. You can do a swab on my hands if you want.'

He knew and I knew and Theresa knew that if he was going to test my hands for gun powder he should have done it yesterday.

'Dee,' Theresa said in stage whisper. 'You are not here as a suspect.' She looked at him, 'Is she?'

'No. Not at this stage.'

The sergeant had crossed the room and was hovering by Hamley's shoulder. He took the opportunity to bend and murmur in his ear. Hamley nodded as he listened. Then, when the sergeant finished, Hamley checked the time and turned towards the recorder. '4.30 exactly. End of interview with Dee Street,' he said, then switched it off.

He put out his hand, standing up at the same time. 'Thank you for coming in. Not planning to leave the country, are you?'

I gave his hand the briefest of squeezes – both our palms were dry. 'No,' I said. He then shook Theresa's hand with more of the same overpoliteness, thanking *her* for coming as well, and suddenly we were gathering up our jackets and our bags and being hustled out of there.

As we approached the first set of double doors I thought, I'll push these open and wake up.

Alas, no such luck.

We reached the double doors into the reception area and, passing through, I glanced around and saw Tim Maguire sitting at the back, at the far end of a line of people, flipping through what I guessed to be the *Police Gazette*. He didn't look up and I did nothing to attract his attention. As we were pushing open the door, though, I glanced back and for a split second caught him watching us (me?) Or was he? He looked away so fast it was hard to tell.

Then we were outside again. Sky above. Traffic. People. Fresh air. *Normality*.

Theresa and I both instinctively kept walking as fast as we could away from there, but whereas I could have done without talking, she was eager to post-mortemise. 'Jesus Mary, wasn't that witness stuff incredible?' she said. I could feel her looking at the side of my face.

I kept my eyes on the pavement. 'Yeah. Amazing.'

'I thought, well, at least he's using a single bold lie to turn you into a suspect.' She laughed.

'Yeah,' I said again. Should I tell her I did go to Janey's? *How* could I tell her?

She was still looking at the side of my face, waiting for me to say something, anything. When I didn't she said, 'Ordinarily I'd call his bluff, but you know that'll prolong things. You still rather get it over with?'

I stopped and the sigh that had been building up in my gut finally escaped. 'Yeah. Yeah, I would.'

She touched my shoulder and nodded. 'Fine.' She pointed to the café just ahead. 'You want a coffee?'

I did but said no on the pretext that Sufiya was expecting me.

Lying to the police is one thing. Lying to an old friend, a protégé, something else.

Seven

The single-storey Gothic-revival schoolhouse with the kids' drawings in the windows was quiet, its main business obviously finished for the day. I peeked at it through the railings, then went through the front gate and crossed the small hardtop yard in half a dozen of my short steps. There was a schoolkeeper's bell beside the door with a note stuck on it. 'Dee,' it said, 'we're at the back. Ring hard. S.'

I obeyed and could hear the long bleat of it, like the moan of a hungry ewe, rolling around inside.

Moments later I heard hard heels clicking on tiles, hurrying my way. Sufiya opened the front door to me with a big smile. 'Dee! Hello!' She gestured me in. It was yet another warm day in this long, dry spring and the hall smelled of feet. A couple of small jackets hung on the low rows of coat hooks and half a dozen pairs of small shoes and boots were lined up neatly, toes against the skirting boards.

'What you working on here?' I asked as she led me into the school.

Over her shoulder she said, 'Getting ready to run our tests on the fabric. At last.'

'Right,' I said. With everything else going on, I'd forgotten about her search for the cause of the birth deformities and miscarriages among her patients.

'The environmental health officer and his assistant are checking out the yard at the back.'

'Nasima came with you?'

She nodded. 'Amin's with the baby.'

'Is the baby any better?'

She paused just long enough to glance back at me. 'A bit. Relatively speaking.'

'And his chances?'

She didn't pause again, just shook her head. It was supposed to be a don't-know shake, but even from behind I felt her pessimism.

We went out the door into the rear yard, which was divided into an open games area and a corner full of swings and slides and climbing frames. At the back wall two men were standing with their heads bent over a clipboard. One looked up, waved to Sufiya and went back to what he was doing. Nasima was sitting on a swing, moving gently back and forth, gazing into her private space. She was so lost in wherever it was that we'd sat down on the swings to either side of her before she registered us and came back. She touched my hand and smiled and said hello, then she and Sufiya had a brief conversation in Sylheti. At the end of it Sufiya turned to me. 'Nasima's husband's cousin told her she saw Janey Riordan the night before she died.'

'Really! Where?'

'Hodder Street. She and a friend and their children were over at the playground site, demonstrating.'

'Good. It's still going on.'

'They can't end it until they get a promise of somewhere else. It's the only place around here for the little ones apart from this school. Besides – taking on the bureaucracy is doing wonders for confidence.'

Nasima said something which even I recognised as 'Hurry up!'

Sufiya cocked her head at her and smiled at me as if to say, There – what did I tell you? Then she hurried up.

'The gate was closed but the padlock wasn't on and they knew there were some men in there working on the excavation. When Janey Riordan arrived they all thought she'd just come to give one of her fiery speeches, exhorting them to suspend the demonstration so the Council had time to make us an offer, as they'd promised they would. But Janey walked straight through the group without speaking to anyone –'

Nasima cut in and said something to her.

Sufiya nodded. 'Like she was ashamed. Embarrassed. Anyway, she went right up to the gate and prised it open and slipped through and pulled it shut behind her. Nasima's husband's cousin and her friend had been about to go home but decided to wait another ten minutes or so, to see what would happen. They stayed twenty, then had to go. They were ten yards up the road, heading towards Brick Lane, when bang, the gate slammed shut behind them. They turned around to look and saw Janey storming away. She was coming in their direction, but glaring at the ground. They did like everyone else and stood back.'

I smiled at Nasima and tapped my temple. 'Smart move.'

She nodded. Then she gestured to Sufiya to go on – finish the story.

'People were beginning to find their tongues again when a car accelerated out of a parking place past Nasima's husband's cousin. She says the white man at the wheel had his eyes on Janey and drove off in the same direction as she walked.'

I whistled. 'Could Nasima's husband's cousin recognise him?'

Nasima shook her head no. Then she mimed that the car was small. 'This colour.' She plucked at her deep red tunic.

'Has your husband's cousin told the police?'

Nasima made a face that said I'd spoken the unthinkable. She talked rapidly to Sufiya. I understood only one word but it was enough to give me the gist: Hamley.

I sighed. 'Unfortunately he's the one in charge of the investigation.'

She shook her head even more emphatically. 'Trust you. Not trust him.'

I could hardly argue.

I reached out and took her hand. 'I'm flattered. Thank you.'

The problem was: what was I going to do with this piece of information?

It was 7 when I got back to the office but Marc's green Mercedes was parked in its spot out front and I found Suze primping in the ladies' room mirror. As I came through the door she was rolling on fresh lipstick. She set down the tube and smiled. 'You survived then?'

'Just.' I came over and turned on the tap. Into her ear I said, 'Either he's bluffing or someone saw me come out of Janey's.'

She cast a weary look upwards and cursed. 'Look – Marc and I are going to go through those ex-Soviet bloc contracts over dinner. Why don't you come?'

I laughed. 'He'll want your undivided attention.'

'Dee. It's not a date.'

'Sure, you *always* put on fresh make-up before meetings.'

'At night, yes, I do. Look, joking apart, he's dying to get to know you better. You could –'

But I put up my palm to stop her. She could protest as much as she liked but I could imagine what the atmosphere would be like, the two of them suppressing their lust for my sake. I could do without it.

Up in my office I looked out and watched the Mercedes drive away. Trouble was, I could have used Suze's company.

I turned to my desk. Reluctance welled. Work was not the answer. I needed to phone somebody, go around to friends and socialise. I sat down to get out my address book and my eye fell on the top message in the pile. 'If you change your mind re meal before

7.30, give me a ring. Shoulder available free of charge.' Signed: Greg Tuttle.

Right, Greg Tuttle, I thought. You are on.

Don Pepes was in Hampstead Village, on the High Street, and Greg was waiting under the sombrero awning. When he spotted me coming, he grinned with his entire huggy-bear being. 'Hi! Hey, you look *great!*' He smelled of aftershave and shower gel in a way that no British heterosexual man would want to. It reminded me of my dad, back when he was well and still working; before he died.

By the time I recollected myself we were inside following a waiter with a Zapata moustache to a rear table. There we warmed up to each other by going through the menu and discussing whether a great Mexican restaurant was possible above the 35th parallel. We decided to perform a taste test on the salsa, tortilla chips and guacamole, followed by ribs and fajitas and cold Sol.

'In a pitcher if you have one,' Greg added as the waiter collected the menus.

'*You're* ambitious,' I said.

'I'm trying to train them to do it right here,' he said.

I laughed. 'So what's this event you need a speaker for?'

'The American High School in London Senior Class Graduation ceremony.'

I laughed again. 'I'm hardly a model American.'

He pretended to look me over as if I were a second-hand car. 'You look just right to me.'

'No, no – I mean I hate to shop, I gave up driving –'

'Great! Tell them that – tell them about going native here. Shake them up.'

It was only then that I thought: school. *Shit.* 'Do you have, ah, "offspring" there?' I asked as airily as I could manage.

He nodded. 'My son, Bill. It's his graduating class.'

I went for it. 'And your wife is with you?'

He shook his head. 'We split up,' he said evenly. 'Before

Christmas. She's in Atlanta with our daughter, Pam. Bill wanted to come with me.'

'For his last semester of high school?' I was surprised.

'Yeah.' He forced a smile. 'He likes the bum she ran off with less than I do.'

I reached out without thinking and touched his arm. He caught my hand and held it and looked into my eyes. Looking back into his I thought, Messy down there. Emotionally raw. Wounded.

The waiter materialised with the beer and I extricated my hand and sat back. The beer was in a pitcher.

'Okay,' I said. 'I'm impressed.'

He poured out two glasses and handed me one, then raised his to me and drank. I did the same. As I set it down again, I said, 'I better say no to the speech. There's too much going on and although it might be over by then – I *hope* it's over by then – it might not be. Thanks for thinking of me, though.'

He shrugged. 'Is this anything to do with that friend of yours who had the accident?'

I took an extra glug to fortify myself and nodded. 'She died,' I said, trying to sound as matter of fact as I could.

He didn't say 'Oh God!' but his expression conveyed the feeling.

'She was murdered,' I said, pushing myself on. I felt my bottom lip wobble. 'And the police – it's as if – as if . . .' Water welled in my eyes and I had to stop and daub at it with the napkin. Get a grip, Dee, I thought. Get a grip.

Greg got up and moved his chair over next to mine and sat down again and put his arm around me. That did it: the tears gushed. I was so embarrassed and so relieved at the same time. He didn't say anything, just stroked the back of my head. This guy might be light years from my type (wherever *he* had gone) but he had a sensitivity you had to admire.

Just at the point when I was together enough again to start worrying about the meaning of that arm on my shoulder, he gave me another stroke and removed it. 'Do you want to talk about it?' he said gently.

Of course I do. I shook my head.

'I'm a stranger. That's what we're for.'

I waved this suggestion away as if I couldn't possibly talk, then proceeded to unburden myself. 'It's just – well, I have reasons for thinking I – I might be being set up for it.'

'What? You're kidding.'

'I wish,' I sighed.

'But who would do that?'

'The investigating officer hates my guts – I've been assuming it's him. Now I'm beginning to think it's the murderer.'

'Any idea who *that* is?'

I shook my head.

He thought a moment. 'So you're a suspect?'

'Nobody's said so, but yes, yes, I am.'

'Well,' he said, thumping the table with the flat of his palm, 'get in there! Figure it out! Prove you're innocent!'

I groaned and leaned over so my forehead touched the table. 'I have *no* energy.'

'That's because it's all tied up feeling sorry for yourself.'

This was too true to dispute. I groaned again. 'Thanks.'

'Look,' he said over my bent head, 'think about it. Let's just say you *were* to try to prove yourself innocent. Where would you start?'

I found I had an answer instantly. I lifted my head up again and straightened. 'At the Inquest, tomorrow.'

'Why there?'

'To see who shows up. I could ask around – see who saw her recently – see –'

'Did you say she was a client?'

'Ex-client. We'd, ah, "fallen out", to put it mildly. She moved her business elsewhere.' The word 'moved' echoed in my mind. That storage box with the Weaverstown file in it – had it gone to the basement?

Maybe, if I had a look . . .

My spirit returned in a great whoosh. I leaned over and gave Greg Tuttle a kiss on the cheek. 'Thanks!' I said. I unlooped my shoulder bag from the back of my chair. 'Look – I know this is rude, but you're right. I should get off my butt and go through my own records.'

'Atta girl,' he smiled. 'We'll eat and then –'

I placed my hand firmly on his arm. 'No. It's all confidential material. I have to check it alone.'

He looked genuinely crestfallen, a man deprived of an adventure, but I held out. The waiter chose that moment to arrive with the tortilla chips and salsa. I took a chip, dipped it and stuffed it in my mouth. 'Delicious. Home-made. Seven out of ten. Take my portion to your son.' I stood up and started putting on my jacket.

He caught my hand. 'What are you doing tomorrow night?'

I laughed. 'I might be paying off this raincheck.' I handed him an invisible ticket.

He liked that. His jolliness returned. 'How's a dinner dance at the American Chamber of Commerce grab you?'

The groan was out of me before I could stop it. 'You're not serious?'

He put on an affronted look. 'What, you mean it's too "square" for you?'

He *was* serious. 'Oh God,' I said, my hand fluttering to my mouth with embarrassment, 'I'm sorry.'

He laughed. 'My son's in the band. He's *good*.'

I took down the details and said I'd look forward to seeing him there. On the whole it was true.

The taxi dropped me back at my office and I was fishing for my keys when I sensed someone watching me. It was twilight and there were loads of people about, so I didn't feel threatened exactly, just a bit spooked. I looked up and took in the scene on Parkway: couples and families and businessmen and businesswomen and tourists toiling up and down the hill. Nobody even glanced at me.

Still, what could it hurt to double-bolt the office door behind me?

Inside I went straight to the storeroom in the basement and over to the 'W' stacks. When I located the Weaverstown Housing Association box I couldn't be bothered to take it upstairs, I just sat at the table there and started flipping through it, from the most recent pages backwards, looking for – who knew? Something I hoped I'd recognise when I saw it.

Two hours later, as I finished with five years ago's leases and contracts and ho-hum correspondence and was proceeding to the excitements of year six, wondering seriously now if I was wasting my time, I finally came upon something that felt like a possible lead: a letter of authority from Janey giving me joint access to a strong box in her name, lodged in a safe deposit facility in St John's Wood. There was a ninety per cent chance that all that would be in there would be deeds, but you never could tell.

I carried on, hope revived: my seam of luck had opened, there had to be something important ahead. But it was all just more unrevealing documents. I took to skimming and half an hour later was flicking through the earliest days of our lawyer–client relationship. Nearly at the end (or the beginning – depending on your perspective) I found a second small kernel of information in a memorandum to myself.

Janey dropped in, no appointment. Speedy like she's been since she got back from Oz and took this Weaverstown HA job. Suspect coke and suspicions heightened by the meeting: she wants a gun. Tried to find out why. Gun ownership so un-English – so un-Janey before Australia. Her excuse: Waterlow Park rapes. Gun means empowerment. Told her procedure for licence. She didn't like that. Had one out in the bush, no hassle.

Wanted to know penalties if caught with illegal gun. Told

her that it wasn't any easier getting one of those – harder in fact. Was worried she was building up to asking to meet one of my criminal clients but she said she had a line on it. I pressed for more. She's very coy. Somehow think it's that son of Evie's – the one she calls the thuggy one – Tim?

This is what's different about her since she's been back: manner more hyper, actions less confident, political. Never thought I'd see her like this. Will try to talk to her about it.

I closed the file feeling awful. So much for the efficacy of my words.

The earlier sensation that someone was watching me didn't recur when I came out of my office and on the way home I was free of it as well. As soon as I unlocked the front door of my flat and walked into the hallway, though, bam: I had a chill. Someone had been in here again, I was sure of it. I practically ran to the living room, where I rushed right over to the airing cupboard, pulled the door open, got down on my knees and looked in the gap.

No. No one had put another glove there. God, I had to watch it or I'd jump into a paranoid deep end and whoever this bastard was who was setting me up would win.

Behind me a male voice called, 'Dee? You home?'

'Grant?' I hurriedly got to my feet and went to look. Grant was standing in the doorway.

'Saw the door open – just wanted to check.'

I walked down the hall to him. 'Thanks. Only me.'

He peered into my face. 'How are things?'

I shrugged and tried to say jokingly, 'I'm becoming an acute paranoic, but otherwise okay.'

'I think you should stay at our place again. Come on – I'll make you another tonic.'

I started to say no, then thought, what the hell, I could do with another good night's sleep. I collected my nightdress and toothbrush (*had* the place been entered again?), relocked the front door and followed him along the landing.

David was on his way to bed with a hot cup of something and a book and apologised for seeming rude. He and Grant had a quick kiss good night, then Grant and I carried on into the kitchen. He sat me at the table, where he'd sat me the night before and where he'd obviously been sitting reading and making notes, and went to see to the boiling of the water and the steeping of the herbs. I picked up his book. '*Hypnotherapy for Jungians*', I pronounced. 'Do you do hypnotherapy?'

'Sometimes,' he said over his shoulder. 'Varies.'

I opened to the table of contents and skimmed through. Use in treating disease, use in treating habits, use in pain control, use in retrieving unconscious memories, use in –

Suddenly I thought, God, if the killer had seen me, either from inside or from outside Janey's flat – and he must have: – how else could he be setting me up? – if the killer had seen me, could I have seen him?

I drifted around in this idea until the smell of camomile brought me back. Grant was holding a steaming cup of dark liquid under my nose. I pushed it away. 'Would you hypnotise me?'

He extended the cup again. 'Ask me tomorrow. Now here – drink this.'

I drank.

Eight

At 7 the next morning I woke up feeling paranoia-free and bursting with the unaccustomed desire to clean my flat – to make it mine again, to reclaim it from the intruder(s).

To get it ready for Hamley.

I left Grant and David a brief note saying thanks, then went home and pile-drove my way through it – dusting, changing the sheets, putting away books and post, bagging up the paper-bank rubbish and the bottle-bank rubbish, picking dead leaves off the plants – for an hour. The result was a better superficial gleam: you had only to open a drawer or a cupboard to see how superficial. Still, it was more or less the way I always tackled cleaning, and it made me feel more in control.

By 8.50 I was at the entrance of the safe deposit facility in St John's Wood, waiting for it to open. I'd bought the *Guardian* and the *Mirror*, both of which had pieces about Janey's murder and the progress of the investigation. Both mentioned, among other things, that she'd 'recently been sued for libel by her former solicitor, Dee Street'.

Just what I needed.

At 9 exactly I pressed the entryphone button beside the double steel doors and, after identifying myself into the speaker, was told to push the door on the right. Inside, the duty officer examined my letter of authority and checked that they had my signature on file (they did); then a young guard with a wish of a moustache and a jaunty street-smart walk escorted me down a dimly lit corridor. He stopped in front of another pair of steel doors and pressed some buttons on the wall panel beside them. We entered a small vault lined with small locker doors and furnished with a single table and a couple of chairs. Leaving me at the entrance, he crossed to the back wall and quickly scanned the middle section. The box he was looking for was at about knee height and when he found it he pressed more buttons, pulled it out and set it on the table for me.

'Press the buzzer when you're finished,' he said.

'Hang on. I won't be a minute,' I said and quickly lifted the lid. But instead of the deeds I was expecting I found myself looking at an old black and white photograph: a couple side by side on a sofa, holding hands and mugging stoned grins into the camera. What took me another moment was recognising that dumpy young woman was myself – and the long-haired guy was Liam.

I'd never seen this picture before.

She must have taken it one of the times she'd visited the house. I closed my eyes, trying to think exactly when, but my memory fed me back nothing.

The guard cleared his throat. 'I'll come back,' he said. This time I didn't stop him.

I opened my eyes and continued to stare at the photo. If only Suze had told me the truth about Liam's disappearance *when* he disappeared. If only I'd known Janey had this picture. I'd never have sued for libel. *Never*.

I couldn't let Hamley get hold of it. Hamley or anyone else. Without a twinge of conscience (okay, *one* twinge) I slipped it into the inside pocket of my shoulder bag.

Underneath was a bundle of papers tied in ribbon and my first thought was, ah, here were the deeds. But no, they were letters, all still in postmarked envelopes, all six years old, all sent from Bethnal Green to her home. I opened one, 'My darling J', it started. Nipples, yearning and love all figured in the first sentence. I opened another: more of the same. I quickly did a spot-check of the rest: yes. Same person, same besotted language.

Lucky Janey Riordan.

Did I know who it was? No one came to mind. Janey'd had her share of lovers since she'd left her ex-husband, Tony, but she rarely talked about any of them.

I set the letters bundle to one side. The layer now exposed consisted of several pages of accounts, photocopied, with hand-written amendments all over them and some notes at the back. The figures weren't in a hand I recognised, but the amendments were in Janey's familiar print.

These I would need to study more closely.

At the bottom of the box was a small newspaper cutting about government moves to regulate the UK–Bangladesh money trade following record reports of theft. I was pondering the possible significance of the big red exclamation mark in the margin when the door opened behind me. I glanced up – the young guard. I instantly started shuffling everything back into the box but he gestured for me to stop, he wasn't coming in. 'I thought you might want to know, ma'am,' he said. 'The police've just rung us about this box.'

'They have a warrant?'

'Well, you know, like, that's confidential,' he said. He didn't move, though; he waited.

I got the message. I fumbled in my bag and found a solitary twenty-pound note, which I held out to him. He grinned and took it and slipped it in his pocket. He was a smoothie, this lad; used to doing this.

'They *do* have a warrant. They're on their way.'

'Thanks,' I said. 'Thanks a lot. I'll just be another minute.'

He shrugged as if to say that was fine by him, then turned to leave. As he was heading through the door, though, I had a sudden thought. 'Wait, hey.'

He turned back.

'Do you know the other person who shares this box?'

He nodded. 'Know she was murdered too.'

'Did she come in here recently?'

He nodded. 'Like I told the police, Tuesday afternoon.'

This time I let him go.

Tuesday afternoon. That meant *after* she'd phoned me. *After* she'd gotten back from wherever she'd been.

Did she remember I had a letter of authority to get into the deposit box, or had she forgotten, the way I had? Were these items a secret between her and herself – or a message to me?

Faced with these imponderables, my instinct was to grab everything I'd found and think about What It All Meant later. I was being set up. Hamley might or might not be playing dirty. I needed every advantage I could get.

I quickly put the things in my bag, closed the lid of the box and picked it up, intending to take it back to its slot in the wall. Its lightness made me pause. An empty deposit box would be far too suspect. Hamley would be bound to ask if anyone else had been to it. Whereas, if there were at least one thing in it . . .

I sat the box back on the table, pulled everything out of my bag again and reconsidered. Photo of me and Liam – had to take that. The accounts – had to have those. The cutting – had to ponder. The love letters – had Janey been killed in a *crime passionnel*?

I took the only possible course: removed one letter (the last one) and sacrificed the rest to the box. Then I put it, the photo, the accounts and the cutting back in my bag and got the heck out of there.

I wanted to avoid thinking about my booty on my way to the office, so I bought the tabloids and went through them in the taxi for items about Janey's murder. By the time I got back I felt pretty good: just one little page six piece in the *Sun*, and that devoted to revealing that the victim in former times had been Red Janey, the Squatter Queen.

Suze was with a client, so I made myself a cup of tea and sat down at my desk and leaned my head back against the head rest and shut my eyes and let in all the thoughts I'd been keeping at bay. Like: what had Janey Riordan *really* been going through the last week of her life? She doesn't pay me, she sacks me when I complain, she libels me out of pique for fraternising with Richard Farmer, she has a rendezvous with him secretly, she does a volte-face on demonstration tactics against him – and then she rings me at seven-thirty a.m. after ten days of silence as if nothing has happened and insists I come over, warning me to be careful I'm not followed.

And what was Richard Farmer up to? The last time I'd spoken to him about the playground lease he was still coming on like Mr Community Good Guy, morally bound to renew it. Why did he pull out? And how did he get Janey to divert so much of the pressure away from him and on to the Council?

Opening my eyes, I got out my notebook and wrote:

Behaviour: Janey.

Then I made a list:

Finances
Reason for wanting to see me
Relationship with Evie
Items in deposit box: her deep secrets?
a message to me?

I paused and thought a moment. Then I turned to a fresh page and headed it:

'People with reason to kill Janey Riordan'.

Unknown ex-lover – for unknown reasons. Jealousy?
Evie Maguire – for the hassle Janey caused?
A bitter local Muslim – with a business deal? (Drugs?)
Sufiya – for the clinic?
Richard Farmer – for revenge?
Suze – for old wounds?

I stopped. This was ridiculous. None of them sounded like a killer and none of the reasons sounded like killer reasons.

I thought a bit more. The photograph was the dirt she had on me. Was the rest of the stuff in the deposit box the dirt she had on other people?

Was extortion at the heart of this?

I picked up the photocopied accounts but this time made myself open them. I've done an accounting course but figures induce in me the same resistance as computer technology: I have to force myself. I was nearing the end of the third page, feeling no closer to whatever story it was these columns of numbers contained, when there was a quick tap on the interconnecting door and Suze came in clutching her ever-present steaming mug. She was looking glamorous again today, as if it were getting to be a habit.

'Look what I found in Janey Riordan's safe deposit box,' I said, waving the pages at her.

'How'd you get into *that*?' she asked, crossing quickly to take them from me.

'Found a letter of authority in the files.' I reached into my bag, took out the love letter and the cuttings and laid them on the desk like they were it. My conscience instantly started ticking me off for gratuitous deceptiveness; lying was getting to be easy. I reached into the pocket of the bag and retrieved the photo of me and Liam back in the year dot and put that beside the other things.

Suze immediately picked it up and scrutinised it. 'God,' she said on a big sigh, 'weren't we all young.' Then, turning it over, she glanced at the back. She frowned. 'Who's "Sharon B"?'

'What do you mean?'

She held it out for me to see. There was a small Post-it note stuck on the back and on it in pale pencil, in Janey's hand, were the words 'Sharon B.'

I peeled it off the back of the photo and studied it. How had I missed it?

Suze was skimming the love letter. 'No signature but it's definitely not from a woman.' She dropped it and picked up the accounts again and sat down in my client's chair and began to read through them.

I wasn't inclined to distract her. She was the one with the knack for figures. I stuck the Post-it on the file flap, went over to the sideboard, switched on the kettle, cleaned my mug and put together a fresh cup of tea for myself. By the time I finished and took it over to my desk and sat down opposite her, she was muttering to herself.

I gave her another minute or two, then leaned in. 'What?'

She tapped the pages and looked up. 'There are two sets of accounts here. One is marked WHA – obviously that's Weaverstown Housing Association. The other's marked WHMP. What's that stand for? Any ideas?'

I chewed the bit of my thumbnail I'd sworn to give up chewing. 'Nope. Sorry,' I started. Then, 'Wait – Sufiya's group. The Women's Health Monitoring Project. If Farmer hadn't pulled out, Janey'd have had a development grant for them.'

'She had it. They paid it to her. Look – she got it in February.'

'Oh, God,' I said. 'She spent it.'

''Fraid so. These amendments show – without any doubt – systematic usage of the project's money to cover the housing association's expenses over that period.'

'Shit,' I said. 'Shit, shit, shit, shit.'

'There's more,' she said. She pushed the pages over to me. 'A month ago she ran out of both pots. The situation got worse and worse and then here –' she leaned over and flipped the pages until she came to one headed 'Receipts'. She tapped the spot where she wanted me to look. 'A couple of weeks ago, three payments were suddenly made – large payments, apparently cash. Over sixty thousand's worth. Both accounts were filled up again.'

'Christ,' I muttered. I glanced down at the notes I'd been making when Suze had come in. How did this new piece of information alter things?

Suze, meanwhile, was off on her own thought train. 'Perhaps she *was* into drugs.'

I shook my head with the quick certainty I felt. 'More likely to be blackmail.'

'You think so?'

I was telling her my reasoning when Natasha tapped and came through from the outer office. She was edgy, as if the world was wobbling a little too much, too often, for her taste. 'Inspector *Hamley*'s here again,' she said.

'Oh God – tell him I'll be a minute.' Before she was out the door again, I'd gathered everything up and stuffed it back into my bag.

'Wait,' Suze said. 'You could be searched too. I better take it.'

I handed her the bag.

'Deep breaths.'

I took three and felt better.

'You want me to sit in?'

I wouldn't have minded, in fact, but before I could admit it her secretary, Annie, came through the interconnecting door, gave us her usual harassed smile and said, 'Suze – the Siberians are here.'

'Wow,' I said. 'I didn't know you'd started doing pop group contracts.'

She laughed. To Annie she said, 'They're early. Ask them to wait, okay?'

But Annie was shaking her head. 'There's some cock-up with their flight. They have to be there by lunchtime and –'

Suze cut her off with a wave. 'I'm coming.' She looked at me for permission.

'I'm okay,' I said, meaning it.

'Good.' She patted the bag. 'I'll put it in the safe. Don't let the little shite get you down.' And she headed through the door.

I smoothed my cream skirt, brushed invisible fluff off the shoulders of my lilac blouse, breathed in and out again and collected myself. This had to be the crunch of crunches. For whoever was setting me up, it must be time for the bloody glove to be found in my flat.

Natasha showed Hamley in and he crossed my small office briskly, without seeming to notice the plants or the stacks of files, and shook my hand. His sergeant came in after him but hung back by the door as usual.

'I'll come to the point, Miss Street,' he said. 'We need to search your flat. Just to eliminate you from our inquiries once and for all, of course.'

'Of *course*,' I repeated, the edge of sarcasm slipping out before I could catch it. 'You have a warrant?'

He nodded.

I told him I had a few odds and ends to tidy up and would be right with him if he'd like to wait outside please. Then I phoned Theresa and told her what was happening. She was just going into a conference and couldn't get away, but she pressed me to name who exactly I might be able to recruit at short notice to be there with me as a witness. There were a few candidates among my colleagues; than I thought of Grant, my neighbour.

Theresa made me promise that if Grant wasn't available and nobody else was either, I'd take Natasha, and that I would phone her and get her out of her meeting if there was any trouble, and that if it all went well, as she was sure it would, I would call her later and tell her about it.

I promised.

It's difficult to stand back and watch a pair of uniformed police officers – even when they're women officers, as these were – go through your phone table and your mail and your hall cupboard memento box and your messy gardening area in the bathroom and the unknown grot at the back of your kitchen cabinets; rifle your photo albums; take your mother out of her frame; check inside your book covers. It's worse when you're getting more and more tense, wishing they'd hurry up with the entrance hall and the kitchen and the bathroom and just go straight into the living room and straight over to the airing cupboard and down on their knees, expecting to rise up clutching 'the' clue, saying bingo, what's this?

The minutes crawled by, each item of my life being turned over with a methodicalness that none seemed to me to merit. Was it supposed that each might be equally important to me? The process exposed them as equally unimportant, the stuff you collect.

It was only when Grant reached out and put his arm around my shoulder and murmured, 'You can go outside if you want. I'll watch,' that I realised how much the tension was getting to me.

I let out the breath I'd been unconsciously holding in. We were finally approaching the sitting room. 'After this,' I said.

Hamley and his sergeant were also muttering to each other – probably planning to drive me over the top with suspense, I thought. They would go over the furniture minutely and pore through the rest of the bookshelves book by book, then do the same to the tapes and CDs, leaving the hot spot till the very end. But in fact they were ready to go for it there and then. They led us across my familiar threshold and made a line straight for the airing cupboard. One of the women officers opened it and, starting from the top shelf, exactly as I had two nights ago, proceeded to examine my towels and tools and spare light bulbs, and feel around the back of my hot water heater, working her way to the floor. Then, on her hands and knees, she again did just as I had: she peered into the gap between the floor and the bottom shelf, using a flashlight to look around.

For a minute I had a heart-stopping burst of paranoia: whoever it was had been in this morning – since I'd last checked. But no. The woman officer got back to her feet and, wiping her hands, smiled at me before saying to Hamley, 'I'll check the sofa and the armchair, shall I?'

I scrutinised his face for a sign of disappointment, of irritation. There was nothing.

I took Grant up on his offer and went out to the landing to breathe for a couple of minutes. They could discover the hidden horrors of my bedroom and my dirty laundry basket without my presence.

Perhaps it wasn't so gratifying without an embarrassee (as I expect we must be known in the trade). Maybe my old tights drawer, with my collection of Best Single Socks of the Past Decade shoved to the back, was too much. In any case, bare minutes later they all followed me out. I got another polite handshake and another polite thanks for my time, even an offer of a lift back to the office. But I'd had enough of Hamley's glutinous company. Enough.

I watched them disappear down the stairs and listened to the sound of their footsteps diminish as they neared the ground level. When the gate to the street clanged shut, I turned to go back in and nearly walked right into Grant, standing so still behind me.

He laughed. 'You forgot I was here. Admit it.'

I laughed. Relief! Over! 'I cannot tell a lie. God – thanks for coming.'

'Allow me to press another remedy on you. I have just the thing for what you're going through right now.'

'What's that? Post-police-search stress syndrome?'

'Mock,' he said, 'go ahead. It's well documented.'

'Who's mocking?' I said. I had a sudden memory of the night before. 'Hey – *will* you hypnotise me?'

He frowned. I obviously sounded more facetious to him than I did to myself. 'What for? To help you relax?'

I glided in a series of sliding side-steps down the landing until I was half-way between my place and his. I gestured to him to follow, and when he had, to lean down so I could speak into his ear. 'I think my friend's murderer is setting me up. I may know who he is.'

This time we had no trouble with tone. His eyes said, 'Wowee zowie!' He put his mouth to my ear. 'He? Not he or she?'

'He for certain. Somehow I *know* that.'

'Right,' he said. 'You're on.'

The smell of fresh pastry hit me as he opened the door of his place and gestured me in. As we passed the kitchen door, I looked in. David was bent over the work surface beside the hob, chopping with practised speed.

'Mmmmmmm,' I said appreciatively. Suddenly being hypnotised seemed a silly idea, a sign of my true desperation.

'Stay,' David said over his shoulder. 'There's plenty.'

I turned to Grant. 'Would you rather eat? I would. In fact, we could forget the –'

'Afterwards,' he said. 'Don't bottle out.'

His office faced south and, if it had been mine, I'd have turned it into a jungle. But leaf green would have spoiled the shades-of-grey effect he was obviously going for in here. He directed me to the great charcoal-coloured womb of an armchair and while I made myself comfortable he pulled the light curtains across, turning the hazy sunshine into a fuzzy glow. He had me close my eyes and asked me to describe the circumstances I wanted to explore further.

I told him about turning down Janey's street in Tufnell Park on Tuesday night and crossing to her house and approaching the front gate; about the anger at realising she'd stood me up; about leaving there in a white heat of a huff. When I'd done that, he thanked me and I noticed his voice had dropped an octave. We would now go through the sequence of events again, he said, only we'd drag each one out as I visualised it, turning the pace of things right down to slooooow mooootion. As much as possible I should also try to imagine that it was day rather than night.

It was surprisingly easy, even though I saw nothing new, as far as I could tell, on the way there. Then I re-lived the realisation at her back door: she wasn't there. The anger welled and –

The next thing I remembered was Grant speaking in his normal voice: '. . . two, *three*.' He snapped his fingers and I blinked and sat forward in the chair. I felt terrific.

'Phooey,' I said. 'Nothing new.'

'I wouldn't be so sure.' He rewound the tape recorder on his desk (when had he turned that on?), then played it back. I heard that mid-Atlantic headcold of a voice I knew to be my own as others hear it. 'I come out of Janey's,' I was saying, 'and I turn left to go back to Dartmouth Park Hill and I notice – I notice that one of the cars parked along the kerbside – it has someone in it, in the driver's seat.'

'Male? Female?'

'Male. But as I'm approaching, he leans over and looks out the window on the passenger side. I see the back of his head.'

'Hair colour?'

'Dark.'

'What kind of car?' Grant prompted.

I laughed. I hadn't a clue about cars.

'New? Old?'

'New.'

'Colour?'

'Dark.'

'Stop the memory there. Look at it closer.'

There was a pause. 'Red.' Another pause. 'Dark red.'

He turned off the tape and tilted his head at me.

But I was already far away, thinking. A dark red car. Nasima's husband's cousin had seen a dark red car following Janey from the playground the night before she was killed.

Nine

Between Marylebone and St Pancras – a bus ride of fifteen minutes – I discovered something I hadn't previously appreciated: one out of seven cars was new and dark red and that same aerodynamic shape. Parked in the immediate vicinity of the Coroner's Court alone there were at least half a dozen that met that description, and as I walked towards the front door one pulled up at the kerb behind me. I waited to see who would get out but it was no one I recognised.

I spotted the local TV news cameraman and sound engineer standing outside the door of the courtroom as soon as I turned down the corridor. I felt myself hesitate: should I put on dark glasses? No. That would call more attention than nothing. I kept walking, passed them, went in. They didn't blink.

Inside I realised why they were hanging around out there – the small room sat about forty and most of the seats were taken. I slid into the back row and from there scanned the backs of heads in front of me. The mix of races and sexes was pretty even, though most of the whites seemed to have either grey hair, white hair or no hair. Over the hushed tones of the general conversation I heard Evie Maguire's unmistakable voice from somewhere down in front.

Presumably she'd organised the turn-out, making sure all the right people came – so many tenants, so many committee, so many representatives of the local community, so many from the political world.

I glanced over to my right and spotted the tall, gangling frame of Richard Farmer coming through the door. He took off his dark fedora and, holding it to his chest, looked around. His eyes jumped on to me, then off me again without any awareness or recognition. As they passed, though, something in them made me wonder if he'd been drinking. He turned back and joined the clutch of people now filling the available standing room just inside the door.

The Coroner appeared and everyone rose and he declared the inquest into the death of Jane Elizabeth Riordan open. The police surgeon was first. Death was not due to a natural cause, the body had been identified by the deceased's father and the post-mortem examination had determined the cause of death to be a single gunshot wound to the head. Then it was DI Hamley's turn.

'What is the status of your investigation?' the Coroner asked him.

'We have had excellent public co-operation and are pursuing several significant leads,' he said.

And that was it – all the Coroner needed to know. He adjourned the proceedings pending the criminal investigation.

As people stood to leave, I scanned the faces beginning to come my way to see if I recognised any. Then, down in front, Evie Maguire stood up. She was talking to someone with her characteristic intensity and a moment later a lean, youthful man with white hair rose beside her, nodding as he listened.

God! Marc Felici. I'd completely forgotten that Janey'd referred him to us. What was the connection?

Tim Maguire materialised between them. Ugh.

My instinct was to make a move before I was spotted. I'd intended to stand outside and watch to see who drove off in the dark red cars – I should get on with it. But as I reached the aisle and waited for a gap, I glanced at the front again just as Marc looked over my way, registered me, waved and turned back to his conversation. I saw him interrupt Evie and point to me. She scowled and slipped her arm through her son's and said something that looked fierce. Marc smiled that smooth smile of his back at her, leaned down and gave her a kiss, shook Tim's hand, said something else and strode towards me.

I got a kiss on the cheek as well. 'Dee, hello. What a surprise,' he said in that round Edinburgh accent of his.

'That's what I was going to say.'

He gestured with a roll of the eyes up the aisle towards Evie. She and Tim and the rest of her entourage were now moving slowly our way. 'Evie Maguire asked me to come for Janey's father's sake. I did a bit of business with him out in Sydney a few years back – before he retired. He doesn't know many people in this country any more.'

I looked around. '*I* met him once. Where is he?'

'Probably waking up from his nap.' He smiled. 'He'll be at the reception.'

'What reception's that?'

'Evie's organised it. If you'd like to come –'

I laughed. 'No thanks. Give him my condolences.'

He nodded. 'How are you holding up?' He dropped his voice. 'Suzannah said the police have had you in.'

'Yes – well – you sue someone and they get murdered, you're in the frame, as they say.'

He sighed and nodded sympathetically. 'If I can help in any way.'

'That's kind.' Perhaps he really wasn't just a well-preserved businessman with hair by Santa Claus and a suit worth my entire annual clothing allowance. 'I need to find the bastard who really did it and get him to confess.'

He pretended to tug his forelock. 'Coming right up, ma'am.'

I laughed.

Evie and her retinue drew level and I glanced over at her. This earned me an arched look from way atop the high throne at the bridge of her nose. Then she clucked her tongue as if to say *I don't know how you have the nerve to show your face here*. She turned to Marc. 'Dad Riordan will be expecting you.' And with that she led her troops off again.

As they passed through the door, Tim turned around and glowered at me, as if to underline that disdain for me was an entire clan thing.

Any will I might have had to run after her and spit in her eye deserted me. It was like the hex of the bad fairy godmother, a thought that reminded me how once upon a time long ago Evie'd been nicknamed (by Suze and Janey in fact) the Wicked Witch of the East. Marc seemed affected by it too. Certainly it took us both a moment to come around.

'I'm sorry –' he started.

'It's hardly your fault,' I said. Then I waved him off.

He hesitated.

I gestured to him to go, *really*.

He kissed my cheek again, said goodbye and went.

I waited a few seconds, recollecting myself. Then I too left the courtroom and went back down the corridor and out of the front door. Three of the six dark red cars were gone. I watched Evie and Tim hurry along the pavement. I began to think they were heading for the tube when they stopped by one of the remaining red cars. Was it theirs? Were they just pausing for a chat?

My ruminations on these and other mysteries were interrupted when a voice from the bottom of the Coroners Court stairs called, 'Dee Street?'

I looked. A guy in a leather biker's jacket and wire aviator-frame glasses put a camera to his eye and took my photo. Then he put the camera down and gave me a smug smile. 'You haven't returned my phone calls.'

I had one option and that was to walk right past him. I went for it, hurrying down the steps and carrying on quickly by him. 'I don't know you,' I said.

He followed. 'Bruce, freelance. *News of the World*.'

I was picking up speed but so was he. 'Look, I have nothing to say –'

'We've been investigating the allegation Jane Riordan made – that you had an association with an IRA member –'

'I'd be careful,' I said over my shoulder. 'I sued her for libel.'

'We understand there's a piccy.'

Wow, I thought. Who told him that?

'Look – talk to me and I'll go away.'

Shaking my head emphatically, I kept walking. Alas, he kept following.

A moment later, desperation escalating (should I pretend to co-operate in an interview? kick him in the balls? phone for help?), I recognised something familiar in a male figure loping in my direction. Hope! I peered at him – who was it? Then I realised: Janey's ex-husband, Tony. The beard was greying and there was only a tonsure's worth of hair left on his head and he was wearing a suit (or at least the parts of several suits) rather than jeans and a jean jacket. But who else would arrive for an inquest ten minutes after it ended?

The recognition abruptly became mutual. 'Dee!' Tony called. He opened his arms. 'God, I wondered if it was you.'

I had a quick peek over my shoulder. The tabloid guy had stopped and was in the process of raising his camera to take another picture. I ducked off the path and, when Tony responded by veering my way, I pointed urgently over my shoulder and said, '*News of the World!*'

He made a thumbs-up sign and tacked back to the path. 'My van's parked near the junction. I'll deal with him and catch you up.'

As I hurried on gratefully, I had a sudden memory of the younger, hairier Tony, blotto on the alcohol and drug cocktail of the moment, knocking the shit out of a guy in a pub. He'd tried to knock the shit out of Janey too, about three times. That was one of the reasons she'd left him. It had happened a dozen years ago, of course, and I'd heard (from her) that he'd mellowed, but still . . .

I turned around to see what he was doing. He was bigger than the journalist – I'd say four or five inches bigger, both vertically and horizontally – and had his arm gripped around the guy's shoulder. He was chatting away to him like a long-lost relative, big smile on his face, but the guy had his camera tucked into his chest defensively and didn't look too comfortable. I had to hope Tony'd outgrown fists.

I carried on.

The van wasn't hard to locate: Tony was known for putting vehicles together from car knackers' yards and letting the seams form where they might. If he'd called his creations art instead of transportation they'd have been candidates for the Turner Prize.

I leaned against his current beast, preparing for a wait, but he was back almost at once. Still hurrying, he unlocked the passenger door and gestured me in. 'Get in the back and lie down.'

I obeyed.

He chucked me a roll of film. 'Thought I'd be on the safe side.'

'You didn't hurt the camera?'

'Not too badly.' He got the thing started and pulled out and did a U-turn that made a couple of cars blow their horns at him with irritation. When he accelerated away I sat up and looked out of the rear window. The photographer was standing there, camera obviously fine, spare film obviously in, taking pictures. I slid back down.

My sigh must have been something because as soon as he was in the traffic Tony said, 'You sound like you could do with a drink.'

The image of a frosty glass of white wine came to my mind. 'You haven't gone into herbal remedies have you?'

He looked in the rear-view mirror and made a face that said 'Blech!' at me.

'In that case,' I said, 'I'd love one.'

*

I wanted to talk to Tony about Janey but not from the floor behind him over the sound of a clonking engine. I lay low and waited until I felt him pull into a parking place and turn off the motor.

I couldn't believe it when I sat up and looked out. I had to climb back over into the passenger seat and peer out the front window to double check, I was so surprised. 'You're not still here!' I started trying to open the van door.

He laughed – 'Wait, I'll get it –' and came around to let me out. When I slid down and stood there on the pavement, still gawping, he began to laugh harder.

It was the house where Janey'd been living with Tony back when I first met her. It's where I'd met Suze too, and where I'd come for Squatters' Network strategy sessions at least once a week for a couple of years. They'd knocked it through laterally to the house next door, so there were five bedrooms plus the sitting room, and they'd run it as a commune, presiding as the ma and pa of the rest of the squatters around there. In those days it had been one of an entire street of decaying houses near Victoria Park. Now it was the only one that hadn't been refurbished.

'Well,' I said. 'You're obviously here for the duration.'

He shook his head as he extracted his key from his jacket. 'Actually, the bleedin' Council finally agreed to rehouse us.'

Even before he got the front door open I heard the murmur of group conversation. 'You'll know some of these folk,' he said, directing me in. 'We're having a little wake for our Janey.'

Like the outside, the hallway had apparently been in decline since I'd last visited there. As I crossed the threshold a single shiver went down my spine. Time. God, that it could move so fast and not move at all – simultaneously.

In the kitchen, where the action always used to be, the action still was. Half a dozen people – four guys, two women, none of whom I'd seen in a decade – were sitting around the table, just like they'd been the last time I'd walked in. It came back to me why I'd never fancied living here: it required non-stop extroversion. The fuel was lots of drink – and not pissy lager, either: serious drink – and lots of heartfelt political analysis. Sometimes a list of headings would even get circulated and minutes taken and the discussions would be called meetings.

Everyone greeted me with surprise and good grace, moving to make a space for me on the bench, taking my jacket, asking how I was, commenting from all directions on how well I looked. And in fact I was grateful for the drink that appeared – whisky and soda – and had (with hindsight) too long a swallow.

The closed door at the back opened and a young, heavily pregnant woman in a long pinafore dress came in. Tony went to her, said something unintelligible into her long straight hair, and guided her over to introduce us. This was Melanie. They'd been married a week ago but she didn't look too happy. The baby was due any moment.

She got herself some juice and padded heavy-footedly back to the other room. When she pushed open the door I saw a couple of other women and heard the sounds of young children playing.

This was new. Back in the old days, babies hadn't figured much. The right to choose had still meant you picked work or mother-hood. Having it all hadn't quite appeared. Putting empty housing into use was the work option. In fact, Tony's efforts to persuade Janey to have his children and stay at home looking after them were the other reason they split up, I seemed to recall.

Tony sat down beside me and the guy at the head of the table – Doug? Dave? Dan? – yes, Dan – lifted his glass: 'To Janey.' I drank another good draught and set my glass down empty. I'd been needing that all day. Now some food wouldn't go amiss. I looked around. Not a bread crust in sight.

Tony said, 'Tell me how the inquest was.'

'Short. It'll reconvene when the police have finished.' I turned to a woman who'd been known as Big Jude back in my day. Now she was Bigger Jude. 'Why didn't you come?'

'In a word? Evie Maguire.'

Dan said, 'That's two words.' She threw an ice cube at him.

'You had a run-in with Evie?'

One of the others – a guy whose name I still can't remember – snorted. '"Run in". Ha! I *said* we shouldn't go near any project remotely connected with her. I knew we'd get shafted.'

Big Jude said, 'We had an "arrangement" with Janey. Did all the repairs to all the Weaverstown short-life places, she gave us an empty to work in and paid us on the lump. She was happy, we was happy.'

'And what? Evie wanted better paperwork?'

She grunted. 'That's what she said.' She finished her drink. 'Her nephew and some of his mates do it now.'

The other woman shook her head and muttered, 'I hate calling other women bitches, but that Evie . . .' She turned to Tony. 'Tell Dee about your flat.'

He waved his hand dismissively. 'It's sorted now.' He finished his drink, refilled it, then stood up and waved the bottle over my glass. Unconsciously following his pace, I drank up and let him pour me half an inch of undiluted Scotch. When there were no other takers, he raised his drink. 'To our Janey – she knew her real friends in the end.'

Oh? I thought, as I raised my glass. Or rather, as I tried to raise my glass. My shoulder felt on the point of meltdown and the end of my nose, I realised, was numb. The walls were beginning to move.

I'd been an ass to drink whisky so fast and without food. I stood up. 'Where's the loo?'

Tony pointed through the door. 'Where it used to be.'

I made my way carefully towards it.

A couple of the mothers in the other room offered me help as I passed through but I picked my way across the children and into the toilet by myself. Once locked in, the people and noises cut off, it came down on me how stupendously woozy I was – and how little I fancied company. When I'd assembled myself sufficiently, I crept out and down the hall to the bedroom at the far end. I would just lie down for a couple of minutes, until everything stopped spinning.

I don't know how long I lay there, but there was a cup of hot coffee beside me when I came around. Ten minutes later I was trying my legs again, though the wall and the tops of the dressers made useful supports. I only paused to look at the stuff on top of one of the dressers because I was resting. Yellowed clippings spilling out of an aged wallet folder. How had I forgotten Tony's archives? The man used to collect everything to do with squatting and use of empty property in general and the Greater London Council in particular. I opened a drawer. Yes, more wallet files – new. The dates and labels said he was still collecting.

I decided that fifteen years earlier must be in the bottom drawer and stooped to open it. Yes. Minutes and correspondence from the late 1970s through to the early 1980s. Funny how he'd kept all this. Did he miss the old days? Did he miss leading the battle? Or was he just a hoarder?

I put the first handful back and took out another. A balled-up wad of paper came out with it and dropped on the floor. I reached down and smoothed it out. There was a line in Janey's round handwriting, crossed out, and the sheet was dated – God! – last Thursday. The crossed-out line said 'GLC derelict and semi-derelict –'

The door creaked as Tony pushed it open and came in. 'Ah. You've rejoined us.' He saw what I'd discovered but his expression stayed impassive.

'What was she looking for in here?'

'Who?'

'Tony. I'm being set up for something I didn't do. I need help.'

'I'd love to give it. If I felt there was something here that would help you –'

'Tell me why she was here. Let me decide.'

'Dee – please. I grow drugs, I don't pay tax, I collect the dole when I work – do you want me to go on?'

'I won't incriminate you. I –'

'It's not you I'm worried about.'

'Well, do you mind if I keep looking then?'

He sighed. 'No. Go ahead.' And he left me.

I took Janey's discarded heading as a pointer when I returned to the drawer. Those were the days when Evie Maguire was a deputy chair of the Greater London Council housing committee and if I needed a reminder it said so at the top of every set of minutes. What it didn't say – but didn't need to, because I remembered – was that it was in her gift to appoint head licensees for empty properties regarded as substandard, the ones that could be repaired and the ones that needed demolition. I rummaged deeper and eventually found the address lists of the places she'd managed. I kept going to the bottom. Here was the rest: the file of licences. As I skimmed through them, one fact of relevance distinguished itself: Tim Maguire had held a very large number.

Of course Evie's nepotism was one of the main reasons Suze had never been able to stand her. It wasn't new.

Could it be that Janey had finally decided to confront her?

It would explain why she'd contacted *me* that last day.

But *murder*? Would it explain *murder*?

Suze came through the interconnecting door the moment I walked into my office. She looked so grim I forgot about telling her my own news. 'What is it? What's happened?' I said.

'Sir Teddy's been in. He was apoplectic about this morning's press coverage. He insisted you go on voluntary leave.'

'I'm glad to hear I can count on the loyal support of my future partners.' I threw my bag on the desk and dropped wearily into my seat. 'Let's fuck 'em,' I said.

She laughed as if certain I must be joking.

'Suze,' I said, 'all Sir Teddy's done since this started is turn the screws. How can I work with someone like that?'

'Wake up, Dee. Aspinall Street will collapse if we blow him out.'

'It won't if we could cut hours and can make someone redundant. It's not nice, I know, but –'

'No. You know how I feel. I refuse to do that to people when it isn't necessary. Dee – it's a few days off, that's all. You can use the time, anyway, to –'

Something clicked and anger flared hot at the back of my neck. 'You told him I *would*, didn't you?'

She looked at me as if to say, *Of course I did – what kind of asshole question is that?*

'Suze! Why didn't you ask me?'

'How could I? You didn't bother to tell anyone where you'd gone.'

'I told Natasha I was going to the Inquest.'

'That ended hours ago.'

I sighed. It was true; I hadn't called in. 'I went out to Tony's.'

'Tony! God, I thought that daft bugger was dead.'

I shook my head. 'Turns out Janey was at his place last week, looking through old GLC housing committee stuff. If she was sniffing what I think she was sniffing –'

She cut me off with an emphatic wave towards the door. 'Go! Pursue it!'

The anger flared again. 'Why do I feel like I'm alone with the problem all of a sudden?'

She put her hands on her hips. 'You're the only one who can sort this out.'

I grunted and picked up my bag again and headed for the door, feeling in a dark messy nasty loathsome detestable mood. The feel of her glance on my back just made it worse and as I was passing over the threshold on my way out it finally got the better of me. I turned around to face her again. 'You could ask Marc what Evie's reception was like.'

From her expression you'd have thought I'd spoken to her in an obscure Chinese dialect. 'What?' she said.

'Evie's reception. He was going there from the Inquest –'

'He was – at the Inquest?'

I couldn't believe it: she hadn't known he'd be there either. It was cruel of me, but at that moment I took distinct pleasure out of her ignorance. I filled her in on what he'd said, then did what she and Sir Teddy had decided in their wisdom was best and got the heck out of there.

Ten

It wasn't until I got home and poured myself a glass of wine and put some peaceful music on and sat down in my armchair and began to let go a bit of the anger that I remembered I had a stupid 'date' with Greg Tuttle. A dinner dance may have sounded intriguingly quaint yesterday, but it was the last thing I felt like doing now. Anyway, I didn't have the clothes to play 1950s Middle America Revisited.

He'd given me his card; now where had I put it? I went into my bedroom and over to the closet. What day had he come to see me? It was the day I found out Janey died – Wednesday. Wednesday I'd worn the pink cotton jacket. I fished in the pocket and found it at once: Amco Engineering, Atlanta and London. I dialled the London number and just caught him as he was leaving to go home.

'Need to extend the raincheck,' I said in my 'and that's final' tone.

He groaned. 'I've really been looking forward to seeing you,' he said.

My debilitated ego fluttered. I laughed. 'It's been an incredibly long day.'

'I bet. I'm dying to know what you found out last night.'

I'd forgotten: I was indebted to Greg for giving me a push. He was entitled to at least the edited highlights. 'Look,' I said, 'the truth is I can't face telling you at a dinner dance.'

'Well! Let's do something else then.'

'But your son.'

'Hey! He'll survive. He'll probably be relieved the old man's not around –'

I was about to be talked into something, I could feel it.

'– Do you play gin?'

'Do I play gin?' I said. 'I was eighth grade all-camp gin champion.'

'Wow. Do you like pizza?'

'I like good pizza.'

'Right. I'll bring my cards and a "good" pizza and a six-pack. You got a video recorder?'

'I've got a video recorder.'

'That's it then.'

Could I have said no to that? All right, in theory I could have said no to that. In practice I couldn't resist, especially when he began to backpedal a bit about missing his son's *entire* performance. I liked what that said about him. We agreed he'd come on over after he'd heard the first set.

The evening was as low key as you'd expect. We started out at the kitchen table, eating and drinking beer, me sketching in the events of the previous twenty-four hours. He was immensely curious and would have explored every detail with me if I'd wanted to talk about it. But when I made it clear that in fact I'd rather discuss something (anything) else (please!), that seemed okay by him. We were struggling to switch over to Favourite Vacation Spots when Grant knocked on the door.

'Just checking,' he said.

I introduced him to Greg and offered him tea but he said no, he'd locked himself out of his car and was waiting for the RAC. Greg said, 'Allow me', and asked if either of us had a wire coat hanger. I found him one, which he set about deconstructing, then he went down the stairs to the street with Grant. Five minutes later they were back. Grant thanked him heartily and went home to ring the RAC and tell them not to bother.

'Wow,' I said afterwards. 'Where'd you learn that?'

'Vietnam,' he said. Then he told me about how he'd sat in a prison cell in a POW camp outside Hanoi in 1971, a nineteen-year-old maintenance mechanic, figuring out ways to break out. He'd become extremely good at locking mechanisms.

'And you've been a successful international car thief ever since,' I interjected.

He laughed. 'I considered it, believe me.'

'But fate intervened.'

'You've heard it?'

I laughed and gestured him on.

'Columbia gave me an engineering scholarship. What about you? How'd you ever get into *British* law?'

I told him how I'd come to London and been homeless and discovered squatting and got involved first with Janey, then with Suze. Somehow that led us to how he met his wife, also an engineer, and how having kids had changed them. I felt so at ease I confessed my new ambivalence about wanting kids at all. It was such a kid-unfriendly age, and I'd made it this far without . . . He agreed: *he* wouldn't start now. Before I knew it the clock said 11 – time for him to pick up his son – and we hadn't opened the cards or watched the video he'd brought. We hadn't touched each other either and as I saw him to the door I put a bet on it that we wouldn't. I was mistaken. Suddenly he was leaning down at me and I was on tiptoe, craning up, my arms around his neck. What lips! It had been a long dry spell since I'd had an erotic kiss, never mind one with that kind of interest and enthusiasm in it. My instinct was to entice him back in and lead him through to my bedroom and have my way with him. That kiss said he'd be unlikely to resist. Then we looked at each other and without a word we agreed: we would wait. Anticipate. Yearn a little.

'Come to the game tomorrow?' he said.

'What game's that?'

He laughed. '*Baseball*. It's baseball season.'

'What, do you play in Regent's Park?'

'Yes, ma'am. Every Saturday and Sunday afternoon.'

'Sure.' I smiled, hoping he'd kiss me again.

My wish came true.

I was up at bat, standing by the plate, bat lifted above the right shoulder of my grey and red baseball shirt, sweat beginning to prickle my brow under my cap. The crowd was chanting my name – *Babe Dee, Babe Dee, Babe Dee*. I swung a couple of times at the air, warming up, then pawed the dust with my cleats and wiggled my butt gratuitously at the fans. The pitcher finally stopped warming up and started to wind up his throw. I stood there, poised to swing. The ball was coming towards me when I realised it wasn't a ball, it was something yellow. *Yellow*. It seemed to slow down and judder, as if the projector was breaking. I saw that it had red on it and then – no, no! flobbity *fingers*.

The killer's glove with Janey's blood on it.

It came closer and closer and when I could almost feel it touching my face, I screamed and woke myself up. My heart was beating against my chest and it was a moment before I could get myself calmed down.

In that moment my mind was invaded by my anxieties. Much as I wanted to go back to sleep, I lay there, wide awake, going over and over everything. By dawn I'd made a few decisions and managed to staunch the remaining nagging thought-flow by reading. When my entryphone buzzer sounded just before 7, I was off in South American magic reality.

I looked out the sitting-room window and saw a police car parked on the other side of the street.

'Sorry to trouble you at this hour, Miss Street,' Hamley said when I answered. 'Didn't want to miss you. I wonder – might we have another look at your flat?'

I griped about the inconvenience and the lack of warning and was tempted to insist he come back at a more convenient time, when I could at least have someone with me. Then I thought, Why prolong it? He had a warrant – and I could handle it. I let them in.

Hamley'd brought with him the woman officer who'd gone through my airing cupboard so thoroughly eighteen hours earlier. He had certain key places he wanted her to search again – kitchen drawers, all my plants individually, cushions and pillows – and the cupboard.

Ah hah, I thought: whoever'd planted the bloody glove obviously hadn't expected it to be gone. I felt a moment's pang of gratification.

It was premature. This time the woman officer not only got on her hands and knees and looked into the gap between the floor and the bottom shelf with her flashlight, she then left it propped down there, took out some cotton swabs, reached down into the area and took a number of samples of the dust and grot.

It hadn't occurred to me that a bit of blood might have rubbed off the glove onto my floor or walls.

(No. That was ridiculous. That was paranoia triumphant.)

As they were on the point of leaving, Hamley said, 'Just one more question. Is it true you lived in Janey Riordan's flat a few years ago?'

'Not quite. I flat-sat for her once for a couple of weeks. Is that what you mean?'

He mulled that over but if he drew any conclusions, he hid the fact well. 'Thanks,' he said. And this time he and his crew really did leave.

As soon as the door shut behind them I did what I'd neglected to do the night before: picked up the phone and called Theresa. We agreed to meet in an hour – enough time for me to have a shower and change.

I was about to set off to meet her when I paused to check out the street again. Looking up at me from the other side was that guy from the *News of the World* who'd sought me out after the inquest. Right, you bastard, I thought. You want to play games?

I headed down the stairs to ground level, slipped out of the back door and crossed the minimalist garden courtyard to the block on the opposite side. When I reached the small gate, I quickly checked the street, first right, then left: no one. I let myself out and headed towards Edgware Road at nearly a run.

The café Theresa'd suggested was near her boyfriend Martin's place in Farringdon and as I approached it I could see the two of them standing in front of it, kissing goodbye. Martin caressed the side of her face – I could see his big smile from here – waved at her and headed off. He only spotted me when he looked over his shoulder to check on her again. He gave me a cheerio wave and continued on his way.

She was grinning as she watched me come towards her. We hugged and greeted each other and she gestured me to enter the café first.

'You don't jog on Saturdays, eh?' I said as I passed her.

She laughed. 'I do usually. But today I'm celebrating.'

'Celebrating?'

She grinned even harder – she wanted me to guess, clearly – and herded me towards the table at the far wall.

I didn't have to think very hard. 'You're not – are you pregnant?' She nodded.

I reached over and hugged her again. Last time we'd talked about it, she'd been thinking of going for fertility tests. It turned out she *had* made an appointment – it was coming up the next week. While we were enjoying The Great Irony of It All, the waitress came and took our order for coffee and croissants.

When she'd left us again, I said, 'I'm glad I've caught you on a hormone-assisted high. I have something to tell you.' I cleared my throat and straightened. 'I – well – it's about the night Janey died.'

The smile didn't leave her face as she said, 'You *did* go to her place.'

I nodded. 'Yeah. Yeah, I did.'

'I had a feeling you had. You want to take me through the real story?'

I started out pretty objectively, describing the last call I'd had from Janey and our agreement to meet at her place and my efforts to make certain no one saw me, coming or going, even though going I was incredibly angry at being stood up. I told her about the little pile of things in the deposit box and my hypnosis session with Grant and my brief hunt for the dark red car and the possible candidates parked near the Coroners Court, and about going to Tony's. It was when I started telling her how sure I was that Janey's killer was purposely setting me up – when I heard myself confess to finding the bloody glove – that my lower lip began to wobble and water began leaking from my eyes.

Theresa shoved our half-drunk coffees aside, reached over and put her hand over mine. 'Jesus Mary, what a nightmare! Well, I'm sure we can get you out of it. We have to. I think Suze is right, though – you have to identify the real killer – prove to Hamley you're being set up by him.'

The sigh that escaped me was long and deep. 'I know what I need to do next. I just wish I wasn't so tired. And feeling a bit under siege in my own home – that *really* pisses me off.'

She plucked her handbag from its spot on the floor next to her feet, opened it and rummaged at the bottom for a moment, then pulled out a set of keys and slid them over to me. 'Use my place.'

I was touched. 'Oh, what? What about you?'

'I'm virtually living at Martin's. I expect we'll both try to sell up now – get a house.' A grin of pleasure about the pregnancy again spread across her face.

I felt nearly as much delight as I reached out and picked up the keys. Refuge! 'That's brilliant,' I said, feeling lighter already. Refuge! 'Thanks a lot.'

She shrugged. 'What is it you "need to do next"?'

'You don't want to know.'

She leaned forward. 'Hey, Dee. This is Tell Your Lawyer the Truth Day.'

I laughed. 'Okay. But remember, you asked for it. I need to get into Janey's flat.'

Bye-bye went the jolly face. 'You're joking.'

'She invited me there,' I said defensively. 'Maybe she had papers she wanted to show me.'

'Yes, well, if so, they're what her killer wanted. Surely he/she took them.'

'Not if he/she hid them.'

'But how will you get in?'

This time when I laughed I shook my head emphatically. 'That you really don't want to know.'

I re-entered my flat the same way I'd left it, through the back, and was glad I had when I got home and looked down at the sidewalk opposite. That damn journalist was still there. While I was packing my overnight case the phone rang: was it him? I went out to listen. The answering machine went through its cycle, then Sufiya started to leave a message.

I picked up. 'Sufiya, hi. How are you?'

'That was my question. Are you well? We have heard you are a suspect. Nasima and Amin insisted I telephone you to find out if it's true.'

'That was kind of them. How's the baby?'

She sighed. 'Holding on. He's a little fighter. Is it true?'

'Tell them I wish it wasn't but it seems to be.'

She clucked disapprovingly. 'But any thinking person can see that that Hamley's having his revenge on you for Amin's case. Can't you get him removed?'

'I wish! If he arrests me and charges me –'

'But that's – that would be outrageous!'

'Yes. Which is why it's not going to happen.' I wanted to change the subject. 'How're things with you, anyway?'

'Good! I've been helping organise what we hope will be the biggest demonstration ever at the playground site. People are saying Farmer sold it to a Canadian developer who means to put up *another* office block –'

'But they can't! The planning permission's for housing –'

'That's what I thought. Still, the rumour's made everyone so angry they're pulling together again.'

'That can't be bad. When is it?'

'Tomorrow afternoon. We're aiming to cover the demolition lorries in balloons and children's paintings. *Come*, why don't you?'

I promised I'd try.

It was still only 11.30 when I opened the door to Theresa's cool garden flat. In her bedroom, unpacking my few things, I decided the bed looked so inviting I'd just lie down for ten minutes. An hour and a half later, when I woke up again, I had to hustle but I felt a lot better. And I needed to: I was about to ask Greg a favour that would make him an accessory to a criminal act – and could put him right off me.

I stuffed a pair of gardening gloves in my bag anyway – I'd need them if I persuaded him – and checked out of the front window: no *News of the World* journalist. No police. No anyone.

A genuine moment of gratification!

Then I set off.

By the time I got to the playing fields beside the Zoo, the game had started. In fact, several games had started, but as the other teams were either kids or women (or playing soccer), Greg's was easy to pick out. As I approached, he stood up from the catcher's spot behind home base, slid back the grille over his face and waved at me with a big smile. While I was waving back, a woman separated herself from the group of supporters sitting on the parched grass and came to me, hand extended. She was a big-haired blonde with an undulating walk and the way she drawled, 'Dee? Hi! I'm Candy' made Greg's accent sound like BBC Standard. 'Greg asked me to look after you and I said, You bet. Come on over here and meet everybody.'

Before I knew it I was in the middle of the group, shaking hands and being offered soft drinks. I even met Greg's son, Bill, an all legs and arms seventeen-year-old with an innocent look you don't expect to see in young men that age these days. This team, I discovered, was the American High School in London, Parents. That group on the other side, they were the teachers.

Attention returned to the game, or theirs did anyway. I pretended to watch but in fact was watching them watching. They'd absorbed me so easily, but did I fit? *Where* did I fit? Wasn't my outer skin now pretty anglicised? Seeing them nudge and murmur and make jokes and laugh with each other – seeing them be physical – I felt a pang. That sociability was the part of being with other Americans I missed the most.

The inning ended 0–0 and in the change-over Greg made his way off the field and to the sidelines. He stopped to chat to Bill *en route* and, watching them, I felt myself warm to the guy again. How could I be considering alienating someone so *decent*?

There wasn't time for anything but big smily greetings and general enquiries into health and well-being either then or any of the other times he got a break. Afterwards (triumphant!), Candy invited me back to her place for the victory barbecue and my hope switched focus: I'd talk to him in the car on the way. But we'd become part of the group and the group asserted itself over the travelling arrangements as well.

Two hours later, after I'd put in a stint with the salad brigade in the kitchen and played volleyball with the leggy teenage daughters of Candy and her zillionaire designer husband, Ralf, and toured their drool-inducing garden (I'd never actually met anyone who occupied an entire detached house in Frognal before) and devoured juicy grilled chicken and had umpteen more conversations about nothing in particular with people who were all that I wasn't, I could feel my sense of desperation escalating. I had to get out of there. I glanced over to see if I could catch Greg's eye and found he was trying to do the same to me. He raised an eyebrow and cocked his head meaningfully towards the door back into the house. I extricated myself from my latest new acquaintance and inched back that way and found him in the kitchen. He took my hand and smiled with full-on huggy-bear fondness. A butterfly broke free in my gut and fluttered up to my heart. Then we both spoke at once.

'I need to talk to you,' we both said.

We laughed and both said, 'You first.'

He gestured me further into the kitchen and over to the sink. To my surprise he even turned on the water. Had I given him my paranoia already?

'I couldn't sleep last night, thinking about you,' he started in a hoarse whisper.

I smiled. 'Funny. I had the same problem – thinking about me, I mean.'

'Look, I have a suggestion, but it could – well, it could be really insulting to you and if it is, you just say so, okay? I'm just trying to help.'

I felt a buzz at the back of my neck. Had he anticipated me again? 'Go on,' I said.

He cleared his throat. 'My skill with locks – if you think it might be any use to you –' His eyes appealed to me to understand.

I tried to show him with mine that I did. Softly I said, 'Are you thinking what I'm thinking?'

We continued searching each other's eyes. If I was wrong, this could be excruciatingly embarrassing.

'I thought perhaps – the dead woman's place –'

I couldn't believe it. I clasped my hands around his upper arm.
'Tonight?'

'Heck,' he said, 'right now if you want. We've got to get you out
of this business.'

Eleven

I wanted to wait until it was seriously dark, so it was 10 p.m. when we came out of the tube at Tufnell Park and headed up Dartmouth Park Hill. We approached Janey's from the opposite side of the street and luck seemed to be with us: her immediate neighbours were evidently out boogying or doing whatever else they did on Saturday nights. The only other person we saw was a guy snoring away in the driver's seat of a parked van.

Greg was as curious as I was about what might be in Janey's and would have loved to come in and snoop around – that was obvious in his almost pantingly eager manner; but one of us had to stay out front and keep watch and, as I knew the flat and had a vague memory of its hiding places, he was it. He acquiesced. We made our way together to the back door and he had it open within seconds using a small bit of wire he'd brought with him. Then he went to stand guard and I put on my gardening gloves and entered.

There were signs everywhere of the police forensic examiners: the chalk mark on the carpet in the living room where Janey's body had curled into foetal position; the traces of fingerprint powder on every surface; the gouged-out hole in the wall above the television where a bullet had been removed.

I tried to put all this out of my mind and see the place as I'd known it. Finally, as I was staring at the bookshelves lining the sitting-room wall, a memory surfaced. I knelt down to the third shelf up on the left, removed the books and bent down to have a look. The hole in the plaster was still there. Problem was, there was nothing in it.

I put the books back and crossed the room and flopped down in Janey's desk chair. What did you want to show me? What? I started looking at the desk top: bills, stamps, stationery, pens, pencils, a pile of magazines and circulars. Reveal it to me, come on, what was it. At the bottom of the magazine pile was a road map – South Wales. I felt a surge of excitement – the operator who'd put Janey's last call through to me had had a South Wales accent. I opened it, hopes high, but there were no marks on it.

I slumped back again and closed my eyes. There'd been another dope hole. Now where was it?

I got to my feet once more and let them lead me into the kitchen, which smelled high with five-day-old rotting food and unwashed dishes. As I held my breath and contemplated it, I was tempted to stop and clean up, just out of respect. Then I decided that was a sentimental indulgence I didn't have time for.

The appliances were fairly new but the room was laid out as it had been when I'd flat-sat here those nine or ten years before. I turned myself towards the door, getting reoriented, and then remembered. I reached behind the Welsh dresser and my fingers touched something – Yes! There was a wallet file stuffed back there. As I pulled it out a film canister separated itself and fell down the crack between the dresser and the sink cabinet. I found the broom and was using the handle to retrieve the canister when I heard a whistle from outside.

Greg.

I got the film, stuffed everything in my bag and quickly went to peer out of the front window into the murky night. Behind the line of cars parked at the opposite kerb I could just make out two male figures, one large and undoubtedly Greg, the other small and unknown, moving and bobbing as if they were jigging or jiving out there. Then I saw the small one's hand rise. Something in it glinted.

Holy shit, I thought. Holy shit. I looked around for a weapon and didn't need to go far: wood stacked up in front of her fireplace. I snatched a stout stick and hurried out the way I'd come in.

By the time I got out to the front of the house, Greg was disappearing down the opposite pavement at a run, chasing after a minute, moving speck. I couldn't hope to catch up but I couldn't stay there. I hurried over to the spot where I'd seen the two men and glanced around to see if either of them had dropped anything. All I found under the dim street lighting was a spray of blood droplets on the paving stone. Alarmed, I was about to set off when I noticed that the guy who'd been asleep in his van had gone. Instinctively I got out a bit of paper and wrote down the licence number. Then I did my best approximation of a jog and headed off in the direction I imagined they'd gone.

Five minutes later, still going but getting anxious that they'd turned up the hill instead of down, as I'd bet, I heard a rasping noise coming from the vicinity of the intersection ahead. I quickly crossed the road so I could check it out from a safe vantage point: it was Greg, leaning against the front bushes of a house, panting to catch his breath. I crossed back over and hurried up to him. He had a tissue pressed to his cheekbone.

'Greg! God, are you okay?'

He nodded and took the tissue away. The cut wasn't big and the bleeding had stopped.

'What was that about?'

He shook his head, getting the last of the panting under control. 'Guy in the van. Watching the house. I went to check him out.' Then, turning to me, 'I sure am sorry, Dee.'

'Sorry! What are you sorry for?'

'Because I didn't find out who sent the bastard.' He pulled himself upright and started back up the hill.

'Where you going?'

'To get the licence number of his van.'

'No need.' I showed him the bus ticket I'd written it on. 'Come on,' I said. 'There's a pub. Let's get a drink.'

Ten minutes later I was half-way through a large glass of white wine and he'd nearly finished his double whisky. He raised it to me and we each took a long swallow. 'Right,' he declared, putting it down and sitting forward in his normal eager way. 'You find anything?'

My booty – it had slipped my mind. I got out the folder and opened it. Inside was a small collection of ancient GLC housing committee minutes, the same generation as the ones in Tony's archive (where I presumed they'd come from) and a single glossy black and white PR photo of Tim Maguire standing in front of a flat-bed lorry that said Maguire Haulage in italic script on the cab door. Judging by his clothes and by the look of the print, it was at least fifteen years old.

'You know who this guy is?' Greg said.

I nodded, still studying it. 'Janey's boss's son. I forgot he had that haulage business.' Then I thought, Hang on: I'd seen him talking to a driver down at the playground site. God, what if –? Could he be working for the new owners of it?

'What?' he said.

But it was too frail a thought yet to utter. 'Nothing,' I said, and despite his look of disappointment, put the picture away. I shook the roll of film out of the canister. 'Wonder what's on here?'

'We can find out easy enough.' He knocked back the rest of his drink. 'Let's get that baby developed!' He started to get up.

I gestured to him to sit back down. 'It's Saturday night. This is the Old World. Things close.'

He wouldn't sit. In fact, he was trying to pull me to my feet. 'My office – there's a photo lab in the building. I'll get hold of the guy.'

'But –'

But there were no buts. We found the phone and he rang. Money quickly came into it, which worried me, but when I tugged his elbow he said not to worry, he'd put it on his expenses. He failed to get the guy to come out now but he agreed to come out first thing the next morning.

We stood out at the kerb holding hands, waiting for a taxi. In my backbrain a little voice was saying, You can't sleep with him. You barely know him. He's on the rebound from his (long) marriage. He doesn't even live here.

I gave him a sidelong glance. He was miles away, thinking his own thoughts.

We'd done a break-in together – that was a quick bonding kind of thing to do. *And* he'd bloodied his cheek for me. *And* he'd had just the one previous owner.

What if he invited me to his place? (Would he do that with his son there?)

A taxi was coming down the road towards us. We flagged it simultaneously, then looked at each other. 'Your place?' said our eyes. We spoke at the same time. He said, 'I've got a relative visiting or I'd –' and I said, 'I'm not at my own flat –' Then we laughed and he kissed me and we lost the taxi.

It was a good nourishing kiss, and although we'd kissed the day before, this felt like the real first kiss of myth, the first kiss ever. The little voice in my head had switched tack and was saying, You need comfort, not complications. Sleep with him, yes, if you must, but Don't Get Involved! But being lectured made me dig further into the kiss, to blank it out. By the time we flagged another taxi we were walking like one body, annealed by sweat and desire.

Theresa's place was a long enough journey to get used to kissing and get the feel of each other's bodies. He had the shoulders and neck of a football player gone to flesh but still working on it. He was broad around the chest and had muscles. He had the early signs of potbelly and tried to suck it in. The pockets of his trousers were deep, American cut, the kind you could put your hand in and use as a glove to play along his thigh.

His hands were moving too and he had a nice touch – gentle on the breasts, feathery as it played up *my* thighs.

How did we pay the fare? How did we unlock Theresa's flat? How did we find the bedroom? How did we nearly suffocate the cat who'd made the mistake of falling asleep under the duvet on the bed? Where did the condom come from? How did we get over the awkwardness?

I remember only one thing for certain: it was so much fun I forgot all about Janey Riordan and slept the soundest and deepest I'd slept in the four days since she died.

The next morning I woke first and looked at him sleeping there. The edge returned. He was a nice man, hunky even, who knew his way around, orgasm-wise. I could take it for what it was. I did not have to get serious.

He opened his eyes and saw me looking at him and reached for me. As he pulled me down to kiss him, I thought: doing without sex was okay, but doing with it was pretty good. Then I stopped thinking.

Afterwards he checked the front window, unprompted, declared all to be clear, and went out to buy us a paper and some juice. About a minute later – no, less, half a minute – just as I was contemplating the shower – the entryphone buzzed. Had Greg forgotten something? Was it someone pursuing me? Should I ignore it?

I decided I'd use a silly voice. 'Yeah,' I grunted into the mouthpiece.

'Dee, it's me.' It was Suze.

Suze! I buzzed her in, then looked around and realised the state of myself and of the place. We'd shed our clothes from the doorway through the sitting room last night and the trail of my things was still there. My hair had formed into woolly dreadlocks, my nightshirt was half unbuttoned and Greg's sports jacket was hanging on the back of a chair. What's more, I hadn't even mentioned him to her.

I'd nearly finished restoring neatness when she rang the front doorbell. I opened the door and she came in clutching a file, gave me a quick kiss, and then, alerted by something, looked me up and down. 'Are you okay?'

'Fine,' I said, patting back my hair. I smiled, so she'd know I meant it.

Frowning slightly, she looked past me into the sitting room, taking it all in as she said, 'Theresa said not to trust her phone. I need your signature on this Siberian joint-venture paperwork.' I shut the door behind her and she went through and headed straight for the jacket. She put her hand on it and turned and gave me a long questioning look.

I winked lewdly at it, but all I said was, 'What am I supposed to sign?'

She opened the file and got out a sheet, which she handed to me. The English was pretty rudimentary.

I frowned over it.

'It's a first-draft translation from the Russian.'

'Can't you get a better one?'

She nodded. 'I'm trying. But I've got to have this for Marc *tomorrow*.'

Greg chose that moment to return. She looked around at the sound of the front door opening and saw him. Even in profile I could see disbelief ooze out across her features. She looked back at me, her eyes big as gazongies. Was she going to laugh? She looked pretty tempted. She got her hand over her mouth in time and cleared her throat.

'Suze – Greg,' I said.

'We met Friday,' he said to me. I must have looked uncomprehending because he added (one word at a time), 'You Referred Me to Her.' Then he pulled a package out of the plastic shopping bag. 'Found some English muffins. You want one?' he asked Suze.

She got herself together and smiled what I recognised as her straining-to-be-polite smile. 'No. No thanks. Just came to get something signed.' She tapped the page in front of me. Reluctantly I leaned over to sign. She leaned towards me at the same time. 'Come out with me.'

I was so startled I obeyed.

In the hallway she whispered, 'What are you doing with *him*?'

'What does it look like?'

She sighed and looked pained.

'What's wrong?'

She shook her head. 'Look, I'm sorry. I know you're in a spot and I'm sure he's – well –'

'Comforting –'

'Yes. Comforting. But he's – he's – Well, I don't trust him.'

'Why on earth not?'

She wriggled with inarticulate ambivalence. 'I don't know. The slick style.'

'I think he's cuddly,' I said. 'Maybe you're being anti-American,' I said. I refrained from adding 'again'.

'No. It's – well – he made a funny comment about Marc too.'

That surprised me. 'He knows Marc?'

She shook her head. 'Met him at a do. Heard of Aspinall Street via him from the sound of it. Implied he's dodgy somehow. Pissed me off.'

'I'm sure you misunderstood.'

'Yeah, well. You be careful.'

'Yeah, well. You be careful too. Maybe he's right!'

'Oh, for – *Thanks*. I'll have you know Marc Felici is one of the people Janey begged money from to repay her misappropriated grants. *That's* why he was at the inquest.' And with that she huffed off.

After her I called, 'Yes, I *am* getting on with the investigation, thank you for asking.'

She carried on without looking back.

I need Suze in a snippy mood. Really need that.

I had to stand there and count to ten and take deep breaths before I went back in to Greg. When I did, I was hit instantly by the smell of toasting buns and fresh coffee. He looked up from laying the table. 'I got the feeling she doesn't like me much.'

'I think it's more that she's very fond of Marc Felici. Very fond.'

'Damn – I had no idea.'

'Why did you tell Suze you didn't like him?'

'It's not "like", "not like". I barely met the guy. His name came up.' He shrugged. 'I've heard things.'

He leaned down and kissed me. I didn't give much. 'I'm sorry,' he murmured in my hair. A ripple of lust shimmied down my spine. Then he tilted my head up and kissed me again. I spent a further half-second resisting (why had he poked his nose into Suze and Marc? I didn't need this), then gave in and got into it. Some immeasurably elongated moment later, just as I was beginning to surface, he opened his eyes and spotted the time. 'We'll be late,' he said into my mouth. 'Unless –' And he kissed me harder.

I kissed back. What a temptation – to shut out reality for another few hours. I sighed and separated from him. 'No. I want to know what's on that film.'

Greg's firm, Amco Engineering, Atlanta and London, sounded big, so I was surprised when his office turned out to be a small two-room suite in Swiss Cottage. The photographic lab was up on the next landing and the guy had left a Post-it note to say he was setting things up.

While Greg went to check out what was what, I studied the photos of his family on his uncluttered desk: a group shot of the four of them; his wife and the two kids; each of the kids separately. His wife separately.

I picked that one up. I could see that I looked a little bit like her.

Greg came back as I was returning it to its place. He saw what I was doing but spoke as if he hadn't. 'I'll go help him in the lab. It'll be faster that way.' He held out his hand for the film.

I found myself reaching very very slowly for the canister, acutely aware that for some reason I didn't want to hand it over. This was evidence. This was my neck. 'Can I come and watch?' I asked.

He frowned. 'It's small for three. Look, we'll get it set up – start the process. Then I'll swap places with you, okay?'

That sounded fair. I gave him the canister. 'Great!' he said, then gave me a big doggy kiss on the cheek and went back up the stairs.

I had another look at the photos of his family. That one of all of them really got to me: seeing him as part of a unit. He must be going through terrific separation pains. And yet, apart from that first evening, when he'd told me what had happened, he'd kept that part of his life to himself.

Did he hope they'd reconcile?

A couple of minutes later he was back. I didn't like his expression. 'What is it?' I said.

'Unused,' he said.

'What! She hid an unused film?' It seemed incredible.

He shrugged, then said, 'Come and see.' He led me up the stairs into the dark room. I went over to the small sink full of chemicals and looked in at the paper: nothing. Not a thing.

It wasn't just disappointment that made me want to be on my own again. A lot had been happening and I needed to catch up with myself – digest. And anyway, I was used to being on my own.

Greg wasn't. 'Someone's after you –'

'It's daytime. I'll be fine.'

'But if you come to the game –'

I shook my head. 'Too much to do. I'll be with people – don't worry.'

'What people?'

I laughed. He had a strong will, that was for sure. 'I'm going to the demonstration at the playground.'

'You think that's safe?'

I shrugged. 'Yes. I do.'

'And then what?'

'Well, *Mom*, I'll probably come home to eat.'

He didn't laugh. 'Do that with me.'

I took a step back. What intensity! I'd had enough of it. 'I'll call you.'

'I'll be out until 6.'

'I'll call you after 6.'

'Really, I'd rather –'

I shrugged and stood my ground. 'See you tomorrow then.'

He sighed and got out a pocket-sized pad and wrote me out his number.

I took it, checked that it was legible and put it in my bag. He reached for me, wanting another deep kiss. I kept it short and made my getaway. Wherever this ambivalence had come from, I could see it had hurt his feelings.

Twelve

At the site of the former playground, demonstrators – mostly either Bangladeshi women with children or young men in their teens and early twenties – were four deep all the way around the perimeter hoarding. On the opposite side of the street, also standing three or four abreast, was a crowd of young white men waving British National Party placards ('Repatriation Now!'). In between the two groups, in the narrow demilitarised zone, a number of uniformed constables patrolled. It felt edgy, as if one false move and boom, riot.

When I got closer I realised the demonstrators had already succeeded in the aim Sufiya had described to me: they'd stopped the demolition work for the day. In the middle of the road was a flatbed truck with a hydraulic digger on its back, covered in balloons and children's paintings. The driver was sitting up in the cab wearing a silly hat and drinking tea from a styrofoam cup.

I studied that vehicle as thoroughly as circumstances allowed but if there was a company name or phone number or location (or anything else) written on it, it was covered up. It seemed pretty ensconced there, so I decided to go look for Sufiya. I joined the demonstration going clockwise and shuffled along, keeping my eye out. As we were rounding the corner, I heard from behind me the noise of an engine starting up. I turned and slowly worked my way against the flow. The long flatbed, fortunately, had the same problems with congestion as I had, but navigating by foot was much quicker and I managed to extricate myself well before it did and hurry off to Bethnal Green Road. There I flagged a taxi and hassled the deeply sceptical driver into agreeing to follow the decorated truck as soon as it emerged.

We waited another five minutes and then, finally, there it was. It inched its way out and turned right, heading north-east. A couple of miles later it pulled over and we had to drive past before finding a spot to pull over ourselves. When it pulled out again and passed us a few minutes after that, the balloons and paintings were gone. On the now-exposed door of the driver's cab it said 'Haulage for Hire, London'. There was no phone number.

We followed for another thirty minutes or so, into an area that would have been an industrial zone if there'd been any industry left. Only the occasional red London bus told me we were still inside the metropolitan boundaries.

Finally the flatbed pulled over by the gate of a lorry parking lot. We drove past and pulled over as well. I watched the lorry driver unbolt the wire-mesh gate, push open the right-hand side and walk back to his truck. He drove it through, got out again, closed the gate, got back in and carried on.

He didn't lock it!

The taxi driver had been watching all this as closely as I had and I suppose I hoped he'd become intrigued or even just interested. Instead he checked first his watch, then the rear-view mirror. 'Right then, love, seen enough?'

'I want to go in,' I said. 'Will you wait?'

He turned to me. His facial expression said it all: no, impossible, was I nuts? He started on about the regulations and his tea and it being Sunday. And I mean, what the hell – he had his life. He wasn't happy at all, though, when I got out and settled with him then and there, despite the generosity of the tip.

As he drove away, I looked up and down the road: no sign of buses now of course. Still, it was light and I didn't mind walking.

I crossed to the gate and only then saw the small sign: Essex Storage and Transport. I slipped in quickly and headed as fast as my short legs could go up to the lot full of lorries.

As I approached I could hear the voice of the driver I'd followed and went towards it, being careful to shield myself behind the trailers and equipment. He was still up in the cab of the flatbed, but he was talking on a phone. 'I wasn't going to mow down women and children . . . I know we're late, you don't need to tell me – Because you *told* me to bring it to Brentwood, remember? What about that other job? – Okay, yeah, I'll hold on.'

He sounded like he was going to be talking for a little while yet, so I set off to have a closer look at the other vehicles parked here. After slipping around for a bit, I concluded my survey as follows: two Haulage for Hire flatbed lorries with no phone number, address or registration details on their cabs, plus two dozen others which belonged between them to six companies. I wrote down the details of the six and tried not to get too excited that one of them had contact offices in both London and south Wales. Then I went back to eavesdrop on my friend again.

Not only had he finished, he'd gone. I heard an engine start up and, ducking back, saw a small blue car emerge from behind the other side of the warehouse and head for the gates. I listened to the various noises of the gate opening and closing and then, after a pause, the car driving away.

I gave him thirty seconds to change his mind and return and, when that passed, hurried down the drive. I threw the bolt on the gate and pushed: it held. I pushed again: it held again. I looked through the mesh: a padlock – *terrific*.

The fence was higher than I fancied and besides had barbed wire at the top.

Well, Dee, I thought, you have done it now. You have really really –. Then I remembered the telephone in the cab of the flatbed truck. I hurried back to it wondering what the odds were that it would be unlocked. One hundred to one? Whatever they were, I didn't have the necessary bit of luck. It was locked up tight.

I went back around the other two dozen, peering in windows for portable phones and, when I saw them, trying the doors. The bad luck held.

The only place I hadn't explored was the warehouse. It was big and windowless and looked an unlikely venue for an outdoor telephone booth, but stranger things have happened. Alas, not that day: it was locked up tighter than the lorries.

Panic was rising from my gut but I beat it back down. There was only one choice: I had to break the lorry cab window. I set about searching for a suitably stout rock and within a couple of minutes had found one.

Then it was just a matter of heaving the thing hard enough, at the right angle. It took me four tries. Just before the fifth I made a secret vow that if it worked I would definitely definitely start back to an exercise class (and I mean it this time). I threw, the sharp corner of the stone connected, and there came the satisfying sound of shattering glass – followed instantly by the sound of an oscillating, high-pitched alarm. No one ever seems to pay any attention to those things downtown, but out here in the middle of nowhere (as it felt) I was certain that concerned local folk were already getting on their Barbour jackets and wellies and setting out to investigate.

What the hell, in for small damage, in for the lot. I took off my turquoise cotton cardigan and used it to poke out the glass fragments completely, then reached in and unlocked the cab. I fiddled impatiently with levers on the dash beside the steering wheel until I found the one that opened the hood. Engines are not my thing – I don't even drive any more – but basic principles of electricity, like 'alarms need connections', I can grasp. I started pulling at various wires and a minute later silence abruptly returned.

I took a couple of deep breaths as I surveyed what I'd done. Then I went back to the cab and reached for the phone.

It was only five-forty – earlier than Greg had said he'd be home – but I tried his home number on the off chance.

On the third ring someone picked up. 'Hi, Greg?' I said breathlessly.

'I'll just get him,' drawled a husky American female voice. 'Who should I say is calling?'

Visiting relative, I thought. Hmpf. But I was in no position to have indulgent emotions. 'Dee,' I said. 'Tell him Dee.'

He came on sounding a bit miffed but his tone changed quickly to consternation when he found out where I was and what I'd done. He promised to set off right away.

Greg pulled up in a dark green American car with left-hand drive one very long hour later. He got out and came over and looked through the stout wire mesh of the fence at me. I was excited and relieved and grateful and anxious to get out of there and, all right, I expected him to just get out his bit of wire and get on with freeing me.

Instead he stood there staring at me with a half-exasperated, half-fond look on his face. 'I don't understand,' he said.

'What?' I said.

'I'd have done this for you.'

I had to laugh. 'I'm not used to asking a man to do things for me.'

'Not because I'm a man. Because I'm fit.'

Ouch! I puffed up my cheeks and put my arms out like a muscle-bound Popeye.

That made *him* laugh. 'I mean it.'

'Yeah, well, you were in the middle of a field in Regent's Park.

Anyway, if I'd stopped to phone anyone, I could have lost the lead. Now, could you just get me out of here?'

He did then finally pull out the bit of wire he'd used at Janey's, but this time he had to fiddle in the keyhole for about ten minutes. As I stood on the other side watching him (confidently!), he muttered, 'This is in case you were getting the idea this always works.'

I refused to lose faith and eventually it did work and I walked out of there and headed for the car while he relocked the padlock. As soon as I opened the passenger-side door I smelled the light scent of perfume. I watched him walk around to the driver's side and let himself in.

(Who was the woman who'd answered the phone?)

He got the car started and, as we drove off, he said, 'You going to tell me what you were doing out here?'

'I was trying to establish whether the new owner of the playground site – a Canadian developer, I've heard – is using Tim Maguire to do the excavation work.'

'And did you?'

'No. But I found another way to check.'

'And what if he is?'

'If he is, Janey'd have felt incredibly betrayed.'

He kept his eye on the road but his frown suggested he needed an explanation.

I said, 'His mother, Evie Maguire, was Janey's boss. She runs her children's lives the way she ran Janey's. If she didn't actually get this job for Tim, she knew he had it.'

The frown deepened but he said nothing.

'I think Janey found out,' I went on, 'and I think it must have made her so angry she threatened to blow the whistle on Evie's nepotism going back to her time on the Greater London Council.'

'Blackmailed her?'

'Yeah. Forced her to help pay back that grant money.'

He glanced at me. 'And you think she was killed for that?'

'It could have been an accident or self-defence, covered up out of fear.'

'How you going to prove it?'

I leaned over and kissed his troubled temple. 'I'm going to start by finding out if Tim Maguire is still in the haulage business.'

He glanced at me again and, taking his left hand off the wheel, put it over mine. 'What can I do?'

I laughed. 'You can let me take you for an Indian meal.'

But he wanted to argue about that too.

In the end we picked up a Thai take-away with everything and took it back to Theresa's. I must say, I hadn't previously appreciated the aphrodisiac properties of eating lemon grass soup in bed.

He didn't stay over that night because he was (and I quote) seeing his son. I thought again of the husky-voiced woman 'relative' who'd answered his phone but didn't have the heart (okay, or the desire) to ask him about it. Who cared, anyway?

The next morning I was waiting at the door of Companies House on City Road when it opened and within half an hour I'd found what I'd come for. Not only was Timothy Patrick Maguire a director of a firm called South Wales Demolition and Haulage (registered office: Cwmbran; headquarters: London), so was his mother, Evelyn Maguire.

Theresa's firm wasn't far from there, so I decided I might as well risk catching her in as spend time finding a working pay phone. She excused herself from a meeting to see me in her office and listened while I put all the pieces of my Tim/Evie theory together for her. When I'd finished she smiled and said, 'Well done. Now how are you going to prove that the unmarked flat-bed you saw at the playground is actually one of Tim Maguire's –'

I shrugged. 'I thought we might ask Hamley to go to south Wales and check it out.'

She laughed.

In fact I was half serious. 'We're on to a whole seam he could be ignoring.'

She thought about that a moment. 'Yes.' She reached for the phone. 'Be good to suss out his position on the Maguires.' She dialled and, when it started to ring, pressed the conference-call button. The ringing at the other end suddenly rang out in her office.

She'd barely identified herself to the police station receptionist who answered when she was put through.

'Good to hear from you, Theresa,' Hamley said with a brusqueness that made the content of the words perfunctory. 'Is Dee Street with you?'

'I'm here,' I said from my corner.

'You were to tell us your whereabouts –'

A snotty retort was about to escape my mouth when Theresa shook her head at me. I bit my lip.

'– We have obtained a search warrant for your office and adjacent rear yard.'

My office. God, had something been planted there now?

Theresa sat upright and said in her most glottal Belfast tones, 'Detective Inspector, you have conducted *two* searches of my client's *home* –'

'It's the confidential material that concerns me,' I said.

'I can assure you we don't propose to read anything at this stage. Now, my officers will meet you at your office. Can you be there in half an hour?'

Theresa gave me a questioning look: should she acquiesce or should she argue?

I shrugged. What could we do? They had a warrant. I whispered, 'More time.'

Into the phone she said, 'Lunchtime would be more –'

'We're under a lot of pressure here to –'

'Two hours.'

'One.'

There was no getting out of it. I nodded.

'Okay,' she said. 'She'll be there. Now, what *I* wanted to speak to *you* about was Mrs Evie Maguire and her son Tim.'

'Oh?'

I leaned forward towards the phone. 'They're playing both ends against the middle,' I said. 'Janey caught them.'

He laughed a single wry sound.

Theresa said, 'So you've established where Tim Maguire was the night of Janey Riordan's death?'

'Indeed we have. In fact he and his mother have both been very forthcoming with us.'

The airiness of his tone made me stick out my tongue at the telephone. Theresa smiled at me and said to him, 'Did Evie Maguire tell you Jane Riordan was blackmailing her?'

'Miss O'Connor, *please* – Miss Street, one hour.' And he hung up.

'Bastard,' Theresa muttered.

I reached out for the phone as she was setting it in the cradle. 'Can I ring my office?'

She gestured 'Be my guest' and switched off the conference button, then she got to her feet. 'Will you be okay?'

'Fine,' I nodded. 'Thanks.' I started dialling.

'I'll ring you at the flat later,' she said, and left me to it.

Suze was there, thank God, though the chill in her voice reminded me we'd fallen out. Well, I didn't have time to deal with that. 'Has there been a break-in?'

'No. Why?'

I said, 'It wouldn't be obvious.'

'What, not another left-something-rather-than-took-some-thing?'

'That's my fear. And Hamley will be there in an hour to search my office.'

'He can't! My Siberian clients are due in about twenty minutes.'

Various sarcastic retorts rushed for my tongue but I restrained myself. 'I'm sorry. I'm on my way but I thought – if you could start looking around.'

Her sigh retained the peevishness. 'I'll get Natasha and Annie to do it. Look, got to go –'

'Wait. You know the "matters" I discovered the other day.' I used the tone she knew meant 'decode *this*' – the one that assumed our phone was tapped.

She responded with a long, mulling silence.

I willed her to think of the papers from Janey's deposit box – the ones I'd given her to put in her safe.

'Friday?' she said at last.

Whew. 'Yeah. Perhaps you could get Natasha or Annie to *communicate* them to Theresa.'

More silence. Then she said, 'There's no "safety" problem if you're worried.'

'Please. I want to study them again.'

She tutted and said (too grudgingly), 'Okay.'

When I got out of the taxi outside my office I was immediately accosted by that guy from the *News of the World*. 'Ms Street! How are things going?'

I kept walking towards the front door. 'Fine. Just fine,' I said over my shoulder.

He kept up with me. 'Who do you think killed Janey Riordan?'

As I reached out to open the door, I gave him my most Medusa-like look – 'Give me a break!' – then let myself in and shut him out behind me.

The meeting-room door was closed and as I passed I could hear Suze speaking. If you knew her as well as I did the undercurrent of stress was palpable enough to crunch.

Natasha's desk in the outer office was vacant but when I entered my own office I found her standing on a stool, going through the upper shelves of my bookcases.

'Anything?' I asked her.

She shook her head. 'Not so far.'

'Did Suze ask you to "communicate" something to Theresa for me?'

'Annie's done it.'

'Good. Great.' I looked around. 'Where haven't you looked?'

Half an hour and one thorough search of both offices later neither of us had found anything that seemed put there to link me to Janey's murder. When Hamley's team arrived I felt more relaxed and confident that they wouldn't find anything either – not unless they planted it there and then. Natasha and I followed them around, watching closely to make sure they didn't. Interest again focused on my plants, though the spaces behind my filing cabinets were also popular.

They were there an hour, and as they moved from my room into Natasha's I paused to look out of the front window. When they'd come to my flat they'd contrived to be discreet about it. No such courtesy had been extended this morning. Two marked patrol cars were parked at the kerb outside our door and, across the street, the News of the World guy had been joined by two other guys, one with what I guessed to be sound-recording equipment, the other with a video camera.

The police apparently planted nothing and apparently found nothing. When they left, the News of the World guy and the guy with the video camera stayed behind. As they were on foot I got away from them by the simple expedient of ordering a taxi.

I gave the driver the address of South Wales Demolition and Haulage's London office and set about rehearsing what I would say to Tim if he were there and agreed to see me. I started out fancying the direct approach – 'Hello, Tim. Did you kill Janey Riordan?' – but by the time we arrived I'd gotten over that.

I stood on the kerb a moment, scanning the street for dark red new-model cars. This confirmed what I'd observed near the Coroner's Court a few days before: dark red was popular this year.

Fortunately I decided to go inside and see what was what before I checked the cars out further. It was just an accommodation address with a hard-looking receptionist presiding over mail boxes for a couple of dozen companies.

On the way out I passed a phone booth that still had a set of directories in it and remembered there was a basic piece of research I hadn't done. There were seven E Maguires and two Ts. I started with the first 'E' and one plumber, one housewife, one Scotswoman, one no-reply later, an answering machine picked up and a recorded version of Evie's overly elocuted voice told me no one was available. I didn't care; I'd learned what I needed.

I caught another taxi and set off for the Putney address that went with the number.

It turned out to belong to a mansion flat in a block near Putney Bridge. Dark red new-model cars weren't so popular on this street as they were downtown; there was just one that I could see, across the street and down about twenty yards. I crossed over to have a look: resident's parking permit, toddler seat in the back. Did Tim Maguire have a little kid now? I bent and peered through the driver's window – nothing legible – and, straightening, glanced over at Evie's building. Was that a curtain being pulled aside on the third floor?

I recrossed the road, went up to the entryphone panel and pressed the bell for Evie's. Nothing. I tried again, leaning on it a bit, then waited some more. Still nothing. I tried another bell, then another, then another. Finally someone answered. 'I'm a relative of Mrs Maguire in fourteen,' I lied. 'I thought she was expecting me. I need to leave a message and I don't seem to have any paper.'

Silence.

'I'm *so* sorry to trouble you,' I added in my most laid-back Californian.

More silence. In fact, so much more that I started thinking

about where I'd go from here. Then a buzzer sounded and I pushed the door and was in.

I climbed to the second floor, where outside number ten I found a pad and pencil. Somehow they seemed a sad comment on something.

I continued to the next floor where Evie's flat was and at the top of the stairs I stepped back to let an elderly woman get by me. As I did so the door opened behind me and Evie Maguire materialised. For half a second I thought she wasn't going to recognise me. Ha! No such luck.

'What do *you* want?'

'Tim. I – Is he –'

'If you don't leave this instant I shall call the police.'

Imperiousness always winds me up. I start acting worse than the person who's done it to me. 'I have a perfect right to be here.'

'You can't harass people.'

'Now look –'

She opened her mouth and, I kid you not, started to scream at the top of her voice 'Help! Police! Help!' It was pure theatre, just a hammy act, but I could hear doors opening above and below us as even the most tentative neighbours were compelled to check out what was going on.

I decided it was time to get out of there.

Minutes later I was hurrying out the front door of the block and back the way I'd come, towards the tube. Just as I reached the junction with the High Street a police car drove past me and, I couldn't help it, I turned to watch to see if it would stop at Evie's.

It did.

I redoubled my speed.

It took me too long to get back to Theresa's. There was an 'incident' at Earls Court and the District Line crawled and lurched before finally terminating there. There wasn't a taxi to be had anywhere and the buses were chock-a-block, so I walked to

Gloucester Road and eventually prised myself into a jam-packed Picadilly Line train. I had to change again at Green Park and when I finally turned into Theresa's all I wanted was a long, tall drink and some mind-numbing television and maybe some comfort food like fish and chips.

I had my key in the lock when Theresa opened the door to me from the inside. I'd smiled before I'd registered the expression on her face: storm-warning, it said. Beware. 'What?' I said.

She gestured me in and shut the door behind me. 'Tim Maguire,' she said. 'His car crashed. He's dead.'

Thirteen

Theresa must have guided me in from the hall. All I can remember is the uprush of anxious thoughts beating their wings against each other. Tim Maguire – the man I was becoming convinced was Janey's murderer – dead. What did it mean?

One thing it meant was that he couldn't continue setting me up for it. That was clearly A Good Thing.

So why didn't I feel relieved?

I found myself taking a long swallow from the large glass of wine that Theresa must have put in my hand. It didn't stop the inner dialogue but it turned it down. That's when I realised we'd come into the kitchen and sat down at the table beside the window. Theresa was sitting across from me, leaning back in her chair, waiting for my speechlessness to pass.

'When?' I managed at last.

She leaned forward. 'Early this morning sometime. Near Newport.'

'Newport, Wales?'

She nodded. 'Not far from his company's head office.'

'How'd it happen? Anybody else hurt?'

'There was an explosion, apparently. The car turned into a

fireball. Luckily the cars behind were far enough away to take diversionary action.'

'My God, how'd they identify him?'

'His number plate and his teeth.'

I thought about flash Tim. Imagine: reduced to licence plate and teeth. I finished the wine and poured myself some more. 'How'd you hear about it?'

'Hamley's sergeant rang me. He said they were "impressed by the coincidence of your allegations about Mr Maguire and his 'accident'". They want to talk to you about it.'

'Terrific,' I muttered. 'Now I suppose they're going to say *I* made his car explode.'

'Well, if you think about it, not many cars just blow up, do they? Either he hit something or –'

'Or someone planted a bomb on him? Jesus, Theresa, that means –'

She nodded. 'He must have made some nasty bugger pretty angry.'

'Ha! Some nasty, powerful, organised-crime bugger from the sound of it. I mean, *blow* someone up?'

She nodded again. 'A terrorist group would have claimed credit by now.'

'Well, frankly, it wouldn't surprise me to learn Tim Maguire was involved with gangsters. They all need truckers, don't they?'

'And if you have a nice legitimate front like clearing building sites –'

'Exactly. Trouble is – which gang? The Colombians? The Jamaicans? The Chinese? God, for all we know it could be the Mafia.'

We each drifted off into our own middle distances for a moment. Was Tim's death related to Janey's? I wondered. Had she gone on from discovering that he'd been excavating the playground she felt was hers to finding out he'd been hauling contraband of some description? Had they both been killed by the same Nasty Unknown?

And did said Nasty Unknown know about me?

I said, 'I'd love to know if Tim Maguire's car was dark red. I mean *before*.'

'I'm not sure there's a delicate way to ask that. There might not even be an answer.'

'It's important.'

She nodded. She knew that. 'I'll do what I can.' Then she lifted the edge of the curtain and looked out the window. Over her shoulder she said, 'That *News of the World* bloke know you're here yet?'

'I don't think so.'

As she scanned the street I had a memory of the police car pulling up in front of Evie's building. Had they been coming to tell her about Tim? I said, 'I hope to God the *News of the World* guy doesn't find Evie Maguire. I can see it: "Lawyer killed my colleague – did she kill my son?"'

Theresa let the corner of the curtain fall and looked at me again. 'Do you seriously think she believes you killed Janey?'

I shrugged. 'She was incredibly rude to me at the Coroner's Court and she completely lost her rag at me for snooping around her flat this afternoon.'

'Could *she* have done it?'

'Unlikely. I could believe she'd cover up for Tim though.'

She thought about that a moment but was evidently no more able than I was to draw a conclusion. She glanced at her watch, cursed to herself and reached down for her bag. 'Martin's expecting me, I'm afraid.' She started to stand up and, in the process, glanced into the bag. 'Oops. Almost forgot.' She took out a file and put it on the table. 'From Suze. I'm also to tell you that Sufiya Khan wants you to ring her. Oh! And Liam Mahoney sends his love.'

'What? You *spoke* to him?'

The horror in my tone made her laugh. 'No. To our mutual friend – I finally remembered who it was. She wanted to know why I was interested, so I gave her a few broad strokes about you. She told him of course – said he lit up when he heard your name. He was glad to hear you'd found out the truth about him at last but pretty appalled by the circumstances. He's an evangelical Christian in Southend –'

'He isn't.'

She laughed. 'I thought you'd like that. Apparently he got "the call" in prison. Anyway, he said if you needed to get away, you'd be welcome there.'

'Ugh. I mean, thanks but no thanks.'

She laughed again and, getting to her feet at last, looked down at me. 'I don't like leaving you here. Why don't you come with me?'

'That's kind of you,' I said. 'Actually – I've got this new, ah, "friend". I'm hoping he'll be over later.'

She grinned. 'Anyone I know?'

I shook my head and couldn't help grinning back. 'He's an American engineering consultant here on a short contract. Not my usual type, but –' I shrugged.

She came around and leaned down and kissed me on the cheek. 'Maybe that's no bad thing.'

I walked to the front door with her and *en route* we agreed to meet outside the police station at two the next day. I locked the door behind her because she'd made me promise I would (okay, and I was nervous. Tim blown up made me nervous), then I went to the hall phone and rang Sufiya at the hospital. I'd missed her, but she'd be ringing in later; I left my number.

Back in the kitchen I sat down at the table again and opened the file Suze had sent over via Theresa. Inside was the stuff from Janey's deposit box, the box she'd visited the afternoon of the day she was killed. This time I'd look through it assuming Janey had found out about Tim's criminal connections. I'd go further: I'd look for some hint she'd found out who they were.

The first thing I pulled out was the small cutting about moves to regulate the UK–Bangladesh money trade. Yes, I thought, *that* sounded Tim-ish. I knew little about Bangladesh – the usual news-derived images of floods, poverty and Islamic fundmentalism – but it was bound to have a mafia. Most countries seemed to.

I retrieved my notebook and wrote a reminder to myself to talk to Sufiya about it.

Next out were the accounts-book pages. Stuck on the front was the roving yellow Post-it with the name 'Sharon B' written on it in Janey's hand. Had Tim Maguire had a Sharon B in his life? Had Janey? Was Sharon B a club or a restaurant? A singer?

I made another research note, moved the Post-it to one side and returned to the accounts. My finger went to the three sums Janey had deposited in the last week of her life to pay back the three grants she'd spent prematurely. My speculation of a day or two before – that she'd extracted some of that money from Evie by blackmailing her about her jobs-for-my-family attitude to power back in her days at the GLC – it seemed weak now.

An earlier idea came back to me: that faced with the need to raise a lot of money fast, Janey'd been driven to a drug deal. It became even more plausible if I imagined Tim Maguire had been involved.

I made another note, then retrieved the love letter with the six-year-old postmark.

Was it from Tim? Hard to conceive she'd have an affair with Mr Yucky, no matter how friendly she'd become with his mother. If only she hadn't been so close-mouthed about her lovers. She'd tell you she had a new one or that she'd just finished with someone, and I certainly knew that she'd had a long, painful run of married men. Beyond that she tended to keep details to herself.

Had she blackmailed one of them for the money she needed? He'd have to have been pretty damn rich.

Marc Felici came to mind. No. If Suze was his type, it was hard to see him with Janey. Besides which, he'd admitted helping Janey out financially. Why extort what comes if you say please?

I found myself thinking about Richard Farmer himself. Back when I'd started doing Weaverstown Housing Association's work and had first met him, I'd had a suspicion that he and Janey were sleeping together. But, if these were his old love letters, surely she'd have tried to blackmail him into compensating her publicly for loss of the schemes she'd been planning to develop? And he was supposed to be Mr Community Spirit. Surely if he'd offered compensation he'd have wanted it to be publicly known?

I needed to compare the letter to a sample of his handwriting just to be sure, but as a hypothesis I rated this one low.

That left another Richard-related set of questions.

What company had he sold the playground site to? How had Tim come to get the excavation contract from that company? Was it coincidence or a link in the chain of events leading first to Janey's death and then to Tim's own?

I closed my eyes and waited but no answers came. I opened my eyes again and slid out the last item, the old photo of me and Liam. This, of course, was different from the other things left in Janey's deposit box – a 'Here, have this back' gesture.

I could be wrong, there could be another meaning, but my head was starting to throb, a clear sign that I'd done enough speculating. I shoved everything back in the file, shoved the file into my bag and went to have a shower.

Twenty minutes later, as I was just getting out, the entryphone buzzer sounded. My hair was in a towel turban already, so I grabbed Theresa's robe and went to answer.

'Hi, sweet Dee, let me in.'

Greg!

I buzzed him in, then checked myself in the hall mirror. Not exactly the way I wanted a new lover to see me. I decided to take off the turban, then stood there frantically finger-combing the tangled result. He knocked. I checked myself again. Maybe with-turban was better. I picked up the discarded towel.

He knocked again. He'd have to take what he got. I hurried to open the door. He was standing there, the compleat huggy-bear, bottle of Californian wine in one hand, bunch of May blossoms in the other. He stepped in and bent down to kiss me. 'I meant to phone first.' It was a long, delicious kiss. 'Mmmm. You smell wonderful.'

My hand of its own accord unpulled my waist tie so the robe fell open. (Not wide open – just enough. A *reminder* open.) I was a little surprised at myself – what movie was *I* in? – and he looked a little surprised too. In fact I almost thought he was going to pretend this wasn't happening. But the hesitation passed. He put down the wine and the flowers, reached over for me, picked me up – no kidding – and carried me into the bedroom.

I'd had a fantasy of some man doing this to me for years and no one ever had. Whether it was because Greg was a foot bigger in height and girth than the string of British guys I'd had relationships with, or whether it was because I was at that point twenty pounds lighter than I'd been when I embarked on the phase of celibacy just ended, or, more likely, whether it was because I had a reputation as a feminist and nobody'd dare do this except a comparative stranger – whatever: this was it. It was coming true.

An hour – two hours? – later he murmured into my hair, 'I guess you had a good day.'

'Diabolical,' I said into his mouth.

'Yeah?' he said into mine.

'My main suspect's been killed.'

He stopped kissing me and pulled right back so he was half sitting up and looked at me, eyes wide. '*What?*'

'Yeah, I said. 'That's how I felt.'

'What happened to him?'

I told him what Theresa had told me about the explosion. When it left him as speechless as it had left me, I filled the silence by telling him how Theresa and I felt sure some organised crime racket must be involved because who else blew people up.

'Wow,' was all he could say when I'd finished. 'Wow' and 'No shit.'

I decided to make coffee. He waved vaguely as I disentangled my legs from his, slipped out of bed, put the robe back on and headed for the kitchen.

Three or four minutes later, just as I was rinsing the mugs and contemplating making toast, he emerged in the doorway, trousers on, barefoot, shirt open. He held his pager out to me. 'Damn thing. Can I use the phone?'

I told him of course, then strained to hear the indistinct murmur of his half of the conversation coming from the hall. The tone made me decide, on balance, that he was being called away. And sure enough, when he returned, I could see it in his face. 'This Paris deal –' he shook his head.

'What deal's that?' I said, suddenly feeling a bit embarrassed. He knew much more about the ins and outs of my professional life than I knew about his.

He waved his hand. 'Boring. Where did I leave my shoes?' He looked around. 'Ah – there they are.' He bent down to retrieve them from under one of the chairs and padded into the bedroom.

'You coming back later?' I said after him. There was more of a pout in my voice than I'd even recognised feeling.

'I'd like to,' he called.

I poured a cup of coffee for myself and waited.

A moment later he re-emerged, fully dressed, and came straight over to me and took my hands in his. 'I really ought to go home. My relative's here another couple of days.' Before I could process that he kissed me. 'Look,' he said, 'there are two things I can help you with. I can get Maguire's Wales office checked out –'

'Can you?'

He nodded. 'I've got a manufacturer near Pontypool. And I can try to find out who Richard Farmer sold the playground to. There's a Canadian developer on the parents' team at the school.'

'Great!' I said.

He leaned down to kiss me again. 'Talk to you tomorrow. Take care now.'

I promised I would.

I locked the door behind him, then went to the window and watched his broad back head for the gate, pass through, turn left and disappear behind the front hedge. I stared into the space he'd occupied, not thinking, just feeling the way my body ached from so much good sex after such a long dry spell and working through the disappointment I felt that there wouldn't be any more today and wondering why I didn't feel more upset that his wife was obviously staying at his flat and that he was going home to her.

Suddenly my gaze was attracted by something in the real vista and I focused beyond the gate, on a figure standing on the opposite side of the street, at the edge of my field of vision. The hair, the glasses, the camera –

Then I realised. The guy from the *News of the World* had found me.

Damn.

I thought about where I was. Like the block I lived in, it was a converted turn-of-the-century tenement, originally built by a philanthropic Victorian charity to house 'the working poor'. Did it have a flat roof like mine? It must. I pulled on some jeans under the robe and went barefoot out to the hall, locked the flat behind me and hurried up the four flights to the roof door. Yes, it *was* like my building.

I went out on to the roof and walked its full length – a city block – to the door at the other end. It was a fire exit and unlocked.

Good. I could get out that way if I needed to.

I recrossed the roof to Theresa's stairwell and when I opened the door at the top of the stairs heard the distant sound of a telephone ringing somewhere below. I picked up speed in case it was for me.

It was.

I quickly got the door unlocked and hurried to answer.

'Dee! Oh, good! I was about to hang up,' Sufiya said. 'How are you?'

I laughed. 'I'd be better if the *News of the World* hadn't found me.'

She groaned for me. 'Are they literally on your doorstep?'

'Across the street.'

'Do you feel unsafe at all?'

Did I? I felt around in myself. 'No,' I said finally.

'Right, well – if it gets too much and you need to find somewhere else, let me know.'

'Thanks,' I said. 'I may take you up on that. Hey – I looked for you at the demonstration yesterday.'

'Did you? I was late getting there – off sorting things out with the mullahs at last.'

'Oh?'

'They've finally finally given permission for us to test the fabric of the Brick Lane mosque.'

'Great.'

'Mmm. Now I'm back to the problem of premises for the health monitoring project. That councillor Janey got to promise the Council would come up with the goods – he refuses to return my calls. I've decided to drop in to his surgery.'

'Good! Yes! Corner him,' I said. Then, 'Oh – before I forget. I wanted to ask what you know about the Bangladeshi criminal scene.'

'Only what I read in the paper, fortunately. What exactly?'

'The money-trade thefts.'

'Oh *that*. – Yes, a lot of my patients' families have lost savings and ticket money.'

'Ticket money?'

'Traders tend to be travel agents. Actually, the Council's been good on this issue. Shall I ask?'

'When are you going?'

'Tomorrow morning.'

'Yeah? I don't have to be anywhere until 2 –'

'Come with me! By all means!' She laughed. 'It might double my chance of getting something out of him. Look, I want to be first in the queue. That means being there at 10.'

'No problem. I'll even try not to bring the *News of the World*.'

There was a longish silence, full of thought. 'I know,' she said at last. 'I'll come and pick you up. Where are you?'

Fourteen

It had been a couple of days since I'd watched a TV or listened to a radio or read a paper, and the next morning, suddenly yearning to know that the world was still out there, I turned on the television breakfast news. Not a lot had changed: war, genocide, disasters and misuse of resources on the international scene; murder, abuse and the effects of the lengthening drought on the national. That was enough, I decided, reaching to switch off.

Then the first local item came on: a young woman reporter was standing in front of the accommodation office of South Wales Haulage that I'd visited the day before. 'A London man, haulage contractor Timothy Maguire, died when his car *blew up* yesterday morning near Newport, Wales.' A photograph of Janey Riordan, alive, smiling, came on. 'At a press conference in just under an hour's time the Metropolitan Police are expected to confirm that Mr Maguire was a key witness in their investigation into the murder of housing association director Janey Riordan a week ago.'

Oh God, I thought. Oh God.

All my worst speculations about Tim Maguire had assumed he was setting me up anonymously. He shot Janey for reasons I was getting close to, he saw me arriving as he was leaving, he went back in and bloodied a glove (or perhaps donated a glove he'd genuinely used), he planted it at my place the next day and he phoned an anonymous tip-off to the police saying he'd seen a small, dark-haired woman in the area.

Had he really had the front to kill her and then identify himself to the police? I thought back to the last time I'd seen him – when was it? Yes, he'd been sitting in the police waiting room when I'd come out after the first – second? – interview.

Had they put him there to identify me?

God, no wonder Hamley wanted to see me again. In *his* current set of speculations, I had no doubt, I'd killed Janey, then killed the person I'd belatedly discovered was the main witness against me. Add his inbuilt predisposition to want me to be guilty and hey presto.

I could feel the tears coming and got angry with myself for not resisting them better. It was stupid. He couldn't possibly think I'd *bomb* someone. I took a swig from my mug of now-tepid tea, picked up my bowl of muesli and began shovelling it into my mouth.

I gagged: it had gone soggy.

I got up, marched into the bathroom and dumped it down the toilet. Then I sat heavily on the edge of the bath and gave in: anger, loneliness, self-pity, despair – I wanted my mother, I wanted my father (what a nerve – being *dead*). I at least wanted bloody Suze.

Fortunately, within five or ten minutes I'd had enough of wallowing and railing. Dee, I told me (trying for the same spirit I use with clients in my position), Dee, it will do you no good whatsoever to fall apart. Then they *will* have you. No, you have to keep going, looking for your chances. You have to remember at all times that no matter what things look like, no matter how they might be twisted and misconstrued and outrageously interpreted, you didn't kill Janey Riordan and you know nothing about how Tim Maguire's car came to explode.

What's more, you mustn't be uncharitable about Suze. Because of all the crap you are going through, she is coping alone with the burden of the firm's debt and the Ducane Stafford negotiations.

In this way I'd more or less pulled myself together by the time the door buzzer sounded at 8.45.

'It's me,' Sufiya murmured into the intercom when I asked who it was. 'May we come in?'

We? I thought. I said, 'Sure', and buzzed her in.

I opened the flat door and waited, listening to the footsteps cross the threshold, the front door close, the footsteps climb the steps. Two of them? The first came into view – a woman about Sufiya's size in a dark blue saree, her face obscured by a matching headscarf. Was it her? I'd only seen her in Western clothes. Then she looked up and smiled and said, 'Hello.'

'Sufiya! I almost didn't recognise you,' I said, laughing, as she came towards me.

She also laughed. 'Good. Wonderful.' She gestured behind her as she stepped past me into the flat. 'Look who I've brought.'

Nasima appeared. She had on a sage tunic over loose matching trousers and a slightly lighter scarf and the colour seemed to accentuate her fragility, which had definitely advanced in the four days since I'd last seen her at the primary school. When she grinned at me there seemed nothing to her but her wide mouth and her huge eyes. I wanted to hug her because of it but she seemed hunched into herself, so I kept my distance but gave her my best smile. 'How's the baby?' I said, miming cradle arms.

She sighed a long wavery sigh and gave a shrug that said so-so. Then she followed Sufiya into the flat. As I shut the door and returned inside after them, it came to me what Sufiya was up to. And sure enough, when I got to the living room I found her unpacking a plastic shopping bag. Piece by piece she handed the items to me: sage tunic, matching baggies, matching headscarf.

'Try them on!' she said when I stood there looking at everything a bit idiotically. She gestured to the bedroom. Obediently I went and changed.

With my hair off my face and the headscarf on I thought I looked pretty convincing in the bedroom mirror, and I loved the loose comfort of the clothes. But back in the sitting room Sufiya wanted to do more and Nasima thought she was right, so I gave in to a layer of dark make-up and put on the sunglasses Nasima had worn on the way in. Then Nasima and I went back into the bedroom and stood side by side in front of the mirror. One of me was equal to one and a half of her, but apart from that minor detail the ruse probably stood a chance. Even better, her brother was at the hospital with the baby, so she was happy to stay at the flat for a good hour. – Long enough.

I checked out of the window: yep, the *News of the World* guy was on duty.

As we were heading for the door I spotted the file of bits from Janey's deposit box. It belonged in the safe back in my office, not lying around here. I picked it up and put it in my bag. I'd have to drop it in.

I felt excruciatingly self-conscious as we walked out the front door and turned right towards the High Street and the tube beyond, but that made me keep my head down, which is what Sufiya was murmuring at me to do anyway. Would he realise? What if he did? What if he ran after us? But, fortunately, all that proved to be just so much unwarranted paranoia. When we got to the first big intersection we both took the opportunity afforded by the traffic light to glance over our shoulders.

There wasn't a sign of him.

The office at the rear of Weaverstown Hall where Councillor Anwar Miah held his brief fortnightly surgery was unadorned, the way National Health Service and British Rail and other government-funded community services used to be when I first came to Britain. In those days spartan meant honest and deep down I suppose I still believed this. We arrived at a quarter to 10, well before it started, but there were half a dozen people ahead of us. Sufiya and I sat in the two remaining chairs at the end of the queue.

Half an hour later we were only a third of the way there and we'd shifted into finding out about each other's personal lives. Don't know why but it surprised me to find out she was a have-it-all superwoman: not only did she have a consuming and useful medical career that had spilled over into community activism, but a husband and two young children *and* a live-in mother-in-law whom she *liked*.

As someone else went in and we moved along a seat, she excused herself and disappeared to find the ladies' room. I leaned back against the wall and glanced to my left, to the person who'd just shifted along onto the seat I'd vacated. She was young and white and she had her head bent over a letter, reading. My eyes went to it and even at that distance I recognised something familiar in the handwriting.

It took me a couple of minutes to figure out the connection, then it came to me. I retrieved the file from my bag, opened it hurriedly and dug out the love letter. I held it down surreptitiously (I thought) as close as I could to the letter the young woman beside me was reading. Yes, the same. Major coincidences like that never happened to me, I told myself. This was extraordinary.

I realised the young woman was looking at me – speaking.

'What?' I said.

'I said, You'd think they'd type, these people.' The accent was broad cockney.

I struggled a moment with this. Did she mean –? What did she –? Then a second understanding came. I cleared my throat but my voice wasn't there. I pointed at Councillor Anwar Miah's office and shook the love letter. 'From him?' I managed.

She gave me a look that said, Of course! What was I, nuts? Then she pointed at a display case on the opposite wall and went back to her reading. I asked her to hold my seat and Sufiya's and, taking her grunt for yes, crossed to have a look. It was a letter in the same hand, thanking everyone who helped with the last campaign and signed Anwar Miah.

Wow, I thought. Wowee, Jesus, wowee. I must have been vibrating with excitement because as soon as Sufiya saw me she realised that something momentous had happened. 'What?' she said as she sat down again.

I grinned and leaned towards her. 'They used to be lovers,' I whispered. 'Janey Riordan and Anwar Miah used to be lovers.'

An hour and a quarter after we arrived, we were ushered into the windowless broom cupboard that was Anwar Miah's consultancy room. It was hard to believe the large bulky man who welcomed us was the same man who'd stood beside Janey in front of demonstrators and promised a replacement playground. I remembered him as much smaller and meeker.

He greeted Sufiya in Bengali, turned to do the same to me – and suddenly seemed to see me under the make-up and scarf. For an instant he wasn't sure where to put himself. Then, recovering quickly, he gestured to the seats as if white women disguised as Bangladeshis were always dropping in on him. In English he said, 'What can I do for you ladies today?'

Sufiya said, 'I'm Dr Khan. I work in Whitechapel Special Care Baby Unit. I've written to you – left a couple of phone messages –' His expression said, 'Sorry – rings no bells.' She pushed on: 'I'm setting up the women's health monitoring project – to research the local miscarriage and deformities rate –'

'Ah, yes,' he said, memory suddenly stimulated. 'Excellent work. Much needed.' He looked at me.

'I'm a – maybe even "the" – leading suspect in the murder of Janey Riordan.'

He made a pained face. 'Innocent, I assume?'

I nodded. 'Have they questioned you about Janey?'

He settled back in his chair, sticking to his cool-dude mode. Inside he must have been fidgeting like hell. 'Yes, certainly.'

I leaned towards him. 'Do they know you publicly promised her another site for the playground *and* space for the monitoring project *and* space for the youth club?'

'Promised to *try* to find other venues – to *try*.'

'I was there,' I said. 'I don't recall the qualification.'

'Yes – well. My fellow councillors certainly do.'

I got out the old love letter and held it up. 'And do your fellow councillors all know how close you and Janey used to be?' He glanced at it but if he took it in he didn't show it.

I spread it out and held it up to his eye level with two hands. This time he had to register it. He tried to keep up his unbothered expression, but I was watching closely and so was Sufiya and we both saw him tighten his fingers on the edge of the desk.

I thought I'd save him the effort of lying. 'She blackmailed you, didn't she?'

'You can't prove –'

'Hey. Half your constituents must have samples of your handwriting.'

He closed his mouth and cast his eyes down at his desk. 'There are more of them, aren't there?'

He didn't see me give Sufiya a conspiratorial glance: we had him. I said, 'I expect the police took them from her safe deposit box.'

A faint groan escaped his efforts to hold it in.

'But so far they don't appear to be concerned about them; because they're concentrating on me. *I* don't have any interest in drawing their attention to them, let me hasten to add.'

He looked up again finally. Irritation was in the lines around his eyes but he sounded relieved. 'What do you want from me?'

'*I* want what you promised Janey,' Sufiya cut in at once. 'New sites for the playground and monitoring project and youth centre.'

'She knew I couldn't deliver that.'

'Come on,' I said.

'It's true.' He put his hand on his heart. 'What she blackmailed me into doing was *announcing* that the community liaison section would give the playground and community buildings replacement priority.'

'What, you mean just say it, not do it?'

He nodded. 'Obviously she *wanted* me to do it as well. But it was more important to her that I make an immediate public announcement that sounded like the Council was committed to helping. Which I did.' He nodded to me. 'I got into huge trouble for it.'

I wasn't about to offer him my sympathy. I looked at Sufiya. 'Does that make sense to you? She just wanted an *announcement*?'

She thought so hard she frowned. Eventually she turned back to Anwar and sighed. 'I want you to offer help and mean it, I'm afraid.'

'Fine. In that case you've got to do what I told her – lean on Richard Farmer, lean on the new owners.'

'Who are?' I asked.

'Don't know. Some American firm.'

'I heard they were Canadian,' I said.

He shook his head, not so much to say No as to say, Oh, he hadn't heard that.

Sufiya said, 'We've been demonstrating at the playground for weeks. Surely that counts as "leaning"?'

He nodded. 'It's certainly more than Janey was willing to do, as you know. I don't want to speak ill of the dead but she made it impossible for me to get the Council to provide alternative sites.'

'How's that?' I said.

'Look. You know and I know that the days of hundred per cent funding are gone. Compensation from Farmer would have given her funds to put in the pot but she told me she wasn't going to press for it – yet.'

'Why not?'

He shook his head. 'Wouldn't tell me. It was all very strange.'

'The health monitoring project would press him for compensation,' Sufiya said.

'You do that and I'll help you find Council premises.'

She put out her hand. 'Good. Fine.'

They shook and he held out his hand to me. 'I hope you get out of your difficulties.'

Somehow I believed him. 'Actually, I have a question too. I'm interested in the money-trade theft issue.'

'Yes?'

'The perpetrators – they're Bangladeshi?'

'Of course.'

'There must be one or two white Europeans involved.'

He appealed to Sufiya with a glance, then said to me, 'You'll appreciate the investigation is confidential.'

She said, 'Dee doesn't deserve to be hounded if there's some piece of information around that might help her.'

He looked down at the floor as if his privacy and his peace of mind were in its worn tiles. Then he looked up again. 'I'll ask around. Where can I contact you?'

I opened my mouth but realised I had no clear answer.

Sufiya said, 'Through me – at the hospital', and gave him the number. 'I'll hear from you by when? Before lunch?'

He checked the clock. 'That's only an hour and a half.'

Sufiya put her hand on my back. 'It's urgent.'

He worked through whatever temptation he felt to put her in her place. 'I'll do what I can as quickly as I can.'

She accepted that.

Outside in the hall, as we walked back along the dingy corridor towards the sunny day beyond the front door, I said, 'You pushed him hard there at the end.'

With a scorn in her voice I'd not heard from her before she said, 'I have no sympathy for him at all.'

'Really? You seemed –'

She shook her head. 'I kept thinking, I know who you are, I've met your wife, she's lovely, your kids are lovely, why did you get involved with Janey Riordan?'

'Lust?' I offered (just a little too fast). 'Boredom?'

She shook her head. 'Status. If he sleeps with power, he acquires power.'

'I wouldn't have thought of what Janey had as "power".'

'White skin, grant money and housing association pull: that sounds like power to me.'

Funny how relative these things are.

I remained behind in Weaverstown Hall after Sufiya left for the hospital and went in search of a pay phone. When I found one I dialled my office. I wanted to make certain Suze was there before I went over. 'Aspinall Street, good morning,' said Jackie in the cheery sing-song way that (we hope) gives heart to troubled clients. It gave a bit to me.

'Whew,' I said, laughing. 'We're still in business, I guess.'

'Dee! Hi! Well, to tell you the truth, I think it's been a bit hairy, business-wise. Don't tell her I told you so, but Suze looks really wrecked. Hang on, I'll put you through.'

Seconds later Suze came on. 'Dee! God! I've been trying to find you for the past two and a half hours.' The tension in her tone said it all.

Shit, I thought. 'Don't tell me,' I said. 'Sir Teddy's thrown another wobbler.'

'"Wobbler" – hunh. He's pulled Ducane Stafford completely out of the merger negotiations. Can you get over here?' She sounded half overstressed and overtired, half irritated with me for being part of the problem.

'Forty minutes,' I said. Then I hurried out to find a taxi.

My disguise was so effective that the pair of colleagues who passed me as I went in didn't even notice me, and when I walked past the reception towards the stairs, Jackie bolted over to stop me. I took off the sunglasses and pushed back the headscarf and she burst out laughing. I was glad somebody'd kept her sense of humour.

Encouraged, I decided to try it out on Suze, knocking on her door and opening it with fanfare accompaniment. Don't know what I was hoping for but it was more than the grunt I got. 'You've got some proper clothes here, haven't you?' she said. No Hello, how are you; no smile.

'Suze,' I said, trying to keep it light, '*these* are proper clothes. All these years I thought this kind of clothing would be restricting and inhibiting and the opposite's true. They're a liberation. They've made me invisible.'

She looked me over, clearly unconvinced. I noticed then that she was wearing the Armani suit she'd bought in the men's department of Harrods during the last sale. 'Well,' she said, 'we've got an appointment with Marc as soon as we can get to his office and I don't think invisibility is quite the note we want to strike with him.'

'I thought I just bust a gut to get here so we could talk about what we're going to do.'

'We will. But Marc has an offer for us and I want you to hear it from him.'

'I'm due at the police station.'

'When?'

'Two.'

She waved her hand: plenty of time. 'Now seriously, Dee, you do have your spare suit here still, don't you?'

I liked her least in this edgy, officious mood and the temptation to get into an argument was as tremendous then as it ever gets. Would I have the energy for the consequences, that was the question. I decided the answer was no.

I admitted grudgingly that I did have a spare suit in my closet and went through the interconnecting door to my office to change into it. On my desk was a note in Natasha's handwriting. 'Ten a.m. Greg Tuttle telephoned. Will be away on business all day and may be gone overnight and tomorrow. Said he's very very sorry and will "catch you later". Left messages at Theresa's and your home number too.'

176

This made me feel even more disgruntled. Partly it was the prospect of lust thwarted; mostly it was curiosity frustrated. Had he started his enquiries into Tim's Welsh office and the purchaser of the playground site? Couldn't he have said so?

And was this message telling me the truth? Was he away alone or was it that he and his wife were off together in Paris (or somewhere equally Ye Olde and Romantick), going through some reconciliation process?

Why had I done this to myself? I was too old to have done this to myself.

Fifteen

Jackie lent me her yellow hat with the big floppy brim and I borrowed Natasha's pink mohair cardigan: they were my disguise for the dash to the taxi, though I saw no sign of my *News of the World* guy. I'd packed my tunic, loose trousers and headscarf in my shoulder bag for later, just in case.

En route I managed to extract from Suze the background to this meeting. After she'd had the horrendous call from Sir Teddy – who'd seen the same breakfast TV news report as I had, it appeared – she'd tried me at Theresa's and when I wasn't there she'd phoned Marc.

'You still strictly business with him?'

She squirmed and glanced at her hands, then over at me quickly, then back at her hands. I took this to mean she'd slept with him but wasn't quite ready to say so.

'Peter?' I said.

She squirmed again and couldn't seem to look at me. 'Off drink, getting fit, unbelievably lovey-dovey. More than he's been in years.'

'Jeez, Suze, poor you.' I laughed. She smiled a fidgety, self-conscious smile. 'So what did Marc say?' I asked.

'He said to fax him our last three years' accounts.'

'Really? Why? Is he thinking he can –'

She looked out the window. 'You wait. He'll tell you.'

We drove through the Park to Paddington and from there to Westbourne Park Road, across Notting Hill Gate and down to Kensington Church Street. Marc Felici's office was over a small antique emporium called Felicitas and Suze herded me over to the window to have a look. It specialised in eighteenth- to early-nineteenth-century mirrors and furniture – most of it Italian and French, some of it English, all of it targeted at American tourists in search of conversation pieces that weren't too bulky to carry home. I spotted a lampshade I'd have had in an instant and as Suze knows my arch non-shopper tendencies she was especially pleased. 'Marc's got an amazing background, you know. His parents were Milanese anti-Fascists. Mussolini sent some thugs to kill his father and they had an incredible escape. They were taken in by an Edinburgh socialist family.'

'Mmm,' I said, trying not to laugh. I hadn't seen her in the first gush of love for about ten years.

Greg's warning about Marc suddenly thrust itself back into my consciousness. Was she being taken for a ride? Would Greg be wrong about something like that? (Could anyone who made love as artfully as he did be wrong about *anything*?)

The brass plaque by the door had a list of company names etched into it. Felicitas Antiques. Marc Felici Ltd (Fine Art). Milan Felix Art Imports Ltd. M. Felici Packers and Shippers (Antiques and Art) (London–Milan). Suze pressed the top one and a moment later we were entering the boss's private lift.

Marc's second-floor suite was an uncluttered space elegantly furnished with a selection of his favourite pieces: a cathedral chair, a tapestry, a carved bench, a globe on his large pedestal desk. He took both Suze's hands and kissed her fondly on the cheek (did she blush? *Suze?*), treated me to his winningest smile, escorted us to seats around the small table at the conference and library end, had cappuccino and small sandwiches in fingers of ciabatta bread brought in. Then, when we were all seated and settled, he looked at me and said, 'What a difficult time you've had.'

'I don't think it's over.'

'No? But if Tim Maguire was the police witness –'

'Then now I'm a double murderer.'

He shook his head of wonderful white hair. Frown lines furrowed the lightly tanned brow. I might be fifteen years younger than he was, but he'd beat me at tennis, no problem. 'No, I'm sorry. You're a reputable lawyer. They can't possibly suspect you of blowing up a car.'

'Ha. I wouldn't be so sure.'

He shook his head with even more emphasis, rejecting my doubts absolutely.

'Well –' I shrugged – 'they're interviewing me again in –' I checked my watch – 'an hour and fifteen minutes.'

Suze shut her eyes and, leaning her head back, groaned melodramatically.

Marc was still shaking his head. 'Everyone who's ever dealt with Tim Maguire – and I include myself – knows that he was a chancer.'

'Not DI Hamley.'

'Well, I'll tell him.'

'Good.'

Suze said, 'What did he do to you?'

He hesitated, as if he'd rather not go into it, then he said, 'It was years ago. He claimed he wanted to get into antiques transport. I gave him a chance. He did it carelessly.'

Ooh, ow, and take that as a warning, I thought. Thank God Suze was a perfectionist.

I said, 'But can you see him killing Janey – I mean, with his own hands?'

'With no trouble. I can't imagine why but I can certainly see him doing it. I intend to tell the police that too.'

'Great!' I said. 'Thanks.'

He gave me another winning smile. 'I may also point out to them that I wouldn't be offering to pay Aspinall Street's overdraft if I thought one of the partners was capable of shooting her clients dead.'

I looked at Suze, who was now beaming at me as broadly as he was. When I was a kid, this was called a snow job. Cynicism reasserted itself. 'Pay our overdraft?' I heard myself repeat.

They both nodded.

'Become our banker, you mean?'

'In effect,' he said.

'And what would you want for doing it?'

His shrug said, Nothing unreasonable. He said, 'Priority for my work – contracts, licensing arrangements, shipping deals, import/export problems and so on. At the moment I've got lawyers spread over half the globe. I would want to consolidate everything under the Aspinall Street umbrella.'

Suze's grin, which I'd thought was full on, managed to grow even more proud. 'It will bring in a *lot* of work.'

I pushed myself to put out a bit of enthusiasm. 'Yes. It sounds that way. It is, though – ah – rather a different *kind* than most of us do now. We'd need to hire new people, which would rather defeat –'

'I thought we could each take some on,' Suze said. 'If we do that, say, fifteen per cent of the time, we can all continue in our own fields the rest of the time.'

He said, 'And everyone who agrees will of course keep her job.'

Suze said, 'There'd be no tampering with the all-woman nature of it, or even the autonomy of it.'

I looked at him. There had to be a catch. 'What, *no* management changes?'

His expression said, Er, not exactly. 'I'd expect to review your structure – Suze has told me it's semi-collective – and I'd want to bring my accountant in. And of course I'd come to your partners meetings on a regular basis.'

I nodded. *Of course*. Mixed emotions welled inside me. He came on so genuinely decent, especially compared to my preconceptions (okay, prejudices) about stinking-rich capitalists. But what did we really know about him?

The rumours Greg had heard: we were going to need to investigate.

'Good. Well. That's very kind,' I finally said. 'I'll need to think about it – speak to the others.'

Suze said, 'Dee – it's our decision, yours and mine. There isn't much time.'

I looked at him, then at her, then back to him. As a pair they were chiselled and handsome. 'Marc wouldn't want us to rush for the sake of it, I'm sure,' I said.

'Absolutely not,' he said. 'The offer's open-ended.' He stuck in another of those smiles. 'Though an indication wouldn't go amiss.'

'Of course,' I said. Then I stood up to leave. 'I better get going.'

Suze hesitated only a moment. Then she too got to her feet. 'I'll come down to the taxi with you.'

I started to tell her she didn't have to, then stopped: she knew that.

We walked along the kerb of Kensington Church Street in the direction of the High Street, looking for an empty taxi. She said, 'We've got to take it, Dee. What else can we do?'

I sighed and kept my eyes on the traffic.

'What's the problem?' she said. I decided not to rise to the exasperated edge. We were both tired and stressed. We didn't need a row.

I shrugged. 'Don't know. Maybe I don't fancy being the appendage of an antiques trader, no matter how global or culturally correct.'

'Jesus, Dee, we won't be his "appendage".'

I shrugged again.

'Come on. It's better than the Ducane deal in lots of ways.'

'Sir Teddy only wanted me to shift into white-collar crime, not commercial contracts.'

She rolled her eyes.

I shrugged. 'Sorry. You know I've got zip interest in that area.'

'Dee, listen to yourself. You'd rather make three people redundant than do a bit of work you don't like to get us out of our hole?'

'No.'

'That's what you're saying.'

I shook my head. 'I'm saying I want to think again about the other options.'

Her short grunt was fat with scepticism. 'We've just done that. There isn't anything else.'

'There are other merger partners –'

She began shaking her head.

'There's short-time working, there's cheaper premises, there's pay *cuts*.'

She kept on shaking her head.

'I'm not saying *forever*.'

'Why at all when we've got this offer from Marc?'

'Who *is* Marc, though? Can we see *his* accounts?'

She sighed and I felt her impatience with me.

I bristled. 'It's a perfectly reasonable thing to ask, Suze. And that's exactly why I have doubts. In my humble opinion your emotional involvement gives you a conflict of interest.'

Now she bristled. 'I am quite able to be objective, thank you very much. Marc Felici's secretary is preparing copies of his accounts for us *and* a load of bumph about his companies right now. Listen, Dee: the bank manager gave us a grace period because – *because* – of the Ducane merger. I need to be able to tell him we have something else in place.'

'You don't need to do it today.'

'If they find out –'

'I'm not going to tell them. You're not going to tell them. Sir Teddy isn't going to tell them.'

Her shrug said, You never know.

I shook my head. 'He pulled out because he didn't want to be associated with a murder suspect. He'll keep schtum about even having had dealings with us.' Then I said, 'Look – I've got to get through this interview with Hamley about Tim. Whatever comes out of it – and, God knows, it could be anything – I'd like to leave worrying about the firm until that's over. You can give it till tomorrow. You could give it till the day after.'

Suze hmmm'd and clucked to herself and hmmm'd some more. Finally she said, 'I want the associates to meet Marc.'

'Sure. Yes. Have him in. I'll be interested in their views.'

That made her a bit happier.

I saw an empty taxi coming and flagged it down. As I got in we went through the motions of kissing goodbye. Our lips missed each other's faces, though, and there was a forced, even chilly feel to our waves.

Through the back window I watched her grow small as we drove away. I couldn't remember a time when we'd been at such an impasse about the business. My sense of our friendship as something founded on rock was shaking way down low where you could only just feel it. What if the tremors grew? It raised the spectre of a situation in which the firm's name might be saved at the cost of its heart.

But it wasn't the time to be studying the holes in my safety net. I turned frontwards again in the taxi and began to compose myself for what lay immediately ahead.

Like me, Theresa tends to arrive on the early side of on time, and we spent about ten minutes meandering along the High Street near the police station discussing tactics. By then I was feeling that, given no further need to appease Sir Teddy, I ought to do what I wanted – what I thought best for me. And what that was was to tell Hamley enough was enough.

'I agree absolutely,' Theresa said when I'd finished. What she tactfully didn't add was that she'd only gone along with co-operating so far because I'd said I wanted to.

Interestingly, Hamley's attitude had also changed. In all our encounters since Janey's death, he'd trowelled on the affability, in an effort, presumably, to be seen as being impartial towards me. I'd wondered in the odd random moment how long he'd be able to keep it up and that afternoon I got the answer: six days. True, the lower half of his face – that is to say, his mouth – was still putting on the act. But when you looked in his eyes you saw a snow-covered tundra all the way to the horizon. More to the point, you saw the bastard who'd stood up in court and incriminated Amin Ali – was it only five weeks ago? The bastard who hated me for being on the team that exposed what he had done.

We were escorted to the interview room in a way that felt just this side of frogmarched and when we were seated he went straight into it, without cordial invitations to tea or enquiries about our comfort. It made an edgier atmosphere than the fake mateyness but on the whole I preferred the honesty of it.

He turned on the tape recorder, dictated the details about the date and time and reminded me that I'd been cautioned and whatever I said could be used in evidence. Then he said, 'Miss Street, let us take a short cut through what could be a lengthy discussion. After you made your allegations to me about Tim Maguire, did you continue investigating him?'

Theresa leaned forward and sideways, cutting across the line of vision between Hamley and me. 'What is the relevance of this question?' She smiled. 'If you don't mind me asking?'

He too leaned, looking around her at me. I said nothing. He said, 'Did you follow a lorry owned by Mr Maguire from the Hodder Street playground site to a depot in Essex on Sunday?'

Theresa said, 'Are you confirming that Mr Maguire was the contractor excavating that site?'

He looked at her, distaste in the purse of his lips, then waved at his sergeant, who was hovering, as ever, in the background. He came forward and dropped a small plastic bag on the table in front of me. Inside was a three-inch garment label that said 'LL Bean of Maine' on it. Turquoise threads hung off each end and there were a couple of splinters of glass stuck to it.

Shit. It must have come off my cardigan when I'd broken the window of that lorry to get at the telephone.

Theresa said, 'What's this?'

Hamley was watching me think. To her he said, 'She knows.'

I said, 'I know that hundreds of thousands of people – millions even – own garments with this label in it.'

'You yourself own several.'

'My mother sends them to me.'

He pointed to the turquoise threads. 'You were wearing a jacket – or a jumper – this colour the first time I came to your office.'

Theresa stood up and tapped my shoulder. 'Come on.'

I got to my feet.

To him she said, 'Do you want to charge my client with anything?'

He stayed seated. 'Not yet.'

'Well, when you do, get in touch.'

And with that she steered me out of there.

Back outside on the street afterwards, she said, 'Well?'

'It's a cardigan,' I said. 'It's in a bag waiting for me to pick the glass out of it. I didn't even notice the tag was gone. Damn.'

She rubbed my back a moment. 'It couldn't be helped. I'm just glad that I said yes to the offer I had first thing this morning.'

'Offer?'

'Liam Mahoney phoned me direct.'

'Yeah?' How was this relevant?

'I'm to take you out to Southend now if you're game.'

I stopped still, feeling peevish. 'I'm even less in the mood than I was yesterday.'

'He saw Tim Maguire's picture on the news. There's something he thinks you should know.'

'He *knew* Tim Maguire?'

'That's the implication.'

I stared into the middle distance, waiting for pictures of my past to roll. When nothing happened, I shut my eyes and waited some more. But I was too tired and preoccupied. I opened them again and looked at her. 'God, what a prospect. Seeing Liam Mahoney.'

That made her smile. 'Is that yes?'

I thought, is it? Why wouldn't it be?

I nodded.

Sixteen

We found a pair of public phones and while she was dialling Liam to say we were on our way and get directions, I rang Natasha to see if there'd been anything yet from Greg. Answer: no. There had, however, been a call from Sufiya. 'The councillor has arranged a meeting for you,' said the message. 'We can see the person today after five.' I told Natasha to phone her back and tell her I'd try to make it to the hospital by six or so.

Our destination was a pub on the A-something, this side of Southend. As we drove along in Theresa's diesel Saab, I told her about my brief experience as a Bangladeshi Muslim woman that morning and my interview with Councillor Miah.

She found his story as extraordinary as I did. 'Janey blackmailed him into lying for her? That's *all*?'

'I think she was just buying time.'

She frowned at the road as she thought about that. 'But why? And why refuse to lean on Richard or the new owner, whoever it is, for compensation?'

I found I had the answer. 'Because Richard had blackmailed her or bribed her into laying off. Richard's crucial to this whole thing, I'm surer and surer of it.'

'Shall we go see him then?' she said. It was so obvious a step I couldn't believe I'd pussyfooted away from it. 'Yes,' I said, 'yes. Let's. First thing tomorrow.'

'Mornings are not my best time at the moment.'

'Oh, God, yes, I forgot you're in the hormone Jacuzzi. How long does it last?'

'Does it go away?'

'You sure hid it well just now.'

'Anger as painkiller.' She laughed. 'Could be a profoundity there. I'll take the first appointment with him I can get, okay?'

I said that was fine.

An hour and a few minutes later Theresa pointed at the roadside pub coming up on the right. 'That should be it. The Angel.' We both squinted. 'Yes,' we both said.

She turned off into the nearly empty car park.

'Where the heck are we?' I wanted to know.

'Nowheretown,' she said. She pointed diagonally east. 'Southend is that way.'

We got out and as she locked up I studied the place: 1950s stucco, school of imitation Swiss chalet. A genuine local, not much visited by tourists, I bet. She came around to me. 'You ready?'

'No. I'm not even used to the idea that I'm about to see this guy again after all these years.'

She laughed. 'That's probably just as well. Come on.'

As we approached the door, a man with double chins and a pear shape emerged from inside and stood in the doorway, watching us. He wore a patch on his right eye and his right arm stopped at the bicep. As you got closer you could see that the right side of his face was a mass of scar tissue, not pretty. He bore no resemblance to the image of Liam I carried in my memory, so it wasn't until we were three feet from him and he grinned and said hello that I realised here he was. Then he extended his left hand to me and said, 'Dee – you look exactly the same.'

The voice could have been no one else's. For the ripple of a nanosecond we were the people we'd been fifteen years ago, unlayered by time and the hurts and woes and stresses of its passing. We were young and healthy and two-eyed and unscarred. Then we were back to now. I took the hand and made myself smile into his eye. '*You* look completely different.'

'Aye, and I'm even used to that sad fact.' He looked at Theresa and asked her if she be she. She said she was indeed and got an equally cordial handshake.

'Let's walk,' he said.

Theresa and I were happy with that idea, so he led us down the drive towards the pavement. When we reached it he glanced at me. 'You still keep a garden?'

I said I did.

'You'll like our wee neighbourhood park then.'

On the way he told us in some detail the story of how the local evangelical church, of which he was a member, had built the wee park on a derelict site. Feeling odd, I only half listened. Here was a road not taken, and look how sad it made me.

Sad but grateful.

The beds in the small public garden were simply planted with pansies and wallflowers and violas but were vibrant with primary contrasts: purples with yellows, reds with greens, orange and bright blue. They seemed to give him heart. When we'd gotten about half-way around he stopped and looked at me. Theresa walked discreetly past us but paused within earshot.

'Since my friend told me your troubles with Janey Riordan, I prayed to Jesus you'd be saved.'

I studied his face for a sign of facetiousness but saw none. 'Ah, oh, well – thank you,' I said. 'Are you talking about my soul?'

He laughed. 'Just your situation. Then I saw that Maguire was involved.' He shook his head as if to say, No wonder there were problems.

'When did you know him?'

His smile turned a bit awkward and self-conscious. 'When I, ah, stayed in your house.'

'You're joking.'

'Heh. I wish.'

'And were you – ah – "active" then?'

'Praise Jesus, I'm afraid I was. I was a new recruit, you know, proving myself.'

I waited for him to go on.

'I was buying guns.'

Theresa was quicker on the uptake than I was. She rejoined us and said, 'From Tim?'

He continued to look at me. 'Yes.'

Fortunately there was a park bench close by. I sat down and let the implications of what he'd just said waft and blow in my mind. 'Tim Maguire – an arms dealer,' I finally managed.

He nodded. 'Among other things.'

'What kind of gear?' Theresa asked.

'Russian, Czech, East German as was.'

'How many times did you buy from him?' she pressed.

'Three times.'

'Did you get the impression he did it a lot?'

'He knew what he was doing. I remember he even had a range of discounts you could get if you introduced him to other buyers.'

She laughed. 'Sounds like Tupperware.'

He nodded. 'There was another scam too. He was setting up his haulage and demolition business. If you found him derelict sites and he got the demolition contract, you'd get so much off gun purchases.'

'You think he was trying to get out of gun dealing?'

'At that point?' He shook his head. 'I'd say he was just getting into it. Haulage and demolition work – good cover. But you know how long ago this was.' He checked his watch.

I suddenly remembered something. 'Did you know someone named Sharon? Her last name started with "B".'

He looked thoughtful for a moment, then shook his head. 'Rings no bells.' He checked his watch again. 'It's been good seeing you again, Dee. I was always sorry, you know –' And he waved his surviving hand over his shoulder towards all our pasts.

I smiled at him and said, 'I think you've just made it up to me.'

He gave me a final long look. Assessing what? I wondered. *His* road not taken? Perhaps. He took my hand. 'The Lord Jesus Christ our Saviour was guiding me,' he said, somehow managing to sound sane and rational when he said it. Then he said, 'Nice to meet you' to Theresa, kissed his fingertips and planted the kiss on my face, gave us a last smashed-up grin, and headed off.

We watched him go, then looked at each other. 'Wow,' I said.

She nodded. She was feeling 'wow' too.

I was sure she was thinking what I was thinking as well, but I had to hear the words out loud anyway. 'If Tim Maguire sold to the IRA, who else did he sell to?'

She nodded again. 'Absolutely. There are hundreds of possibilities. And if Janey got wind of his business –'

I thought of her last phone call and the operator with the South Wales accent. If she went to his head office and found proof he was dealing arms – Then: revelation. 'I've got to go there!'

She put her hand on my shoulder and I realised I was dancing around, flapping like a penguin. 'Let's talk it through calmly,' she said, and pointed me towards the car.

In the two minutes it took to get there I managed to get my body under control but my mind was out there, running hard.

– If Janey found out Tim was dealing guns, who would that threaten? Answer: Tim.

– Could she have found out who was supplying him? That would threaten him *and* them.

– If 'they' were an organised criminal group, wouldn't 'they' kill her – or make him kill her – and blow him up for his perceived treachery?

– Could 'they' have been the ones parked outside Janey's that night in the dark red car – the witness who saw me come and go?

I babbled these further ruminations to Theresa as we put our seatbelts on. 'The problem is, how to prove it,' I finished.

'How to prove it and live.'

'Yeah.'

We both lapsed into our own cogitations as Theresa retraced the route back to the A-something and pointed us towards London.

As we rejoined it I said, 'How's this? I phone up South Wales Demolition and Haulage and pretend to be a potential customer from the States needing a job done fast.'

'Haulage of American widgets from Cardiff docks type of thing?'

'Yeah. And storage. Insist on seeing their facilities.'

'What are you imagining you might find?'

I closed my eyes and leaned my head back and thought. 'Warehouses,' I said at last. 'Patrolled by private security guards. On-site alarm system only.'

'Nothing wired to the police?'

'Maybe a bit. For show. Or maybe nothing. They keep their heads down. The guns could be in with the legitimate stuff or they could be off somewhere on their own.'

'And a visit probably wouldn't reveal any of it.'

'Maybe not – but maybe. You know how research can go.'

Theresa said, 'Mmmm. Yes. True. But you can't do the recce yourself. If you are being set up by these people, they know you. If they're not actually at Maguire's company, they'd be told if an American woman made an appointment to look around.'

I opened my eyes and looked at her again. 'Damn.'

'How about this,' she said. '*I* phone up and pretend to be a Northern Irish customer and *I* do the recce.'

'And they say, fine, come on by – and because of me a pregnant woman goes into a possible organised crime set-up of some kind on her own. Un uh, no way. How about this? We send along a couple of big strong testosterone-rampant types?'

She laughed.

'I'm serious! What about our old friend George?'

'I thought he was still out in Cape Town. Actually, I know a new woman agent who'd be good.'

We spent the rest of the journey running through ideas and possibilities and by the time we reached outer London had a rough plan: she would do the pretending over the phone, we would both aim to go on the recce, and we'd recruit a burly investigator to assist us. We got so enthusiastic we pulled over at a public phone so Theresa could make the call to South Wales Haulage. It wasn't that long after 5 but no one answered.

As we got closer to London, my optimism began to slip. Theresa urged me the way I urged clients in my position: resist depression, think positive. We had this strong Tim line. We would confront Richard. *And* there was the chance that I'd learn something useful about Bangladeshi money-trade fraud.

'There's the mysterious Sharon B too. I've hardly started on her.'

'Exactly,' she said. 'One of these avenues has to clear you. How can it not?'

It was 6.20 when Theresa dropped me at Whitechapel Hospital and I hurried to the Special Care Baby Unit, where I found Sufiya in the overstuffed little cubicle that was her office, head down over a word processor. She was still wearing her saree and scarf from the morning, though the scarf was loose on her shoulders, no longer covering her thick, dark hair.

'I'm just updating the draft of my new report on our local miscarriage rate. The BMJ is interested, did I tell you?'

'Fantastic! How long do you need?'

'Twenty minutes. Half an hour.' She nodded at my suit and smiled. 'Back to normal, eh?'

I patted my briefcase. 'I've got it with me. Shall I wear it to wherever we're going?'

She thought a moment. 'Yes. Yes, why not.'

I went into the ladies' room and transformed myself.

When I'd finished I came back and sat down at the other desk. It was covered in books and reports and papers and, ever nosy, I glanced through them. Asbestos, gas works, leaded petrol, building materials, building chemicals, other chemicals, sewage. Global studies, British studies, London studies, Spitalfields studies. Ethnic groups.

Finally she said, 'There. Done. If I hurry, I might get out of here before I think of something else.' Then she realised I'd been sniffing her research. 'Find anything interesting?'

'I'm just amazed to see the mountain of written evidence spelling out how unhealthy it is around here. I mean, having to fight to prove it –' I shook my head. In Dee World, my private Utopia, this kind of thing would never happen. 'Oh, and I realised – no mention of the playground. It ever been tested?'

'It's on my list, but lower down. Always been residential. You ready?'

'Who's this we're going to see?' I asked as we set out.

'Sheikh Nasir. He's one of the elders of this community – travels back and forth to Bangladesh a lot. Not someone I'd have thought would know about fraudulent practices, but –' she shrugged – 'who knows.'

The address Councillor Miah had given her turned out to belong to a small shop-front travel agency called Dhaka Express, about a ten-minute walk from the hospital. There was a handwritten sign in the window listing prices for flights to India, Pakistan and Bangladesh, with various Middle Eastern destinations en route, and a rack of mirror-cloth dresses and chiffon sarees just inside. The shelf next to the window was full of Indian books and shoes and knick-knacks for sale.

When she realised this was where we were going, Sufiya stared at the premises thoughtfully. 'Dhaka Express – this is where several of my patients lost money. I thought it went out of business.' It did seem closed – no lights on – no people – door locked but we knocked hard a few times anyway and waited.

Eventually a door at the back opened and a young Asian man in a trendy suit came towards us. He and Sufiya exclaimed simultaneously, both surprised to see each other *here*, and when he opened the front door they immediately broke into enthusiastic Sylheti. Sufiya then quickly introduced me. This was Ashraf Ali. He shook my hand. 'Sorry,' he said. 'The doctor treated my wife.' He gestured us in.

As we followed Sufiya murmured to me over her shoulder, 'This is lucky for us. I didn't realise his wife is the granddaughter of Sheikh Nasir.'

The office we crossed was undecorated (unless the two curling posters of Dhaka and Bombay counted as 'decor') and contained one large desk covered in small, discreet stacks of paper, an old IBM computer, a couple of telephones and a fax machine. The rest of the space was taken up by a small waiting area.

Ashraf led us through the door he'd come out of, and into the even pokier back room. Into this had been squeezed a kitchen sideboard and sink with water heater, a photocopier, a few chairs and three large filing cabinets. As we entered an elderly man bent over a drawer straightened and looked around at us. He was no taller than me, five foot two or so, and wore a brown lunghi and kurtha and an embroidered topee hat. His hair and narrow chinstrap beard were pure white.

Ashraf spoke to him while Sufiya stood by, smiling. This was obviously the news about her link with his granddaughter, for he immediately grasped her hand and shook it many many times as he thanked her.

A young woman had slipped in behind us and was making tea

even as we were being offered some. As we sat down and waited for it, Sheikh Nasir and Sufiya continued to talk. I'd have drifted off but I caught 'Janey Riordan' and found myself looking interested, as if I understood. I certainly got the tone – it was a long, earnest story from his side. Tea was served and I got through half mine at once – that condensed milk made it so sweet and delicious, like cream soup, and the salty snacks were wonderful. I hadn't eaten, I realised, all day.

Eventually Sufiya broke off and turned to me. 'He knew Janey well. He and his family are original tenants of Weaverstown Housing Association. He has one of the refurbished houses near Hodder Street playground.'

'He sounded quite heated. What –'

'They had fallen out. He felt WHA should have been speaking up more about the racist attacks against Muslim people in the area. He felt it should be run by Bangladeshis now, not English. And he's heard about her misuse of the community's grant funds and her affair with Anwar Miah. He feels she was proof that women should be covered.'

'He must like me then.'

She rolled her eyes and smiled. 'No comment.'

'What does he have to say about the money trade fraud?'

She nodded 'Hang on' and turned back to her conversation with him. I had a refill of the wonderful tea. Ashraf asked me what I did and I told him and he realised he'd heard of me because of Amin Ali's trial. He was studying law and a dozen questions poured out. We were moving on to why I was dressed Bangladeshi style when Sufiya turned to me again.

'The fraud here at Dhaka Express happened when a new person took over. He offered amazing deals – cheap discounts on tickets and a double-your-deposit scheme for people wanting to send money back home.'

'A what?'

'If you gave him, say two thousand pounds, he'd send four

thousand to your family and you'd pay him back in low-interest instalments. Hundreds gave him everything they had – and he vanished with the lot.'

'Ouch. Painful.' I gestured to Sheikh Nasir. 'And?'

'He and his family lost the most. They came in to run it and restore its credibility. Devised a rescue. All okay now.' She smiled. 'I hope you want to know how, because he's going to tell me. Do you want to go get something more to eat? You look starving!'

When I admitted that I hadn't eaten all day, Ashraf took me in hand and led me back out of the shop and down a few doors to the take-away. A bulging vegetable samosa took the edge off and I was considering the vegetable curry when I looked out of the window and thought I saw Amin Ali passing on the opposite pavement.

I told Ashraf I'd be right back and hurried out and across the street. 'Amin,' I called out when I was five feet away. It got no response but I was so sure it was him that I assumed he just hadn't heard me. I picked up speed and managed to catch up with him. 'Amin!' I said again.

The young man I'd thought was Amin looked at me with a disdain of which Amin was probably incapable and, in a broad cockney accent (of which ditto), told me to f – off.

I skulked back to the curry shop and was relieved to see Ashraf hadn't been watching. It was the kind of thing I did from time to time that made me feel old and embarrassed for myself. It stirred my liberal guilt too; surely there were racialist undercurrents in mistaking one young Asian male for another?

We returned to the back of the travel shop just as Sheikh Nasir was finishing his story.

'Well,' Sufiya said, 'to rescue Dhaka Express, he and his family had to sell most of their land back in Bangladesh.'

'Was that easy?' I said to him. 'Is there much of a market?'

'No,' he said, 'but an English – Mr Maguire – he helps us. He buys it all.'

Sufiya's face expressed the frisson both of us felt. 'Tim Maguire?' she asked.

Sheikh Nasir peered into her eyes. 'Yes.' He peered harder and with sudden anxiety said, 'What is it?'

'He's dead,' she said. 'He died yesterday.'

He reached out and grasped his grandson-in-law's hand. Then he again spoke in rapid Sylheti to Sufiya. Her expression grew more and more concerned and she asked a single question, which I knew to be 'Why?' a couple of times.

'What?' I said, desperately wanting to understand. 'What?'

'The spring floods in Bangladesh have been terrible this year. Tim Maguire was helping them get medical supplies for their families back home. Malaria pills, antibiotics, vaccines, equipment.'

'Medical supplies!' I said.

She nodded. 'He took payment entirely in land out there.'

'This week – medicine this week,' he said, sounding truly pained. Then he reverted once more to his own language.

'He wants to know where it is,' she said. 'How will they get it?'

I told Sufiya to tell him I had an idea where the goods might be. If I found them, I would let him know.

We saw ourselves out.

Guns, medicine, land: the question wasn't what had Tim Maguire dealt in, but what hadn't he?

Seventeen

The *News of the World* guy was in his spot across the street from Theresa's block of flats – I could see his camera and the gold of his wire-frame glasses from the corner, half a block away. Worse, he was chatting to a woman and another guy.

– Passers-by? Other journalists? – Yes: other journalists.

– Go home? (No: police.) Go to Suze's? (No: couldn't face Peter.)

– Brazen my way in? – The disguise had gotten me out. (But I'd had Sufiya with me then.)

– Reason to brazen way in, as opposed to bottling out and (say) checking into a hotel or B&B: the prospect of at least talking to Greg, maybe seeing him if he was back.

Once a romantic teenage girl, always a carrier of romantic teenage girl syndrome.

I pushed my hair back and adjusted the scarf, slipped on the dark glasses – it was a bright evening and the front of Theresa's block faced west – hugged my case to my chest, breathed carefully a few times and set off.

Ten yards later I heard Sufiya's voice in my mind – Don't walk so fast! Be upright! Glide! – and made a few adjustments. The worst part was crossing into their clear line of vision. At least one of them was bound to watch me just because I was a person approaching the building.

I stayed cool up to the front door, right through pulling out the key and inserting it in the door. Unfortunately it didn't seem to fit. I tried the three other possibles on the ring, then fumbled for the other set and went through the three on that with no better luck. The feeling of three pairs of eyes on my back was growing.

I made myself breathe and started through it once more. This time I remembered something Theresa had said about sometimes needing to lift the knob and that made the difference. The key I'd thought was right was. A moment later I was inside. I was tempted to look out but waited until I'd let myself into Theresa's and locked the door of the flat behind me.

The answering machine light was in spasm but I kept going into the front room. There I hunched close to the wall, out of the sight-line of the tabloid squad, and made my way to the window. When I reached it I looked around the edge of the curtain. The three were engrossed in conversation again.

I wouldn't be able to put the front lights on, but who cared. I checked out the back to make certain there was no one in the garden or on the other side of any of the adjacent fences. All clear. Then I hurried back to the hall to listen to the messages.

The first was from my mother: she'd spoken to Suze, who'd evidently told her I was having a hard time over a case but no more. She wasn't worried, not really, but on the other hand – if I wanted her to come over, or if I wanted to come home to LA, I should just say the word.

Good old Mom.

Next came Suze, who even as she said, 'Dee, hi, me', sounded deeply weary. 'It's Tuesday – ah – two hours and twenty-six minutes since we talked. I've just had a call from the bank manager, who wants an urgent meeting to, quote, discuss contingency plans in the event that our merger negotiations fail, unquote. Got the distinct impression he knew. – Ring me asap.'

Damn. I hit pause, dialled Suze's home number, waited while it rang two, three, four times. When the answering machine picked up, I cut off the connection. By now she'd have dealt with it without me.

The messages tape came back on and immediately there it was, his voice: 'Hi, doll, where the heck are you? Your secretary is sick to death of me, I've tried your home, I've tried this number three times. I hope you're okay. What a drag I had to leave, eh? Even bigger drag is, my main meeting isn't till late tomorrow, so may not see you till the day after.' There followed some kissing noises and a promise to ring in the morning 'sometime'.

Disappointment is a stiff formal word for my feelings at that moment. Hollowed-out is too melodramatic. (The day after tomorrow!) And to complicate matters, irritation: he'd offered to do those two pieces of research for me and, okay, so I was going to Maguire's Welsh office myself now anyway; but that still left the buyer of the playground site. The least he could have done was mention – acknowledge – that he'd offered to find out these things for me and hadn't.

I decided to have a shower and while I was in there found myself imagining a good old heart-to-heart telephone conversation with Mom. She'd met Janey – she'd be horrified. She'd be even more horrified at the idea that I was being set up. She'd want to know who by. She'd want to pick through all the evidence pointing to the real murderer. She'd get indignant on my behalf and I'd feel bucked up. Trouble was, then she'd say she was getting on the next flight.

And, I thought as I got out of the shower, I couldn't trust the phone. So when I called her I just told her about Janey – didn't mention that I was a suspect. She sensed something else going on – kept asking me why I was at my friend's apartment and not my own – but I bluffed and made do with feeling bucked up simply by the sound of her voice.

I dreamed Greg and I were going to a funeral which I believed was his wife's. He insisted I wear a short black dress with pearls and this wig of purple punk hair and he showed up for the service wearing his grilled umpire's face mask, his wife and son in tow.

It was a relief to be woken up by the ringing of the phone. I checked the time in passing: 9.30. I'd slept ten hours straight.

'Dee – sorry to wake you.' It was Theresa. 'Bad news.'

My thoughts went to Maguire's company. 'Oh God, it's closed.'

'What? Oh. No. Haven't even checked that yet. It's Hamley.'

'Oh, ugh. Worse.'

'Unfortunately. The lab tests show a trace of Janey's blood in the back of your airing cupboard.'

'Shit, shit, shit.' Why hadn't I just turned in that damn bloody glove when I found it? (Reminder: Because Tim or the 'they' who killed him would have made sure Hamley nailed the whole thing on me *then* instead of now.)

'So, apropos our planning in the car, dot dot dot,' she said.

'Yeah?'

'I'm going to get straight on to making the contacts now. Better give me a couple of hours.'

I shivered. Thoughts of this 'they' were suddenly giving me the creeps. 'I don't fancy hanging around waiting *here* for two hours.'

'Absolutely. Get out of there. Remember the café where we went after we jogged? I'll pick you up there at noon.'

After hanging up I went back to the sitting room and looked surreptitiously out of the front window: *News of the World* wasn't there, but the guy he'd been talking to the previous night was.

Maybe he wasn't a journalist. Maybe he was 'they'.

I decided to play it super-safe: not only would I wear my Bangladeshi disguise, I'd go over the roof, down the far stairs and out the door at the other end of the block.

The Central London Reference Library was where I ended up. In the hour and twenty minutes I spent there, I found a whole heap of old press articles about Richard Farmer and Farmer Enterprises. Most writers succumbed to his charming public face, his capitalism-with-a-conscience message. A fair slice thought he was a slimy operator with a gift for telling people what they wanted to hear.

There wasn't a single mention of Tim Maguire or his company.

Evie's name came up often in the older indexes, when her GLC work made her controversial. In more recent years the context was more likely to be the official opening of a block of flats.

A book review of a new children's novel called *Sharon B* by a young Australian woman caught my eye and I stopped in at Waterstones to buy it on the way to meet Theresa.

I got to the rendezvous spot exactly on time and waited five minutes before deciding it might be better to go inside. I was sitting by the window sipping hot tea, nearly finished with the large print *Sharon B* and wondering what conceivable relevance a story about a guinea pig could have to Janey Riordan's murder, when I heard a car horn tooting. I looked up: Theresa's car was idling at the kerb, door open. She was gesturing to me to come on, hurry up.

'Sorry I'm late,' she said as I got in.

'That's okay. What's up?'

'Not a lot.' She glanced behind her, double-checked in the rear-view mirror and pulled out into the traffic. 'The phone at South Wales Demolition and Haulage has been ringing engaged since I started trying it. Operator says it's working.'

'So: someone's there.'

'We can hope. It could be off the hook. *And*, all the burly types I know are unavailable at this short notice.'

I sighed. This wasn't starting off too thrillingly.

She said, '*But*, fear not. We'll be fine, I'm sure. I've brought Martin's Swiss Army knife along just in case – it's got all this fishing stuff on it, it's a hoot. Obviously not an offensive weapon –'

'"Oh, no, officer, just for camping."'

'Absolutely. It's in there.' She nodded at the bag sitting on the armrest between us. 'Brought my little camera too. Oh, and there's a note from Suze for you on top – see? There. That's why I was late. She phoned and when I said I was seeing you, she faxed it over.'

'Dee,' it said, 'I'm meeting the bank manager at 9.30. Sorry you can't be there. Marc understands that you're still thinking about his proposal but he said we can use it to buy time with the bank anyway. That's what I'm going to do. Wanted you to know. Hope you're bearing up. Love – Suze.'

Jeez, I thought, when I'd re-read it. On the face of it, she'd simply done what she had to. Underneath she was making it even harder to turn Marc down. I started gnawing on my knuckle the way I do when I get anxious. She couldn't bulldoze ahead. She couldn't do it unless I agreed. She –

'*Dee!*' Theresa said as if she'd been saying it and was repeating it with her voice raised to get my attention.

I looked up.

She reached over and pulled the knuckle out of my mouth. 'What is it?'

I told her, then, about what was happening to Aspinall Street and the division between Suze and me and the reservations I had about accepting a financial offer from someone she was having a brand-new affair with (I was pretty sure) and the position she was in between the two men. At the heart of it all, though (I realised as I said it), was this bitter nut of hard feeling that Suze was going too fast towards something that was a tangent for us, out of a combination of panic and lust and midlife crisis.

Theresa, friend to us both, said, 'And because she loves the thing the two of you have created.'

I couldn't dispute that, but I couldn't hold back a sceptical grunt.

'Well,' she added, 'you always have had very different styles.'

Analysis of the connotations of that simple observation occupied us as far as Swindon, where we hit a tedious stretch of jammed traffic. When we got to the other side, Theresa said, 'Suze will end up in Parliament – you know that? She's just what her precious Labour Party needs.'

I sighed. The future was a time that started about ten minutes hence and got fuzzier and fuzzier the further into it I tried to see. Suze's ambitions had a way to go before they ripened. Meanwhile –

Theresa said, 'Have you thought of starting again?'

I laughed, though the resulting sound didn't have much humour in it. 'I haven't faced the end of this round.'

She gave me a sidelong glance, full of meaning.

Unfortunately I didn't catch what that meaning was. 'What?' I said.

'*I'm* thinking of setting up my own firm.'

I nodded; I knew. She'd been thinking that the way everyone who gets fed up thinks it. 'But a baby –'

'Doesn't change the fact. And you and I–'

But I could finish the sentence. She and I worked in similar ways. (I'd trained her; it wasn't surprising.) I tried to imagine pulling the plug on Suze that way, expecting it to be impossible. Actually it wasn't that hard.

Something else to feel guilty about.

I ended up just shaking my head. It was beyond me. 'If I wind up in prison, even just on remand – this will be one more wasted fantasy.'

'Not true,' she said. 'If you're convicted, okay. But charged – that we can deal with.' I looked at her; the heartfeltness was genuine. Was it blind faith?

'Thanks,' I said. 'That's kind. Maybe later. When this is over.'

She shrugged. 'It's just a thought – in case you need something to cling to.'

A lawyer who'd worked at Aspinall Street back when Theresa had been my clerk now worked for a Bristol firm and we toyed with the idea of stopping in to see her. We abandoned the plan when we hit more traffic on the outskirts, and instead picked up teas to take away and made do with reminiscing about our old colleague.

There was more traffic at the Severn Bridge – a lorry had jack-knifed – and we decided to decide it was funny, not ominous. By the time we finally crossed we were running eighty minutes late.

Theresa put on as much speed as she dared – we didn't want to get stopped by the police or blow a tire or take any risks at all – and half an hour later we were veering off a roundabout at Caerleon, heading for Cwmbran. I dug out the registered address of South Wales Demolition and Haulage Ltd and by dint of asking directions about three times we got ourselves there. It was exactly 4.50.

The good news was that the registered address was part of a warehouse complex. I'd started worrying that we'd find the office, then have to trace the storage facilities somehow. The bad was that it was closed up tight.

I, of course, had to get out and go up to the gate of the chain-link fence that surrounded the place and shake it a few times, to make absolutely positively certain that the message of my eyes was the true message. Unfortunately, it was. I peered in, hoping for a sign of movement. It was futile.

I put my hands on my hips and squinted first down the road, then up the road.

Theresa leaned her head out the car window. 'What do you think?'

I pointed back the way we'd come. 'Let's go into that petrol station. I'm thirsty and the people there might know something.'

It turned out to be one of those stations with a shop selling groceries, tobacco, stamps, liquor and newspapers. This time we noticed what we hadn't when we'd passed it: a number of flatbed lorries were parked out back. We decided to check inside the shop first.

There was a mother and daughter team on duty at the counter. As we picked out juice and sandwiches, Theresa murmured, 'Which one do you reckon?'

'Mum. You want to talk?'

She shrugged. 'Fine.' Then she took the goods and went up to the check-out with them. 'Afternoon,' she said, smiling from one of them to the other and back again. If this had been America they'd have been serious contenders in the local mother–daughter competition. Both wore the same make of powder blue blouse with Peter Pan collar, both had their blonde hair done in a 1950s bouffant. Only the skin quality told you they weren't sisters.

'Afternoon,' said the mother. She was probably my age.

The girl smiled and went back to reading her *Torrid Romance* or *Stud Hero* or whatever it was magazine. She must have been just out of school.

'Any idea where I can find whoever runs that "South Wales Demolition" place?'

Mum concentrated on checking our things through and sticking them in a bag. 'Sorry. No.'

'Are there any drivers with those lorries out back?'

Mum's shake of the head said she had no idea. But the daughter glanced up and said, 'They've been there since lunchtime.' Clearly this was unusual.

Mum shot daughter a look telling her to button up and I had a sudden memory of being twelve and flying from LA to Boston and getting a bus to Maine, where my grandmother lived. There'd been some shops in those parts where the old (generally) women (generally) who served (if that was the word) behind the counter had turned reticence into an art form. This mom would one day be in their league.

Theresa reached over to the counter display of chocolate bars and picked out a couple, which Mom added to the bill.

'Thin people,' I muttered.

'Pregnancy: the world's best excuse.' She smiled.

We made our way around to the back, where there turned out to be four huge flatbed trucks, two loaded with stuff, two empty. The drivers weren't hard to find: they'd made a table out of a couple of upended milk crates and a piece of ply, set it up in the shadow of the back of the garage and were in the middle of a card game so intense they didn't even notice the sound of our feet crunching the gravel on our way over to them.

One of them looked a little bit like my last serious boyfriend, a tormented psychiatrist called David Blake, and on that irrational basis I gravitated towards him.

They suddenly all heard us at the same time and all looked up. They said things like 'Ladies!' and 'Greetings!' and 'What have we here?'

'Cheers,' Theresa said. She'd gravitated to a guy who looked like a hound dog. 'I was hoping to talk to somebody over the road.'

Much shaking of heads. 'Owner snuffed it a couple of days ago,' the hound dog said. 'Been closed ever since.'

'I see. So that's why the phone's been engaged.'

'Off the hook,' said the old boyfriend lookalike.

'Ah – and why are you gentlemen parked here?'

He leaned her way and winked. 'Security lads have buggered off. We're waiting for someone to come and unlock so we can put this lot in.'

'What d'you need doing anyway?' hound dog asked her.

'Oh. I've got a couple of derelict outbuildings –'

'You want to try Llewelyn's in town – the High Street.'

Before she'd even thanked them they'd gone back to their card game.

We looked at each other. We were thinking the same thing again. *No security guards.* We headed back towards the car and had barely taken two steps when she murmured, 'We can get in there.'

'It's a risk,' I said.

'It's the kind of opportunity you couldn't hope to plan for.'

'It's the kind that wouldn't cross my mind. What'll we do, wait for the guy with the key?'

She laughed. 'I had something a bit more "proactive" in mind.'

I wasn't sure what she meant exactly but there was no chance to ask: she picked up speed and gestured to me to hurry up and follow her. When I caught up she was standing at the roadside, scrutinising the perimeter fence of the South Wales Demolition and Haulage compound opposite. I scrutinised it too. On that side there was a bank with a fence on top. We were looking at a fifteen-foot barrier.

Theresa said, 'No barbed wire. It isn't even electrified.'

I was horrified. '*You* might be able to climb that . . .'

She shrugged. 'It only needs one of us. And look, getting out's a doddle.'

'You're winding me up, aren't you?' I said.

She shook her head.

'Theresa, you can't, not in your condition.'

She laughed. 'My "condition" hasn't affected my fitness – not yet.'

'Come on. If you fell –' But I couldn't finish the thought, never mind the sentence. Abruptly one of the lorries switched on its engine and we both looked back that way.

I heard myself mutter, 'I'd rather play Trojan horses.'

It was supposed to be facetious but she said, 'Good idea', like I'd been serious.

Curse you, loose tongue of mine. Curse you. 'That was a joke, Theresa.'

'Or as a Freudian would say, your unconscious speaking the truth. We have to get in there somehow. That was the point of coming, wasn't it?'

She was right, of course. Absolutely right. I nodded. 'Yeah,' I said, 'sorry. Nerves.'

The lorry engine abruptly cut out.

Theresa said, 'Why don't we have a wee peep at the far one – with the load parked towards the street.'

'Good idea,' I said. 'Let's go.'

She headed off. My feet, however, turned out to be rooted to the spot.

When she realised I wasn't with her, she stopped and sighed a fond, exasperated sigh at me and began to rummage in her shoulder bag. She pulled out the chocolate, broke off a couple of bits and thrust one at me. 'Eat that.'

She had the other bit and we sucked and waited for the sugar to do its artificial thing.

It worked. 'Okay,' I said a moment later.

We walked along the road in front of the garage to the flatbed with its load facing the street. It was stacked with large wooden containers and nobody was around – in fact, from the sound of the voices the drivers' card game was getting contentious. We went right up to it and poked around. There was space to hide between the last two rows and Theresa was looking seriously on the point of climbing in when I had a sudden thought.

'Let's move the car,' I said. 'Pretend we've left.' I'm pretty certain it was just an excuse, a way to buy time. But Theresa seemed as grateful for it as I was.

'Oh, shit, yes,' she said instantly.

We headed back along the road, passed the garage again, and turned into the side area where we'd parked just behind an arriving car. We quickly collected Theresa's Saab and drove off the way we'd come. We rounded the turn and within yards spotted a lay-by. 'This will do,' she said, pulling in.

My chicken nature was scratching away in me hard again. 'Oh God, Theresa,' I started, 'let's think about doing this.'

Then we heard the sound of the lorry engines, all four of them, coming to life. We both cursed, got ourselves out of the car, locked the thing and hurried back to the turning. There we stopped and watched: the great long flatbed trucks were negotiating their way out of the drive of the garage on to the road. They turned right, one by one, and headed away from us, towards the entrance to South Wales Demolition. When the first one reached the gate, the others formed a queue behind it. When that was organised, they all shut off their engines again.

The last in line was one of the empty ones – and even I could have run and jumped on it with little trouble. But there was no point – I'd have been completely exposed. The one in front of it, though, had a load of some kind. Not as tall as the wooden containers, but something.

Should we go for it? I wondered. Or was this mad?

'Are we going to go for it?' Theresa asked me.

I shook my head. 'It's mad. The driver of the one behind it will see us. And the women in the garage –'

'– Won't be surprised to see that one of those two bold women is chatting up a driver.'

I wasn't with her.

'Look,' she said, 'you distract the bloke in the last lorry. Wait till he finds out you're from the States. I'll sneak around and get in with the load in front of him.'

'But that means – you could end up in there on your own.'

She laughed. 'Yes!' Then she watched my face as the feelings I couldn't seem to get my tongue around played out (I have no doubt) in my expression. She said, 'You got any other suggestions?'

'We could forget it.' But even as the words came out of my mouth I knew they weren't true.

The front truck started its motor. 'No guards,' she said. 'It's light enough to take pictures. Last chance. Going, going –'

'Promise to let me in if you can?'

She laughed. 'Promise to get me out?'

I didn't think that was real funny. But never mind. I dusted off my I'm-just-a-visitor persona and went to distract the last driver with chat. Where exactly was the other demolition place? Yes, I was an American. Yes, I'd love to hear about his trip to New York twenty years ago. We were on the story of his brother-in-law's efforts to emigrate when the gate opened. The driver wished me well and turned on his engine to drive in. I watched the four vehicles accelerate up the small incline and go in through the gates.

I walked slowly behind them until they were all through. Theresa was nowhere to be seen.

It was crazy. I couldn't let her be in there by herself. This chicken inside me was going to have to go.

A man in overalls closed the gate behind the fourth truck and, though he must have seen me standing there watching, ignored me. His own car was parked just outside the fence. I kept my distance, but issued him orders by telepathy: don't lock it; follow the trucks; don't hang around; don't get in your car.

Can't really claim credit, but he did head up the incline behind the trucks on foot without locking the gate.

I blew a kiss to the cosmos. The adrenalin was starting now.

I waited until the trucks and the gate man had all disappeared, then checked to see if the women from the garage were watching me. They didn't seem to be.

I slid through the gate.

I was good at this bit, having done it in that lorry park in Essex, but I still expected someone to shout 'Halt' at me any moment. No one did.

When I got up to the warehouse that fronted the road there wasn't a flatbed to be seen. Obviously they'd driven around the back, so I followed, keeping in the shadows of the building. Reaching the rear, I discovered a complex much larger than it had seemed: six warehouses around a central parking bay. Three flatbeds, each loaded with a digger, were parked there already.

As I got nearer to these, I saw that one of them had a plain 'Haulage for Hire, London' sign on it – no address, no phone number – just like the one involved in the excavation work at the Hodder Street playground. The trucks I'd followed in were still heading for their respective warehouse destinations and I was behind them, so I took a chance and hurried (scuttled, even) across the tarmac in their wake. Once in the shadow of the Haulage for Hire vehicle, I snuck around it to the driver's side: the window had a piece of wood wedged in it. It was the same truck I'd damaged two or three days ago out near Brentwood – the one where I'd lost the label of my cardigan. I pushed the wood in. If the phone was still there . . . But it wasn't.

The trucks by now were backing up to four different warehouses. Theresa's chances of getting caught looked high to me, seven out of ten, and increased when I saw that her truck was actually backing completely into the warehouse it was positioned in front of. As I watched, it disappeared and a minute later the driver emerged. He pulled down the roll-up door and seemed to spend a lot of time crouched down, fiddling with something.

Oh, God, was he locking it? I had an awful sense he was. The three other drivers, by contrast, all just parked their vehicles in front of various warehouse doors and headed for each other.

From behind me somewhere another man shouted at them. For a minute I thought he must have seen me, but his attention was on them. 'Hurry up, you lot,' is what I think he said. I peered around the truck for a look – it was the guy in the overalls who'd showed up to let them in. My guess was that he was now going to drive them back to wherever. I waited, listening to their footsteps and their voices growing louder as they approached my hiding place and passed by. I turned and moved along my band of shade so I could watch them leaving. Out through the gate – closing the gate – locking the gate (oh, God, what had we done?) – getting into the car and shutting the doors – driving away.

Paranoia kept me to the shadows as I made my way to the warehouse where I thought Theresa was. Thanks to the early evening sun I could see the chunky padlock even at a distance and when I got there I banged on the roll-down door, which, like the rest of the building, was made out of corrugated pre-fabricated stuff of some kind. 'Theresa?' I said.

She banged back. 'Dee! Thank God!'

'You okay?'

Her laugh was nervy with relief. 'I was *beginning* to worry. What's the padlock like?'

'Big.'

'Any surveillance cameras anywhere?'

'Not that I've seen. What's it like in there?'

'Okay. *Smelly*.'

I sniffed the air and caught something faint. 'That sulphur smell?'

'Yeah, and mustiness.'

'What's in there?'

'Barrels.'

'Of?'

'God knows.'

'Hey! You've got the camera. You could –'

'Done it. They're covered in dirt, most of them.

'How's the ventilation?'

She laughed. 'Look down.'

I did. Four white fingers were wagging at me from the floorline of the building like under-sea polyps. I knelt to look closer. There was a gap the size of a mousehole where door frame, edge of prefab building and ground weren't aligned.

I reached to grab hold of her fingers but she withdrew them. A mini-shovel from a Swiss Army knife appeared in their place. 'I'll dig the space out and hand you through the knife. You can try to pick the lock with it.'

'Oh, yeah, unh hunh. Theresa, we could expire of dehydration before we managed that.'

'There's another load of stuff coming in the morning. If the worst comes to the worst –'

'Ugh. I don't fancy an all-nighter here. Let's see if I can find something to snap the hasp.' I told her I'd be gone a few minutes and wandered off in the direction of the closest warehouse, scanning the ground for rocks. I collected four, from small to large, before I was half-way there and went back to see what I could do with them. I suppose, unconsciously, I was confident from my success with a rock at the lorry depot in Essex. This turned out to be a mistake. All I managed to do was flatten the hasp against the door surround, making the padlock in a way even more impregnable.

'Shit,' I said, dropping the guilty rock.

'Hey,' she said, sticking her fingers through the now slightly bigger hole. 'I can practically palm it now. Look, point the keyhole into the gap.'

I did. 'Okay.'

She gripped it with her fingers and I saw it begin to jiggle. She was fiddling at it with what? A cuticle stick?

'I'll do that,' I protested.

'Leave me be. See if you can get in anywhere else. You need to find those guns.'

'Yes, but –'

'Dee – piss off. When I get out of here we're going to rush around taking a few quick pictures. Go find them.' And she went back to jiggling her cuticle pick in the padlock.

'If they catch us –'

'We've got ten hours. We can bloody tunnel me out in that time if we have to.'

I headed out again for the next warehouse along, this time looking where I was going instead of scrutinising the ground. The flatbed loaded with wooden containers was parked in front of it and, as I approached, I dared myself to climb into it. Theresa had made it look so easy. And she was right: this situation was not to be wasted.

I heaved and grunted more than she did, but I managed it. Once on my feet again and dusted off, I checked to see how possible it might be to prise open any of the containers with my bare hands. Answer: not possible at all. But in searching through them I discovered that between the low edge of the truck and the adjacent row of containers someone had dropped a small claw hammer.

I picked it up and immediately started to smash one of the crates open. The effect was like the lucky quarter in a one-armed bandit: out spewed a rain of stuff that rapidly piled up by my feet. Only the stuff wasn't coins, it was tablets. My blow had gone through the wood and ripped a bag of tablets.

Here they were: the medical supplies, some or all of which must have been destined for Bangladesh.

I jumped (okay, picked my way cautiously) down from the truck and went back to tell Theresa the news.

'Brilliant,' she said. 'Look – try prising the hasp with the hammer, why don't you?'

I tried and tried again and tried some more. 'Won't budge,' I said.

She thanked me and shooed me away again. I went to have a look at the hasp on the padlock of the warehouse next to this one. It was much flimsier and not flattened and four or five swift whacks later it snapped off. I pushed up the corrugated roll-down door and went in. More high wooden containers – dozens and dozens, side by side and floor to ceiling – filling the place.

In about the middle of the building I went at another container, at random, with the hammer – a couple of whacks and it opened. I cannot lie: I was hoping for a rain of Kalashnikovs. Instead a wrapped package toppled out at my feet. I picked it up: a framed something. I unpeeled the layers of paper and bubble plastic protection and felt the object inside. A mirror? I groped for the parcel behind it and unpeeled that: a serving bowl. In the one behind that was a tray.

So: Tim Maguire might have lost Marc Felici's business transporting antiques, but he'd stayed in the field anyway.

I thought: Hard to see Tim as an art lover. There had to be another scam here.

Forgeries? Pieces stolen to order?

The next warehouse had no lorry backed up to it and instead of a truck-width door it had an ordinary one. The plaque said 'Registered Office, South Wales Demolition and Haulage Ltd. Owner: T. P. Maguire'.

This was it: the place with the answers to all my questions, even the ones I hadn't formulated. I peered in the door: a couple of desks, computer, several phones – and a row of security monitors, turned off, lining the far wall. A notice on the door warned that the alarm system was wired to the police station and dogs were on guard.

Untrue as this patently was on both counts, the door was impossible to force. Maybe when we got Theresa out . . .

I continued on to the next warehouse. It and the two remaining ones all had a row of inch-thick padlocks at the base of their roll-down doors. The guns, I decided, were in here.

I went back to check on Theresa and found her digging at the ground with one of the Swiss Army knife blades. She'd already created a fair-sized hole. 'That lock's hopeless,' she said. She tried to wedge a black thing through but it wouldn't quite fit.

'What's that?'

'The camera. Get one of those rocks. Scoop from your side.'

It took us another half-hour but eventually the gap was big enough. She pushed the camera through – 'Go on, Dee. Go for it' – and carried on digging. I paused – wanted to say what I felt – that it was ridiculous, we'd never get her out this way. She kept at it with such determination, though, that it seemed an act of bad faith to stand there. I hurried off to retrace my earlier circuit and take pictures.

Thirty minutes later, when I returned, she'd stopped digging. 'You okay?' I said.

'Yeah, I just felt knackered all of a sudden.' She yawned. 'Need a little rest.'

'You warm enough?'

'Got my jumper,' she mumbled. 'Just be ten minutes.'

I know people whose favourite pastime is dozing but Theresa I'd never thought of as one of them. I was a bit worried that she was breathing something in in there, then thought, no, she's right by the gap. She has access to air. This was just pregnancy tiredness catching up with her after all that driving and all this drama in here.

As I listened to her breathing become regular with sleep, I wondered: should I try to get myself out of here over the fence? Hope I managed it without breaking anything? Hope there was a pay phone outside the garage? Try Theresa's Martin? Trouble was, he was a new man, not a hero type at all.

I would have to try Greg, really.

I mulled this option again and suddenly its fatal flaw reared up. In the unlikely event I managed to climb over the perimeter fence and survived, I'd be unable to climb back in because of the incline of the bank on the road side. Leaving Theresa alone in here was unthinkable.

We simply had to wait and hope for a chance to sneak out as we'd snuck in. Failing that, we'd have to declare ourselves and ask for help.

I swivelled and sat on the ground, my back against the wall. I expected to be awake all night and began in my mind to compose the complete unexpurgated letter to my mother. Dear Mom, you'll never guess what's happened –

The next thing I knew I was jolted awake by the sound of voices in the distance.

– Male voices.

– Two of them.

The stars were dense and bright but there was no moon and the heat had faded from the air. The smell was stronger than I remembered. *Was it why we'd both fallen asleep?* I shivered, then tapped the door with the handle of the hammer. 'Theresa,' I whispered. 'Wake up. Someone's coming.'

She moaned. I whispered to her again. This time she came to. 'God, I feel dreadful,' she said.

Alarmed, I said, 'Can you stand up?'

I heard her grunt and strain and move about. 'Yeah,' she said at last.

'They're coming this way. I'm going to hide. If you get a chance to escape, take it, okay?'

She mumbled okay and I heard her move again. I stole back across the lot to the shadow of the empty truck where I'd sheltered when I came in. The voices were coming nearer and I could see the narrow glow of a penlight torch. I ducked back.

Two dark human shapes, one tall and thin, one shorter and bulkier, passed about twenty feet from my refuge. They were walking at a good clip, heading determinedly for somewhere.

Keeping myself well back, I followed. They went right up to the office door that had proved so resistant to my force. The taller one held the light on the door and the other one knelt and began to fiddle with it the way Greg fiddled.

– Greg.

Could it be that his 'business trip' had involved a piece of research for me after all?

If so, I ought to hurry straight over and let him know I was here too.

If not, on the other hand . . . If this was just wishful thinking . . .

Eventually they got the door unlocked and disappeared inside. I needed to get closer – close enough to hear them even if I couldn't see them. That would clarify things. I moved quietly and tried to catch a glimpse of them through the office window from a distance. It was useless. I crept nearer and nearer and abruptly the office door opened again and the tall, thin man came out carrying a large briefcase. He called out, 'That's all we need – leave it alone, leave it alone.'

I knew that voice. It was Richard Farmer.

What was he doing here?

The other man came out and to my increasingly desperate eye seemed to have exactly the right huggy-bear build. They crossed the parking area in the direction of the three warehouses with the row of padlocks at the bottom. They opened the first and disappeared inside for what seemed like quite a long time. Then they came out and disappeared into the second for about the same length of time. They re-emerged and headed on to the third. There they didn't dwell, which caught me a bit off guard. I was close enough at this point to see that they weren't putting the padlocks back on – that is, close enough to be seen. I darted out of sight again.

They arrived at the warehouse I'd broken into – I heard their exclamatory tones of voice when they found the smashed lock – but after about ten minutes they re-emerged and headed at last to the one where Theresa was. The thin beam of light travelled over the roll-down door to the front. Then, after a pause, I heard the sound of the door being rolled up. The torch light was beamed around inside. Even from a dozen yards away I could see stacks of barrels. They went in.

Come on, Theresa, get your butt out of there.

I waited and waited. There was no sign of her.

I didn't want to blow our presence here or put maybe-Greg in a weird spot by revealing myself (or put myself in a dangerous spot if it wasn't Greg), but I wanted to get her out of there and us out of this place. If I had to do something outrageous . . .

But I was worrying unnecessarily. I heard light footsteps. 'Theresa?' I whispered.

'Here,' she said faintly.

I went towards her voice, and in a couple of paces bumped into her.

'I still feel terrible,' she whispered.

'Stomach pains?' I said, probably too alarmed.

'No, no. Just wrung out. Knackered.'

'Not surprisingly,' I said. 'How about deep breaths.'

'I have.'

'Again.' Then I waited while she ventilated, in out, in out, in out, three times. 'Now come on,' I said. 'Let's get out of here.'

I concentrated on pulling her along and then, when we were out of that front gate, I pointed her towards her car. I stopped in passing to have a look at the padlock. No Greg-style wire here.

Theresa's car wouldn't start but while I was alarmed, she seemed too groggy to care. She crawled over into the back seat and said, 'The garage'll be open soon. They'll fix it.' Then she was asleep again.

I slouched down in the front, telling myself not to get anxious. Ten minutes or so later a dark VW bus drove by us. The two men leaving? That was my instinct, but I waited another half an hour before daring to get out and go back to the gate and check. The padlock was on again.

I had no idea what the time was – it could have been 11, it could have been 4 – but I went to the darkened garage shop and knocked on the door. No one was there. I spent between then and six, when the shopkeeper family finally arrived, pacing back and forth between the car and the shop.

I made up a story about how we'd broken down late last night, but told them the truth about Theresa being pregnant and not feeling well. The mother's previous crustiness gave way. She made her husband first check the car (which of course now started immediately), then give us a tow into town, right up to the front door of the hospital emergency section.

Unlike London, where you can sit for hours waiting to have your 'urgent' matter seen to, a gynaecologist appeared immediately and took Theresa in for an examination. Afterwards they brought her porridge and orange juice and tea.

It was hospital standard but it made a dramatic difference. But then, it would, given the diagnosis: she had low blood sugar levels because she hadn't eaten anything the day before except a mouthful of chocolate. She was given a lecture about being lucky this time and needing to take care of herself and the risk of miscarriage if she didn't. Initially she tried to argue that she was fit and used to camping out, that sleeping in her car in mild weather was luxury. By the end she was nodding and saying, Yes, of course, she'd be more careful.

I just felt guilty for getting her involved in the first place (okay, okay, she'd insisted on driving, but I was the reason). To make up for it I tried to persuade her that we must take the train home, but by then she was feeling better. Resting, she reminded me, wasn't something she enjoyed, and anyway, leaving the car here would mean so much hassle it would give out any benefits there might be to not driving.

She won.

Eighteen

The nearer we got to London the more difficult it became to ignore the problems I'd left there. I was innocent but probably about to be arrested; I had seen the medicine and art *objets* in Tim Maguire's warehouses; I knew where the guns probably were. But I had nothing to prove that he or his suppliers killed Janey Riordan. In fact, all I did have was a single hope: that it *was* Greg who'd been at the warehouse, that he now had papers belonging to Tim, that something in them would save me.

I said, 'I think I better move to a B&B. I need a few clothes from your place.'

We drove up Edgware Road towards Kilburn and as we turned off the High Street she said, 'I'll drive by the end of the road. You look.'

I obeyed. 'A possible police car and possible press,' I reported.

We decided that she'd be the decoy. I adjusted my scarf, smoothed my trousers, slipped on the dark glasses and let her drop me a couple of blocks away.

By the time I got there she was standing on the pavement in front of her block talking with two men. Even though all I had were back and side views, I knew they were Detective Inspector Hamley and his sidekick.

As per our plan, I went to the entrance at the far end of the block, the one from which I'd exited that morning, and pushed the top bell. I identified myself to the person who answered as a friend of Theresa's who needed access and she buzzed me in. When I'd made my way to the top landing, she put her head out her door, looked me over and pointed me to the door leading over the roof. Obviously this wasn't the first time Theresa had sent a fugitive this way.

After I emerged into the open air I stayed well to the back as I crossed to the other end, so I couldn't be seen from the street. I slipped into the roof door of Theresa's stairwell without any problem and hurried down the stairs to the ground floor.

I assumed she hadn't been in yet herself and had my key out, but when I got there her flat door was ajar. Funny, I thought. Then I pushed it open. The place had been turned over. Not as comprehensively as it might have been – TV and video and stereo system and computer were still there and most of the furniture was upright. But the desk had been ravaged and there were papers covering every surface in the sitting room. I spotted the briefcase I'd left here the other day, open and empty. My papers were in this mess – that or they were gone.

I thought about how much I'd written down while I'd been here and decided, not much. And Janey's papers from her deposit box were back in the safe at Aspinall Street.

I sighed heavily and picked my way over the contents of the upended waste basket to the telephone. The tape had been removed from the answering machine. Shit. Greg, Suze, Theresa herself – they'd all left messages. I wondered: was this about theft? Was it about unnerving me? Or was it about planting listening devices? I started checking around picture frames and under chairs and was on my knees taking apart an adapter plug when Theresa came in the front door.

She took in the mess. 'Oh my God –'

I stood up and went over to support her. 'It's not as bad as it looks,' I said, leading her to a chair. When she dropped into it I crouched beside her and put my arm around her. 'I'm really sorry, Theresa. Having me as a client hasn't exactly brought you good fortune.'

'Hey,' she interrupted, giving me a smile, 'this is nothing compared to the time I came home to graffiti in pig's blood all over the wall.' She shook her head. 'The irony of it is, if I report this, the police will take you away.'

'So that was Hamley and Co.?'

She nodded.

'Do I want to know what he said?'

She shook her head. 'You want to come up with something concrete to clear yourself and/or point him conclusively to someone else.' She looked around at the mess again and sighed. 'Well, I think this has decided me.'

'What?'

'It is definitely time to sell this flat.' She leaned over and started picking up pieces of paper. I started to help her. She grabbed my wrist and stopped me. Just from the pressure I knew she was going to tell me something serious. 'Go, Dee. Get the film developed. Sort out whatever else you can as soon as you can. Call me at –' she mouthed the word 'Martin's' inaudibly – 'Yeah?'

I nodded and left her to sift and tidy and check for listening devices on her own.

I retraced my route over the roof, down the stairway at the far end of the block and out of that front door. Then I fled.

The first phone box I came to I rang my neighbour Grant.

'Dee! Oh God,' he said.

'What is it?' I asked, even though I had a good idea.

'Your flat –'

'Is it bad?'

'Just papers, but they're everywhere. David's put a board over the door.'

'Oh no, it wasn't kicked in?'

''Fraid so. Don't know how we didn't hear it.'

The next call I made was to Greg's office. He wasn't there but his secretary had a message. 'He says it's urgent he sees you. Are you free tonight? Where can he phone you?'

'Is he coming back to his office?'

'In about half an hour.'

'Well, I'll come there then.'

I stopped at the first clothes shop I passed and bought a blue skirt, a rose-coloured silk blouse and some matching pink espadrilles to counteract my dark feelings. When I tried them on and caught sight of myself in the mirror I thought it was someone else. Theresa wasn't the only one forgetting to eat – and for me, that was really saying something.

I wore my Bangladeshi salwar khamiz over the new clothes in case Greg's office too had been sussed by the police and the tabloids and whoever it was who'd broken into Theresa's flat and my flat. It didn't look to me as if anyone was standing around furtively, but then, if they're good at the job, you don't see them. I crossed the road and rang the bell.

Alone in the lift I used the opportunity to shed my other layer again. Then I did my best at a grand entrance. It was wasted: he wasn't back yet.

He arrived about twenty minutes after I did, just as I was tucking into another article in the current *Engineering Age*. The warm starburst of lust that shot across my gut when he came in made me get to my feet and kind of gawp, hangdog, at him. He showed me into his small, sparsely furnished office and shut the door before putting his arms around me and giving me a bear hug. You can forgive a guy a lot, I find, if he gives good bear hug.

'I been worrying about you,' he said into my hair. 'Where you been?'

I thought back over the two days he'd been gone. 'Ha!' I mumbled into his broad shoulder. 'You name it.'

He nuzzled down and gave me a kiss. It went on and on and when it was over I felt like stripping off and undoing his fly and and and – Instead I leaned back and looked at him. He had a slight dimple in his chin which I'd never appreciated before. I touched it with my index finger. 'You going to tell me about your amazingly successful research on my behalf?'

The face he pulled was Guilt Exaggerated. He grabbed me back to his chest again. 'I'll do it tomorrow, I promise. It was impossible from Paris –'

I pushed back again. 'Paris?'

He laughed. 'Eiffel Tower? River Seine?'

I disentangled myself from his arms and dropped into the nearby chair. 'The *whole* time since I last saw you?'

'Not every single minute, but, yeah, most of it. My secretary managed to find out who bought the playground site – Americans as it turns out – but that's all.'

Rats. I'd convinced myself it had been him and Richard Farmer in that warehouse complex in Wales.

'What's the matter?' he said.

– Good thing I hadn't launched myself at him from out of the darkness.

So who had it been?

He tightened his grip on my shoulders. 'What?'

I shook my head. 'I went to Maguire's company's headquarters in Cwmbran myself. Yesterday. I –'

'You went there? But I said I'd –'

'You went away.' I said it (I think) as fact, not as accusation, but he got defensive.

'I had to go –'

'I understand that. But I'd heard all this stuff about Tim Maguire. I could be arrested any minute. I needed to check it out.'

He let go of my shoulders and in a couple of strides crossed the room to the single window, where he stood staring out. I almost thought I could see smoke pumping from his ears and eyes, though why I wasn't sure. What I suspected, unfortunately, was a latent me Tarzan, you Jane macho streak.

'And?' he said across the distance he'd just created.

I wasn't going to let him get a rise out of me. 'And Theresa drove me. We had to sneak into the damn place and then she got locked in a warehouse.'

'Jesus,' he muttered.

'In the middle of the night two guys showed up –'

He turned around. 'While you were *there*?'

My resolve collapsed. My rise rose. 'I told you. Theresa was locked in. It was pitch dark! One of them had your build and fiddled with the office lock, the other one was tall and thin and sounded like Richard Farmer.' But no sooner had I said the name than the full sense of the hollowness of my fantasy hit me. Unconsciously I'd begun to count on those papers from the South Wales Demolition and Haulage office. How could I have? Panic – fear – hopelessness all welled up. I didn't want to cry. I was a grown woman. Anyway, if I cracked now, would I ever get myself back together?

Greg recrossed the room and sat down beside me and rubbed my back, up, down, round and round, up, down, round and round. It said he was sorry and wanted to make up. It said at the first opportunity he wanted to go to bed with me. His hands got firmer and hotter and the rhythm steadier and steadier and after, I don't know, a minute, two minutes, I slid into the sensation and forgot my problems, forgot the friction of a moment before. Mmm: wonderful. He began to ease off and in that instant I recollected the piece of information he *had* given me: the purchaser of the playground site was American.

I looked up. 'So what's the name of the company Richard sold the playground to?'

He kissed my temple. 'Etna Global Holdings Inc. Based in Newark, New Jersey. I need some coffee. You?'

Did I nod? No matter. He gave my back a final pat and went out.

As soon as the door shut behind him and I was alone in the room, self-pity surged again. Did I have the energy to get myself going on another stray bit of information? I felt so weary. Tears began to rise once more. I fished in my bag for a tissue but all I found were bits too grey and shredded to use. Damn double damn.

Greg had left his partially unzipped overnight bag on the floor by the chair where I was sitting and I reached over to it and looked inside in case he had any. I didn't see one and slipped my hand in for a quick feel around. My fingers touched a thin metal tube and I pulled it out: a penlight torch.

I stared at it, remembering the thin beam I'd seen as I'd hid behind that truck in that warehouse compound in Cwmbran. Penlight torches are common things. Finding he had one didn't mean anything.

I was still holding it up when I heard him opening the door. I dropped it back, wiped my eyes with my hands and straightened.

Mustn't get paranoid. I'd be suspecting Theresa next.

He sat down close beside me and held the mug right in front of my eyes. I took it.

'So fill me in – what'd you find out about Maguire?'

It was an obvious thing to ask but the suspiciousness, once roused, had an effect. 'Well, he didn't always haul legal goods,' I said, keeping it vague.

'What, drugs?'

I nodded. 'Among other things. Actually – what's the time?' (Why was I being like this?)

He checked his watch. '4.30. I'm due at a meeting, but I was hoping tonight –'

'I'm not going back to Theresa's. I need a safe place to stay where Hamley won't find me.'

He hugged my shoulders. (My dad used to do that. The comforts of men.) 'Leave it to me.'

My ambivalence eased; the lust reasserted itself. 'But what if you're called away again?'

He gave me a kiss that worked its way right through any remaining defensive crust in about two seconds. 'I won't be,' he said into my mouth.

I decided I believed him.

We agreed to meet again back here at his office at 7.

He told me to help myself to the phone, then kissed me goodbye and headed off. I noticed then that his shoes looked dirty: not unpolished but dirt-y. (Stop it, Dee. Stop it.)

I dialled Sufiya at the hospital and the nurse who answered went off and tracked her down.

'Dee! I've just been thinking about you. How are you?'

'Managing. I've got news for your friend Sheikh Nasir. I located his goods.'

'Fantastic! Where?'

'I'll tell you when I see you. Would you come with me to see him again?'

'Yes, certainly. Were you thinking of coming soon?'

'Now, actually.'

'Good, yes. If you get here soon *you* can do *me* a favour.'

'Oh?'

'Richard Farmer's coming to see me at five. Wants to talk compensation, he said.'

'Great! I'll be there.'

'Good.'

'Hey – your house hasn't been broken into has it?'

'Not my house, my office. Last night. You don't think it's connected to you?'

'My flat, my solicitor's flat, your office. Was anything taken?'

'The computer disks with my report and research notes on them.'

'Oh, what! Were they the only ones you had?'

'Fortunately not.'

'What about listening devices – have you checked?'

'No.'

'Will you?'

'Of course, but I – look, I know this means it's coincidence, but my instinct is that it has nothing to do with you and everything to do with what I have to say about environmental pollutants in this area.'

I'd lost track of which number warm rainless spring day we were up to – forty or forty-five – and when a bus passed I hopped on, even though it meant a longer journey. It dropped me off opposite the hospital and, hoping to catch the lights, I hurried towards the kerb. I just missed them.

Stuck there, I turned away from the traffic fumes and idly checked out the nearby pub. My eye just caught the dark blueness of the nose of a VW bus parked at the rear. I thought of the VW bus that had passed us in Wales and walked towards the corner to give myself a better view. Its tall driver was standing on the tarmac beside the door of the vehicle, back to me, stripping out of overalls. Underneath were distinctly Richard Farmer-style casuals. 'Turn around, turn around', I muttered. But he threw the overalls into the bus and locked the door, then put on a baseball-style cap and headed inside, without giving me a look at his face.

I headed after him and was reaching for the handle of the glass entrance door of the pub when I saw my reflection. I was wearing my Bangladeshi clothes, including the scarf and sunglasses. Whoops. Slipped out of character.

Two guys coming out gave me the old English bulging eye (we're pretending we're not looking but believe me, we are *shocked*).

'Ladies' room?' I said.

Their relief was instant; all was explained. 'End of the corridor, love.'

The corridor took me past the bar entrance, where I stopped and looked in. This time I could see the guy in profile and it was Richard

Farmer, no doubt about it. In the time it had taken me to follow him in there, he'd been served a shot glass of something yellow and Scotch-looking and was downing the last mouthful. As I watched he put the glass on the counter for a refill, knocked it back and did it again.

Richard wasn't known as a boozer. Anyway, the intensity of it smacked of binge. He was in a state about something.

I decided against accosting him here. Better to wait – confront him at the meeting.

Five minutes later I was waving through the ward door at Sufiya, who was standing among the incubators about half-way down, talking to a couple of women. Neither of them was Nasima.

I watched her extricate herself and come towards me.

'Listen,' I said without preliminaries when she'd joined me in the hall, 'I just saw Richard in the pub. He's getting seriously tanked up.'

'Is he? You know, I thought he sounded drunk on the phone. He –' But at that the doors from the stairwell opened and in he came. He didn't register either of us, just headed straight past and into the ward and proceeded to trip on something, possibly his own foot. I thought he'd go headfirst but Sufiya caught him and he regained his balance. He used it to push her aside and continued into the ward. Unable to stop him, she ended up more or less supporting him. He paused to look in each and every incubator, and when they got to the far end, he reached into his inside jacket pocket, withdrew an envelope and handed it to her. Then he turned around and walked back through the ward. He looked as if he were having to hold his breath; he was certainly walking fast by the time he came through the doors and hurried past me, heading for the outside world.

My instinct was to follow but I paused to make sure Sufiya was okay. She was still standing in the same spot, looking into the envelope he'd given her. I took a breath and went in there and pulled her out.

The envelope was full of cash. She saw the look on my face and tried to speak not just once but twice. Finally she squeezed out, 'He said he was very very sorry about the babies.'

'Good! Glad to hear it! With a nice fat donation . . .'

'I don't know if you can call this a "donation". Dee, it's fifty thousand American dollars.'

I quickly gave her the news about the medicine for Bangladesh to pass on to Sheikh Nasir and hurried off after Richard. In his condition, how far could he get?

He was as easy to find as I'd hoped. He was sitting in his small VW bus in the parking lot of the pub, staring out the front window at a wall and drinking beer from a can. Despite the warm stickiness of the day, the windows were all rolled up. I slipped off the scarf and glasses and tapped on the glass beside his head. 'Richard,' I called. 'Yoo-hoo.'

He frowned the way drunk people can when faced with a demand to communicate. Where was he? Who was I? What was going on? Then he blinked a couple of times at my clothes and started on the hard task of rolling down the window a few inches. A familiar sulphur smell hit me at once – the smell of the warehouse in Wales where Theresa had been trapped.

Proof! And how typical: proof that disappeared in the air.

'Why did you give Sufiya Khan all that money?'

His head wobbled heavily on his neck like a turtle's. He was struggling to keep it upright.

'If you feel so bad about the playground,' I said, 'why don't you cancel the deal with Etna Global.'

He shook his head in that turtly way and looked down at his hands. I decided to hell with this and walked quickly around to the passenger side, intending to slide in beside him and confront him. It was locked. I knocked on the glass but his attention was fixed to the floor. I followed his gaze and saw a pile of papers stacked where a passenger's feet would go. Could this be what he'd taken from the South Wales Demolition office? I had to know.

I went back around to the driver's side and tried to stick my hand in through the three inches of open window but it jammed at the elbow. Enough of this fart-assing around. 'Richard!'

He kept staring.

'*Richard*! What is going on?'

He turned and looked at me from somewhere far far away.

'What deal were you doing with Tim Maguire?'

He started to roll up the window, the task seeming to cost him an immense effort. I stuck my elbow in the opening to stop him. 'I'm going to be charged with Janey's murder, Richard. If you know anything about it, anything at all, you have to –'

But at that I noticed he was listing sideways. I tried again to stick my hand in, just enough to grab his collar, but he had already keeled too far to the right. A moment later he'd passed out.

Great. My best chance so paralytic with drink he knocks himself out – in a locked car where he could frigging *cook* to death – at an angle that could make him choke to death.

And before he'd told me a single thing.

What had spoken was his behaviour and, judging by that, our Richard was one hell of a torn-up guy.

I used the phone in the pub to summon an ambulance, then waited close enough to make sure he didn't do something like vomit and inhale. When I heard the sirens I put my scarf and glasses back on and got out of there.

This time when I got to his office Greg was waiting for me at the front in a taxi. I went from mine straight into his. As the driver took off, Greg put one of his ex-football player's arms around me and slipped my scarf off so that it fell from my hair on to my shoulders. 'Funny,' he said, smiling at me. 'I never thought of this style of dress as particularly erotic before.'

I kissed the lips he was sticking out at me. 'Where are we going?'

'For a little taste of back home.'

This turned out to mean the Marriott Hotel in Swiss Cottage – the one with the full-sized pool, the Jacuzzi, the sauna and a big sign saying 'Ask about a Massage.' I wanted the lot, in order, ending with the massage. 'Ask who do you suppose?' I said, looking around.

He took my hand. 'Ask me. We do a special service for fugitives from justice on Thursday night.'

'You're on.'

Up in the room he did turn out to be an amazingly good masseur. I drifted off into sensation land, that liquid place he'd sent me with the back rub earlier, the place we'd gone making love. I came to to find his lips on my right breast, his hard penis swinging teasingly over my pubic hairs. Then he traced a line with his tongue down my breastbone and across my stomach that made me shudder in its exquisiteness and tantalisingness and whether he entered me or I surrounded him I couldn't tell you. We were all touches and kisses and lickings and spit for God knows how long and I truly absolutely and completely forgot everything else for the first time since Janey Riordan died. We then had a shower together – a good, strong, American shower gushing from the mains supply – and while I was soaping him down, well, let's just say we made those sheets pretty wet.

The plan had been to go down to the buffet – it was TexMex Nite – but in the end we had a sandwich sent up and got into drinking the wines in the mini-bar and talking about our childhoods. I can't even remember falling asleep.

I woke abruptly at four a.m. feeling dehydrated and headachy. I lay there wishing myself into either getting up or going back to sleep, but neither happened. Finally I disentangled my legs from his and forced myself first to sit up and, after a brief rest, to stand. Then, very very carefully, I coaxed one leg to move in front of the other. I aimed at the bathroom and willed myself there on the promise of an aspirin. Alas, all that was in my bag was an empty packet.

Greg's shaving kit was sitting there and I should have known better than to open it, given what had happened when I'd looked in his overnight bag. But never mind, I'd forgotten that. I fished around in it and came out with another pouch tucked at the bottom of it. It didn't look like medical stuff, but who knew? I unzipped it – and there in my hand found an enormous wad of American dollar banknotes.

Nor was that all. Beneath the money was a Serbian travel document with Greg's picture in it. The name was Gregor Kostiĉ.

Jesus. Had I been conned or had I been conned?

It's a measure, I'm sure, of the process of anglification I've gone through living here that I didn't rush across the room, grab 'Gregor Kostiĉ' by the collarbones and bash his head into the headboard, demanding that he explain; if I'd spent my adult years in LA, if I'd been in this situation there –. Instead I got dressed quickly and quietly and put my few things in my handbag and got the hell out of there.

He was lying to me. He knew Richard, he'd been at the warehouse. The cash, the warehouse – shit shit shit. And the name! Who was he?

It wasn't until I was crossing the darkened lobby, heading for the main entrance, that I remembered I had nowhere to go. I stopped and contemplated going back.

No. Screw that.

In fact, screw them all. I was going home.

I was wearing my own clothes but couldn't be bothered to look around when I got out of the taxi. What did it matter who saw me. (How had I so misread him?)

Upstairs I unlocked my boarded-up door, expecting the worst. In fact, Grant and David had collected the papers into piles and that small act of thoughtfulness made all the difference. My answering machine was blinking for its life – spasm overdrive. I ignored it, headed into the bedroom, stripped off my clothes and fell into bed.

Two hours later I was woken abruptly by the sound of heavy fists banging on my front door.

I slipped into my robe, tiptoed quietly down the hall and peered through the spyhole: Hamley, his sergeant and a woman officer. Had the moment come? I opened the door.

Hamley said, 'Ah, Miss Street, sorry to wake you. We'd like you to accompany us to the station – if you wouldn't mind.'

My hand went to my hips, so that from one elbow to the other I filled my doorway. 'Are you arresting me?'

'Yes,' he said. 'Yes, I am.'

Nineteen

Take a criminal defence lawyer whose major cases the past decade all involved people charged with serious crimes they didn't commit. Put her in her clients' position. She'd keep a grip on herself, right?

Especially if she'd seen it coming and gone to meet it (right?).

Alas, at the moment I stepped (was pushed) into the client role, I realised how profoundly my experience of the criminal justice system had eaten away my capacity for faith in it. A pure client, one who'd never done my job, could believe that once a police or courtroom mistake had been pointed out, all would immediately be put right. I knew how rarely it happened like that.

Names, faces, years in prison swirled up around me as if a stink bomb had exploded in my mental filing cabinets. All those people whose courage I'd admired. All those lost years.

How many times had I thought, No way could I get through what this person or that person's been through.

God help me now.

A second, ten seconds, ten minutes – I have no idea how long we stood there. It's the nature of that kind of sulphurous swirl that all you remember is the smelly blur of it, and the sensation of the moment elongating and stretching and swinging over your head like a jump rope.

Hamley could easily have taken advantage of my unmoored, vulnerable state. Hell, he'd taken advantage of Amin Ali's and I had to suppose it was one of his repertoire of tactics. Instead he waited.

When the haze began to disperse inside me, he seemed to know. Only then did he recite the formal caution, using the old wording: 'You are not obliged to say anything unless you wish to do so,' he said, 'but what you say may be put in writing and given in evidence. Do you wish to say anything?'

Given the emotional stew slopping around inside me, I'd have been wise to exercise my right to silence. If I'd known it was really going to be abolished, I'd have done it on principle. In my new shoes I wasn't that rational or that prescient. 'You won't get away with this,' I said. 'I'm innocent.'

He glanced briefly over his shoulder at his sergeant, who I now realised had a notebook open and a pen ready. At this signal he began to write. Hamley looked back at me once again and smiled. That phrase of Aldous Huxley's about a "giaconda smile" came to mind. I might not be singing, it said, but I was a canary, and he was satisfied.

He gestured to the woman officer and practically within that same moment she was at my side. She didn't put a hand on me but I felt physically constrained at once.

He said, 'My colleague will come with you while you dress.'

The lawyer me shouted through the haze with her old outrage at the client me: You don't have to take this crap! Do something!

'I'm phoning my solicitor,' I said.

'Of course, of course.'

In my bedroom I stared into my closet and felt no desire to wear anything in there. I reached for the familiar clothes of yesterday, strewn over the chair. My minder looked a bit repelled by that and it cheered me.

Out in the sitting room I phoned Theresa. On the sixth or seventh ring, just as I was getting seriously anxious that she'd already gone out, she answered. The heart that's usually in her voice was missing, as if the battery were conking out, but it was early and I'd obviously woken her up and I was bursting with myself, me, my problem, help! She said she'd set off as soon as she got herself together.

The next thing I remember is hurrying down the last few stairs of the flight to the ground floor, following Hamley towards the front entrance of the block. Abruptly he stopped and turned and pointed my attention to the gate and stepped aside so I could see past him. I stopped too – and had a full view right out into the street.

On the opposite sidewalk was my *News of the World* guy with what looked like three, maybe four companions. He was leaning across the hood of an old brown banger parked at the kerb, fiddling with a big lens on his camera.

I turned back to Hamley, who gave me another of those damned smiles and said, 'I suggest a blanket.' His sergeant stepped forward and thrust a nubbly grey hospital model into my hands.

'Jesus,' I muttered. 'You tip off the press, then you –'

'Excuse me. Your headline-worthiness is down to you.'

'Yeah? Well, maybe I'll try to sell them "The Detective Inspector's Revenge".'

At last a fissure of emotion appeared in his cool, calm collectedness. 'You think you've been set up? Show me the evidence.' He nodded at the blanket that the sergeant was still holding out at me. 'If you want it, take it.' He pointed left through the wall. 'The car's fifteen yards that way.'

I contemplated the nubbly grey fabric again. Of course he'd leaked the story. He knew as well as I did that, however I played it with the tabloids, I'd lose. If I hid under the blanket, my dignity would go. If I went out there barefaced my anonymity would go.

I sighed. Much as I hated people coming up to me on the street thinking they'd seen me on a game show, on balance it was dignity down the pan. I refused the blanket, lifted my chin and said I was ready when they were.

Hamley and his two minions each tried to get me to talk again during the journey but I kept refusing to be drawn and finally they gave up and left me alone. I curled down into my corner of the back seat, as far away as I could get from the woman officer beside me, and began to prepare myself for what lay ahead.

By the time we arrived at the station I'd decided that I wouldn't waste what little energy I had getting het up or provoked about anything purely on principle. I'd need it all just to get through the bureaucratic procedures. When I was out on bail (I had to assume they'd bail me) and home again and could consult Theresa and Suze at my leisure, then I'd get into the point-scoring.

Anxiety about my immediate position was also out for now on the grounds of energy inefficiency.

As a result I picked my way through the routines at the station feeling disembodied, as if my consciousness were hanging out up there on the ceiling with the security camera. Look, there I am, coming through the station door into the foyer. There's Hamley buzzing reception and identifying himself and leading me inside and along a corridor to the desk presided over by a bright young sergeant. Words go back and forth (bzzz bzzz murder, bzz bzz Janey) and some are even addressed to me. Hearing's not clear from this angle but from the rhythm I know I've been cautioned again.

I'm put somewhere, given a glass of water (hey, lunch!), wait. In the time that passes I mull the various truths I could choose to reveal in my defence. The libel that wasn't. The last phone call from Janey. The visit to her flat the night she was killed. The bloody glove. The evidence that Tim Maguire dealt in guns – years ago to Irish nationalists; more recently, to the Serbs.

I wonder: what will telling some or all of these truths mean for me? For Suze? For the firm?

I'm shunted to a detention room where the same woman officer who watched me dress at home now asks me to take off my clothes, which I do, piece by piece, until I'm down to my overwashed-grey bra and underpants. Then she asks me to extend my arms out from the shoulder and spread my legs and she feels me over top and bottom.

I do not say to her, What a job, eh? though if I had just a little more energy I would.

I watch her tip out my handbag and spend forever itemising everything from my keys and diary to the old receipts and bits of lint on the bottom. Then I'm shunted back to the desk sergeant. The words I again don't catch but I've heard plenty of formal charges in my time and, recognising the form, I could imagine the content. First the accusation: I, Dee Street, am charged with causing the death of Janey Riordan on 30 April between blah blah and blah blah. Next, a description of me: thirty-seven, five foot two, American and British nationalities, eyes hair blah blah blah, and last, the itemised list of the receipts and lint and blah blah they'd taken from me.

The pause at the end I know means, Do you understand?

I nod. What's more, I decide the time has come to return to my body. Hey presto, no sooner thought than done. Suddenly I'm back talking to the desk sergeant eye to eye.

I said, 'So: how long do you think I'll be here?'

'We need your fingerprints and your photo and it says here the inspector has a warrant to search your flat –'

'God, not again.'

'If this is a second search –'

'Third.'

'Mmm, must want to get into the fabric.'

'Oh God, my floorboards.' I'd only finally sanded and varnished them after how many years there?

He finished his mental calculating. 'That takes us up to about three, and then there's the identification parade.'

This implied they had a witness – *another* witness besides Tim – and my instinct said they were lying, it was a ploy to unnerve me. They couldn't compel me to go through an identity parade, either. Trouble was, if this case lived long enough to be tried, God help me, the court could be told I'd refused to co-operate and it would count against me.

As the anxiety rattled up my spine and neared my heart I remembered my vow not to let it loose. I got a hold on it and wrestled it back down into its box and endeavoured to move quickly on. 'And can I be bailed after that?'

He slipped the documents into a wallet file and shrugged. 'I'd have thought the inspector'd want your passports.'

Conditions of any kind meant a magistrate's hearing, which meant getting to court by four at the latest. *And* it was Friday. If they didn't get me there by closing time today, they could hold me until the court opened again on Monday.

No way did I want that.

'I can arrange for them to be with the court for this afternoon.'

He smiled and I could see he'd been taking giaconda lessons from his boss. 'We'll try. No guarantee.'

An hour later I was still waiting my turn to be fingerprinted, sitting in a queue that seemed to move forward one seat every twenty minutes. On duty today, folks, the slowest fingerprinter in the entire Metropolitan Police force. I was five seats or one hour and forty minutes away, trying to come to terms with the idea that I really truly in all likelihood *would* be in a cell all weekend, when the desk sergeant came to get me. Theresa had arrived.

I'd practically forgotten she was coming, that I wasn't in this absolutely alone.

They took me to the underfurnished interview room where she was waiting and before the door had even closed behind me she was giving me a big hug and apologising for being so late. We were the same height but she was small and normally rippling with fitness. That morning all I could feel were her bones.

We separated and I held her at arm's length. Her skin was the most wrung-out white I think I've ever seen pale skin be, and translucent. 'Are you okay?' I asked her.

'I wish.' She walked with careful steps back to her chair, which was on the right of the small table. As soon as she sat down she sneezed three or four times.

'God,' I said. They'd taken my bag so I couldn't even offer her a tissue.

She had her own. 'I never get colds,' she said. She blew her nose. 'Never.'

'It was that damp smelly warehouse, it must have been. Shit! I'm sorry Theresa.'

'It's not your fault.'

'But I –'

'You didn't make me do one of the stupidest things I've ever done in my life.'

I sighed for her. 'You've been to the doctor?'

'That's why I was late.'

'What'd he say?'

'He told me to go back to bed.' She squeezed my hand and imitated her healthier self laughing. 'I love this. You're arrested for murder and we talk about me.'

'I think you should do what your doctor ordered.'

'Yeah, well, I'll just lie there worrying about you unless I know what's going on. Turn up anything new since yesterday?'

Greg. The truth about Greg. Should I tell her that?

Tell her what? That I'm a mug?

I looked around. Was the officer on the other side of the door listening to us? Was our conversation being piped into a neighbouring room?

She watched me, read my thoughts. 'This is the best we're going to get, Dee.'

I sighed; this was obviously true. I decided to put off the mortifying stuff until later. 'More on Richard Farmer.'

When I paused there she gestured to me to go on, tell her. I ahemed and cleared my throat but still couldn't get myself to speak. It was incredible, what I was about to say. A guy like Richard Farmer – a businessman who'd spent a decade cultivating a good-guy-in-the-community profile – why would he be involved in gun-dealing? And with a scumbag like Tim Maguire? Never mind be involved with murder?

She leaned over and pretended to press an 'on' button on my shoulder. 'What more on Richard Farmer?'

'I think – think he's behind this.'

'What, you think *he* supplied Tim Maguire with guns and medicine and and and?' Her scepticism echoed my own.

'Yeah. He was definitely the English man I heard at South Wales Demolition yesterday night. He has a VW bus like the one that passed us just after we settled into your car *and* it's got the same smell in it as that warehouse you were locked in.'

'Shit, you're joking.'

'I'm not! *And* he's on the booze. A serious bender. I watched him down three shots of Scotch in about ninety seconds. Then he went to Sufiya's ward, wept over the babies –'

'No.'

'Seriously. After his catharsis he gave her a wad of American dollars for the clinic.'

'Did he really?' She stared at the floor, chewing on her thumbnail, thinking. A minute or so later she said, 'A guilty conscience like that suggests he's new at all this. Don't you think? Personally, I'd find it easier to believe. Here he is, under financial pressure like the rest of us –'

'On a mega scale.'

'Yes, so mega he has to sell assets, but maybe he can't do it fast enough – he needs more – so he does some illegal deal with Tim Maguire –'

'And Janey finds out.' Various loose wires in my brain magically found connections. 'Or maybe –' I said, getting excited, 'maybe she went in it *with* him. They were both under the same intensity of financial pressure. Perhaps they decided to work together.'

'Yes, I like that even better! Maybe they did one deal together and later he tried to drop her in because in spite of the deal his company still wasn't making it. He had to sell more assets. The playground had planning permission. It was obvious.'

'And she went further than he expected in response. She blackmailed him.'

'Yes, and he killed her.'

We both nodded and went quiet, turning this scenario over. It had drama and it fitted somebody – but Richard? Hell, I wasn't sure it fitted Janey.

'You think he could be doing another deal now?' she said.

'Mmmm. What else was he doing at the warehouse in the middle of the night? Tim's dead and the receiver's coming in to clear the place. He has to seize his chance.'

'Right. Well. Guess it's time to start doing some serious digging into his finances. Anything else?'

I saw myself with Greg, making love that drove all thought away. Was he buying medicine like the Bangladeshis – or guns like the IRA?

I ought to tell her.

She waved her hand in front of my eyes. 'Yoo-hoo.'

I cleared my throat. 'Listen,' I started.

Then she began to sneeze again – and sneeze – and sneeze. Four – eight – twelve. I was seriously starting to worry (sixteen) when at last she stopped. 'God!' I said.

When she finished blowing her nose again, she laughed. 'Whew!' The next moment a bolt of pain flashed across her face and she bent double, clutching herself around the midriff.

I was on my feet and over at her side before I even knew it. 'What? What is it?'

She was struggling to control her breathing and had no spare capacity to answer.

I straightened and headed for the door, intending to get the guard's attention, to get her to go for help.

'No,' she croaked. 'I'm all right.'

'You don't look all right,' I said. But I paused.

'A stitch. Going.'

I stayed where I was, waiting to see if this was true.

A couple of deep breaths later, she gestured to me to come back, sit down. I decided I would, and there I waited another elongated moment.

At the end of it she said, 'There', and raised her torso upright again. There was dampness on her brow and she rubbed it off with the side of her hand.

'You look awful,' I said. 'I am your client and I am instructing you to go home now, this minute.'

'I can survive till we get you bailed.'

I shook my head. 'Hamley wants conditions. They're dragging their heels. Face it, I'm here all weekend.'

'No way.'

'Theresa, he's getting even with me.'

'I can't let him –'

'You know the fight it would take to stop him. I can't let you risk –' I was going to say miscarriage but couldn't get the word out. I searched for a substitute and finally said – 'your health on my account. What for? It's a couple of days. I can survive.'

In the end we arrived (okay, typically) at a compromise: on her way out she'd have a go at Hamley about bailing me without conditions, something he could do any time, without going to court. If he agreed, she'd come back and tell me in the next half-hour. If he refused, she'd send Suze around with a care package later on and come back herself as soon as she felt better. Whenever the bail hearing was set on Monday, she'd be there.

After she left I was escorted back to the pre-fingerprint waiting area, where I'd of course lost my place. Three people movements (one hour) later, I accepted that my prediction was coming true: I really was going to be in this police station, in a holding cell, for the next seventy or more hours.

My turn arrived, my fingerprints were taken and I moved on to waiting my turn to be photographed. Waiting for lunch followed, followed by waiting for a briefing session about the identification parade (in which all participants are expected to do a lot of waiting around).

Mid-afternoon sometime I was summoned from the detention room and taken once more to the underfurnished interview room. This time it was Suze who was there. The sight of me in the doorway must have been truly pathetic because she crossed to give me a hug even faster than Theresa had.

'Jesus, Dee, how are you?'

I stuck out my arms and examined them. 'Still here.'

She scrutinised my face, as if wanting to make absolutely certain of that. Then she pointed to the table. A large Harrods carrier bag was sitting in the middle of it. 'Care parcel,' she said.

I went over and had a look. New underwear, new jeans, new T-shirt, new nightdress, two novels, one true crime, a range of magazines, the morning papers, a pack of cards, a bag of fruit, other stuff. 'Wow,' I said.

She reached in and pulled out a box I hadn't registered: Belgian chocolates. 'From Marc's special stash. He sends his best wishes, by the way. When he heard you'd been arrested he was absolutely appalled.'

'I told him being a reputable lawyer wasn't an invincible shield.'

'Well, he's certain they'll let you go.'

'Will he piss off if they don't – that's the question.'

She shook her head and sat down. 'No way. He came in eyes open. He's in for the duration.'

'What if I have to defend myself by explaining the whole set-up? Including –' I mimed pulling on a glove.

'You won't.'

'Don't ostrich. I might.'

'Okay. Well, in that case I think it would bother me more than him. He's solid. He's been to the office, met people, written a letter to the bank manager – oh, look, and I asked him about your "boyfriend".'

I'd managed to forget Greg Tuttle for however long it had been – an hour, an hour and a half? 'Yeah? And?' I asked without much enthusiasm.

'Never heard of him.'

Another Greg lie.

Obviously he'd been manipulating me. Me or us. The firm.

But what for? How did I or we figure?

How did I let myself be conned?

Suddenly I felt Suze's hand on my shoulder. She'd reached across the table. 'Dee? What is it?'

'Nothing.'

'But you're crying.'

I touched my cheek. She was right. That was it – all I needed. The tears really started.

She hurried around the table and started stroking my back. 'Is it about – about Greg?'

I sniffed and nodded. 'He's – he's not who he claims he is.'

'Who is he?' She leaned her ear closer to my mouth.

'A Serbian. A, a dealer. Here buying arms, I'm sure of it. With American currency.' It sounded ridiculous when I said it like that. Over the top and hysterical and unlikely. But I've been involved in situations before that have sounded like that.

Suze passed no judgement. 'That American accent he has sounds pretty genuine to me.'

'Maybe he's an American Serb. Serbian Americans must support the Serbs in Bosnia the way Irish Americans supported the IRA. Fund-raise. Organise supplies.'

She watched me while I wiped my eyes with my sleeve. 'Are you upset because he lied to you or because you think the Serbs are bullies?'

'Both. *And* because he used me. Ten minutes after I told him about Tim's car blowing up he said he'd been paged, made a call and rushed off. He obviously found out from me that his supplier was dead.'

She nodded and mmmm'd and then mulled this over for a good half a minute. 'What's the name of the company Greg says he works for?' she asked me finally.

'AmCo Engineering, Atlanta and London.'

'And what about that company he told you Richard sold the playground site to?'

'Etna Global Corporation, New Jersey. Can you check them out for me?'

She reached for her jacket. 'I can certainly try.'

I had my choice of position in the identification parade and chose the third spot from the left, out of nine. All of us were women between thirty and forty, full-figured, dark-haired, not too tall. The three of us who looked the most alike (i.e. like me) were asked to step forward and stand first facing left, then facing right. Despite the anxiety this loosed from its cage, though, that was it, and twenty minutes later, when we were told to relax, I didn't get the feeling I'd been positively identified by whoever the witness was.

We were told we could go at exactly 4.30 and Hamley was there, waiting, so he could personally escort me to the holding cell. The look on his face suggested the experience compared favourably with orgasm.

I've been in countless cells just like the one at that station, but only of course as a visitor. When the door shut behind me I stood at the entrance and saw it anew: the narrow camp bed, the basin sticking out of the wall, the bars on the windows, the pus-yellow walls. God, if this fit-up against me proved unstoppable, I could be in a cell like this for the next twenty years. – Then deported!

What a vision: once proud civil liberties defender ends days as bag lady on Santa Monica beach.

My care package was on the bed and I went to have a look at the books. Rifling through I realised Suze had brought me paper as well. I seized on the pad and pen, sat down on the foam mattress and, without reflecting, started, 'Dear Mom, You'll never guess what's happened.' An hour later, when they pushed the gruel they called 'tea' through my flap, I was still at it.

Twenty

Some indeterminate period of time passed – enough that I was half way through the pad – when my cell door was thrown open and Hamley strode in. The earlier equanimity was gone and so was the smile. He looked clench-jawed, the way he'd looked in the Old Bailey after he'd lost the Amin Ali case. Sniffing change is part of my job and the smell was strong around him. Apart from anything else he'd left the cell door wide open.

'You can go,' he said.

It sounds ridiculous but I had to get him to repeat it. He gestured to my bag and then to the door. 'Go.' He was not happy.

But now that I was here voluntarily, I was in no hurry. 'Why?'

'Had a confession.' He turned to leave, pointing to his sergeant as if to say to me, Talk to him about it. But he wasn't getting away with that, no sir-ee Bob, not after what he'd put me through. I hurried after him and tapped him on the shoulder. 'From who?' I demanded.

He kept moving, ignoring me. I dogged him. 'You owe me an explanation.'

That penetrated. He stopped and turned around and squinted

at me from the far-off land of Deep Anger. 'Richard Farmer – he killed himself. Left us a letter admitting Riordan's murder.'

Unlike my capture, my release is an experience I remember in minute detail. Brief as my incarceration was, my freedom still came as an exhilarating thrill. You know what they mean by its 'taste' when it happens to you – that first intake of breath outside the cell is exquisitely delicious.

I went to collect my bag and possessions at the desk where I'd checked in. Along with them came two phone messages from Greg, wishing me well and asking if he could visit. Whatever my paranoia about him, he hadn't been the one setting me up. But I crumpled the notes and threw them in the bin anyway. He was still a liar. He was still probably a Serbian and definitely a dealer for the Serbians in a war where they were the aggressors.

And what was he to me? A three-night stand that I'd enriched with the usual fantasies. I told the clerk that if Mr Tuttle rang again he shouldn't be told of my release.

'We tell the public what we tell the press, ma'am.'

'I see. Well, when will you tell the press about this?'

He glanced at the clock over the door: 7.30 p.m. 'Not before the morning now.'

I couldn't believe it: breathing space.

On the way out I found the public phone and dialled Theresa.

'Terrific!' she said after I told her the good news. 'We have to celebrate. I'd invite you round tonight, only –'

'No, no, I know you're ill. Just wanted you to know. Take care.' After cutting off, I dialled the office. Suze just might still be there.

Sure enough, she answered on the second ring. After the initial yip of excitement when I told her what had happened, she turned and repeated the news. I heard Marc say, 'Marvellous! Excellent. Didn't I tell you?'

Damn! I'd been hoping to catch her on her own. Stupid really.

Back with me again she said, 'Come out to dinner with us.'

No, I thought; she and I were going to have to resolve our differences about his offer to bankroll us before I was going to feel easy socialising with him. The prospect was too much for me at the moment, on top of everything else. I realised, in fact, that, more than anything, I wanted to go home to my little flat, see what they'd done to my floorboards, soak in my bathtub, read my mail, listen to my music and watch my TV. Celebrations could wait.

'Thanks,' I said. 'I'm pooped. How are you fixed tomorrow?'

'I can offer you breakfast, I can offer you lunch, but I'm going off on a tour of Marc's little "empire" at tea time – be gone till Sunday night.'

'Lucky you.'

'I'll say. He's taking me sailing too.'

I could hear the flutter in her voice. Suze the flinty northern realist (her own words!) who'd been known to get at *me* for romanticising life. But never mind. She and I needed to talk sooner rather than later. 'Lunch it is,' I said.

So sensitised had I become to my tabloid shadow that the moment I walked out the door of the station I could feel him watching me from across the street. But this time, instead of taking steps to avoid him, I headed straight for him.

'They've come to their senses and dropped the charges,' I said. 'Someone else's confessed.' Then I had the satisfaction of seeing it dawn on him that he'd wasted a whole week of his time. He tried to suggest otherwise, bluff that there'd be a fee for me in Now I Know What It Feels Like Says Criminal Lawyer. I knew and he knew that that was what certain of my British friends term a load of old bollocks.

I walked away feeling quintessentially free and liberated. Everything was heightened: the fullness of the trees, the glorious-ness of the windowboxes, the endearingness of red double-decker buses, the eccentricities of my fellow citizens – and the thrill of not being tailed.

Home again (home!) the first thing I did was have a good look at my floor. In fact, only four boards had been lifted and only a couple had suffered. It was better than I'd expected, better than I could have hoped.

Behind me a voice said 'Knock knock' and Grant came in. I told him my good news, which got me a hug. Then he told me how he'd stopped the police from destroying my floor by showing them his and proving nothing could be hidden under it. That got him a hug.

'David's making goulash. Can I tempt you?'

I looked around again. It might not be the wreck I'd feared but it needed attention. I begged off.

As I closed the door behind him the blinking light on the answering machine tried for my attention. Sorry, you can wait too.

I selected some all-out get-down music, turned it up good and loud, filled the watering can and boogied around the place, feeding my poor dry plants. When I finished, or after that I brewed some fresh coffee and for an unprecedented second time in a single week went through my flat tidying and sweeping and washing and throwing away. Finally I phoned out for a pizza and Coke and plonked myself in my overstuffed armchair and turned on the news. I caught the end of the national stories and stayed tuned for the 10.30 London regional bulletin.

Suddenly, item three, a picture of Janey appeared behind the baby-faced male newscaster. 'There's been a new development in the case of murdered campaigner Jane Riordan. East End property developer Richard Farmer, a business associate of the late Ms Riordan, was found dead earlier today in his Broadgate office. In a letter he left on his desk, he confessed to her killing. We go now to our crime correspondent, Atar Uddin. Atar?'

Pictures of a reporter in front of Farmer Enterprises came on. 'Atar, is there any indication yet of a motive?'

'Well, Malcolm, I've spoken to the Detective Inspector leading the investigation, but as you would expect it's up to the family to release the details. All we know is that Richard Farmer specifically vindicated Dee Street, Jane Riordan's former solicitor, whom the police apparently charged with the crime only this morning and had in custody at the time Farmer killed himself.'

'So Dee Street has been released?'

'Yes – several hours ago.'

So much for the police's control over stories.

I counted to ten slowly, the time it takes to punch a number on a phone. It was late but –. Sure enough, on eleven it started to ring. Two old friends in a row who'd not known about any of it, followed by my secretary Natasha, who promised to come by the next morning with some urgent bits and pieces, followed by my ex-boyfriend David, who I learned had been engaged, unengaged and engaged again since we'd split up.

Disengaged from now on, he said.

High with all the stimulation, I forgot when the phone rang yet again after I'd just put it down that it could be Greg. Then I made the mistake of sounding glad to hear from him. It was only when he said he wanted to come over then and there that I remembered I had no intention of seeing him again ever. I didn't do a very honourable job: just said I was tired and had a lot of sorting out to do.

An Englishman – even a Scotsman or a Welshman – would have let it go at that. Greg put on a jokey voice and said, 'That sounds like the brush-off to me.'

I didn't laugh, but was less direct than I might have been. 'Greg – please. I just need a bit of space to catch up with myself. I'll call you.'

'Wait! Why'd you leave this morning?'

'I woke up with a headache. I couldn't find any aspirin. I looked in your washbag.' I gave him a couple of seconds to realise the significance of that. 'Bye now,' I said, and hung up.

Then I turned the answering machine back on, contemplated a piece of toast (no), flicked through the channels (no), and decided the time had come to crawl under my duvet and slip away.

Just before I went to bed I phoned my mother. It was three in the afternoon in California and I got her in from the garden.

'Honey! Hi! Boy, have I been thinking about you. Are you all right?'

This time I told her the whole story. Already it sounded like a fairy-tale.

When I got into bed at 11.45 I expected I'd be out of it on contact with the pillow and remain out of it for at least eight hours. Instead I got eight minutes. Then someone down on the street started leaning on my entryphone buzzer and I was blatted back to consciousness.

Phones you can shut off. Assholes buzzing you, like burglar and car alarms, are another order of problem. I ignored it as you have to do, assuming whoever it was would get bored and go away. But it went on and on and finally, angrily, I got up and stormed out to the hall and snatched up the handset: 'If you don't stop I'll phone the police.'

'It's lies,' said a female voice enunciating too carefully. 'All of it. Lies.'

'What? *What* is lies?'

She started tapping the buzzer, chanting 'lies, lies, lies, lies' in rhythm. Finally I put on my robe and went down to the entrance gate to see who the hell it was. She was a vaguely familiar blonde, dripping wet. The long dry spell had ended: it was dumping down.

'Look,' I said as I approached her, 'it's pretty late. Who –' Then I connected her face with a setting: Richard Farmer's office. She was his secretary, the one whose sister I'd represented. I opened the gate. 'What is it?'

'Richard. It's all lies.' And with that she broke down and began to cry. I hustled her in and coaxed her up the stairs. Her unsure step and the smell of alcohol vaporising off her told me she'd chosen to grieve for her dead boss in his own style.

In the flat I got her wet coat off her, sat her on the sofa and reheated the coffee. I refused to let her talk until she'd come down a bit on the caffeine and rinsed her wrists for ten minutes under the cold tap in the kitchen sink.

'Okay,' I said when she looked ready. '*What* is lies?'

My kitchen is small, with no room even for a table. I was resting my behind against one counter and she now leaned back and rested hers against the other. 'Richard – he couldn't kill Janey Riordan. He couldn't kill himself.'

Love, clearly. Of what level and kind? 'But he left a note I understand –'

She let out a bray of scepticism. '*Typed*, they say. On the word processor! Richard didn't know how to turn it on, never mind use it.'

I stuck out a psychic foot and prodded the field between us. Eggshells: tricky. 'But he was pretty depressed, was he not?'

She nodded.

'So –?'

She looked down at her hands. She was clutching the dissolving bit of paper towel she'd used to dry her wrists. 'But he loved – he loved his wife and children. His sweet little boy –' She lifted the towel to wipe her eyes.

I pulled off another one and handed it to her.

'– And he'd never *shoot* himself.' She blew her nose.

Shot himself. This was news. 'Is that how they say he did it?'

She nodded. 'The gun – they say it killed Janey Riordan too.'

I closed my eyes and reminded myself of a few truths. I was free. I was enjoying being out of whatever I'd been dragged into or been set up for or just fallen into. I didn't need to go back.

I opened my eyes again. 'Why are you telling *me*?'

'Because someone has freed you at Richard's expense.'

I thought, If my revered boss had killed himself, would I want to come up with a reason, any reason, to deny it? I said, 'But who?'

She shook her head. 'I hoped you might find out.'

'But this is police work.'

She wrinkled her nose. 'I told them all this and they said the gun angle was right and his signature was on the letter and there were no suspicious circumstances.'

I sighed. 'Look, I sympathise, I really do, but I can't afford the time. My business is in trouble and –'

'What's your hourly rate?'

I told her.

'I'll pay you twice that.'

It was bravado. She earned a secretary's wage. Anyway, I didn't want to get into this. 'I have nothing to go on,' I said. Instantly I thought, You're lying. You know he was with Greg in Wales.

She leaned across the kitchen at me. 'There is one thing. He was worried – very worried – the past five or six weeks.'

'I'm not surprised. He had financial problems. He was catching flak from the community for selling the playground to solve them.'

She was shaking her head. 'He lived with financial problems. He was used to "flak", as you call it. This was something more. Different.'

'Like?'

She continued shaking her head. 'He didn't want to talk about it. He started drinking a lot.' She smiled quickly – she knew she was one to talk.

'You have any idea why?' I asked.

'Mmm, I think it had to do with some properties he bought off the Greater London Council – you know, just before they got rid of it.'

'Properties? Plural?'

She nodded again. 'He had to buy a parcel of about a dozen just to get hold of the one he wanted over in the City.'

It came back to me then. That's why he'd been so willing to lease the playground and nearby semi-derelict housing to Weaverstown Housing Association. It was the unwanted bit of a job lot. 'Why?'

'He had me look up the records and he realised a certain GLC councillor had been involved with all of them.'

'Which one?' I knew the answer, I just wanted to hear her say it.

'A Mrs Evie Maguire. After that her awful son came in –'

'Tim? The one whose car exploded?'

'That's him. Richard had several meetings with him.'

'Had he known him before?'

'No. And he was obviously uncomfortable with him, but he and Mrs Farmer – God, she must be a wreck! The line's been engaged all day. Anyway, they even went out to Tim Maguire's "cottage" in Wales a couple of weeks ago.' She wiped away a new eruption of tears. 'He started drinking heavily when he came back.'

I had to feel for her and my instinct was pushing at me to say I'd help her. My reason, on the other hand, was pulling at me to forget it all, get on with my life.

I waited for the battle to rage between urges. Finally I said, 'Nothing formal.'

She gave me a grateful grin. You're nuts, Dee, I thought. Nuts.

I let her use the sofa for what was left of the night. When I finally stirred myself about 8, she had gone. She'd left a card signed 'Denise' and scrawled 'Thanks' across it with her home number underneath.

I looked out of the window: the rain had become mizzle, turning the morning grey. Normality in south-east England.

More messages had gathered on the answering machine but again I ignored them and dialled Theresa.

Martin answered. 'I'm sorry, Dee,' he said, sounding not at all sorry and very short of patience indeed, 'she's very very poorly. She needs – Oh God – go back.' He put his hand over the mouthpiece. A moment later Theresa came on.

I told her about Denise and her claims.

'Come over,' she said. She sounded like she was operating on five amps. Maybe five.

'No. Look. It can wait. I just wanted you to –'

'You wanted advice. Come. Please. I could do with distraction.'

I caught a taxi to the address she gave me in Farringdon. Martin answered the door and was just barely polite to me.

'Up here Dee,' her voice called from above.

I went on past him up the stairs to the bedroom. It was a bare wood and leather, manly type of house, without any of the softness of Theresa's own place. She was tucked up under a huge maroon duvet with only her head showing. I sat down on the edge of the bed. She stuck out a hand and I clasped it. 'This looks like pretty serious flu,' I said. 'You okay?' It was a stupid question, but one you have to ask.

She shrugged. 'Surviving. You first.'

I gave her the detailed version of Denise's visit.

The moment I'd finished she said, 'You want to know what I think? I think you should hand this over to the police and concentrate on putting this whole episode – Janey Riordan, Tim Maguire, all the loose threads of it – behind you and think about the firm, the future. We waste so much time, all of us.' She sniffed and bit her lip against tears.

I brushed her hair off her forehead. 'What?' I asked her as gently as I could. I had an awful premonition of the answer.

'The baby,' she sniffed. 'I'm bleeding.'

I sighed heavily. 'Oh dear.'

'Martin's sure it's because I spent that night out.'

'Mmm, he didn't look very happy to see me. Are you having tests?'

She nodded. 'This afternoon. I may need to decide to have a – an – to decide to –'

I told her to shush then, I knew what she was saying. We just sat there a while holding hands. Eventually she dozed off.

The rain started up heavily again just as I got back to my flat: I remember because I had to run from Marylebone station. I'd gotten out of the habit of carrying an umbrella – that's how long the dry spell had lasted. The front gate was ajar, but other tenants' visitors are careless and it happens so I didn't think anything of it.

On the walk up I was preoccupied knocking the water off my jacket.

'Hi,' said a male voice in front of me. I knew it was Greg even before I looked up and saw him. If the day carried on like this I could end up applying to go back to that holding cell.

'Hi!' I got out my key and started unlocking my door.

'Can we talk?' he said. He obviously meant inside my flat.

I felt pulled two ways. No and yes. But there was no contest really. I turned my back to him and returned to the task of letting myself in. 'Not now,' I said. 'I told you on the phone –'

He took a step towards me. 'But I want to explain. It's not what you think.'

I got the door open and felt safer. I faced him again. 'Oh? You lied about being at Tim's warehouses. I know you know what he dealt in. What am I supposed to think when I find a Serbian passport and a wad of cash?'

'You could give me the benefit of the doubt and think I might be dealing in medical supplies.'

I shook my head. 'You wouldn't have hidden something that noble and humanitarian. Besides, I saw you go into the munitions stores with Richard.' I started to shut the door. 'Let me ring you next week –'

He covered the ground necessary to stick his foot in the door. 'Please. I promise you, this isn't what it seems.'

I don't like feet in my door. I glared at his until he moved it.

'Look,' he said, and he got out the Serbian ID and pointed to it. He mouthed something I didn't catch.

'What?'

He moved his lips silently again. 'Fake' he was saying.

'So who are you?' I whispered.

He shook his head; he couldn't tell me, not here.

I stared at him. Words were absolutely beyond my capabilities. Then I thought, Don't trust him. The next instant I'd closed the door on him. Leaning against it, I sighed a deep, relieved, grateful sigh. What a perfectly judged bit of psychological manoeuvring on his part. Plant a doubt – turn everything on its head – hint at conspiracy – watch Dee Street buy it.

Well not this time.

He pushed in the letter flap. 'Please,' he whispered. 'If you come with me –'

I laughed. I obviously looked younger than I felt. He thought I was born yesterday. I knelt and pushed the flap back at him. 'I want to know who you are.'

I heard him sigh. There was a pause and some fumbling noises and the next moment he pushed a plastic card through the letter flap. It was an ID issued by the US Justice Department. Greg Tuttle, Special Investigator.

Oh, that's great, I thought. Just great. I spend a dozen years earning a reputation for winning cases against the British police and I go and sleep with an American super-cop. It was a toss-up which made me feel dirtier and more used: the thought of him as a Serbian arms dealer or this.

And what if both cards were fakes?

The entryphone buzzer suddenly blatted by my ear. Startled, I fumbled to pick up the handset. Was he beating me down with plausibility so a companion could finish me off? What is the line between paranoia and sensible behaviour?

'Dee? You there? It's me, Natasha.'

Another voice said, 'And Maggie.'

'We've all come,' said Simone and Gita and Debbie.

Saved! I laughed with relief and buzzed them in. Then I took the risk of opening the door. He'd either lunge or – 'I've got visitors,' I said. 'We'll have to continue this another –'

You could already hear their voices rising as their feet came up the steps.

He said, 'Have lunch with me.' It was a plea.

I shook my head. 'Busy.'

'Tea then. Three o'clock? Look, I'll bring the guy I work with. He'll tell you.'

I agreed to meet him and his colleague at the cake shop near his office. He disappeared down the stairs just as Natasha and the others appeared. All were soaking wet because Debbie had insisted on using the umbrella to protect the biggest bunch of flowers I'd ever seen in my life.

'Have I died?' I asked as she handed them to me. They know to laugh at my jokes. I rewarded them with an offer of coffee.

Another laugh went around. Five pairs of eyes looked at me with a fondness I hadn't seen there before, or hadn't noticed. 'We were just saying that what we missed most was your coffee.' She handed me a shopping bag. I knew from the smell it was fresh ground beans. They'd picked up milk and real chocolate chip cookies as well.

They filled my small sitting room and their wet coats filled my bathroom. It was great listening to them talking and laughing as I worked in the kitchen. God, I'd actually missed our meetings.

Natasha came in. 'You not listening to your messages on purpose?'

I shook my head.

'Right,' she said, 'I'll go through them', and disappeared again. Oh, to be taken care of!

I took the tray and coffee out to the sitting room, handed it around, sat down, reached for a mug and a cookie. 'So,' I said, munching, 'what do you think about our new banker then?'

They all took deep breaths simultaneously and glanced around at each other. Then Debbie looked straight at me. 'We're all thinking about finding other jobs.'

I felt like Jerry when Tom's just pushed a concrete block off the top of a multistorey building straight on to him. I realised how little I'd been thinking about the firm, really thinking about it, the past week. I mean, I knew I had doubts about the Marc deal, but that the others would have some too . . .

They were all waiting for me to speak. 'God,' I managed. I looked at them one by one. Suze and I had been putting this team together for years one way and another. Immigration, family, tenancy, contracts, industrial tribunals, sexual and racial harassment, local authority law, judicial reviews – we had specialists in them all. And we were all equally committed – in spite of being told it was no longer necessary – to seeing that the women clients we'd gone into business to serve got the most out of the legal system.

'But if you all go – I mean, the whole idea of taking the loan was to save your jobs.'

'But it's not that simple,' Debbie said. 'We'll have to work for this Marc character.'

Maggie was nodding. 'We'd have to put in a lot of time doing joint venture contracts.' She wrinkled her nose.

'But I understood it would be fifteen per cent of the work –'

'It's grown,' she said. 'Grows every day.'

Simone said, 'And there's no guarantee to our jobs. I've seen the documents.'

I put my head in my hands. This was worse than I'd imagined.

I felt one of them leaning towards me. 'We've been talking again about going on short time.' Debbie's voice.

I looked up.

She gestured to Gita. 'We had a meeting with the tutor of the financial law class Gita's taking.'

Gita nodded. 'He said we could take pay cuts and/or could each be employees three days a week and self-employed the other two days. And/or we could even each invest a small amount.'

I looked at them. 'You'd rather go that way?'

They all nodded.

Simone said, 'We'd have come sooner, but obviously –'

'That's okay. I'm glad you told me now. I'll tell Suze how you feel –'

'Ah – actually: I think she knows.'

'She knows? But that doesn't – I mean, your jobs are the whole point.'

They shrugged, like they wouldn't be too certain about that if they were me.

'I'm seeing her for lunch,' I said, glancing at the clock. 'I'll talk to her.'

Twenty-One

After they'd gone I discovered the list of messages from my answering machine that Natasha had transcribed and left by the phone for me. The third to last one had a big star beside it.

Sufiya Khan: left her congratulations and said Sorry, has sad news. Nasima's baby died in the middle of the night. The body's in Brick Lane mosque all today, the burial's in the East London Muslim Burial Grounds late this afternoon. You'll be welcome.

I closed my eyes and saw the dim ward and the rows of incubators and the brown-skinned babies in imperfect bodies and the anxious young mothers, half – two-thirds? – unable to speak English, going through all this and feeling acute alienation. In the far corner, in a chair by herself, I could just make out the frail stick figure of Nasima.

I would try to go.

When I'm stressed out, I eat. Suze cooks. Judging by the spread she'd prepared for us – homemade minestrone with an entire deli counter of esoteric salamis and obscure Italian cheeses, fresh bread with garlic butter, pea-sized green olives in herby oil – she was extremely tense, though, as usual, she didn't seem it at all.

She sat me down and poured me a large glass of Chianti Classico, then poured one for herself. She held hers out: 'To liberty!'

I clinked it with mine. 'And to the future.' We both drank. 'Mmm. Delicious,' I said.

'Marc's favourite,' she said, pulling up a chair opposite me. 'Brings it back from Italy.'

'Where's Peter?'

'At his sister's. Not speaking to me. Try the olives.'

'Has he moved out?'

'I don't know. I don't want to know.' She picked up the dish of olives and thrust it towards me. End of subject.

I took one, but of course one meant two meant a handful. Munching them brought up memories of a sunny beach in Sardinia I'd visited maybe eight, ten years ago. Perhaps that's what I needed. I said, 'Did you manage to find out anything about those two American companies?'

'I tried.' Then she gave me an affectionate smile and leaned towards me so we were almost nose to nose. 'You can stop investigating, Dee. You're free.'

'Ha!'

I told her about the middle of the night visitation from Denise and the things she'd said about Richard's behaviour.

'Oh God, you didn't say you'd carry on?'

The sarcastic edge put me right on the defensive. 'I didn't say I wouldn't. And then Greg was at my door this morning.'

'What did he have to say for himself?'

'He showed me what he claims is his real ID. It said – you mustn't mock – it said that – ah – he's a US Justice Department agent.' I stopped and waited for the wild incredulous Aspinall whoop I was expecting.

Instead her expression composed itself into thoughtfulness. 'Mmm, yes,' she murmured, 'that would be one explanation.'

'For what?'

'For why the database whizkid I went to couldn't get a line on either of those companies. Does he expect you to take his word for it?'

'He says he has a colleague who'll vouch. In theory we're meeting for tea this afternoon. Not sure I'm up to it.'

'Not surprisingly! Make the bugger wait. I'm curious what he has to say, though, aren't you?'

I was and I wasn't. I shrugged.

She got to her feet. 'Oh. Ah. Before I forget – I've got something to give you.' She left the kitchen, heading for the bedroom, and was gone a couple of moments.

She came back carrying a file, which she set in front of me. 'The loan documents, your set,' she said. 'Plus bumph on Marc's companies. I almost stuck a copy in your care parcel yesterday.' She laughed. 'Decided it would be mean.'

I opened the file and flipped through it while she sat down again and started making herself one of her usual hyperactive person's food-mountain sandwiches. The deal looked pretty flawless on paper, no doubt about it.

As she was sawing her creation in half I closed the file and looked at her. I watched her study the half in her hand, calculating the angle it should enter her mouth. I said, 'Debbie and the others came to see me first thing.'

She pulled back from the bite she was about to take. Her good humour exited left. 'Oh Jesus, here we go.'

'Did you know they're all keeping their eyes out for other jobs?'

She dropped the sandwich back on the plate and shoved it away. 'They're exaggerating.'

'I don't think so.' I strove to keep my tone absolutely neutral. 'They said they'd be willing to work fewer hours.'

My delicacy was in vain. She threw her napkin on the table. 'Goddamn it, Dee, I've worked my arse off putting this deal together.'

One two three four five six I couldn't let myself be drawn nine ten. 'It shows. It's a terrific deal and I appreciate all the effort it's taken, especially doing it on your own, without me –'

'Exactly, and I say, if they want to leave, fuck 'em. We keep six associate positions and two partners.'

I was sceptical we'd hold positions without bodies filling them. 'But remember how long it took us to put this group of individuals together.'

She folded her arms across her chest and glowered out the window. There'd been another lull in the rain, but from the darkening sky it was gearing up to start again. There were going to be floods somewhere in the south-east tonight, you could tell.

Over her shoulder she said, 'We built one group, we can build another.' She faced me again. 'It's Debbie and Simone, isn't it? They both have this, this prejudice about "all" rich people.'

'I get the feeling it's more to do with a certain perceived patriarchal style.'

She cast her eyes towards the cosmos, as if saying to God Almighty, see? What'd I tell you about this woman. 'That's rubbish. I'm not a patriarch, you're not a partriarch, we're the partners, nothing's changing.'

'Calm down, Suze. Everybody wants us to get this right.'

'"Calm down"?' She pushed her chair back. 'Dee – Marc has done mountains of work on this. He cancelled a big selling trip to be here for me – for us – while all this's been going on. He's organised capital, he lent his credibility to our bank, he –'

'Okay, we'll compensate him. It won't be much, but –'

She stood up and went into high flail. 'He doesn't want compensation, he wants to work with us, he wants input, he wants –'

'I thought he wanted the best for Aspinall Street.'

'That's the same thing to him.'

'And that's the worry, don't you see? "To him". From his point of view.' I shut up a minute, composed myself and started again.

'Look, I'm just saying that keeping our independence might really be the most important thing here.'

She began to pace up and down in front of the dining-room window, combing her hair back with her fingers. 'I can't believe this,' she said to the cosmos she'd appealed to earlier. 'We stand to lose enough work to keep two associates busy.'

I just shook my head. She wasn't getting it. Hammering the point would be a waste of time. 'Well,' I said lightly, 'we don't need to decide this today.'

She stopped and looked at me, half disbelieving, half contemptuous. 'Put it off, put it off, that's always your solution, isn't it? If we'd found someone like Marc a year ago, when I told you we should, but oh no, oh no –'

I stood up as well. 'Suze! For God's sake. We both decided on the strategy. Why are you blaming me?'

'Because you never want to change anything. God, you're supposed to be the zippy Californian and I'm supposed to be the parochial Brit, but I swear –'

But I stopped hearing, just stood there and stared at her, studying her face, the aggressive body language. It was some stranger standing there, not my best friend, not my business partner.

Unbidden a memory came of the heightened sense of liberation I'd felt when I'd walked out of that holding cell. It had been less than twenty-four hours before. Why was I doing this to myself already? I didn't need this shit. I picked up my bag and slipped the strap over my shoulder.

'Where are you going?'

'To a funeral.' I shoved the duplicate set of loan papers back across the table at her. 'Ring me when you're prepared to be reasonable.' Then I walked past her and out the front door.

I caught the first bus heading towards the East End and sat at the front on the top deck, staring unseeingly out at the rain, thinking about me and Suze. She couldn't accept the loan from Marc without my consent. I couldn't restructure without her. We couldn't stay the same because the bank would foreclose and Aspinall Street would be wound up.

Contemplating that made my heart hurt.

Without Aspinall Street, without Suze's friendship . . . I didn't know if I could even stay in London – stay in Britain – if I lost those.

By the time I got off the bus at Aldgate East station, however, I'd decided such negativity would get me nowhere. I had to be positive. Suze had always been obstinate and prone, if truth be told, to having her head turned. I had brought her around before. I could bring her around again. She'd eventually have to see it: selling off a slice of ourselves when we didn't have to – it was stupid.

On the pavement outside the Brick Lane mosque, where on dry days old men milled around by the wall, I stopped to get out a scarf and put it on with one hand while holding up the umbrella with the other. I was nervous, in fact. I'd only been into mosques as a tourist. I had to hope it would be apparent what to do.

I approached the stairs, preparing myself for the unknown, letting other people pass me even as I took the first step. I was hesitating towards the fourth when Amin Ali came out of the door at the top and started down. He was moving fast, almost running, and his attention was fixed on where he was going. I wouldn't have intruded but my need for advice at that moment was greater than my sense of propriety.

'Amin!' I said as he drew closer.

He didn't respond and I was about to say his name again louder as he passed me; then I noticed his snazzy, un-Amin-ish suit and remembered mistaking someone else (this guy?) for Amin near the samosa shop a few days before. I shut up and carried on up the steps and a moment later I was glad, for just as I reached the landing and paused for a break in the outcoming traffic of visitors and worshippers (mostly male, mostly of a distinguished age) so I could slip in, I saw Amin again – only this time it really was him.

He too was moving fast, but spotted me before he hit stride and stopped. 'Dee. Good see you,' he said in his careful way.

'I'm sorry about –' and I gestured inside.

He tried to smile. 'Thank you.'

'Is Nasima here?'

He shook his head. 'Coming later.'

'How about Sufiya?'

He pointed down the road. 'Big emergency. Playground. Dr Sufiya, everyone –' He motioned for me to come, follow him. I accepted the invitation.

The hugeness of the crowd milling in front of the hoarding was obvious from a couple of blocks away: all those umbrellas. It reminded me of Pavarotti in the rain at Hyde Park, wet Wimbledons, the last big miners' strike. You're serious in this country if you defy a downpour.

Close up most of the umbrella carriers turned out to be female and Bangladeshi and I recognised many faces from earlier demonstrations. Down in front, trying to whack the padlock off the gate with a hammer, was a clutch of men. Amin was hailed by a group of friends and, after checking that I didn't mind, went off to join them.

I was struck by the smell in the air and stopped to sniff. Was it –? I moved closer and sniffed some more. Yes, it was a thinned-out version of *the* smell from the warehouse in Cwmbran.

Sufiya materialised at my side. 'Awful, isn't it?'

'Hi! I'll say. What is it?'

'Here. I'll show you.' She steered me away from the crowd and along the perimeter hoarding towards the back of the site. The smell began to get stronger and stronger until finally I'd had enough and stopped. She stopped as well and pointed to some oily-looking stuff foaming out of the gap between the bottom of the corrugated-iron fencing and the ground. It had flowed across the pavement and was making a small pond in the street.

The smell was making my eyes sting and as I backed away to escape it I began to sneeze. Theresa, I thought. Theresa, flu, bleeding.

Theresa, pregnancy.

Miscarriages, infant deformities.

Jesus, Jesus.

Sufiya waited while I reached for language, formulated a sentence. 'This is it, isn't it?' I finally managed. 'The cause of the miscarriages and the birth defects?'

'That's a conclusion I'm not allowed to jump to. The British National Party could have dumped it here last night.'

'Come on. Tim Maguire was excavating it. It –'

But just then a cheer went up from behind us and we both looked around. The umbrella-covered crowd mass began to heave.

She said, 'The padlock.'

We hurried back to see.

The crowd was nearly through the open gate when we joined it and I followed her as she set about weaving through the crush of people. We ended up right at the edge of the large hole where the playground used to be. This was awash with the same oily foaming stuff that was leaking out of the back.

Maybe Richard Farmer really had killed himself. If he knew what was going on – Or worse, if he was responsible.

I started to say as much to Sufiya, then realised she was no longer beside me. I looked around. She was back by the gate, talking to a guy with a neat moustache and rubber boots who was in the process of pulling on a protective overall. I remembered the moustache from that day in the primary school: the environmental health officer.

He opened his case and retrieved a small megaphone and began to ask people to leave, please, because this could be a toxic chemical and they could be endangering their health. When maybe only perhaps a tenth of them responded, Sufiya took it from him and spoke urgently in Sylheti. That did it. People started to shift.

I got involved in keeping everyone calm and directing them to the pavement and in closing off the site. Many of the women were demanding to know what it all meant, so Sufiya ended up on the outside of the gate explaining the possible medical implications.

I stayed inside and trailed around after the environmental health officer while he took samples and recovered bits of broken barrels – broken blue barrels, very like the ones in the warehouse where Theresa'd been trapped. He didn't mind me doing this so long as I wore a mask like his and didn't ask him to talk, and one way and another Greg and tea went from my consciousness.

When he finally locked his sample box and headed out of the site, I ran ahead and waited at the gate. He pushed up his mask as he approached me.

'Definitely toxic?' I said.

'Oh, aye, it's that all right.'

I pushed the gate open for him. Everyone had gone. Sufiya had obviously persuaded them they'd be safer elsewhere. 'Been buried here a while you think?'

He nodded. 'I'd say so.' He headed for his van.

I followed. 'Any way to tell how long?'

'Not from the waste material itself. From the corrosion on the containers – maybe.' He got in the driver's side and set his sample case on the passenger seat.

I knocked on his window so he'd roll it down. When he had, I said, 'Just a ball-park figure?'

'Until I've completed the tests, I shouldn't –'

'Please. I won't tell anyone. Three people have died for whatever this stuff is.'

He sighed. 'Ten years at least, I'd say.'

I watched him drive away. My ears felt hot and a marching band seemed to have taken up residence in my gut. Ten years ago: when the Greater London Council still owned the site; when there were still crumbling houses here, too far gone even to squat.

– When Evie Maguire was the housing committee deputy in charge of derelict property.

Twenty-Two

The old squat, so alive with yesteryear eight days ago, looked abandoned now, right down to its open front door banging in the breeze. Standing there staring at it from the pavement, it was almost as if I'd imagined my whole previous visit here after the inquest. Then a large tea-chest with legs – Tony's? The jeans made me think so – appeared in the doorway. It wobbled out, kicked the door shut behind it and felt its way with its feet to the steps, which it then took precariously. I got there in time to open the gate and caught a flash of grey beard: definitely Tony.

'Oh – Dee! Thanks.' He hurried along the pavement as if by speeding he would reduce the weight of his load. (Do we get more or less wet if we run through rain?) The art installation he called his van was parked around the corner and I went ahead of him again and opened the rear doors. It was so full of stuff you'd swear this extra chest would never fit.

I stood back and watched him struggle with it until eventually he made it fit. He shut the doors and, leaning against them, wiped his brow. 'Whew. You happened along at the right time.' Then he peered at me. 'Thought they'd nicked you.'

'There wasn't a jail in all the west that could hold her,' I said in my 1940s American radio serial voice. 'You look like you could do with a nice cuppa.'

'New place is the closest.' He gestured towards the passenger side door. Then he commanded himself forward with a silly military-band drum-major gesture: a man running on his reserve tank.

They'd moved a mere two blocks away, to a flat in the bottom half of a house in a mid-Victorian terrace identical to the one they'd left. Or identical except for the substantial sum the local council had spent making it habitable.

When I'd first come to London, the local councils did this for thousands of tenants a year. Nowadays getting one put you in the same category as winners of the Reader's Digest prize draw.

'Wow,' I said, staring at it out the van window. 'How'd you get this?'

'Janey. Twisted the arm of some council bloke.'

I remembered Anwar Miah in his narrow cubicle office, saw him squirming as he took in the fact that I knew Janey'd blackmailed him over their old affair. Clearly he hadn't told me everything Janey had demanded for the return of his letters. It was a nice touch.

Tony held the low gate open for me, then hurried ahead to the front door of the flat. He gave me the big grin of a man truly pleased with himself, then thrust the door open. The smell of fresh paint, faint outside, was stronger in the corridor, which was full of unpacked boxes.

As I followed him in I heard grizzling and a moment later Melanie appeared in the first doorway off the hall, baby in her arms. She looked sickeningly like the ads say new mothers are supposed to look, pink and happy, hair loosely tied back, long pinafore dress trailing. My recent ambivalence about having kids fell away and for a moment I was aware of my clock (*only a few years left – better hurry up*). Then I thought, *But you've just seen off yet another prospective father*. I bent over for a closer look at the baby – a boy, born the day after my visit a week ago – and started chucking him under the chin and examining his fingers. Tony continued past us and into the next doorway.

Melanie said, 'You must be relieved, eh?'

I laughed. 'Absolutely. All they need to do now is charge the *right* person.'

'But I thought – didn't that developer guy leave a letter saying he did it?'

'His secretary says the confession's bullshit, a fake. Janey's killer strikes again, basically.'

'Christ, come *in*.' She led me into the sitting-room-in-progress, where she'd established residency, I could see, in the one real chair. I was drawing up a packing crate when Tony rejoined us bearing three mugs of tea, a packet of biscuits tucked under his arm. I relieved him of it and a mug and parked myself on top of my crate. He dragged another one over to the spot on the other side of Melanie and swapped her a tea for the baby.

I said, 'I'm hoping you'll tell me what you didn't feel able to tell me last week – about what Janey found in your archives.'

Melanie gave a couple of quick nods at me like she quite agreed and swivelled her head around to Tony. He ducked not quite out of my sight-line and gave her a dark look that I read as Keep your mouth shut. She gripped his arm and bowed her head so that it was resting on his biceps and I heard her whisper something to him which, from the tone and brevity, sounded like an urging. He murmured something back impatiently: *No.*

I said, 'Look, I'll guess and you can tell me if I'm right.' I didn't wait for an answer, just paused for half a second so no one could say I hadn't, then ploughed on. 'Janey Riordan came to you because she found out the playground she'd run under licence for the past seven years, and had been busting a gut to develop, was sitting on contaminated land. She probably learned this straight from the owner, Richard Farmer, who I suspect hadn't known about it that long himself. He seems to have decided to pretend he'd sold it to some mythical American corporation so he could get it cleaned up. His mental and emotional state can be judged by the fact that he honestly seemed to believe Janey'd accept his story and go quietly. When the campaign against him built up so fast, he arranged to meet her and told her the secret. I saw them get together.' I stopped there and looked expectantly from one of them to the other.

Tony'd begun to jiggle the baby. He said, 'I don't want to get involved.'

'Tony – honey – come on –' Melanie started.

I said, 'You are involved. You helped her.'

'I let her help herself.'

It was a cheap shot but I gestured to the baby. 'Yes, and she realised all those Bangladeshi babies on the special care ward with birth defects – including the one whose funeral is about to start in an hour or so – she realised those babies were deformed and that spontaneous abortions were so high in that neighbourhood *because of* what was buried under the playground. I've just seen that stuff in the daylight and, believe me, it even looks malignant.'

The baby suddenly cried out – in his agitation at what I'd been saying Tony'd overjiggled it. He handed it back to Melanie, got to his feet and headed out the door without so much as a glance at me.

'Oops,' I said. 'Was I too fierce for him?'

'Don't worry,' Melanie said, 'give him a few minutes.' She unbuttoned the top of her dress, released a breast, shifted the baby into position and began to nurse. There was an endearing awkwardness to the routine, motherhood with an L-plate.

Moments later, Tony came back through the door and sat down beside Melanie and the baby.

'You okay?' she asked him.

'Fine. I'm fine.' He looked around her at me. 'I'm telling you and no one else. If it comes back I'll know where it came from.'

I nodded.

'Okay – well, you're right. This guy Farmer told her what was really going on – said his company would go under if a contaminated land scandal hit it. Janey didn't need it underlined. She could see that if she blew the whistle on the situation there and then, the local people, her tenants, would be the losers. There'd be investigations and court cases and years would drag by and the stuff would still be there and people would still be living near it, even if not playing on it. His idea was to close it on the pretext of a sale – stop people using it – clean it up, present the evidence to the authorities, then go public.'

'Attract the kudos instead of the blame.'

'Exactly. Turn things around. And *do* something *now*. He asked her to help and she couldn't say no. She agreed to subvert the locals' campaign – divert it away from him and that site and redirect it on to the council and the issue of an alternate site. That would get the demonstrators away from the contamination and buy him time to get it excavated and removed.'

'But wouldn't it also make it easier for whoever put the stuff there to get off scot free?'

'That was Janey's worry,' Tony said. 'But Farmer wasn't interested. They didn't have the resources to go hunting a needle in a haystack, he said. Leave it to the bureaucrats later, after they'd gone public. She said, But surely, as he'd bought it from the Greater London Council, there'd be records. He said he'd looked – it was the first thing he'd done. There wasn't a hint or a clue in them. He was so insistent she stay away from the whole issue that she told him she would.'

I said, 'And beetled right over to your GLC archives.'

He nodded. 'And within an hour or so found out Tim Maguire had held the licence on the terrace of houses that used to be there. They'd been totally uninhabitable, scheduled for demolition, in such bad nick that even squatters weren't interested. The basements would have been perfect places for illegal dumping.'

'Incredible,' I said; I could easily imagine how shocked she must have felt. I was shocked and I didn't have the personal involvement she had with the Maguire family.

Tony said, 'The irony's what really got her, you know? Here was this Richard Farmer guy using Tim Maguire now to remove waste Tim had dumped there himself fifteen years or whatever earlier.'

'She supposed Richard didn't know this?'

He nodded. His expression said 'unfortunately'. 'She decided to see if Tim held any more licences –'

'I found her list,' I said. 'He had dozens, didn't he?'

'Oh, at least.'

Melanie looked up from the baby. 'And all thanks to his mum – that's what really really got her. We were in the archives bedroom at the old place and she sat on the bed and put her hands over her face and started bawling her eyes out. God, I felt so sorry for her.'

'It was something else,' Tony said, 'seeing the penny finally drop with her about Evie. How many years had people been trying to tell her?' He shook his head.

Melanie said, 'I started to worry she wasn't going to be able to stop, you know? It was like – like – heartbreak. But eventually she began to calm down and we left her on her own for a bit. I was worried she hadn't eaten, so I made her some lunch –'

'And when I took it in to her,' Tony said, 'she was sitting there, dry-eyed, a look on her face like she'd snorted four lines of grade-A coke. "Tim Maguire," she says to me, "doesn't have the wit to set up this kind of scam. There's someone else behind this. And his mother's going to tell me who it is."'

'Wow,' I said, 'she went and confronted Evie?'

He nodded. 'Evie denied nepotism. Any contracts Tim had, she said, he'd won on his own merits. The rest of it was fantasy. She didn't want to hear it.'

'So Tim was deceiving his mother too?'

'So she implied. Janey wasn't entirely convinced. Anyway, she started "monitoring" Tim Maguire's movements, as she put it.'

'With what intention?'

'Finding out how he meant to get rid of what he excavated from the playground.'

'Good. Yes. That's what she must have been doing when she phoned me from south Wales.'

'She went there – definitely.'

'Terrific. Did you see her again?'

'Once.' He reached into his shirt pocket and pulled out a photo and handed it to me. 'She left this with us.'

It was a picture of a container ship at a dock, taken from far enough away to show the whole vessel plus the dockside at either end of it plus a bit of the surrounding portscape. The figures in it were specks. The name of it was too small to make out.

Tony tapped the name area. 'She tried having it enlarged but it didn't work.'

'So she didn't take this picture?'

'No.'

Without looking up from the baby, Melanie said, 'I think she broke into that guy Tim's office and stole it. I could be wrong, but that's the feeling I got.'

Tony said, 'Her theory was that Tim was going to export the barrels and contaminated soil he'd excavated from the playground on this container ship.'

'Export it? Really? I'd have thought incineration was easier. Isn't there a big toxic incinerator somewhere in south Wales?'

'She went there,' Melanie said. 'They said they didn't do business with Tim Maguire. He wasn't licensed to carry toxic waste.'

'I see.' I looked at the photo of the container ship again. 'Had she identified the port?'

He shook his head. 'She reckoned it was probably Cardiff, though.'

That was two big pieces of information they'd given me. To have tried for more would have been greedy. I gathered my bag and my jacket and stood up. 'Thanks. You've been a great help.' Then I stroked the baby's cheek again and left.

Ten minutes later I was in a phone booth in the tube station, writing down the number the computer voice of directory inquiries was reciting to me. When I had it I took a moment to attempt to assemble my thoughts, then dialled. On the sixth ring Evie picked up and said 'Hello' and enunciated her phone number in her hammy overdone way.

'Evie,' I said, 'hi. It's Dee Street. Look, I –'

'You,' she said, as if I were a trail of slug mucus. 'Stop interfering. You've made enough trouble.' Then she hung up.

I redialled and got a busy signal. Well, I thought, I know she's home. I could go there and try to waylay her – ask her what Janey said to her about nepotism and what she said back and who does she think shot Janey and who does she believe blew Tim up. Then, if it seemed appropriate, I'd ask her straight about her own role in the burial of that waste.

It was unimaginable that a woman who'd devoted thirty years to the cause of low-rent public housing would knowingly allow such a thing to happen, no matter how loathsome an empire-builder some people found her. And she'd had two children herself – surely she wouldn't countenance death and damage to babies?

Or was that naïve? Was I just clinging to old idealism about sisterhood when I knew there was increasing evidence that power was an equal-opportunities corrupter?

– Probably. –

We would have to see.

I headed for the tube.

Thirty minutes later I emerged at Putney Bridge station and found my way to the mansion block where Evie Maguire lived. I stood on the pavement opposite and looked up. It was mid-afternoon and the mid-May sky was that luminous waterlogged grey unique to the

British Isles. No lights were on in any of the windows I thought were hers, but no lights were on in any windows. I pressed her bell and waited. No reply. I tried again – waited again.

Definitely not answering.

Deviousness had worked the last time so I gave it another try. I buzzed the same neighbour and said I was visiting and couldn't find my front door key. It worked again.

I climbed the two flights slowly, using the time to psyche myself up for a confrontation. If she threatened me with the police the way she had the last time, I'd stand my ground, call her bluff, tell her in my loudest, most authoritarian voice why I'd come – embarrass her into talking to me. What else could I do?

I arrived at her door. I'd forgotten there was a spyhole. She'd be able to see it was me, pretend not to be there. I stood to one side, stretched out my arm and tapped with my index finger knuckle. Then I ducked back and put my ear close to the door and listened for creaking floorboards: silence.

I darted back and then crouched and listened. More silence.

Okay. Two could play at this. I'd wait.

I sat down on the bottom step of the flight leading to the next floor and fished the novel I was reading out of my bag.

Ten pages later a woman came down the stairs behind me and, as I moved to let her pass, asked who I was waiting for. I said Evie.

'Away,' she said. 'Left, oh, half an hour ago.'

Phooey: right after I'd phoned her. 'I'll wait,' I said, prepared to dig in overnight if I had to.

She held up some keys. 'You could be here a while. She said she'd be gone indefinitely.'

I wanted to interpret Evie's flight as an incriminating act – an admission of guilt – but of what order? There was no way to know. Agitated, frustrated, I headed back to the tube at a fast pace, burning with emotional turbulence. I would go to Paddington station and get on the next train to south Wales. I would quickly revisit Tim Maguire's warehouse complex, just in case people were there clearing it out. If no one was there or no one would tell me, I'd continue west and visit the ports one by one, starting with the four most likely: Newport, Cardiff, Port Talbot and Swansea.

I'd identify the ship in the photograph, I'd trace the owner, I'd trace links to South Wales Demolition and Tim Maguire, I'd take my own pictures with Theresa's camera, which was still in my bag. When the environmental health officer identified the chemicals that had been taken away, I'd get hold of all the research on all the side effects of all of them. I'd assemble the best possible case for the women who'd miscarried or had infants born with defects, so they could sue the person or people who'd poisoned their lives.

I was starting to draft the legal aid application in my mind when I got to the station and saw the time: 8.15. The last train would have left by now. I checked the ticket office: yes, it was too late. I'd have to wait until morning. The first train stopping near Cwmbran left at 7.30 a.m.

I caught a taxi and had it take me home via my local take-away, where I stocked up on a tikka and a vegetable curry. While I was dragging myself up the last flight to my landing I thought I could hear the indistinct voice of someone talking to my machine. Curiosity made me hurry.

Sufiya.

I got my key in the lock, my door open. She was saying '– as late as midnight or first thing tomor–'

I picked up and said, 'Hi! I was just thinking about you.'

She laughed. 'Oh?'

'I thought, She'll want to know, can her patients sue for damages?'

'You're right, I do.' She laughed again. 'But I decided to wait until after I'd had the test results from the environmental health lab.'

'What changed your mind?'

'Nothing. I'm ringing about something else. Nasima.'

'How is she? How was the funeral?'

'As you'd expect. We're just leaving. She wants to stop in and see you on the way to her parents' place.'

'Really? Why's that?'

'It's to do with her brother's trial.'

'God, what–'

'She wants to tell you herself.'

'If he did murder that cop, I don't want to know.'

She laughed once more.

'I'm serious,' I said.

'That's not it. Half an hour, okay? We won't stay long.'

Not entirely reassured, I returned the phone to its cradle and spent a couple of futile moments gnawing my thumbnail. Then I saw there were several more messages and decided to mend my ways and listen to them. The first was from Debbie, wanting to know how the meeting with Suze had gone. The second was from Greg, saying he'd wait another hour and really hoped I'd come. The third was from Greg ninety minutes later telling me I must give him a chance to explain.

I switched it off in the middle. I wanted to know his side of the story, of course, but the bastard had used me. I could wait to hear it. In fact if I *never* heard it I'd survive.

I rang Debbie back, even though it was now the middle of Saturday evening, and told her about the argument Suze and I had had about the loan from Marc and the attached strings. She promised to talk to each of the others and organise a meeting for first thing Monday morning. 'We all want to keep Aspinall Street going,' she said. 'We'll sort it out.'

I said 'Mmm', as if I was sure we would. Inside I wished I could feel as confident.

Nasima didn't want to come in, she wanted to walk. She and Sufiya both had on black saris and headscarves but on Nasima the absence of colour evoked the eternal void of loss. Her focus was distant, as if she really just didn't know what was happening to her.

As the three of us headed up Lisson Grove towards Bell Street, I said to her, 'I'm sorry about the baby.'

She shrugged and gave me a half-smile of thanks. Then she spoke quickly in Sylheti, her tone of voice sounding old and wise as she told Sufiya what to say to me.

It was simply this: when people were assembling at the cemetery for the funeral, Nasima had been looking for Amin and thought she saw him coming out of the men's toilet. When she went to talk to him, she found the man wasn't her brother.

'I've seen the same guy!' I said. '*Twice*. He even fooled Nasima, did he? That makes me feel better.'

'He's a cousin apparently – came here when he was small. She'd heard he lived in Bradford and never looked him up because she never liked him. Turns out he's been in London since last year.'

Pieces were stirring in my backbrain. I stopped walking and looked at Nasima. 'Are you saying what I think you're saying? This other Amin – you think *he* killed that policeman?'

Nasima shrugged, then she nodded, then she shook her head.

I turned to Sufiya for an interpretation.

'It could be,' she said. 'That's the point: it could be.'

'The police still falsified notes to set Amin up,' I said.

Nasima nodded. Sufiya nodded.

'But it's quite possible they didn't pluck him at random from the crowd, the way it seemed,' Sufiya said. 'The eyewitnesses – their evidence may have been the truth. They saw the cousin strike the policeman who died. He looked like our Amin. They saw our Amin and mixed them up.'

Wow, I thought. I'd pretty well decided that Hamley hadn't set me up for Janey's murder. If he hadn't set Amin Ali up either –

– If I'd been as wrong about him as he'd been about me –

I, Dee Street, was going to have to eat crow.

'Do you want me to tell Hamley?' I asked Nasima.

She nodded. 'Arrest,' she said to me in English.

'Okay,' I said, trying to sound light and upbeat and as if I ate crow at least once a week. 'I'll talk to him on Monday.'

Such was my eagerness the next morning that I arrived at Paddington in time to walk on to the first train to Swansea. What I didn't get a chance to do was read the schedule. It turned out to be the milk run: three and a half hours to Newport.

It gave me plenty of leisure to review my plans, as a result of which, when we finally chugged into Newport station, I stashed my bag in a locker and hired a taxi to take me to the docks. There I scanned the scene for the container ship in the picture Janey'd left at Tony and Melanie's. It was easy: there was nothing that size.

The driver agreed to take me to Cwmbran and a short time later the tops of the warehouses came into view in the distance. We passed the lay-by where Theresa had tucked her car and I turned around to look at the car parked there now: something familiar? No – just another newish dark green sedan. We passed the garage and shop: no lorries parked in the lot this time.

I spotted the entrance gate to the South Wales Demolition and Haulage complex ahead and pointed. The driver spotted it too and slowed, preparing to cross the road and pull up in front of the gate. It looked shut up tight but you never knew.

We crossed and pulled up. The padlock was on. Damn.

The plain old stubborn need to double-check the message of my eyes made me ask the driver to wait while I slid out of the taxi and walked up to the padlock to give it a tug. I noticed the bit of wire sticking out of it just as I was reaching for it.

Greg. Of course – that dark green car in the lay-by was his.

I grabbed hold and yanked. It slipped apart.

The driver had no desire to know what I was doing, nor any to sit there while I did it. He said he'd wait for me up at the garage, but he insisted I pay him for the journey so far. I saw him drive off, certain he was heading for the horizon.

I turned back to the gate. It might not be Greg in there, or it might be Greg but undercover. Until I knew I'd keep myself to myself.

I went through the entrance, propped the padlock back together behind me and hurried up the small incline, wishing Theresa were with me like last time (to lead!). I felt exposed on the drive, and was glad when I finally reached the shadows of the long building that faced the road. I stayed with them until I rounded the corner to the back.

And there I was faced with my prime worst-case scenario. There wasn't a lorry anywhere and all the warehouse doors – every single one – were rolled up. The place was deserted.

I had come too late.

This fact released a worry I'd been doing my best to suppress: that I would fail to stop the export of the toxic stuff excavated from Hodder Street playground. That the ship's owner and users would get away before I identified and traced them.

Had Greg, in whatever guise, gone with it?

If so, why was the lock propped open with a wire? Why was his car parked on the road?

I decided to do a quick check of the warehouses and, keeping to the shadows, shuffled silently to the nearest. It was dark inside but its emptiness was beyond doubt. I crossed the exposed pavement to the next, which was the same, and the next, and the next. The absence of even a hint of another person, never mind containers or lorries, led me to the provisional conclusion that my fantasy about Greg being here had been just that, fantasy.

I peeked into what must have been my fifth warehouse. The smell hit me at once, fainter than when Theresa had been locked in here, much fainter than the oily gurgling stuff in the hole at the playground, but recognisable none the less. I stood in the doorway and stared into the darkness. The least I could do was find a bit of corroded barrel to take to the environmental health officer who was testing the pieces from the playground. A match would prove –

Then I heard the moaning. God – where was it coming from? I stepped further in, one step, another step, and listened.

Silence.

Had I imagined it? I took another step. No. There it was again, ahead of me. (Greg?)

The acoustics in the place were weird, and my sense of direction hadn't really advanced since I was a Brownie Scout. I decided to walk around following the inside of the walls and, doing it that way, was practically next to the sound when it came again.

It was the darkest part of the warehouse and I had to feel my way with my feet. Four or five paces later I touched something soft with my toe and knelt to feel with my hands. It was a man and he was in foetal position. I found his face and when my fingers recognised the dimple in the chin, I knew: Greg.

I felt for his pulse. My first aid skills harked back to the same scouting era, but yes, there was one. But his hand felt sticky in a way that made me uncomfortable. I put my ear to the general vicinity of his mouth. He was breathing but it was shallow. 'Greg,' I said in a loud whisper. 'Greg.'

He rolled his head and moaned again but didn't open his eyes.

A moment later I was back on my feet and heading towards the door. A sudden thought made me stop and turn around, go back and fish in his pockets, or at least the ones on top, that I could get to. In the second one I found a set of car keys.

I moved so fast after that that I was half-way down the drive, heading towards the gate, before I caught up with myself. I looked for my taxi in the parking area outside the shop but couldn't see it as I rushed inside. I had my story all prepared – an explanation for how I happened to be needing to get a second friend to hospital from this unlikely spot – but the woman at the counter looked through me as if she'd never seen me before in her life. I cancelled the explanation. 'Help!' I said. 'There's a man unconscious up in one of the warehouses.' I glanced down at the hand I'd touched him with and saw the red traces. 'He's bleeding.'

She immediately came out of herself and took over. First she phoned the ambulance and, that sorted, pointed at the door. 'Go and stay with him. Here –' She went into the back room and came out with a couple of blankets.

I took them and ran all the way back.

The next five minutes were long and slow and full of worry about Greg's hand, which I rubbed between my own but couldn't get to warm up. When the ambulance finally arrived, though, I'd worked out what I needed to do next. I directed them to him and waited until they'd confirmed that he was alive – which, thank God, he was, if only just – then said to the medic in charge, 'I need to get something from the car. It's back at the lay-by. Can you pick me up there?'

He said that would be fine.

I unlocked the passenger door and bent to look in. Neat. Tidy. Coffee cup in the rack by the radio, couple of music tapes, pack of gum, road atlas. I opened the glove compartment: a woman's cosmetic bag.

Either he was a transvestite or these things were another woman's. Like – his wife's.

I slammed the door (cheating lying bastard) and went around to unlock the trunk. Also neat. Fishing rod. Waxed jacket. Wellington boots. Thermos. I felt in the jacket, looked in the rod case and the bait kit and the boots and the thermos. I checked the spare-tire hold, the jack, the window cleaner and rags. Nothing.

There was a plastic ground sheet stuffed into the recess behind the fishing gear. I pulled it out, shook it, opened it up. More nothing.

I was about to put everything back when I bent down and peered into the recess between the trunk and the back window of the car. Was that something black back there, or just lining? I had to use the fishing rod case to reach in and prod. Yes: something.

I manoeuvred it out. It was a small black sports bag, heavier than it looked.

Jackpot?

The ambulance was coming down the drive. I undid the zipper: wallet of photos, Walkman recorder and cassette tapes, a folded-up US Justice Department report entitled 'Organised crime and the international toxic waste trade'.

Definitely jackpot.

I stuffed my own smaller purse into the black sports bag, hoicked it over my shoulder, shut the trunk, relocked the car and was ready when the ambulance rounded the corner and stopped to pick me up.

Twenty-Three

When we arrived at the accident and emergency entrance of the hospital, we pulled into the spot right next to a waiting police car and as I stepped out of the back of the ambulance after the stretcher two plain-clothes detectives appeared at my side, eager to talk to me.

They had to wait – what choice did they have? – while I saw Greg through admissions and followed the stretcher as far as the emergency room door. Then they had to wait some more while I got some sweet black coffee down me in the canteen. I'd decided to fall back on old reliable, the nearly truth, and managed, despite how rattled I was feeling, to enhance the illusion by couching my co-operation in a deal: I'd tell them everything I knew if they promised not to leak any of it to the tabloid press.

The senior of the two put his hand on his heart and said yes, absolutely.

So I told them my mostly truth: I'd been a suspect in a murder case in London and an American engineer friend – the man I'd found unconscious in the warehouse – had become overly concerned to help me; his investigations had led him here, where I'd been led myself earlier, before the whole thing had been solved;

he'd phoned and said I must meet him, I'd agreed, I'd come, and I'd found him there.

I gave them Hamley's name as a reference, I told them Greg had a son who must be worrying where his father was, I gave them the phone numbers they needed.

The junior of the pair went off to call. The senior got me to repeat certain parts of the story and this time took notes.

Five minutes later the junior one came back. Greg's son, Bill, was heading for London Airport even as we spoke. He was glad to hear I was with his dad and hoped I'd be here when he arrived.

'Yeah,' I said, 'of course.' At the same time, though, I was thinking, How long could I stay here? I had to know how Greg was, but all the evidence was on its way to mysterious dockside x, if it hadn't already been loaded on to unknown container ship y. Could I let it get away?

Then I wondered: had Greg solved x and y?

His bag: I had to examine the stuff in his bag.

The police finished their questions and the junior one saw me back to the accident and emergency waiting area. As soon as he'd left I hurried into the ladies' room, picked a cubicle, locked the door behind me, sat down on the toilet, propped the heavy bag on my lap and reopened it. I lifted out the wallet of photos on top and slid the pile into my hand. The first four were pictures of the South Wales Demolition complex as I'd seen it the first time – full of lorries and containers and activity. The next three were shots of a couple of the lorries at a dockside, in front of a container ship that looked like the one in the picture Tony'd shown me – the picture Janey'd left with him.

I remembered the roll of film I'd found in her flat, the one Greg's friend and Greg had gone to develop, the one Greg told me didn't have any exposures on it. Something I hadn't thought about before took on new significance: Greg had gone out to buy the Sunday papers. Had he bought another film and swapped it for the real one?

What a stinking rotten bastard of a bastard.

Had his *whole* come-on to me been about him getting access to what I knew? If it had – (Grrrr.)

I forced my attention back to the pictures. The next was the same ship face on, no lorries anywhere. Hmm, maybe Janey'd been getting into ship aesthetics. I flipped to the next: same picture, telephoto lens. This time I could read the name of the ship.

The *Sharon B*.

The ladies' room door burst open, banging back against the wall, and a woman's voice said, 'Dee Street? Is there a Dee Street in here?'

I was so off in my thoughts that the noisy summons made me start physically. The jerk of my knees disturbed the balance of the sports bag, which before I could stop it rolled off my lap and fell to the floor, dumping stuff on its way.

I cursed. 'Here.' I swept a handful of stuff back in the bag, then realised I had my priorities wrong. I reached over it, unlocked the door, stepped across it and went out.

The nurse, obviously only hovering there mid-flight, said, 'Mr Tuttle is in surgery. He'll be taken to the private wing post-op. If you'd like to wait there.'

'What's the surgery?'

'Removing the bullet.' She pointed to the double doors at the end of the corridor. 'It's through there.' Then she was gone.

He'd been shot.

That made one shooting, one car bomb, one faked suicide (by gun) and now another shooting. I thought of the title of the report in Greg's bag; 'organised crime' could well be involved here.

I turned back to the cubicle and knelt in front of the toilet to repack the sports bag. Automatically I opted for pulling everything out and, that done, glanced into the bag. That's when I noticed the zipper running around the edge of the bottom. There'd been a false bottom in his wash bag – maybe he had favourite tricks? I reached in and unzipped it. Underneath the false bottom, packed into stiffener, was a small handgun.

– Fat lot of good that had done him.

I zipped it back in, put the wallet of photos on top, then reached for the folded US Justice Department report. Here was bound to be information on what Greg was working on. But the type was small and my focus on it unsteady. No. This wasn't the moment for reading it.

I retrieved the Walkman, earphones and tape cassette from under the toilet. The cassette was unlabelled, so I opened the Walkman; inside was a tape with a 'D' on the tag. The Walkman had a dink on the top but worked when I tried it. 'D' was definitely a speech tape. Listening I could get into.

I closed the bag and got to my feet, thinking that was everything. Then I saw a pamphlet had escaped on to the floor. This month's tides tables for south Wales. I looked up today. There was a checkmark beside it: not high until early evening.

If the *Sharon B* hadn't sailed already – if it was still loading – if it was the right ship (if if if) – then there might still be time for me to find it.

The waiting area in the private wing was first class: sumptuous, hushed, underoccupied. Three of us shared it the whole time I was there, each on our own vast sofa-sized chair. I kicked off my trainers and stretched out my legs, then put the headphones on and pressed 'play'.

The burst of background noise – phones over printers over voices – says office. A voice recognisably Greg's speaks close to the microphone, which makes me decide he's wearing it. 'Hi, I have an appointment with Richard Farmer.'

'Just take a seat.' Richard's secretary, Denise.

There is a fade out, then a fade back in.

Denise says, 'Mr Tuttle? Mr Farmer will see you now.'

Footsteps. A door closes behind him. Hands slap into each other. 'Greg Tuttle. Thanks for seeing me.'

A creaky noise: they're sitting down? Richard: 'I try to meet engineers.'

Greg: 'Heh heh, the truth is I'm not an engineer. Here –'

There's a pause and then Richard says, 'US Department of Justice, eh? Well, what can I do for you?'

'I'm investigating a global racket in toxic waste disposal. Most of the waste's generated illegally in America.'

Richard laughs. It's an inappropriate, slightly hysterical sound.

Greg's surprised by it. 'You find that funny?'

'Said without irony – yes, I'm afraid I do.'

'I don't think you'll find my news too amusing. I'm sorry to have to tell you this, but you're a victim of this racket.'

'I?'

In the silence that ensues I can picture Richard's long unsmiling face. I hear what sounds like a dry throat swallowing. 'How's that?'

'Some of this waste is buried under one of your properties.'

The next pause is even longer. I fancy I can feel Richard thinking. Finally he says, 'Which one?'

Greg's tone is gentle. 'The corner of Hodder.'

Richard scrapes back his chair. 'Not the playground.'

'I'm afraid so.'

'It's under the *whole* thing?'

'Yeah.'

'Since when?'

'Probably since it was derelict houses.'

There's more scraping of chair, followed by the sound of feet pacing up and then back, up and then back. Richard mutters in the background of the recording field. I make out, 'I don't believe it' and 'Those kids!' and 'Farmer Enterprises won't survive it.'

Greg comes in again here. 'I have a plan that could help you – provided you're willing to help us –'

The recording stops there and the tape runs silently for several seconds. Then a new extract starts.

'Tim! Richard Farmer.' A distant voice says something indecipherable. This is a phone call and Richard now seems to be wearing the microphone. Obviously he'd agreed to help Greg. 'Yes – good to meet at last,' he's saying. 'Look – I have some work I'd like to throw your way. "Special". Can we meet again?'

Another fade out. A silence. Then the sounds of a bar – clinking glasses, an antique Beatles song by the Muzak Orchestra, loud conversation. 'Tim. Thanks for coming,' Richard says.

Tim: 'Good to see you again. What's the problem?'

'Got some nasty stuff buried under one of my properties.'

Tim makes sympathetic noises. 'I'm not supposed to remove that nature of material without notifying –'

'Of course. I'm willing to pay.'

'Really. It's more than my job's worth.'

'You'd be part of a construction contract. It would look like just another excavation job.'

Tim says nothing for a moment. 'I see,' he says finally. 'Well – perhaps.'

A bartender asks what they'll have and they order.

Richard says, 'I'd want you to take it far away, so no one ever finds it.'

Tim: 'No problem. Where is it?'

Richard: 'Hodder Street. Your old patch.'

Tim coughs a fake, buying-time cough. 'Used to manage a lot of places in those days. Keep-the-squatters-out kind of thing, you know.'

'You wouldn't forget this. Terrace of two-up, two-downs. Big basements.'

Tim pushes out some more fake coughing. I can imagine him squirming and wriggling.

'Goodness,' Richard says, 'have some of this.' Glass clinks, liquid's poured. The coughing stops.

'Ah.' Tim smacks his lips and sets the glass down.

Richard says in his quietest, most authoritative tone, 'There'll be no charge for this job, am I right?'

There's a pause before Tim says, 'Of course.'

The tape ended and the machine clicked off.

Well, I thought, as evidence went, it wasn't bad. This must have been what Greg was going to give me if I'd kept our tea date the afternoon before. 'D' was me. I turned the tape over and started the second side.

Footsteps hurry, almost running; they stop, there's a loud metallic scraping noise, they resume again. Richard's voice: 'Tim! Sorry I'm late.'

'For God's sake, man, close the gate! If any of those Bangla birds see us in here –'

'At midnight?'

'Hey, that damned vigil they ran was round the clock.'

The metallic scraping noise happens again, followed by a reverberating bang.

'Now I can't see a damn thing,' Richard says. There's a click. 'Ah – thanks, that's better.'

'There's the hole there – see.'

Richard: 'Right.' Both of them walk a dozen, fifteen paces and stop again. 'The smell's odd,' Richard says. 'Wonder what was in it.'

Tim: 'No point thinking about it. Out of sight, out of mind.'

'Mmm. Wait, wait, train it there again. To the left. A bit more. A bit more. There: that's a barrel, isn't it?'

'Where? I don't –. Oh, yes, I see.'

The footsteps start again and walk swiftly becomes run. When they stop again they're both panting.

'Jesus, three of them,' Richard says. If his anger is acted, it's pretty convincing. 'If someone else had found them –'

'They didn't,' Tim says. 'I'll see to them. Don't worry.'

There's another fade out, a silence, then a fade in. We're back in the hubbub of a bar, this one with country music in the background. We're also back to Greg wearing the microphone. He says, 'So, have you had a chance to check my references, Mr Maguire?'

'Tim, call me Tim. Yes – yes, I have. You understand: I didn't expect an American accent.'

Greg laughed. 'That's why they use me. Customs officials don't expect it either. So, can you get everything for me?'

'Of course, no problem.'

'Really? Quantity was the problem for my usual source.'

'Well, it's not ours.'

'Terrific! When would you deliver?'

'A week from receipt of the first payment.'

'Fan-tastic.' He slaps Tim on the back. 'My bankers want to give it direct to the supplier. You can arrange that?'

There was a muffled spluttering and a cough. 'He doesn't normally meet customers. In fact –'

'But I will be his biggest customer, won't I?'

Tim cleared his throat and must have nodded.

'And I'm going to open up the Balkan markets for him if he's sweet with me.'

Tim must have nodded again.

Greg said, 'Well, it's just polite to meet me, then, yeah?'

'Yes, but I don't think –'

'You tell him no meet, no release of funds – simple as that.'

'Right. Yes. Well. In that case.'

I clicked off and thought a moment about that last scene. Surely that was what it was all about for Greg: the sting, the set-up of Tim's supplier. I clicked back on. A city street, heavily trafficked. Two sets of footsteps, walking quickly.

Richard: 'Why have you come? I thought we weren't to meet until –'

Greg: 'It's an emergency. Tim is dead.'

One set of footsteps stop. Richard: 'Oh, what! How?'

The other set stop. Greg: 'His car blew up.'

'Jesus, they got him.'

'Yeah. And what's worse, I don't know if he set up the meeting for me. I need your help.'

'The meeting with the supplier? How can I help? I don't know him. Or her.'

'Actually, you do.'

Richard laughs. 'Come on.'

Greg: 'I'm serious.'

There the second side ended.

I leaned my head back on the sofa arm – shut my eyes – contemplated the story told by the sequence of extracts I'd listened to. Greg recruits Richard, Richard entraps Tim for him, together they manoeuvre Tim into introducing 'Gregor Kostič' to the organised crime boss who supplied him with guns and probably with medicine, art works and whatever else he could sell.

Hmm. And Janey found out.

Then what?

Despite Tim's death the meeting goes ahead? The venue is the warehouse complex? Greg takes Richard there beforehand so he can get the evidence he needs from Tim's office. Then Richard is killed. Greg goes to the meeting with the supplier anyway.

Judging by what happened to him, Greg's Serbian cover story didn't stand up at the crunch. The supplier had been tipped off or saw through it or maybe he or she just didn't like being seen by customers.

Re the 'or she' idea – consider again: Was it Evie? Why had she run away if she was innocent? Trouble was, devious a person as I thought her to be, organised crime connnections still didn't seem to me to fit. Was that a testament to my imaginative shortcomings, or to the effectiveness of her front? Or was it just common sense telling me that sixty-year-old women probably had less power in criminal hierarchies than they did in legitimate ones?

Perhaps I'd missed some clues about her.

I replayed the first side and listened to it through again; then I replayed the second. I was engrossed in note-making when the nurse came to tell me Greg's operation was over and it had been a complete success. He was still coming round – he'd need another twenty minutes or so – and he'd be weak, so I'd be able to see him, but only briefly.

The anxiety that had germinated inside me when I'd found him and had been growing in my gut even while I'd been trying not to think about it, vanished, *poof*, like that. I shook her hand and thanked her for telling me, then shook harder and thanked her again. When she'd escaped me and my embarrassing Yank gush, I decided a celebration was called for. I would take myself to the canteen for a cup of tea.

The first sip was heaven. I had a second to Greg's health, then reached into his sports bag and pulled out the Justice Department report called *Organised crime and the international toxic waste trade*. I was ready.

I turned to the introduction. 'This interim briefing paper report covers one aspect of the on-going investigation into the affairs of the Atlanta, Georgia branch of the Banca Nazionale del Lavoro, an Italian-government-owned financial institution'.

Unh oh, 'Italian-government-owned'. *That* sounded like a euphemism.

'That aspect is the Bank's laundering of funds generated by the black market trade in toxic waste, especially the American export end of it. The nature of this trade is that it overlaps with the arms and drugs trades, so this report inevitably overlaps too. The focus, however, is on BNL Atlanta's involvement in the illegal toxic waste trade on a country-by-country basis.'

I flipped ahead to the Great Britain section, subtitled 'The dirty man of Europe'. The first couple of pages outlined the 'regulations vacuum' which for the past thirty years had made the UK so attractive to waste traders and so repugnant to environmental pressure groups. Then: 'As explained in the section on Italy, the Sicilian Mafia created the European trade in illegal toxic waste, helped by the lax export regulations in Italy. Great Britain quickly became one of the favoured dumping grounds because of the regulations vacuum. After certain American Mafia families formed trade links with certain Sicilian counterparts, much of the waste buried in the UK came from American sources.

'Although the Italian government had to bow to European Community pressure and brought in the tightest waste trade control measures in the Community (see Chapter 4), the Sicilian Mafia operational headquarters simply relocated to Libya. The British also tightened regulations under EC pressure, but in truth the trade to the UK fell off in the late 1980s because of a shortage of burial sites.'

Wow. There it was, spelled out in hard copy. Not just any old organised criminal group. The godfather of them all.

How the hell did Tim Maguire get involved with the Mafia?

I skipped ahead again, to a section called 'Operating methods': 'A key feature of the trade everywhere is old-fashioned entryism: individual Mafia organisers have settled in key cities around the world, becoming part of local communities, ingratiating themselves, developing local reputations, taking over local businesses and running them as "fronts". According to our sources this method has traditionally worked well in the UK, because of the premium the British place on secrecy.'

Here was the answer to my question: South Wales Demolition and Haulage, Tim Maguire's company, was a front organisation.

Again I found myself wondering about Evie. Active participant? Deceived mother? There was one person who had to know. I checked the time. He might even be awake by now.

Greg Tuttle looked almost as shrunken tucked up in his bed in that private room as he had in the stretcher in the ambulance. Skin translucent, no energy at all coming off him. Deracinated. When he was back to normal all my anger and ambivalence about him was bound to rise again. But for the moment I just had to feel sorry for the poor bastard. I reached for his hand and, touching him, thought, Ah, here's change, his skin's warmed up.

He opened his eyes and the corners of his lips lifted in a way that in a stronger person would have been a smile. I felt a slight pressure on my fingers that would have been a squeeze. He said something with what would have been a voice. I leaned over, so my ear was near his mouth. 'What?'

'My bag – car trunk,' he said.

'Got it.'

'Tape?'

'Yup, listened. And read that report. I wish you'd felt you could tell me from the start what you were doing – but, professionally, I can understand.'

He pressed his head back into his pillow a bit, as if getting the measure of me somehow. His eyes were barely slits but I saw a question.

'What?' I said.

He cleared his throat. 'Did you – connect?'

'About Tim?' I nodded.

A small grunt escaped him and he shut his eyes again but didn't release my fingers. I waited and, as I did so, could feel his grip getting tighter, as if he were summoning all the energy he could muster. Finally, eyes still closed, he said, 'There's something else. I shouldn't tell you, but –'

I laughed again. 'But you owe me.'

His sigh was neither confirmation nor denial. 'Is – my jacket – there?'

I looked around. It was on the chair behind me. He wouldn't let go of my hand but I managed to turn around and pick it up with the other one. I laid it on the bed.

'Sit,' he said. He pushed my hand so I knew he meant on the edge of the bed. I sat.

'Breast pocket,' he said.

I rummaged in it and pulled out an old photo. A couple in formal evening wear, arm in arm. The woman's gown caught my eye first – shimmering royal blue, cut low on high breasts, revealing, glamorous. Only then did I register the face. 'Evie,' I said. 'God, this must be twenty-five years ago.'

'And?'

I looked at the man. Dark hair, styled long back and sides in the manner of the day, moustache, beard –. It was the eyes that made me pause. I knew the eyes.

I imagined the face clean-shaven and abruptly saw that the hair colour was misleading. Turn it white and there he was: Marc Felici.

Stray pieces I hadn't even realised were part of my puzzle suddenly fitted together. God Almighty, how could I not have seen? Mr Wonderful himself, the benefactor of cash-starved service groups like housing associations for Bangladeshi immigrants and law firms for underdogs and God knew who all else.

Evie had been his first connection, back when she had power over a stock of empty property.

Greg had tried to warn us.

Oh, God – and Suze was with Marc now, at this moment, as I sat there. The adrenalin of panic rushed into my bloodstream. My legs stood me upright of their own volition.

Greg opened his eyes again. The energy summons had worked. He seemed more present. 'What?' he said. He sounded more present too.

'Suze,' I said. 'She's with him. She's in danger.'

He waved his free hand at me as if to say, Relax, sit down. 'Suze is in less physical danger from Signor Marc Felici than anybody on the planet. You're a close second.'

I stayed on my feet. 'That's ridiculous. The guy's probably killed dozens of people.'

'Not recently. He uses henchmen.'

'Janey, Tim and Richard might call that splitting hairs.'

'Tim killed Janey. I'm the only one Marc personally shot. He's so out of practice he thought I was dead.'

'So did I! That's the point. Are you telling me he's too polite to shoot women?'

'No, I'm telling you he wouldn't sully the reputation of the law firm he needs to fulfil his expansionary ambitions – not after everything he's done to save it so far.'

Well, that made me sit down again, let me tell you. 'Wait – wait,' I said, not wanting to believe I'd understood him. 'You mean –? Not –?'

He nodded. 'You guys are the perfect front. That's why Marc Felici went to so much trouble to clear your name.'

'*He* did? Hang on, I'm not following –'

'Tim killed Janey Riordan to stop her telling the world about his waste business. He saw you arriving as he was leaving and he saw his chance and took it.'

'The story of the guy's life.'

'Yeah. The bad luck for you was that that cop, Hamley, wanted to believe him.'

'The good luck for me was finding the evidence the bastard planted in my flat.'

'The good luck for you was that Marc Felici was chasing Aspinall Street. Poor dumb-ass Tim. He must have thought Felici'd be proud of him for putting you in the frame.'

'Oh, yeah, poor Tim.'

He laughed. 'You have to feel kinda sorry for old "Felich" too. I bet when he had Tim blown to smithereens he never imagined you'd be suspected of that. On the other hand, the fact that you were gave him a chance for total control over Aspinall Street. He took it, then killed Richard and had him leave a confession that would clear you once and for all. And here you are – out.'

It was all too much for me. My whole perception of things – upended, overturned. I had to move from the edge of the bed to the chair, be physically on my own while I reran everything he'd just told me – digested it – imagined coming to terms with it.

Aspinall Street – almost a Mafia front. Three deaths and my

freedom – all down to manipulation for advantage in an invisible business world. And Suze – still enamoured of the man Marc Felici was pretending to be.

How would she take the news that he was the exact opposite?

I knew how I'd take it.

I came out of myself enough to look over at Greg. He was looking back at me. The sympathy I'd felt for him moments ago, the 'poor sod' sentiment, I recognised being returned.

He said, 'Me and my partner have been working with MI5 and a special unit of the local police. They're arresting Marc Felici late this afternoon. The amount of stuff we've got on him, when we get him back to Atlanta, he'll have to turn state's witness.' He kissed the air at the sweetness of the thought.

'Yeah, well, I'm happy for you, but what about Suze? If she's caught up in it, she might get –'

'They know she's with him. She'll be okay.'

The cynical grunt escaped before I could stop it.

'She will be. My partner's good.'

It escaped again. 'He left you to die.'

He smiled and shook his head. 'He phoned the ambulance on his way. It's thanks to him I'm here.'

'Excuse me,' I said. '*I* phoned the ambulance.'

That took him aback. 'You? You came to the warehouses?'

I nodded. 'Haven't they told you? You'd almost bled to death. You'd been there four or five hours.'

He withdrew his hand from mine and tried to push himself into a sitting position. He almost managed it. 'What time is it?'

I checked my watch. '3.30.'

'God, is it? It's happening now.'

'Where?'

'Cardiff.' He dropped back down to almost prone again. 'Christ, I heard the emergency services in this country were screwed up, but this is ridiculous.'

'They came fast enough when I called. Maybe your partner didn't –?'

'No. No, he's never let me down. Is my beeper there? Right pocket.'

I reached in, found it, checked it. 'Nothing,' I said.

'Well,' he said, sounding heartier than he looked, 'honestly, he won't let Suze get hurt.'

'Physically, you mean. Emotionally she's going to feel like a ton of crap has landed on her from a great height.' My legs acted of their own volition again. I stood up. 'Where's the bust happening?'

'At the harbour. There's a container ship –'

'The *Sharon B*?'

'Yeah. But by the time you get there they'll be at Cardiff Central police station. Go there. Tell them "Operation Eagle".'

I couldn't help smiling – it sounded so 'Boy Scouts Grow Up'.

He saw my amusement but just shrugged. It was serious enough to him. 'Bring Suze back here if she wants to talk.'

'Thanks. I'll see how she feels.' I bent to kiss him on the cheek.

He turned his head so the kiss would land on his lips, but I was quicker. As I straightened, though, he managed to grasp my hand. 'We need to talk.'

'Absolutely,' I said, but I extricated my fingers. 'I'm pretty sure there's evidence on that container ship that'll help the women who used the Hodder playground sue for damages. If you can get me to it –'

'Yes, of course. Anything you need. I meant about us.'

'I'm still working on the realities at the moment,' I said. 'The fantasies will have to wait.' It was supposed to be flippant but he looked wounded. I laughed to indicate it was just a joke and then, because I didn't know what else to do, I headed for the door.

Twenty-Four

Despite hold-ups – finding a taxi took ten minutes instead of two, there was awful traffic in the Cardiff suburbs – half an hour later I was walking up the steps of the central police station in Cardiff.

The woman at the reception desk wrote my code words on a slip of paper and disappeared into the inner sanctum. I sat down to wait and began to think about Suze, imagine her state of mind, how she must be feeling by now. Would she go back to Peter? Would she want time on her own? My flat didn't have the space she was used to, but I'd offer her my sofa, certainly. My shoulder and ear as well.

God, she must feel terrible.

The receptionist returned. 'I'm sorry,' she said, 'no one's heard of this.'

Obviously I didn't take her word. I'd lived here a long time, I knew about bureaucrats who took pleasure in being unhelpful. I insisted, I demanded, I persevered. In the end I wore her down and made her fetch a uniformed officer, superintendant somebody. I explained that Operation Eagle was a joint Anglo-American one involving organised crime, I explained that I was a lawyer, I explained that I just wanted to rescue an innocent party. He nodded and hmm'd and umm'd but his answer was the same as the receptionist's: he didn't know anything about it, he couldn't help me.

Part of me thought, Suze is back there in some room being interviewed and he just can't be bothered to find out. The other part thought, If Suze isn't back there, something's gone wrong. The impossibility of establishing the truth one way or the other increased my irritation. I bit back a snotty remark – made myself stay calm. Perhaps (I told myself) the arrest had simply been delayed. It wouldn't be the first time.

I caught a bus heading towards the docks and asked the driver to let me off at the container ship area. Fortunately that meant something to him.

I thought finding the *Sharon B* might be tough but it wasn't. There was only one ship loading on the bridge that clear Sunday afternoon and she was many times more megalithic live than in her photographs. I stood there on the quay watching as empty chains were cranked upwards from above by the arm of the derrick, then reeled back towards the dockside, where a couple of crew were standing waiting to catch them. Half a dozen containers remained: almost ready to sail.

It didn't feel to me as if there'd been a major arrest here in the past hour. Everything was too normal.

I walked towards the ship as if I were small and invisible and knew where I were going. I got as far as the bottom of the steps.

'Oy!' a voice shouted to me from the distant main deck. 'Help you?' It was attached to a crew member.

'I'd rather not shout,' I shouted.

At my shoulder another male voice said, 'What, they lose you off the coach, love?'

I gave him a big smile and played to his assumptions. 'I'm looking for a Scottish guy, Marc Felici? He said to look him up. This is his boat, isn't it?'

He grinned a great patronising me-hearties of a grin. 'We call this a "ship".' He pointed towards the water. 'The marina's on the other side there. That's where he keeps his "boat".'

It's so easy to make some people feel big. 'And he is?'

'Not here. If he was here he'd be telling me off for talking to you.'

I walked away from the container bridge and headed back to the road. There was no bus coming so I set off on foot, following the signs to the marina. I had fantasies and fears about disappearing into the freight wilderness but eventually I spotted the tips of masts in the distance.

When I got there at last I sought out the harbour master in his office and continued with the Yank tourist act. 'Hi! I'm looking for a friend of mine? She's got spiky hennaed hair, big smile. She's here with a guy called Felix? Feleech?'

He checked a registrations book. 'The Syracuse. Berth thirty-seven.'

'They're here?'

'The schooner is. I couldn't say where they are.' He pointed left along the dockside berths and I took this as an invitation to go check for myself.

The Syracuse was pretty damn big – sixty feet, eighty feet, who knows, BIG. The two main masts looked like ancient oaks. The cover over the windows and boarding area said no one was home but I called out anyway. There was no reply.

I walked back out and along the marina's edge, thinking. Had Greg been befuddled by the anaesthetic when he'd told me about Operation Eagle? Had he thought today was yesterday or tomorrow? Or had something gone as badly wrong as deep down I was worried it had?

Where was Suze? Was she all right?

I decided I'd better find a phone and ring him.

I could see touristy shops up by the road and headed that way. I was perhaps a quarter of the way there when I heard a familiar voice, high and sharp with surprise, call out, 'Dee? Is that you?'

I turned. Suze was alone, coming towards me. She had on shorts

and a sweatshirt but somehow – the earrings, the bracelets, the bag
– she looked chic. I ought to have grabbed her by the arm and run
with her but bumping into her like this was so much the last thing
I'd expected that I didn't have all my wits marshalled. 'Suze? Are
you on your own?'

She gestured behind her, towards a teashop. 'Marc's just paying.
What are you doing here?'

'I need to talk to you. Alone. Just you and me.' Damn, there he
was, coming out of the door.

She laughed. 'You're amazing, Dee. Anybody else I'd row with,
they wouldn't come all this way to sort it out.'

'Row?'

She laughed again, assuming I was joking.

Suddenly I remembered: yesterday. We'd argued about the firm.
It felt aeons, a lifetime, ago. I glanced at Marc – he'd seen me and
was taking long strides towards us. I turned my back to him.

'It isn't that,' I said, 'it's – you've – we've –' The words dried.
What could I say to her? Your cultured philanthropist is a lying
scheming Mafia boss? It would backfire. It was going to take
preparation and persuasion to get her to see the truth.

Then the chance was gone: he was there. Why hadn't I made her
run? What now? Where were Greg's partner and MI5 and the local
police?

He draped his arm possessively over Suze's shoulder and smiled
at me. 'This can't be coincidence, surely?'

She looked up at him fondly. 'She heard about the tour, decided
to come.'

'Tour?' I said.

'Marc's got antiques going out on a ship over at the docks. We're
going to have a look – check they've packed the containers okay.'
She bulged her eyes at me in a way that I took to mean, Men,
humour them.

My problem was that at that moment I couldn't conceive of
going anywhere with Marc Felici. And oddly enough, it wasn't fear,

it was loathing – the thought of that toxic soup under that playground. Even more obscene was the idea that the stuff was probably headed for reburial in Bangladesh. And the thought of how close he'd come to using Aspinall Street as a front . . .

Marc said, 'I'm sure Dee isn't interested in a container ship.'

But by then I'd decided I couldn't let Suze go into that thing with him by herself. Greg might be right, she might be physically safe with Marc, but her soul was in peril.

I rehoicked the strap digging into my shoulder and realised I was still carrying Greg's sports bag. I remembered the handgun in the bottom of it. We wouldn't be defenceless, anyway. 'Actually,' I said, 'I'd love to come along.'

He drove us back to the container ship area and as we pulled up on the quayside, he pointed to the top of the three-level cabin area at the stern end. 'I need to see the captain, so we'll start up there and work our way down.'

What he didn't say was that he meant for us to use the external built-in ladder steps between decks. For someone with tendencies to vertigo, everything after the first flight of metal stairs leading from the quay to the main deck was done on will and the only thing that got me up the last flight was the twin determination to stay close to Suze and keep an eye on Marc.

The captain was poring over papers when we finally arrived at the eyrie known (I saw from the sign) as the compass bridge and Marc immediately went over and got involved in poring with him. Winded and half in, half out of myself as I felt, it was the moment I'd been waiting for. I gestured to Suze to follow me to the windows, but she was already on her way.

Arriving first I looked out over the ship, which even from above seemed the size of a city block. Between where I was – in height, a little below the top of the smoke stack – and the distant bow were hundreds of identical containers neatly arranged in groups – and that was only the top layer.

I felt Suze come up behind me. 'You going to tell me why you're here?' she murmured.

'Let's go downstairs, eh?' I murmured back.

But Marc's antennae were on. He glanced up. 'Just coming. Won't be a minute.'

Damn.

The official tour resumed a minute later: across the compass bridge to the internal staircase and down to the crew quarters. Beds, cupboards, laundry facilities. Marc enticed Suze over to a stack of new mattresses and must have made a suggestive remark, because I heard her giggle.

I resorted to looking out the window again, this time on the dock side. The almost empty industrial harbourscape, set against the pink mackerel clouds, had a surreal beauty. The last container was being hoisted off the pavement and I watched it clear the side and swivel towards its target spot, swinging back and forth. The crew on the main deck rushed to steady it and guide it into its slot.

'Yoo-hoo,' Suze called from the doorway. I turned in time to catch Marc putting that possessive hand on her shoulder again, just to underline who had the power. I didn't exactly hurry towards them, but I made my way in that direction. As I was walking I sent up a(nother) telepathic message to Greg's partner/MI5/the local police: I'm ready! Save us now!

We didn't dally in the mess hall or entertainment lounges on the main-deck level but passed through and headed down the stairs into the hold. This flight felt long thanks to the declining effectiveness of the yellow sodium lights the deeper we went. At the bottom my first impression was dampness, and as I shivered and hugged myself, Marc went and felt the walls with the flats of his palms, then stooped and felt the floor.

He cursed, gestured to us to come on, and hurried across to the opposite side of the corridor that ran around this level. Suze automatically hurried after him and by the time I caught up he was huddled with a group of crew around a section of containers.

Suze was leaning against the corridor wall, watching, and as I approached she sighed and shook her head for my benefit. 'This is apparently what happened the last time – all this dampness in the hold.'

I gave her a look like, Oh, really? Poor him, but I was thinking that this might be a true porthole of opportunity. For the first time Marc seemed to have forgotten Suze and I were there. I pointed down the corridor and gestured with my head for her to follow me. Then I set off. She started after me but he called her name.

'Just come,' I muttered, but too under my breath for her to catch.

'Hang on,' she said. Her tone said even she was getting impatient with his overattentiveness, but she turned and went out to him.

I carried on along the gloomy corridor between the shell of the ship and the great mass of containers. I first noticed the familiar smell at the point where I realised there was only one more light on ahead; after that, the dark abyss. Nevertheless, I began to walk faster, sniffing harder and harder. The smell seemed to be coming from that unlit area at the back. Had they packed those messy leaking barrels from the playground in ordinary containers? Surely not.

On the other hand, anyone who'd let pregnant women near this stuff wouldn't worry about strapping male crew.

Suddenly, ahead of me, a wall with a garage-sized door in it loomed. I went and put my nose to the crack between the frame and the door. The smell was definitely stronger in there.

I realised now there were footsteps approaching behind me and stopped to listen – one pair, proceeding cautiously into the murk, as I had. 'Dee?' Suze said. 'You there?'

'Here!'

She arrived holding her nose. 'God, what is that horrible smell?'

I gestured to the door. 'This is what was buried under the Hodder Street playground until only a few days ago: as yet unspecified toxic waste, generated maybe fifteen years ago in America. The source of Sufiya Khan's high incidence of miscarriages and deformed babies. Put there in the first place by Tim Maguire, then unburied and transported here by him.'

'Jesus,' Suze whispered. She stared at the door, shaking her head. 'Jesus.' You could practically see the various implications shifting and merging and parting in her brain. 'What a coincidence. Marc will be furious – his antiques on the same ship.'

The moment had come. I put my arm around her shoulder. 'Suze,' I said, preparing to speak both gently and directly. 'Suze, Marc is responsible for it.'

'What do you mean?' She stepped out of the physical contact with me.

Not a good beginning. And was that the sound of footsteps? I pressed on. 'I found some tapes and a report Greg had. It's Marc the US Justice Department is after. He's a big Mafia don – he's in the waste trade –'

'Oh, for – and you believe *them*? Dee – don't you see? Every powerful person with Italian connections is being called Mafia at the moment. Your confused feelings about Greg – which I understand! Don't get me wrong! – they're blinding you to a smear campaign.'

I felt desperate. This had gone wrong, irretrievably if I wasn't careful. The footsteps were getting louder and closer. 'Okay,' I said, pointing to the far end of the wall, where the darkness was deepest. 'You hide, I'll ask him.'

'I'm not playing games about this.'

'Do you want to know the truth?'

She hesitated.

'Come on.' I grabbed her by the arm and more or less pushed her out of the dimness into the dark. Then I went back to the locked door and retrieved Theresa's little camera from my bag and started pretending to set up a picture of the locked door.

Marc emerged from the other direction. 'Dee! What are you doing?'

'There are illegal goods on this freighter,' I said. 'Arms, medicines, toxic waste for burial –'

He touched the locked door. 'And you think they're in here?'

I nodded.

He reached in his pocket and pulled out some keys. 'Okay.' He unlocked the door and pushed it open. I got a blast of the smell. And what was that grunting noise?

'Come,' he said, reaching for my elbow, 'have a look.'

I shook his hand off and backed away from him, away from the open door, down the corridor, holding up my camera with my right hand. My finger was on the flash. I could blind him with it –

He continued moving towards me in a way I'd have found truly menacing if I'd been on my own.

'I have proof that you know all about the contraband on this ship,' I said. At the same time I slipped my hand into Greg's sports bag and touched the gun compartment. 'From the US Justice Department, which has been investigating you –.' The words 'and your Mafia connections' got stuck in my throat.

It didn't matter. I'd said enough to stop him. His glare penetrated the murk between us like a laser. I began undoing the zipper. 'Is this a blackmail demand?' he said.

Oddly enough, I hadn't appreciated that that's what it would sound like. 'Yeah,' I said.

'And how much do you require to keep quiet?'

I knew without having to think. 'Enough to pay off the Aspinall Street debt. No strings.'

He was silent, considering this. I sensed more than saw Suze coming out of the shadows to look at him. Over the years I'd known her I'd seen her through some big emotional traumas: loves, losses, deaths, mistakes, betrayals. But heartbreak – well, I don't know if it had happened to her since she was sixteen. Yet there it was now, pouring off her.

Despite her obvious distress, I thought she was going to be able to hold on – I certainly wished she would: I might get the cash out of him. But then he felt her approaching behind him and turned. For a protracted moment none of us spoke. Then he sighed and said; 'You just couldn't leave well enough alone could you?' A gun appeared in his right hand and with his left he grabbed Suze by the wrist and thrust her into the room. Then he did the same to me. He gave her a look of regret, shook his head at me and slammed the door on us. We heard the key turning in the other side and footsteps retreating away down the corridor.

I would have started banging on the door and shouting to try to rouse attention but I'd seen Suze's face just before the door had closed. Pain – hurt – humiliation. I went to her in the dark and gave her my shoulder. She put her head on it and wept. 'What a mug,' she kept saying. 'What a stupid mug.'

I kept patting her and murmuring, 'You're not the only one.' I expect this made me feel better than it did her.

She was moving into the angry phase, beginning to mutter 'that shit' and 'that bastard', when I again thought I heard the grunting.

'Shhh,' I said. 'Listen.'

We listened together but there was only quiet now.

Suze started to cough. 'God, that smell is foul. I won't be able to stand this for very long.'

I opened my mouth to say that was probably the idea when there was a thunderous bang, followed by the grating effort of the gears struggling to mesh and move. Then – they stalled.

The full weight of our predicament landed on us both.

'I hope you've got some ideas,' she said, trying not to sound desperate.

'As luck would have it –' I quickly undid the zipper on the bottom of Greg's sports bag and lifted out the gun. I'd only ever held one gun, years ago, in LA, and I hadn't liked the feel of it then either. I located the lock on the door with my hand, made Suze stand back and aimed. Then we waited. Eventually there was another loud bang and the gears began struggling again. I fired. Failure. I fired again. Better – there was now a hole below the lock, letting in yellow corridor light. One more shot: half the door panel vanished.

Aim I might not have, but a punch that lands is still a punch.

Suze and I together pulled and kicked the door and finally forced it open and stepped out into what suddenly seemed like wonderful fresh air and bright light. Abruptly the engine noise ceased again.

I lifted my arm to point in the direction we'd come when we both heard the grunting noise.

'That is definitely human,' Suze said, looking back into the room we'd just escaped from. I looked with her. The section was full of containers just like all the others on the ship. She stood in the doorway and shouted out, 'Hello? Anybody there?'

Silence. Silence. Silence. Then – more grunting.

'There,' she said. She pointed left and headed back in.

Three more call and response exchanges later we were going towards the very rear of the locked-up area, the very rear of the ship. We'd left the door open so we benefited a bit from the corridor light. Suze was ahead of me and I heard her say 'Jesus', sensed her kneel. I joined her and even the little I could make out made me want to look away: four men lying side by side on their backs, gags around their mouths, handcuffs on both ankles and wrists. Three of the four were unconscious. We hurriedly untied the gag of the fourth, who gasped and coughed and said 'Air' even as I was moving around to put my hands through his armpits so I could drag him out of there. Suze bent to lift his feet but he yelped, 'Ow! No! Not the legs!' and she backed off.

Out in the corridor we propped him upright against the wall and, under what passed for better light, I realised who he was: the guy Greg had told me ran the photo lab near his office, the one who'd supposedly developed the film I'd found at Janey's and declared it unused. He hadn't spoken at the time or I'd have realised then that he was American too.

'The others,' he said, but Suze and I were already heading back. 'Careful – the legs,' he called after us.

The next guy was big and it took both of us to drag him. From the hip joints down he was like a cloth doll with ripped seams, feet flopping at unnatural angles.

'Jeez,' I said. 'This has been done to them. On purpose.'

'Please, Dee,' Suze said, and hurried to put distance between us and, I suspect, between herself and that thought.

When we had all three of them out and their gags off I realised I knew another of them. I pointed to his comatose body. 'He's a tabloid journalist,' I said to Greg's partner. '*News of the World*.'

'He's MI5,' he said. 'So's the big guy. The guy on the end, he's FBI. You got a gun, I guess, eh?'

But I was too busy making yet another conceptual readjustment (MI5!) to reply.

'Yeah,' Suze said to him.

He held out his manacled wrists. 'Shoot these mothers off me.'

I lifted the gun, then had second thoughts. 'Wait. If we use two bullets to free you,' I said to him, 'that would leave us one.'

'And that's if we're lucky,' Suze muttered.

He laughed, a single sarcastic syllable. 'I'd just need one if I could stand up.'

I waited for her to ask him why he couldn't and for a couple of moments I thought she was on the point of it. In the end she just coughed.

She had to know. I had to know. 'What's happened to your legs?' I asked.

'See for yourself,' he said, gesturing to them.

My innate squeamishness asserted itself. 'I'd rather just hear about it.'

'I don't even want to do that,' Suze murmured.

He said, 'You know about "kneecapping"?'

Suze made a repelled face.

'That's what he did to us first – so we'd "co-operate" in the "debriefing".'

I let out a long breath. We could all die here; I hadn't faced that idea till now. We were in the ancient realm of the male mysteries, more bloody and malevolent than anything I'd encountered in fifteen years of often bloody, often malevolent criminal defence work.

'What happened to the police?' I asked him. 'Greg said –'

'Greg's okay?'

I nodded. 'Just.'

'They set him up – that's when I knew. The local fucking pigs are in Felici's pocket. The plan called for fifty or sixty of them to turn up and bust everybody – the captain, the cook, crew – not forgetting Felici himself.' He sighed. 'Sold us right down the Swanee.'

Suze turned away. It had to be tough, taking all this on. I rested a hand on her shoulder.

To him I said, 'But the crew don't know what's on board, do they?' Letting x-dozen people in on it didn't sound the way to protect a secret three people had died for.

He shook his head. 'But they'll have seen things that'll make sense when they understand what's going on. Look, I don't want to be rude to you ladies, but while we're down here yacking, he's getting away.'

Suze said something unintelligible.

I rubbed her back. 'What?'

'I said, He won't leave until he knows this ship is on its way.'

On cue there was a third thudding clang. This time the gears meshed and the engine turned over once – twice – three times – four times. (Uh oh.) Then it failed again.

Suze looked up. To me she said, 'We can't stop him. How can we stop him?' To Greg's friend she said, 'You were going to use a whole armed police force to do it. We're two amateurs with three bullets.'

He sighed at the truth of this. 'If you could just get to a telephone –'

'And ring who?' Suze said. 'You just told us the local bill dropped you in it.'

Then it came to me, the way realisations do: first all was confused, the next moment all clear. 'Wait, wait,' I said. 'We're not just two amateurs with three bullets. And there is someone we can call.' I put the gun back in the bag and slipped the strap over my shoulder. 'Come on,' I said to Suze.

By the time we reached the door at the top of the stairs leading out of the hold on to the main deck, Suze was happy with everything but one crucial detail. 'You can't seriously mean to ring Hamley,' she said.

'Why not? He's the head of the murder investigations.'

'He set you up! God, he was probably bribed too –'

'No,' I said. 'He was manipulated the same way I was.' I almost said 'by Marc' but censored myself in time.

'Come on. He set Amin Ali up.'

I told her about Amin's lookalike cousin.

'He still falsified interview notes.'

'Yes – and he'd love to get rid of that blot. He'd love to solve the Janey Riordan murder too. Anyway, who else is there?'

She named a senior officer up in Yorkshire we both respected and another out in Norwich. There was another down in Devon and –

'But we'll have to go into lengthy explanations with all of them about the whole Janey saga. Hamley knows the story. He's desperate to solve it. He'll drop everything and come.'

She looked disgruntled. I was right and she knew it, but she didn't like it.

It would take more time than we had to change her mind. 'You ready for this?' I said, putting my hand on the door, ready to push it open a crack and catch a glimpse of what was happening in the crew mess, which we thought was on the other side. The best-case scenario was that it would be empty and the phone would be right there, working and available. We'd nip in, make the call and head for the metal stairs down to the dock.

I pushed and looked through the crack. I thought half our wish had come true: it was empty. I was still trying to spot a phone, contemplating going in to look, when we heard distant hubbub and the doors on the opposite side of the mess opened and crew members hurried in and shaped themselves into a queue at the food counter.

'Damn,' Suze whispered. She was looking over my shoulder.

'It'll be okay,' I said. 'You can do it.'

'What if they *are* all in on it?'

'They're not.'

'*Dee.*'

'Okay – maybe they are. You've got to persuade them to help. What's our choice?'

She took a deep breath and nodded. Then she looked down at her feet. She was preparing herself. Who knew what really might happen? Finally she looked up again and nodded. 'Okay,' she said, 'ready to boldly go.'

'You'll be great,' I said. Then I boldly pushed the door full open and we went through.

By this time men – all the crew we'd seen so far and saw then were male – were selecting tables and sitting down with their teas and their coffees and their bits of cake.

'Hi,' I said in a loud voice to the room at large. 'We're looking for a phone. There one at this level?'

'Bust,' someone called.

'There must be one somewhere.'

'Captain's got a mobile.'

Suze and I looked at each other. We'd gone from best-case to worst in thirty seconds.

'What you doing down the hold?' one of them called out.

'Yeah. Them's the birds was with the owner.'

Suze looked at me, alarm in her eyes. 'Owner,' she said. 'He's the *owner*?'

'Now,' I said to her. 'Do it now.' I went and got a chair and pulled it over so she could stand on it.

Righteous anger vanquished her earlier nervousness. She stood on the chair the way I'd seen her stand on other chairs – and soapboxes and tables – at countless public meetings over the years. 'I'm here to tell you men,' she began, 'that the cargo on this ship is illegal.'

The laughter was universal and rotund.

Suze looked stricken. She stepped down off the chair while they were still laughing and said to me, 'They know. We guessed wrong. We got it wrong.'

It did look that way, but I pushed her back up on the chair. 'Be more specific,' I said.

She raised her head and tried again. 'I'm not talking about guns,' she said. 'I'm not talking about medicines. I'm not talking about fake antiques. I'm not even talking about drugs.' She stared around the room.

The laughing stopped.

'I'm talking,' she said, 'about toxic materials that were under a playground in the East End of London for the past decade. I'm talking about chemicals that have damaged the unborn babies of immigrant women who used the play area over the buried waste barrels. I'm talking about spontaneous abortions and deformed infants that live a few weeks or months and die in agony. I may be talking long-term cancer rates too – there's no research on that yet.'

'You sayin' this stuff's on this ship?' someone called.

She nodded.

'Is that what's locked up downstairs? The smell?' someone else said.

I said, 'Four government agents, two American, two British, were locked in with them till we let them out a few minutes ago. They've all been tortured. Go down there – see for yourselves if you don't believe me.'

One guy who'd been in the queue for tea suddenly bolted and ran as fast as he could back out the door. He didn't head down the stairs to the hold, however, but up. Three other guys tackled him and managed to prevent him leaving.

'Thanks,' she said. 'What we need now is for volunteers to do the same thing to Marc Felici.'

'We'll lose our jobs,' someone said.

Another guy said, 'This job is already gone.'

'Yeah, good riddance,' said another.

Knots of men began talking among themselves. Suze got down off the chair. 'What do you think?' she said.

I shrugged. It sounded a good enough pitch to me, but then, I was biased.

Discussion went on another minute. Then we had our first volunteer, followed by another, followed by another. In the end, as we'd hoped, virtually the whole crew joined us.

The consensus was that Marc was still up with the captain while the engineers worked on getting the ship going.

Suze turned to me again. 'I want to lead. You got any objections?'

I shook my head.

She held out her hand. 'Give me the gun.'

'We want him alive, Suze.'

'*Dee* – give me a break.'

Reluctantly I handed it over. Twenty of us followed her up three flights of stairs to the compass bridge.

The noise of our arrival inevitably went before us and as we were nearing the top the door opened and Marc Felici stood in the doorframe. We all paused except Suze, who continued up another couple of steps before coming to a halt and staring at him. For a long, skin-prickling moment it might as well have been just the two of them. Then he vanished, the door swinging shut behind him.

Several of the crew members shouted, 'We'll stop him', and hurried on to block the other way out.

'How's your nerve?' I said to Suze.

'Fine,' she said in a clenched tone that suggested she was stoking herself on her anger again. 'Just fine.' Then she continued on up the stairs to the door and kicked it open. I hurried after her. The captain was there, telling the dozen or so bulky men swarming around him that they had just lost their jobs.

Then the other dozen crew members surged through the doorway opposite us, Marc in their collective grip. Just as they got him there, though, he shook himself loose.

Suze lifted the gun and pointed it at him like she knew what she was doing. I was glad to see that a lifetime watching American TV cop shows actually had some use.

Unfortunately, he seemed to have watched them too. Instead of doing the sensible thing and stopping there and then, he ignored the threat and kept on walking towards her. Suze held her ground. 'Stop or I'll shoot,' she said, as if she'd made up the line.

He didn't stop. And by God, Suze pulled the trigger.

She got him in the thigh.

The captain made to go to Marc's aid. Suze waved the gun at him, though, and he opted to stop. 'Dee,' she said, 'make that call.'

Twenty-Five

Fortunately, I'd forgotten it was Sunday afternoon. If I'd remembered I'd never have dialled Hamley with such certainty that he'd be there and been so unsurprised when I was right.

'Ah, Miss Street, you caught me just as I was clearing my desk.'

I felt a twist of anxiety. 'Really? Where you going?'

'This time? Essex. To push paper.' He didn't add 'thanks to you' but that's what his pause seemed to say.

The twist tightened. 'You're still in CID now?'

'And for several hours more in fact.'

I laughed, nervous with relief. 'Good! I've got a murderer I want to hand over.' Then I sketched in the main details about Marc and the American Justice Department investigation and the problem with the local police in Wales.

He didn't need to hear any more. 'Tie him up,' he said. 'Put him somewhere he can't get away. Give me –' he paused to calculate – 'give me two hours.'

After hanging up with him I made another quick call, this one to summon medical help for the intelligence guys with the broken legs down in the hold.

By the time I got off the phone and hurried back across the

navigation area to Suze and the group of crew surrounding Marc and the captain, they were doing what Hamley had advised: binding the captives' wrists behind their backs with rope.

Marc was ignoring the onlookers, speaking to Suze in his sincerest, soothingest baritone, trying to sweet-talk her. It wasn't what it appeared. She shouldn't spurn his financial offer. The future could be phenomenally prosperous for her and the firm, regardless of what happened to him.

It was obviously crap but resisting it was hard for her, I'm sure – heart and loins are so amoral, so a-rational. The battle her head was having for control was there in her eyes – in her hesitancy.

It was to help shore up that side that I said, 'Maybe we should see how Marc and his friend here like the smell.'

She gave me an instant's dumbfounded look, as if that were the cruellest, most wicked idea she'd ever heard in her entire life and how could I even think it, never mind suggest it. Then she re-remembered what they'd done. She began to laugh. 'Yes!' she said. 'Yes!'

Marc, for a change, looked alarmed. 'Suzannah, my dear,' he tried, 'there's no need –'

But she'd turned and was selecting four burly guys from the crew. 'Let's take them downstairs,' she said. Then she gestured to everyone to follow her.

I ended up bringing up the rear of the long queue down the three flights to the mess deck, then down the further flight into the yellow-lit hold and along the damp corridor to the lock-up at the back. When I finally got there I found Suze sitting by the door clutching her knees and looking wearier than Sisyphus. From the faraway rear of the compartment I could hear the voices of the men who were settling Marc and the captain near their retribution. The captain was screaming his innocence.

Three or four yards from Suze a crew member was on his knees beside Greg's partner, trying to saw through the handcuff chain with the hacksaw blade on a Swiss Army knife. The other three men had all come to, thank the Lord, though so far as I could see them in the murk, they were still pretty out of it.

'Hey,' I said, pointing to the handcuffs, 'we've got Marc's gun now too – we're up to nine bullets.'

'Right,' Greg's partner said, 'let's get these mamas off.'

I turned to retrieve our gun from Suze and realised she'd gotten to her feet and was beginning to walk away. I hurried after her.

'You okay?'

She nodded and kept walking, eyes on the ground.

'Can I have the gun?'

She handed it to me and carried on moving.

I stopped and watched her walk away. If I felt shitty, how bad did she feel?

Hamley had commandeered a small plane at the London end and a helicopter at the Cardiff end, which meant he and his six associates – three plain-clothed, three uniformed – boarded the *Sharon B* exactly 116 minutes after I'd summoned him, four minutes under his predicted arrival time. I was there, waiting for them, at the top of the metal stairway leading up from the dockside to the main deck and, after the hastiest of hellos, showed them down into the hold. There it happened – the moment the past few weeks had, underneath, been building towards: Hamley dragged Marc to his feet, recited the caution into his face, informed him he was under arrest, led him away.

Only when that essential business was over did I again go in search of Suze. I found her up in the navigation room where we'd apprehended Marc and the captain, staring out the window in the direction of the sea. 'How are you?' I said to her back.

She turned around and shrugged. Then she attempted a smile. 'Has it – happened?'

'Yeah.'

'How soon can we get out of here?'

The answer to this turned out to be 'quite soon'. Hamley

interviewed me first and Suze second, then offered us a driver and car to the station. I persuaded him to send one of his officers with us and take us to Newport to see Greg.

Suze continued to be withdrawn on the journey and I didn't intrude. She needed to make sense of what had happened, go through blaming herself, try to come out the other side. Trouble with doing it her way was, in the aftermath of capturing Felici I felt pretty wobbly myself and the prospect of facing Greg Tuttle – well, emotionally I didn't know where to put myself. I'd have loved to talk about it. Instead I ended up going over and over the course of my relationship with him in my mind, looking for signs that at least the feeling between us might have been real.

When we got to the hospital, Suze came out of herself enough to ask, 'You okay?'

I nodded 'yes', then tempered it with a shrug 'maybe'. 'You?'

She nodded and half smiled. Then she shook her head.

'Glad we're so clear and forthright, aren't you?' I said.

She laughed, then looked like she might cry.

'Could you just wish me luck?' I said.

'Sure,' she said. 'Only what is luck in this case?'

I sighed. That was the precise nub. The part of me reared on romantic comics imagined me and Greg falling into each other's arms – the love-conquers-all scenario, 'all' here being defined as my hurt over his deceptions. What the heck, I understood the professionalism in it. I too had to keep confidences. I too would lie to someone I loved to protect them.

But there was another, darker part and it was full of resentment, even vindictiveness. He was an untrustworthy bastard, it said, that was the short and simple of it. It was all just an impersonal power trip to him.

It was visiting time in the hospital and people were coming and going. I knew where Greg's room was, so I led Suze past the receptionist and into the private ward. The closer I got the more the upbeat, optimist, romantic side moved to the fore. I started walking faster and faster.

'I'll just wait out here, shall I?' Suze said from behind me. I could hear the affection in her voice.

'Yeah,' I said (fool that I was).

Outside the door to Greg's room I paused to smooth my jeans and straighten the big shirt I was wearing over them and fluff my hair with my fingers. I caught a drift of voices – from Greg's room? From the one behind me? The acoustics were confusing. I leaned my ear to the door to check but still couldn't tell. Then I gave up – what did it matter? – and tapped on the door with my knuckle.

'Enter,' he called. His voice had energy in it again.

I pushed the door open and saw him sitting upright in bed, big smile on his face. Beside him to his right was his son, Bill. I stopped there, moved by the father–grown-up-son tableau. It lasted only a moment. When he saw me his smile stayed on his mouth but a look of alarm seized his forehead, wrinkling it from the eyebrows upwards. He glanced the other way and brought his arm and hand back to the centre. 'Dee, hi,' he said. 'Come in, come in.'

I pushed the door completely open and saw the woman on the other side of his bed. She looked a lot like me – it was uncanny to recognise that so quickly about her.

'Dee,' he said again, his face reddening under the spread of a blush. 'This is Maryanne.'

'His wife,' she added, keeping her eyes fondly on him. I recognised the husky drawl. This was the same woman who'd answered the phone in his flat that time I got locked in the truck depot out in Brentwood. Then she turned and smiled at me. 'Thanks for saving him. I was missing him anyway. This made me see how much.'

I wanted to gag, tell her not to be ridiculous, wives who left these days left for good, they didn't come back.

Greg, still red-faced, said, 'Sit down, sit down, Dee – here, move closer to your old dad, Billy boy.'

I sat because my knees wanted to.

'What happened?' he said.

'When?' I asked. That's how out of it I was.

'The bust.'

I glanced at his two relatives. This was classified stuff.

'A broad sketch,' he said.

Ten minutes later he was lying back against his pillow, a look of elation on his face. 'Hot damn,' he said. 'I can't believe we've got the mother.'

'Er – not quite. There's the small matter of the British judicial system – not known for speed or simplicity.'

'Yes, of course, we'll have to negotiate over him. But by God, when he testifies for us, there won't be any East Coast Mafia left.'

His wife patted his shoulder and her proud smile grew prouder. I suddenly became aware that I'd done my duty and could go. A new ache twisted in my gut: yet another sandcastle of possibility – washed out in the tide.

I got to my feet and bent for a perfunctory kiss into the air above Greg's cheek.

'So soon?' he said.

'Suze is waiting.'

'God, what state's she in?'

I looked him right in the eye, heedless of what his wife might see and deduct. 'We're both in quite a state,' I said. Then I waved to Billy boy and Maryanne and turned to go.

'There could be a nice reward,' he called after me.

I almost didn't stop – it was a ploy, I thought. On the other hand, if it weren't . . . I turned back around. 'What?'

'A reward. He got the better of *us* and our strategy. If it hadn't been for you –. There's a case. I'll argue it.'

'The firm,' I said. 'You know the state of it. Is it – much? I mean, will it make a dent?'

'Get rid of half of it, no sweat. If we get him to testify and you make a contribution there – maybe more.'

'Wow. You're not joking?'

'Not joking.'

'Cross your heart and hope to die?'

He put his hand on his heart and nodded.

'Thanks,' I said. I think I even smiled. 'We'll be happy to accept if you succeed.' Then I turned again and once more headed out.

He called, 'I'll be in touch!'

I didn't look around.

On the train journey back Suze and I talked about Marc and Greg and took turns picking ourselves apart, vying for the stupid-sucker award. I got into great generalities about testosterone and what it did to the male psyche, but Suze reckoned she'd have the same problems with any sexual relationship, no matter what gender the other person was.

The closer we got to London, the less she spoke of Marc and the more she mentioned her husband, Peter. What should she say to him? Did the fact she'd had an affair mean her marriage *ought* to end? When she'd got involved with Marc she'd been feeling for a long time that she'd 'fallen out of love' with Peter, but since he'd really stopped drinking he was like the Peter she'd fallen for all those years ago.

In the end she decided to sleep on my sofa and leave the real decisions until the morning. Her mind would be fresh and there would be a dozen hours rather than three separating her from her feelings of humiliation.

But then, having made that pledge, the first thing she did when we reached the flat and I got the front door unlocked and gestured her in was make for the telephone. Did I mind if she rang 'just to see how he was'?

Twenty minutes later I'd checked over my plants and washed the dishes and she was still talking to him. Five minutes after that, when I was chopping onions to start the pasta sauce, she came in to the kitchen, apologised profusely for messing me about like this and said she was going home. Peter was calm. He blamed himself. He wanted to talk.

She left and I looked down over the railing on the landing at the street, waiting for her to emerge from the gate. When she had, she looked up and waved. 'Good luck!' I called down in a loud voice.

'What's *that*?' she called back up to me. Then she waved again and hurried away.

My neighbour's door opened behind me. 'Ah hah, thought I heard you,' Grant said. The oilcloth apron he had on over his shorts and T-shirt said meal preparations were going on in his household too. He was clutching a white letter-sized envelope in one hand. 'How's it going?'

'It's sorted.'

'What, bad guys behind bars and all?'

'Yep.'

'Great!' He gestured into his place. 'You eaten?'

I hadn't but I nodded anyway. I'd had enough of people and talk for one day. Antsiness had set in; I needed time on my own.

'I'm bushed,' I said. 'Why don't you guys come for a meal tomorrow night – I'll bore you with the rest of the story.'

He laughed. 'You put it so charmingly, how can we say no?' Then he remembered the envelope. 'Your friend Theresa dropped by while I was lighting the barbecue.'

She'd written just four lines: 'Dee, I lost the baby yesterday. How did you ever get over it? Martin and I are going away for a few days. Will call you when get back. Love, *xxoo*.'

The next morning, my first back at the office in ten days, I went to survey the hummock of messages beside the mountain of files in the theoretically clear patch of my desk. On top was a fax from the Justice Department, Washington, DC, informing me that 'discretionary reward money would be forthcoming' and naming a figure that would certainly take the pressure off us for another six months. It also told me that Greg Tuttle had been flown back to the United States for emergency medical treatment.

That's when I discovered how many Greg hopes I still harboured, despite a night's sleep. Okay, he was married, they went, but he and his wife had split up before. And the fact that we lived in the same city meant there was always a chance of bumping into him.

But not now.

I dropped into my chair and was digging myself into muddy melancholy when the phone rang and saved me from myself. It was Sufiya and she was pretty excited.

'Dave, you know, the environmental health officer who sampled the playground? He got a lead on something from the barrel manufacturer and he's had an emergency team in the lab non-stop the past thirty-six hours. He's coming over. I was wondering, do you want to come?'

But I was already on my way.

We met in the small café in Whitechapel Art Gallery. Dave could barely eat his carrot cake for grinning.

'There's a range of tests still to do,' he said, 'but I'm reasonably sure they'll confirm that the main toxin in that brew removed from under that playground is oxcyllium.'

'What's that?'

'A heavy metal. Used in missile guidance systems. Fifteen years ago, ten years ago, its use globally was so restricted only a handful of labs in the world – all of them in America – worked with it.'

I sat forward. 'A handful?'

He nodded. 'It's not going to be easy proving which one had the accident, but –'

'But it's possible in the lifetimes of all those young Bangladeshi mothers.'

He kept nodding. 'Oh, yes. Absolutely. Possible even in the next year.'

I shook his hand. 'Thanks,' I said. 'I needed a case to get me back to work. Now I've got it.'

That evening's edition of the *Standard* contained a news item on page seven headed 'Charity Leader Apparently Drowns'.

A dark red Renault found on a beach near Plymouth last evening by Devon police belongs to Evie Maguire, chair of Weaverstown Housing Association. Shoes were found at the shoreline and steps led into the sea. No body has been found but Mrs Maguire was said to have been distraught at the sudden death of her son a week ago and the murder of her business partner, Janey Riordan, four days before that.

Personally I believe she got out of the country.

Three days later I had a fax from Greg. He opened with the business: Marc Felici's singing was exceeding their hopes. Thirty-five Mafia bigwigs from New Jersey alone were in deep doo-doo. Then, the personal stuff: he wanted me to know, he said, how much he'd loved me when he met me and how much he loved me still and how much he'd never thought he'd be one of those men who went on about loving two women and the angst of choosing between them for the sake of the offspring. I had set new standards of sexual pleasure for him, he said. 'On that level alone, I'll never ever forget you.'

That made me cry, I'm afraid.

Then I crumpled up the selfish bastard's note, struck a match and set it alight in a saucer. When it had burned itself to ashes, I found I felt much much better.

The Women's Press is Britain's leading women's publishing house. Established in 1978, we publish high-quality fiction and non-fiction from outstanding women writers worldwide. Our exciting and diverse list includes literary fiction, detective novels, biography and autobiography, health, women's studies, handbooks, literary criticism, psychology and self help, the arts, our popular Livewire Books series for young women and the bestselling annual *Women Artists Diary* featuring beautiful colour and black-and-white illustrations from the best in contemporary women's art.

If you would like more information about our books or about our mail order book club, please send an A5 sae for our latest catalogue and complete list to:

The Sales Department
The Women's Press Ltd
34 Great Sutton Street
London EC1V 0DX
Tel: 0171 251 3007
Fax: 0171 608 1938

Also of interest:

Meg O'Brien
A Bright Flamingo Shroud
A Jesse James mystery

Jesse James has learnt never to rely on the men in her life.
When the going gets tough, they're sure to leave. Just like
the grandfather she never knew. But now her grandfather
is back – if the man who knocked on her door is who he
claims to be.

He's a down-and-out conman, a liar and a thief, but he
needs Jesse's help. 'Gramps' has swindled a dangerous man
and is in hiding for his life. Against her better judgement,
Jesse allows herself to get involved. But once the man who
claims to be her relative is safe, Jesse herself becomes the
target of a vicious, cold-blooded rage . . .

**'A wise-cracking, street-smart heroine in the
V I Warshawski mould...Fast-moving, feisty
and fun.'** *The Sunday Times*

**'A verve and naturalness unmatched since Sue
Grafton teamed up with a Gatling gun.'** *Clues*

**'Meg O'Brien is a real find. Credible characters,
wonderful dialogue. A bestseller.' Ted Allbeury**

Crime Fiction £5.99
ISBN 0 7043 4463 7

Hannah Wakefield
The Price You Pay
A Dee Street crime thriller

In search of an expert witness for a tribunal to free
Carlos – a young Chilean exile – from mental hospital,
London-based solicitor Dee Street comes across
consultant David Blake. But events take a deathly,
unexpected turn when the bodies of Carlos and David's
wife, Amanda, are found in compromising circumstances
in a lonely country cottage. The police suspect David of
murder and it's up to Dee to get him off the hook.

The list of potential killers is long – from Amanda's
volatile boss to a random burglar caught in the act.
And what of Dee's growing and highly unprofessional
attraction to her client, David…?

'Lively, entertaining and legally accurate.' *Guardian*

'Excellent and original.' *Daily Telegraph*

'An engaging first person heroine with real depth
and a distinctive voice.' *Time Out*

'Enormously attractive…Friendly, ordinary,
honest, doubtful, with an unself-righteous integrity,
this voice is intimate and even sexy.' Nicci Gerrard,
Women's Review

'Riveting.' Patricia Craig, *London Review of Books*

'Witty, thrilling and compulsive. More please.'
Tribune

Crime Fiction £4.95
ISBN 0 7043 4072 0

Anne Wilson
Truth or Dare
A Sara Kingsley mystery

Caroline Blythe has always seemed the epitome of success.
A journalist, wife and mother, she is confident, assured,
sophisticated and self-contained. So why should she
suddenly turn to Sara Kingsley – an overworked, underpaid,
community counsellor – for help? And what's behind her
concern for a 'friend' who's involved in a dangerous affair
with a married man?

Unconvinced by Caroline's story, Sara insists there is
nothing she can do. Then Caroline is found dead of a drug
overdose – and questions start to surface. Who was the
'friend' Caroline had been so anxious to protect?
Was her death suicide or murder? And is Sara herself
partly to blame? Despite the pressures of work and single
motherhood, Sara feels impelled to undertake a perilous
investigation that, if she dares, may bring her closer to the
truth…

Crime Fiction £5.99
ISBN 0 7043 4461 0